W9-CUV-719

**VOYAGE TO NEW WORLDS WITH THE
BESTSELLING AUTHOR OF *EVERLASTIN'*
AND *DUSK BEFORE DAWN!***

"I demand to be allowed to go home." Brehan stared at the man in front of her. He was a good foot taller than she was, and that, combined with the massive breadth of his chest and shoulders, dwarfed her. The giant stared down at her as if she was a petulant child.

"I haven't the inclination to stand here and argue with you. You may convince yourself that you are as independent as you like, but you will obey the constitutions of this society."

"I'll fight you with everything I have."

"To what end, little one? It's futile to oppose me."

"If it takes the rest of my life, I'm going to make you choke on those words."

He gave her a measuring look. "You're out of your league this time. Don't ever underestimate me."

With that, he walked away. Her knees grew weak and she sank down on the bed. She wanted to cling to the hope that she was dreaming, but her every nerve had been receptive to the giant's mere presence. Despite everything, something in him called to her.

Throughout her life, she had emotionally and physically battled against anyone who'd tried to dominate her. And now to be a prisoner of such a formidable male . . .

"His life is about to take a turn for the worse," Brehan vowed.

ALL'S FAIR IN LOVE AND WAR . . .

**NOW IF BREHAN COULD JUST DECIDE
WHICH THIS WAS . . .**

ROMANCE FROM JANELLE TAYLOR

ANYTHING FOR LOVE   (0-8217-4992-7, $5.99)

DESTINY MINE   (0-8217-5185-9, $5.99)

CHASE THE WIND   (0-8217-4740-1, $5.99)

MIDNIGHT SECRETS   (0-8217-5280-4, $5.99)

MOONBEAMS AND MAGIC   (0-8217-0184-4, $5.99)

SWEET SAVAGE HEART   (0-8217-5276-6, $5.99)

ONE BRIGHT STAR

Mickee Madden

Pinnacle Books
Kensington Publishing Corp.
http://www.pinnaclebooks.com

PINNACLE BOOKS are published by

Kensington Publishing Corp.
850 Third Avenue
New York, NY 10022

Copyright © 1997 by Mickee Madden

First Printing: February, 1997
10   9   8   7   6   5   4   3   2   1

Printed in the United States of America

Dedicated to my family; Meeka; Diane; Phyllis; my mother-in-law, Terri, for planting "Katiah's" seed; Kitty for putting me on the right track; and Cindy, for keeping me there. Special thanks to my editor, Denise, a woman whose faith in my writing has opened the door to my dreams, and who has tried her best to teach me that patience is not necessarily a dirty word.

IN WHAT SHAPE shall come Doom to man, in all his varying species across the universe?

She walks among the unsuspecting, waiting for her reign to begin.

This human who comes to be known as *Katiah,* hosts mankind's imminent destruction. But her creators didn't count on her human half possessing such an indomitable will. . . .

Chapter One

The last door had closed to any hope of justice.

At twenty-five, Brehan Tucker was burnt out on humanity. Her life's purpose had met its end. Not even the rag magazines would listen to an account of what truly transpired within the walls of the Marson Estate. She had no way to satisfy the rage within her, short of murdering the woman responsible for the atrocities against the wards of the orphanage—past and present.

Standing barefoot on the promontory near her cabin, she ignored the cold, salty spray of the breakers crashing against the face of the cliff. The Atlantic Ocean and the sky had turned to gun-metal gray with the advent of night, except when an occasional display of sheet lightning lit up the gloom. A hearty breeze flapped her nightgown and her waist-length fiery hair against her tall, slender body. Her arms crisscrossed against her chest, she clutched the corners of an old shawl to keep it secured about her shoulders.

The hypnotic thrashing of the surf beckoned her. She'd always loved the roar of the sea, the way the sound pulsed through her and made her feel as if she were a part of its turbulence.

This night it held a different meaning for her.

Escape. From the rage. From the futility of life.

To allow the sea to swallow her up seemed a very right thing to do. If she could let go of her strong survival instinct for just a few moments, she could end what never should have been given life.

I DON'T LIKE THIS PLACE.

The abruptness of the inner voice within her head gave Brehan a start. "Go away."

WHY ARE WE HERE? I WILL NOT PERMIT OUR END.

Nothing was private anymore. Not even her thoughts. Since she'd noticed that inner voice several months prior, Brehan'd had to practice building up mental walls to ward off the voice's constant intrusions. Not only was what she believed to be her conscience a nuisance, but it even claimed a name of its own.

Di'me.

"Go to sleep—or whatever it is you do."

PROTECT US.

The only protection I need is from you. You're driving me crazy.

NOT ME. THEM. YOU WANT ESCAPE FROM THEM!

"I want . . ."

Brehan fell silent. In her heart, she longed for serenity within herself, but it seemed impossible. With Di'me, her rage had developed a hair trigger, one that was growing ever more difficult to control. Brief blackouts. Forgetfulness. A sense of nonexistence at times. Premonitory dreams which visited her sleep and awake hours, far more frequent and purposeful than those she'd had as a child. Her sixth sense had also magnified, tuning her into the thought waves of outsiders.

WE HAVE A PLACE, NOT ON THIS WORLD.

This elicited a low laugh from Brehan. "Di'me—"

NEVER SPEAK MY NAME!

"So long as you're in my head, I'll say whatever the hell I please."

Stepping toward the edge of the cliff, Brehan met with an invisible wall. Her hands went up. She could feel something smooth and solid erected in front of her. She reached higher, but could not find its end.

"Did you do this?"

ARE YOU ASKING IF YOU HAVE THE ABILITY TO PROJECT A PSYCHIC WALL, OR IF I AM CAPABLE OF SUCH WONDER?

Brehan's tongue lapped up the salty liquid on her lips. "Just answer me."

YOUR SUBCONSCIOUS IS ATTEMPTING TO STOP YOU FROM MAKING A FATAL MISTAKE.

"Then I can tear it down."

She concentrated on the wall until an acrylic-like image of it focused in her mind, then she strained to absorb it back into the compartments of her imagination, from where she believed it had originated.

WE HAVE PURPOSE!

The image evaporated.

We know what yours is, don't we?

TO PROTECT US.

To taunt me.

Again Brehan conjured up the image, but again Di'me distracted her, shattering her concentration.

PATIENCE! HE IS COMING FOR US!

"Who is this *he* you keep talking about!"

A fey sensation moved within Brehan, as if some vaporish thing were trying to settle more comfortably. She'd experienced this kind of internal fluctuation before. Since Di'me's arrival. Brehan had no way of knowing the spore of her alien legacy had prematurely awakened—an entity which she erroneously mistook for a loud, annoying conscience. An entity conceived of evil intent, who awaited her time to take over the human vessel and begin the reign awaiting her.

WITH HIM COMES THE ESCAPE YOU DESIRE!

Brehan became as still as a statue when her psychic abilities zoomed in on a scene. On her mind's screen, she saw a young man standing in front of a stone wall, his hands behind his back as if bound. His eyes were enormous with fear. His thin shoulders trembled.

A choked cry escaped Brehan. In conjunction with multiple gunshots in the vision, searing sensations penetrated her torso, face and arms. The young man dropped to the floor, dead. Brehan fell upon her knees and wailed, "Jimmy!" The psychic link severed. Weakness washed through her, teetering her on the brink of unconsciousness until a thought surfaced through her grief.

Tapping into a reserve of stamina, she made her way down to the sandy beach. Twenty-odd yards back from the shoreline, she burst through the front door of the cabin. Joy Lowery, who was sitting on a green plaid sofa, dropped the newspaper she'd been reading and jumped to her feet.

"Get your stuff packed, fast!" Brehan ordered, tossing her shawl across the back of the sofa.

"Whoa! What's going on?"

"Where's Lisa?"

Joy hesitantly stepped up to Brehan. "What's wrong?"

"He's dead!" With the outburst, Brehan braced her folded arms against her middle. "And it's my fault."

Joy's coffee coloring paled significantly. "Who?"

"Jimmy Conway. Pitts had him killed. Now she's after us."

"How do you know this?"

"Dammit, Joy, how do I *know* anything, huh?" Brehan drew in a breath to steady herself and glanced about the parlor. "I was out there on the promontory, and saw his death in my mind. A-a firing squad opened up on him."

"Oh, God."

"Twenty years old. Dammit, he was twenty years old!"

"Bre . . . it's not your fault."

"The hell it isn't!" Tears misted Brehan's eyes despite her struggle to suppress them. She began to pace. "He knew I was desperate for hard evidence. He took too many risks!

"What the hell is going on there, Joy? It isn't just the physical and mental abuse, or the mysterious disappearances of some of the kids anymore. I couldn't see the firing squad or their guns, but I knew they were there. What kind of covert operation is Pitts involved in?"

"You're scaring me."

Brehan stopped short in front of Joy. "We're next. Pitts is sending someone after us."

Casting a fearful, dazed look off to one side, Joy murmured, "Where will we go?"

"I'm not sure. Hasn't Lisa gotten home from work yet?"

"Wh-what happened at the governor's office?"

"He wouldn't see me." A bitter laugh escaped Brehan. "They all think I'm some kind of lunatic. God forbid anyone should attempt to tarnish the institute's reputation. We're on our own, kiddo. I just wish to hell I hadn't gotten you and Lisa involved in this mess."

"We moved in on you," Joy said tremulously. "It's not like you haven't tried to get rid of us."

Although Brehan had never shown open affection for any living creature, right now she wished she could let go and throw her arms around Joy. Instead, she clipped, "Get packed. We'll do Lisa's stuff and be ready to leave the instant she gets home."

"She went to see Jakes."

The stoked fireplace insert filled the room with warmth, but it felt as if a block of ice had manifested and lodged in the core of Brehan's gut. "What?"

"She didn't go to work today." Releasing a ragged breath, Joy made a feeble gesture with her hands. "She-umm, she called Jakes and arranged to meet him at the club."

"Why?"

"Bre, we've been worried about you. She thought if Jakes re-hired you, it would get your mind off Pitts!"

"I quit for a good reason. The man's a slime ball."

"But you love to sing. We thought—I thought—maybe you'd left in one of your moods."

A deadpan expression slid down over Brehan's features. "One of my *moods*?"

"It's not just your blackouts anymore. Your eyes turn this eerie color—"

"Not that again," Brehan dismissed impatiently as she turned and headed for her bedroom. Hastily, she stripped out of the nightgown and donned a dark green sweat suit and a pair of flats. When she returned to the parlor, Joy hadn't budged. "What time did she go?"

"Sometime around noon."

Brehan glanced at the mantel clock. "It's after nine. No telling what that slug has done to her." She reached for the car keys hanging on a hook near the door, but Joy clamped a firm hold on Brehan's wrist.

"You can't go."

"The club's been closed for renovations for the past two weeks," Brehan informed heatedly. "That's why I didn't bother giving notice, and *that's* why Lisa's in trouble. So, are you coming or not?"

"Give me the keys. I'll go."

"You couldn't handle him."

"Brehan, the other night you dreamt you *killed* Jakes, remember? Too many of your dreams have come true. If I had my own car—"

Brehan's right hand sliced through the air in a gesture of finality. "Either get your butt in the car, or wait here for us to return!" she bit out, then flung open the door and ran out into the night.

Joy numbly stared after her. It was seldom she or Lisa had tried to stop Brehan from doing something she wanted to, but this time, Joy had a sickening fear of what this night would bring.

Propelling herself forward, she shouted, "I'm coming!" and slammed shut the door behind her. She crossed the porch and beelined for the moving vehicle. Although Brehan didn't slow down as she backed it up, Joy managed to open the passenger door and throw herself onto the front seat.

Hastily closing the door, she asked, "Jakes wouldn't really hurt her, would he?"

Brehan skirted the car across the sand and didn't speak until the wheels were upon the tarred incline of the road behind the cabin. "He's capable of anything."

"I feel like I'm gonna be sick."

"Stick your head out the window."

"We could stop at the police station—"

"He owns the damn cops!"

The smaller woman shriveled against the back of the seat. "I'm scared."

Glancing at Joy, Brehan said in a kinder tone, "Don't be. I know how to take care of his kind."

Joy lapsed into silence throughout the rest of the eleven-mile drive. When they arrived at the club, Jakes' Spot, they found the doors were locked. Brehan didn't have any qualms about breaking one of the basement windows and climbing through. Joy reluctantly followed. Brehan was aware of her friend's trepidation, but she was also now linked with Lisa. Phantom pain thrummed on parts of her face, arms, left shoulder, and abdomen, letting her know she was too late to spare Lisa from Jakes' fists.

The thought thundered within her skull, echoed harshly off the wall of her tenuous control. Through a thickening red haze, she found her way to Jakes' office door. Light shone through the upper opaque glass panel. Gripping the knob, she said to Joy, "Stay here." She paused before going in. Her senses were still under assault by Lisa's pain. She couldn't sever the link. She was also sensitized to Jakes' vile presence, and it taunted her darker side to fully surface. Knowing she couldn't hold back the rage much longer, she flung open the door and crossed the threshold.

Immediately, the scene before her came into sharp focus. Lisa stood across the room, behind a black leather love seat, her fingers gripping its back. She looked in Brehan's direction with lifeless, pale blue eyes. Her short blond hair was disheveled, tangled. Welts mapped her wrists. Her blouse hung in strips, exposing darkening bruises on her left shoulder and upper arm. Blood trickled from her nostrils and a split lower lip at the left corner of her mouth. Swelling and discoloration marred her right eye.

The second figure, Malcomb Jakes, was standing closer to Brehan. He turned in her direction. A moment passed, then he slapped a hand on his large oak desk and released a guffaw that made his corpulent middle quiver beneath a stained, dingy shirt. His dark slacks were in a heap on the floor. Pale, thick legs mapped with varicose veins hung beneath green and white striped boxer shorts. Garters held up dark socks. His black shoes were shiny.

Jakes' beady eyes lit up mockingly as his tongue swept along the inner lining of his puffy lips. "I'm up to a foursome," he chortled.

HE MOCKS US! KILL HIM!

Trembling with rage, Brehan walked to within arm's reach of the man. She could not sense an iota of remorse in him for what he'd done to Lisa. His eyes had their usual sadistic gleam. Behind Brehan, Joy stood at the threshold, staring at Lisa in shock and horror combined.

"Joy, get her *out* of here!" Brehan ordered.

The sharpness of Brehan's tone dispelled Joy's fear-induced stupor. Going to Lisa, she placed her hands on the dazed woman's shoulders and urged her toward the door.

His head remained fixed as Jakes' eyes grotesquely strained in the direction of the two women. A wicked smile split his face, prompting Brehan to reach for the desk telephone. The instant his hand shot out toward her friends, she lifted the telephone and slammed it against the side of his head. Only a brief whimper of a sound escaped him. He bobbed on his feet, stunned. Blood trickled from a gash above his temple. When Joy and Lisa were at the door, Brehan tossed the makeshift weapon beyond the desk. She was turning to leave when Jakes' fingers bit into her shoulder and forced her around.

"Not so fast, missy!"

Brehan shucked off his repulsive touch. "The 'good ol' boys' aren't going to get you off this time, you bloated roach."

Jakes teetered. He was a man nearly as wide as he was tall, which was two inches above Brehan's six-foot stature. He was not accustomed to anyone standing up to him, especially a woman. He usually got what he wanted out of the women who came to his club looking for their "big break," whether it was through promises of fame, intimidation, or physical violence against them. Brehan alone had escaped unscathed to this point.

"I'll kill you, Tucker!" he hissed, his bloodshot, faded blue eyes lost in the fatty folds surrounding them.

Years of physical and mental abuse culminated within Brehan and focused on this one man. Even without Di'me egging her on, she felt compelled to push Jakes to the brink. "If you think you're man enough."

Jakes lunged forward, his massive hands clamping around her neck. He squeezed tighter, determined to crush the life out of her. Brehan experienced momentary panic before plummeting into a familiar darkness—

Di'me surfaced. To conceal the exchange, she lowered the eyelids of the shared human vessel.

Confusion caused Jake to relax his hold. The strength he'd applied to her neck should have crushed the bones, but it was as if an invisible, impenetrable shield were around her neck, protecting her. He dropped his arms to his sides and mentally groped for an explanation.

Too late, he felt icy fingers curl about his thick neck, their inhuman strength forcing him to his knees. The fingers tightened, cutting off his oxygen supply. He couldn't struggle. He had no will to resist. His protruding eyes rolled up in his crimson face, and fear gripped him.

Luminous amber eyes impaled his face; inhuman eyes, framed by a livid visage.

"Brehan!" Joy cried from the doorway. Propping Lisa against the doorjamb, she ran to Brehan's side and attempted to break the death-hold. "He's not worth it!"

Brehan resurfaced, dazed and unsteady. She was unnerved to discover Jakes kneeling in front of her, and her fingers tightly imbedded within the moist folds of fat covering his neck. "Lisa?" she asked in a strained whisper of a tone.

"S-she's in shock. Bre, we gotta get outta here."

Brehan looked down at Jakes' mottled face and felt a shudder of disgust course through her. Releasing him, she turned to leave, but Jakes' hand shot out, grabbed her ankle, and she toppled to the floor.

"Bre!"

"Stay with Lisa!"

Joy hesitated before she ran back to Lisa.

Panting, Brehan rolled onto her hands and knees. Despite his bulk, Jakes was quicker to get to his feet, and drove the toe of his shoe into her rib cage. Pain exploded throughout her torso. Collapsing to the floor, she curled into a fetal position, and folded her arms against her midriff. Blood pounded against her temples, matching the pulsating rage yawning within her again.

Nearly hysterical, Joy cried out Brehan's name.

"He's mine!"

OURS! Di'me hissed.

Through a film of tears, Brehan saw Jakes' foot positioning to deliver another blow. The darkness again vied to claim her, but she resisted and managed to roll onto her back. With all her strength, she drove her heel into Jakes' groin. Shrieking, he fell back. He braced against the ledge of the desk and fondled his testicles in a futile attempt to alleviate the terrible pain.

With an arm held against her rib cage, Brehan unsteadily scrambled to her feet. At first she found it impossible to straighten up. Then, breathing in shallow spurts, she finally forced herself upright.

The sound of a drawer opening set off an alarm inside her skull. Turning around to face Jakes, she found a gun leveled at her face. Beyond the cold glint of the muzzle, she focused on Jakes' maniacal eyes.

"Sing about this, you whore," he wheezed, waving the gun beneath her nose.

Brehan probed her mind for fear. Nothing. Not a qualm to ruffle her. Everything that had been said and done since the moment she'd entered this office, was merely a replay of the dream she'd had a few nights ago. The pain was washing out of her body. It was as if she were suddenly outside of herself, watching someone else go through the motions.

"Either y'ain't got the sense to be ascared, or y'ain't human!" he spat, his teeth discolored with blood.

Deathlike coldness swept through Brehan before she found herself once again falling into the darkness. Di'me returned, and by a tenuous thread Brehan's human programming supplanted the furies of the true identity. The instant Jakes drew back on the trigger, she grabbed his wrist and wrestled with his arm until the gun was aimed upward. One bullet fired into the ceiling. Joy and Lisa screamed. Committed to harvesting the dream's sowed visions, Di'me wrested the automatic from Jakes' grasp. He raised a fist in retaliation, his lips curled back from his teeth, a gurgle-snarl vibrating in his throat. Di'me drew back on the trigger and emptied the clip into his chest and gut. Each discharge of the gun caused him to jerk. Each bullet penetrating him widened his eyes a little more until, gawking at her as if frozen in a moment of incredulity, he collapsed to the floor at her feet.

Temporarily satisfied, Di'me withdrew and Brehan awakened to a moment of spiritual soaring. With a sharp intake of breath, she tilted back her head and waited until the incredible sensation began to wane. Physically, mentally, she gloriously tingled. Earlier, she'd been willing to walk into the sea to prevent the release of her rage again. She'd been willing to forsake life and seek absolute severance from a species she was growing increasingly intolerant of. She had no way of knowing that, whenever Di'me surfaced, a residue of the entity's furies remained to cloud her judgment. Otherwise, she would have questioned the rapture she was experiencing at Jakes' expense, at his expiration.

Although she was human, Brehan was little more than a womb to nurture Di'me's development—a womb to camouflage and position Di'me among those she was so cunningly designed to annihilate.

Savoring a deep sense of gratification that Jakes would never lay his hands on another woman, Brehan dropped the weapon to the floor and turned to join the two young women across the room.

A deluge of rain and hail greeted the women when they fled the back entrance of the club and crossed the parking lot to where the drab green Ford Falcon waited in the gloom of the moonless night. Unnaturally quiet and subdued, they climbed into the car and began their journey home.

By the time Brehan was maneuvering her Ford along the dark, twisting, coastal roads of Hull, Massachusetts, a full-blown storm was beating down on the vehicle. Lisa, sitting center on the front seat, was tearfully contemplating the fact that there seemed to be no world beyond the scope of the headlights. Joy sat alongside the blonde, gazing bleakly out the side window gnawing on a thumbnail.

Buckling beneath the oppressive silence, Joy said,

"Brehan—" but the sentence was lost to a moment of panic when the rear of the car slid to the right on a sheet of ice.

The instant the vehicle came to a stop, Brehan exclaimed, "Dammit to hell!" She shut off the engine and pressed her brow to the wheel.

"Maybe we should walk," Joy suggested.

Brehan sat back, grumbling, "Too far." Her feet ached from the cold. The car heater was on the bum again. "We're still about four miles from the cabin."

Testily turning the ignition key, Brehan shifted into first gear and lightly pressed down on the gas pedal. The rear tires spun. Slapping the steering wheel, she hissed, "What next!"

After her fifth, futile attempt to rock the car out of its rut, she turned off the engine and asked Joy to hand her the blanket on the back seat. Once Joy had passed it to her, she slipped out the door with it.

"What's she doing?" Lisa asked.

Joy pressed her brow to the cold glass of the window. "Using it for traction." She could barely make out Brehan's outline through the rain. A shiver coursed through her. The downpour and impenetrable darkness served to deepen her anxiety.

"Do you think Jakes is dead?"

"I don't know." Joy cast Lisa a look of concern. "How are you holding up?"

"I can't stop shaking."

"Lisa, did he—"

"No. He would have if you guys hadn't come when you did."

Joy rubbed her hands along her arms for warmth. She could not shake a nagging suspicion that something more had happened at Jakes' office than was readily apparent. "You're a mess."

Gingerly, the blonde dabbed at her swollen lips with the back of her hand.

Joy glanced woefully out the window again. "I don't

think she realizes what's happened yet. Maybe she thinks it's another one of those dreams.''

''My car's still there.''

''Don't worry about it.''

A shadow of fear passed over Lisa's youthful face. ''Did you see her eyes, Joy? They turned that yellowish color again ... like when that car nearly hit her the other day.''

Joy allowed a shiver to run its course through her. ''It's all getting too weird—like a dream we can't wake up from.''

A sob caught in Lisa's throat. ''What's going to happen to us?''

Before Joy could respond, the driver's door opened. A chilling gust of wind hurled rain and hail at the two women. Brehan flopped in behind the steering wheel, soaked to the skin, her sweat suit plastered to her body. She simultaneously slammed the door with her left hand, and turned the ignition key with her right.

''This better work,'' she muttered as she lightly stepped on the gas pedal. When the car began to ease forward, she released a slow breath and settled back against the seat.

''When we get home, I'm going to park my butt on the stove,'' she said. Her chattering teeth and shivering lent a vibrato to her speech.

''What happens then?'' Lisa asked.

''I drown my insides with hot coffee.''

Joy leaned forward enough to look at the driver. ''We have to call the police.''

''No.''

''Bre, we can't just pretend the shooting didn't happen!''

Brehan cast the women a look of annoyance. ''No police. Jakes has affiliations with the mob. If he lives, he'll send his goons after us. If he dies, and we've turned ourselves in, his people will make sure we never live to see a trial. Our only hope is that he dies without mentioning names."

"Oh God," Lisa breathed. "This is all my fault."

Her gaze riveted on the road ahead, her shoulders drawn in from the unbearable cold, Brehan asked, "You okay, Li?"

Sobbing, Lisa stiltedly nodded.

A tingling sensation began along Brehan's spine. They were on the last stretch of road. A half mile up ahead was the access road which led to their cabin on the beach below. She eased on the brake, wary of the treacherous curves on the downgrade. There was a coldness in her bones she was sure had nothing to do with her sodden state or the weather.

Then the imaginary red light in her mind's eye began to flash, warning her of danger.

"Listen carefully," Brehan began, her grave tone awarding her Joy and Lisa's full attention. "Should I lose control of the car, bail out. Understand?" She glanced to her right and, after noting their strained nods, she concentrated on the road.

Her knuckles turned white as her fingers tightened on the steering wheel. The danger was very close. She could smell it, feel it, as though it had substance, as though it were an entity breathing down the back of her neck. The dream had ended with Jakes dropping to the floor. What awaited them now was unknown, a fact which greatly disturbed her.

Her nerves were raw. To her, the storm was an extension of the emotional gale twisting within her. Clenching the steering wheel even harder, she made the pain in her hands keep her reflexes alert to driving, and less to the chimerical impressions bombarding her mind.

I must get them home, she thought. Her teeth locked as an awning of thunder roared above the vehicle, sounding like a succession of detonating cannons.

The stormy night began to conjure up hallucinations. Brehan believed she saw glimpses of ghostly images zipping around the car, and it felt as if something were now gnawing at the base of her spine.

The right-side tires touched upon the gravel shoulder. Correcting the deviation with a cut of the steering wheel, she blinked hard. Water trickled down her face from her sodden hair and weighed down her thick dark eyelashes.

Keep your eyes on the road! Forget Jakes. Forget the storm.

She squirmed on the seat. Needing audio distraction, she turned her head to say something to her friends—

A scream ejected from her throat.

The car swerved near the edge of the road before she was able to right it again.

"What's wrong with you?" Lisa cried, her eyes wide with fear. Brehan's scream had shaken both women, Joy to the point of clutching the dashboard.

Brehan had heard Lisa's query, but the voice was as surreal as what she'd thought she'd seen. Teeming tension, exhaustion, bad temper day, it could all be responsible for her imagination going off the deep end. But her consternation magnified when an overpowering stench seemed to rob the car's interior of air. Gagging, she swung a frantic look to her right.

Two corpses sat beside her, ravaged, as if by fire.

Pain in her left arm jerked her head around. Curls of smoke were rising from blackened, crisp flesh.

It's not real! her mind lamented.

Then Di'me released the guttural warning, HE'S COMING!

First, Brehan's intuition warned her of nearby danger, then she caught sight of a figure standing off the roadside ahead. As the headlights closed in, she saw a man leveling something in front of him. By the time she realized it was a rifle, it was too late. A report rang out. Another. The front left tire exploded, and it was all she could do to hold onto the lugging steering wheel.

Multiple forks of lightning descended from the darkness and struck the road just ahead of the vehicle. Lisa and Joy's screams became one as Brehan instinctively swerved the car to avoid the blinding flash. The Ford surged into the air from the cliffside and began a two-hundred-foot plummet.

Lisa's scream rang out throughout the descent, ending with the simultaneous crash and explosion.

Chapter Two

Crackling sounds invaded Brehan's dark lofty realm. Acrid smoke assailed her nostrils and she reluctantly opened her eyelids. At first the flames and black smoke didn't register in her mind. Coughs wracking her body, she stiffly rose into a sitting position. Her chest ached. The right side of her rib cage throbbed.

In a stupor, she cranked up onto her feet and stared at the remains of the car. There was nothing left of it to identify. Its nose-dive into a boulder had rendered it a charred, mangled heap of smoking metal.

She gazed upward. It was early morning, the heavens an abstract canvas of orange, red, and gold. A warm frolicsome breeze swirled among the dunes. Even the smell of coming winter was missing.

The air held . . . *The air held* . . .

Bewildered and lost in the moment's uncertainty, she absently smoothed the front of her sweat suit and regarded the surrounding hills of sand. Then her memory returned, catapulting her into the uncompromising claws of reality.

"Omigod," she whispered, her gaze ascending the craggy walls of the cliff.

The strident sound of the car settling, sent a chill of fear through her. Stumbling to the front of the Ford, she stared beyond the shattered windshield. She tried to reason that this was just another nightmare, but dream or reality, what she saw on the front seat snapped the remaining fibers of her logic.

There were *three* burnt remains in the car. The one behind the steering wheel was still gripping it, its mouth agape, locked in an unfulfilled cry for help.

Pain in the soles of her feet drew her gaze downward. She stood barefoot atop a patch of shattered windshield, discolored with blood. *Her* blood, she realized, numbly stepping back onto sand. She wondered fleetingly what had happened to her flats. Then, desperate to put some distance between herself and the maddening perplexity of the accident scene, she clambered up the side of a dune and stood on its granulose crest.

The unexpected shrill cry of a gull wrenched a scream from her, and her scream unraveled what little control she had left. She succumbed to a sense of complete helplessness and dropped to her knees. Hot tears filled her eyes.

"Jason, look!"

Seeing a man and woman approach the wreckage, Brehan stretched out on her front. She soon recognized Cara and Jason Cruthers, neighbors who lived two miles north down the beach from the cabin.

"Jason, could they be the girls from the cabin?"

"I don't know. God, what an awful way to die! Hon, we'd better get back and call the police." Taking his wife's hand, Jason urged her to run alongside him.

Staring after them, Brehan whimpered, "I'm not dead."

When the couple were no longer in sight, she rolled back down the dune and scrambled to her feet. For an indefinite time, she stared at the devastated figures inside the vehicle. Again and again, she mutely counted the occupants, until the cold of fear began to warm to a swell of raw denial.

She was alive!

"I don't know who or what you are," she said in a clarion voice, pointing a trembling hand at the monstrosity behind the wheel, "but you're *not* me! And I will not accept that *they* are Lisa and Joy!"

Long moments stretched painfully by. Her green eyes riveted accusingly on the aberrant scene of the wreck, Brehan inwardly struggled to come up with a feasible explanation. The only possible answer was that she was still asleep. What had happened in Jakes' office, the accident, were the uncontrollable workings of her imagination. Her dreamings, the window of her precognition, had ruled her most of her life.

But doubts continued to plague her.

Although her dream world was very real, *this* moment transcended the bounds of substantiality. The acrid smell of smoke, the breeze playing against her skin, the sand biting into the wounds in the soles of her feet, were not figments of her imagination, but realism in its cruelest form.

Still, she was not in that car, and she had to cling to the possibility that Joy and Lisa had also escaped.

The corpses . . . ?

With a guttural cry of anguish, she began to run as fast as her legs would move. Only once did she look back to see a curl of black smoke in the distance.

HE KNOWS WE'VE SEEN THROUGH HIS PLOY! RUN FASTER. HE'S WAITING FOR US!

Di'me's urgent tone inadvertently slowed Brehan. A few yards farther she came across a dark shape in the sand, and lifted into a hand what turned out to be one of her missing shoes. Her heart began to pound faster and louder behind her breast as an image raced through her mind, one of her sailing through the air, clinging to a mass of lights.

Not lights. Something she could not identify. And she had clung to it.

It was somehow tied to Lisa and Joy.

Flinging the shoe aside, she lit into another run. It seemed an eternity before the old, uneven porch of the cabin welcomed her. She reached the front door and threw it open. Her fears made her forcefully close the door behind her, as if to shut out the Grim Reaper she had miraculously cheated.

The parlor was shockingly cold, prompting her to lay a fire in the fireplace insert. When it had risen to dancing flames, she numbly stared into them through the bay-front glass until a thought penetrated her stupor.

Check the bedrooms.

DON'T BOTHER. THEY'RE GONE.

Brehan cast a furtive glance in the direction of the bedrooms. *Gone? No! They're asleep. And so am I.*

WHEN ARE YOU GOING TO LEARN TO TRUST ME?

Drop dead.

Defying the voice, Brehan crossed the cabin on shaky legs and peered into the larger of the two bedrooms, which Joy and Lisa shared. She swallowed past the tightening in her throat. There was no one in the cabin but her.

Tears pressed at the back of her eyes, forcing her to tap into her inner strength to steel herself against the grief trying to overwhelm her. She walked to the back of the sofa and fiercely locked her fingers onto its worn upholstery.

"Lisa? Joy?"

Silence responded, a silence so dense it seemed to press in on every side of her. She had wanted to sever her ties with her roommates, but not like this. Her own death would have been acceptable, but not theirs, not when they had so much to live for!

Anger at the injustice of it all speared her through

the heart. Crimson stole into her cheeks. The emerald green of her eyes became unnaturally bright.

"I want them back!" she wailed, turning in place, her face lifted to the heavens, her fists held against her abdomen. She had never believed in God. Could never bring herself to believe in any divine being capable of ignoring the pain and suffering of the innocent. But something preternatural *was* toying with her, she was sure.

"Do you hear me! *Bring them back!*"

A familiar clicking invaded Brehan's consciousness. Although the reliable imaginary red light was not there to warn her of danger, there was a deep-set awareness of something foreboding hanging over her. Something, she sensed, that had nothing to do with Jakes, or the supposed accident.

The pain throbbing in her feet made a bid to distract her.

"It has to be a dream," she rationalized, flexing her hands at her sides.

TRY WAKING UP.

"Shut up!"

Brehan's sorely chafed nerves made it difficult for her to sort through her thoughts. "I . . . I remember the sensation of the car sailing through the air, but I would be dead, wouldn't I, if it had actually happened?"

I SAVED US.

Images flickered through her mind. The memory of falling was too vivid, but yet another vied for her full attention. Of something tugging at her from the inside out. Something unseen. Unnatural. Something . . . *powerful.* It had tried to touch her soul. That's when she had let go.

Feeling nauseated and emotionally wired, she glanced about the deathlike stillness of the cabin. "I've gone mad. I-I must have snapped after I shot Jakes. Or did I shoot him? Lisa! Joy!"

HE'S HERE! I KNEW HE WOULD COME BACK FOR US!

Di'me's shrill voice caused Brehan a violent start. Then the clicking sound reared up once again in her mind. As if compelled, she glanced into the fire and saw a superimposed image of a grinning skull. Edging around to one side of the sofa, she looked up in horrified fascination at the ceiling.

The imaginary red light began to flash before her mind's eye. The hairs along the back of her neck squirmed against her sensitive flesh. A breath lodged within her throat. The air, it seemed to her, was being sucked from the room, but with a forceful yank on her willpower, she managed to resist the impressions toying with her reason.

"Paranoia's setting in. I'm going to wake up." She headed toward her bedroom. "Lisa and Joy are asleep. We'll all wake up and fall into our usual routines."

She was about to cross the threshold when the cabin plunged into inky blackness. Pivoting on a heel, she faced the parlor, her senses heightened by a keen sense of danger.

Light returned.

An unnatural effulgence.

It dimmed, but Brehan's vision was impaired by an aftermath of white lights flashing before her eyes. She gripped the doorjamb to keep steady on her feet, and squinted upward. Luminous tentacles were coming down through the ceiling and hovering above the main room. She watched the descending appendages with morbid fascination. Although her feet were rooted to the floor by fear, her mind was cloaked by a fey awareness of familiarity in what was happening.

A mass of multi-hued lights replaced the ceiling as the squirming snares steadily closed in on her. At first she was mesmerized by the luminosity, her heart intermittently pounding and fluttering behind her breasts.

Then the reality of her predicament ignited her survival instinct.

Running across the room to a tri-legged table supporting a brass antique lamp, she stopped only long enough to evaluate the position of the tentacles. As one wormed through the air toward her, she grabbed the lamp with both hands and flung it with all her might. The lamp exploded on contact with the light entity. When she determinedly threw the table, it met with the same fate.

Above her, the cloud-mass rumbled and shifted and rolled. Something within it touched her mind and tugged at her will—a feeling not unlike what she'd experienced when the car had been plummeting from the cliff.

Running for the front door, she flung it open—

A tentacle slammed it shut.

A different kind of fear seized her as she pressed her back to the door. As if testing her fortitude, one of the appendages began to stroke her jawline and neck. When she was unable to tolerate what she considered to be a violation of her person, she struck out at it with the back of her hand. Her action only prompted three other appendages to caress her throat, waistline and left thigh.

"Stop it!"

The tentacles withdrew only enough to hover in front of her. Brehan's fiery gaze cut upward to regard the main body of the entity. Outrage rushed like boiling blood beneath her skin. An erratic pulse drummed at her perspiring temples. Without a thought as to what her next action would later cost her, she lunged to one side and flung herself through a single-paned window to the right of the door. The sound of shattering glass dimly embraced her awareness. Shards ripped through her skin during her momentum, gouged and fell upon her as she struck the coarse, weather-worn planks of the porch. Pain radiated through every part of her body, but the sight of light tentacles seeping through the front of the cabin, prompted her onto her feet.

The pounding of the surf became her beacon as she broke into a run. Glass was imbedded in her feet, but she couldn't stop. She didn't need to look behind her to know the *thing* was following, closing in. She could sense its presence through every fiber of her being. Electricity crackled in the air, moved along her bare skin.

Then a deep, male voice boomed within her skull, "It's futile to run."

Her nostrils flaring, her lungs ached with the strain of breathing. She riveted her concentration on the waves in front of her. The breakers rose high, curled, then crashed to the shore, over and over, the sound of them unnaturally loud and vibrating beneath the sand.

She dove headlong into a cresting wave, only to be crushed beneath its descending weight. She turned and rolled, her arms and legs flailing to find something by which to anchor herself. Sea water passed into her lungs. Frantic, disoriented, she fought to break the surface. Nearly on the verge of unconsciousness, she felt her liquid blanket surge and roll her over once again. Through a gray haze, she became dimly aware of something tightening around one of her ankles. Solidity moved beneath her back. Shortly, she realized she was being dragged onto the beach. Salt burned her eyes. Coughing seized her as her lungs strained to expel the water she'd swallowed. Her limbs were strangely buoyant with numbness.

The instant she realized the mass was moving over her, she made a feeble attempt to roll away. But before she could fully get onto her side, the main body of the intruder lowered, and the tentacles swiftly formed a succession of bars around her.

This time, she sensed the entity was not playing with her. Its impatience crackled in the air, sparkled like thousands of white-hot stars within the mysterious mass. With a cry of desperation, she kicked out at it with her free foot.

"You will hurt yourself if you continue to resist me," the male voice warned telepathically.

Tentacles smoothly wrapped around her arms and legs, pinning her to the cold moist sand. Whatever was threatening her, she was not about to cow to its phenomenal existence. She struggled with even more determination to win her freedom, her torso arching up, and her limbs fiercely jerking against their bizarre restraints.

The mass became very still.

Breathless, her heart slamming against her chest, she mentally counted away long seconds. She sensed a hesitancy in the predator, which instilled a false hope in her that her predicament would soon be over. But then she sensed something else . . . something she couldn't quite define until two other appendages began to fondle the contours of her face.

"Bastard!" she hissed through clenched teeth.

A bluish glow began to emanate from the mass as it lowered itself to within inches above her. Warmth washed over her, delivering her from the biting chill of the air on her sodden body. Against her will, she felt herself relaxing, as if basking beneath the summer rays of the sun. Her ebbing anger and fear left her oblivious to the tentacles which were slowly coiling around her body.

Exquisite sensations burst along her skin. Burning ice pumped through her veins. Her mind fumbled for an explanation to understand the forceful stimulation of her awareness. Pulse upon pulse built rapidly within her until she was nearly overwhelmed by an instinctual hunger to cling to the entity.

"You cannot deny me," said the deep voice as the mass drew her upward into its cloudlike, glistening underbelly.

Upon entering the womb of the main body, an explosion of ecstasy swept through her. Pictures flooded her mind. Of a huge aircraft. Of men whose faces betrayed innocence and shyness. Of Lisa and Joy, among other young women. And of a giant of a man who was strangely familiar to her—a man whose quest would forever change her life.

Momentarily, there was no pain, no fear, no feeling at all. Losing all sense of existence, she screamed within the confines of her mind.

It took an indeterminable time before Brehan was able to soar up through the veils of sleep. Conflicting dreams of towheaded angels had plagued her. They would be trying to console her with softly spoken words, or holding her down and talking around her of her state of mind. She had fought them in the dreams, but the wingless angels had possessed unyielding strength.

Strong, yet gentle. Blond, yet silhouettes. Angels, and yet . . .

Awareness of a sexless voice droning on and on about a world called Syre, caused her to consciously linger a while longer in twilight.

—The catastrophic return of Feydais two hundred years ago forced an acquisition of breedable human females—

Frowning, Brehan slipped closer to wakefulness.

—Eleven hundred twenty-three males survived the devastation—

—With this last acquisition the foundation of the new world will be complete—

Brehan opened her eyes to find a broad, red beam of light scanning her from head to toe, and back again. A squeal of surprise escaped her. The beam zipped upward and disappeared into a circular fixture in the ceiling above her.

—Med Chambers is now apprised of your alertness—

Stiffly drawing herself up into a sitting position in a large bed, she dazedly looked to her left. The sexless voice seemed to be coming from a mechanical structure which occupied most of the wall.

—Would you care for refreshment or a change of attire—

—Your jersey is torn—

Brehan looked down. A jagged tear went from between her breasts to the curve of her left shoulder. Lifting her right hand, she clutched the material closed and glowered at the machine. "Where am I?"

—Aboard the *Stellar*—

Waiting for the haziness to leave her mind, Brehan eyed the spacious room. To her right was a mirrored vanity with a spiral-legged chair. Occupying the same wall was a carved highboy with filigreed knobs on the drawers. Colorful moving abstracts adorned softly lit panels composing the walls. A high-backed chair stood in the corner by an archway.

Memory of having thrown herself through the window of her cabin prompted her to inspect her feet. The soles were smooth, unblemished. And although there were rips in her sweat suit, not a scratch was visible on her skin.

—You were repaired—said the computer, as if divining her thoughts.

Brehan glowered at the machine, then slipped from the bed on the right side and peered around the corner of the archway. Off to her right, beyond a second archway, was a bathroom containing a single commode and a large open shower stall. No doors. She was turning back into the main room when she became aware of a hum vibrating beneath her feet. Crouching, she placed a palm to the floor. The vibration was undoubtedly of mechanical origin.

Syre? Brehan knew of no such place. Aboard the *Stellar*?

Standing, she tried to deny what her logic was telling her. This was not a spacecraft. The angels were not alien beings. She was asleep, caught up in the strangest dream of her life.

—Christie has arrived—

—I was preprogrammed to admit her—

The wall paralleling the arch separated. That in itself was startling, but Brehan was completely taken aback when a young, small-built woman stepped into the room.

"I'm glad to see you're up," the stranger said pleasantly, but there was wariness in her dark blue eyes. "My name is Christie Warner."

"You're . . . human?"

A smile of understanding touched upon the lovely woman's face. "From Orlando, Florida, actually."

Brehan swallowed past the tightness in her throat. "What's the story here?"

"The counseling programs will answer your questions and help you to adjust."

"Adjust to what?"

Christie arched a pale brow. "Your computer should have been feeding you the data while you were under."

"Something about . . . a world called Syre."

"It's our destination." Christie walked further into the room, her hands casually clasped at the small of her back. "This voyage is the last. The skeleton crew is what remains of the single males. Counting the Syre men, Erth, and the acquisitions, there are twenty-two of us aboard."

Brehan's mind struggled to digest the information. "You-ah, seem pretty casual about this."

"I wasn't at first. I've been aboard for over ten years. Quite honestly, I barely remember my life on Earth. I was matched with Barrit shortly after I was taken. He's the medix—a doctor—which is why we have remained aboard."

Brehan stiffened noticeably as an image flashed through her mind. "I remember being subdued by angels."

"Barrit and Manak were forced to restrain you the first time you came around. They were concerned you would hurt yourself." Christie's gaze settled on the white-knuckled hand at Brehan's breast. "Would you like to change into something—"

"What happened to my two companions?"

"Lisa and Joy are in comp counseling with the other singles. If you'll come with me, I'll take you to them."

Christie led the way into an elliptical corridor, its walls, ceiling and floor comprised of gray, lit panels.

"Kousta is from Epalar," Christie explained, slowing her stride to walk alongside Brehan. "She's aggressive and blunt, but if you ignore her, you shouldn't have any problem with her."

"Epalar?"

"It's a world in the C-Keps System. Deboora is a Luthi from the Poorht System. The rest of the women are from Earth. The previous trek had an assortment of characters from neighboring regions. Sharing our cultures sure passed the time away."

Brehan remained silent when the smaller woman stopped and touched a pyramidal disc built into the wall to her right. A section of the wall slid aside—an exit/entry unit she would later be told was called an E wall. She immediately spied the other singles beyond the threshold. Nine of them, including Joy and Lisa, sat around a large oval table. Each wore a wireless contraption over their ears. As Brehan stepped further into the room, she noted that their eyes were closed and their expressions oddly rapt.

"The comp counselor is stabilizing their psyche to adjust to long space flight."

"Programming," Brehan said bitterly.

"No, it's not brainwashing."

"The hell it isn't."

Christie felt a chill course through her at the intensity in the green eyes staring at her. "The mission is about life, Brehan. The Syres are a very simplistic people. Their world has never known war, civil or intergalactic." She released a sigh and ran a gaze over each of the women. *"Our* cultures certainly can't boast of such a history."

Brehan's gaze moved to Lisa and Joy—riveted on Lisa, who showed no sign of her ordeal at Jakes' office. The young women were sitting beside each other, oblivious to her presence. Brehan strongly sensed a state of peace within them that she'd never before experienced, but it was false serenity, born of programming, a fact which heatedly stirred her blood.

Then she experienced something very like a shadow passing over her. Turning her head, she looked into the pale blue eyes of a woman sitting to her right. She read a palpable threat in those eyes, an instant dislike for her she couldn't quite grasp. The woman removed her headgear and rose to her feet. She was nearly as tall as Brehan, but boxy-built and muscular for a woman. Her angular face supported thick lips, an aquiline nose, large eyes, and dark eyebrows that were mere slashes. Her unruly hair was short, dark with golden tips.

A soft beeping sound drew Brehan's gaze to a small blinking box attached to Christie's wide belt. "I'm being paged to Med-C," the blonde sighed. "Brehan, you must let the program finish for your friends. If you interrupt the process, they'll become disoriented. I'll leave you in Kousta's care. She'll show you how to use the headgear."

Kousta's nostrils flared contemptuously. "She isn't one of us. I can feel it." She tapped a large fist between her flattish breasts. "It was a mistake—"

"What are you afraid of?" Brehan bluntly asked Kousta.

"I fear nothing. Certainly *no one.*"

"Kousta." Christie's stern tone brought both women's gazes to her. "Can I depend on you to help Brehan, or not?"

A moment passed before Kousta gave a reluctant nod. Although Christie felt apprehensive in leaving Brehan to the woman's care, she had no choice at the moment. "Brehan, if you need anything, feel free to contact me."

Brehan only stared at the smaller woman. Her insides were knotted. The blood flowing through her veins felt like liquid fire. She remained perfectly calm until Christie entered the corridor and the E wall closed after her, then she looked again into Kousta's eyes and was given momentary pause at the hatred burning in them.

"Don't put yourself out on my account," Brehan said sarcastically, walking around the table to where Lisa and Joy sat. Removing their headgear and tossing the implements on the table, she gripped each of their shoulders and gave them a mild shake. "Come with me. We're not staying here."

Lisa's blue eyes smiled up at her. "You're awake. Isn't this wonderful?"

"Wonderful," Brehan echoed testily.

"We're going to be given husbands," Joy said wistfully. "Life mates. We can have all the babies we want."

Brehan sucked in a breath when both Lisa and Joy replaced their headgear and lapsed once again into the program. She looked across at Kousta's smug expression and considered belting the woman just to relieve her frustration before it boiled over.

"They belong. *You* . . . don't," Kousta snarled.

Brehan couldn't have agreed more. Keeping half an eye on Kousta, she went to the exit and placed her hand in front of the pyramidal unit. When the wall opened, she hastily stepped into the corridor and glared at the woman until the wall sealed.

She had no idea where she was running to, only knew that she had to keep moving. Jakes, the plunge from the cliff and her attack from the *light thing* was a day in the park compared to the reality of being trapped aboard a spacecraft. She couldn't count on any help from Lisa and Joy. Once again she was pitting herself against the establishment, the powers that be. But this time she wasn't sure what the establishment entailed.

Her feverish thoughts caused a psychological haze to cover her eyes, and it was due to this she plowed into a solid object. With a grunt of surprise, she felt herself teetering backward until strong hands gripped her upper arms and steadied her. The features in front of her remained a blur for a few seconds longer. She could only make out what appeared to be a halo—

Her vision sharpened on the concerned expression of a man slightly taller than herself. The halo proved to be a mane of pale blond hair which fell nearly to his shoulders. Eyes as black as night searched her flushed features. Eyes which displayed a large measure of curiosity, and a small measure of wariness.

One of the wingless angels?

Backing up until her shoulder blades met with a wall, she clung to it and scowled warningly at him. Her heart beat at an alarming pace. Not from her run. Not even from fear. The man was certainly the most attractive male she had ever encountered, but it was more than his startling appearance that rattled her. He was definitely one of the angels she'd dreamed about, his striking features exuding an innocence she had never seen in another male's face. His skin was golden. A cleft bisected his chin. His nose was straight and perfectly proportioned to his perfect face.

One corner of his chiseled mouth quirked up in a grin, and she felt her temper surface. "Do you find me amusing?"

"Forgive me," he said respectfully, with a slight bow of his head. "I was remembering the struggle you gave me when you first arrived."

Although Brehan made a valiant attempt to compose herself, her eyes betrayed her confusion. "You're Christie's—"

"No, that's Barrit. I'm Manak, a single." His cultured voice made a bid to ease her nervousness. "Would you like me to order you a jersey?"

Brehan hastily clutched the material together at her

breast, the gesture eliciting a flicker of amusement in Manak's eyes. "Why aren't you with the others in the Counseling Chamber?"

"I refuse to be programmed."

"There is nothing to fear here, Brehan."

"Only fear itself?" she challenged bitterly.

He was silent for a time, his gaze keenly studying her. "You're doing yourself a disservice—"

"I will not be programmed! Who is responsible for this abduction? *You?*"

"I guess I am in a way. It *is* for my people that you and the other women have been indoctrinated."

"Are you . . . human?"

He smiled almost shyly. "Yes. Humans span the universe in all shapes and sizes."

"I want to talk to the party responsible."

"Erth is our *Katian.*"

"My world . . . ? I don't understand."

Manak obligingly spelled Erth's name. "The pronunciation is coincidental."

"I want to see him."

"I'm afraid this isn't a good time. We're about to begin a meeting in regard to the pending matching."

Brehan's heart rose into her throat. "Matching? You mean pairing, don't you? Then *now* is definitely a good time to confront this . . . *Katian* . . . because I have no intention of being a part of this mission."

"I must advise you to—"

"Now!"

Drawing in a fortifying breath, Manak conceded, "As you wish." He reached to activate the pyramidal mechanism by her left side, and was quick to note her reflex stiffening. To further test her curious reaction, he attempted to place a hand on her arm.

Compulsively, Brehan struck out at his arm with the back of a fist. "I don't like to be touched!"

The E wall slid aside. Manak calmly clasped his hands to the small of his back. "As you wish, my lady." He lowered his voice and added, "But may I beg of you to heed your temper when addressing Erth? He does not respond well to aggressiveness, especially in a woman."

"Then he erred supremely when he decided to abduct me."

Manak glanced within the room at the assembly looking his way, then met the fiery green of the woman's eyes. "Come with me," he said, gesturing beyond the threshold.

Turning from the wall, Brehan fell into step beside him. The instant she saw what lay beyond the threshold, her spirit waned and her steps faltered. High on the wall to her right in the spacious room was a row of blank screens. Directly across from her, a window spanning the width of the wall gave a startling view of star-speckled blackness. Positioned out from the wall to her left was a long table with chairs, from around which stood a group of men, all staring at her with blatant surprise.

Brehan's feet moved of their own accord, closing the distance, while her mind tried to grasp the fact that all the men looked alike. Blond. Golden skin. Dark, riveting eyes. By the time she came to a stop a short distance from the table, she was able to discern slight facial and hair-style differences. A slow burn began in her chest when one of the men at the far end of the table came toward her. His hair was combed back from his face, and although he, too, bore an air of innocence about him, Brehan noted an element of shrewdness in his eyes when he stopped in front of her.

"She was in the corridor," Manak supplied.

"You're Barrit, the medix," Brehan said stiffly.

"Yes. I tried to calm you when you first awakened several days ago."

Several days ago? The lost time further unsettled her. "I wish to speak to your leader."

"It would be best to wait—"

"Now! I demand to be returned to my people!"

"We are your people now," Barrit said evenly.

A retort died on Brehan's lips when a machine exited a division in the wall to her right. Gliding across the room, it came to hover a short distance from her. The body of it was a good four feet long, two feet wide. Numerous lights and metal configurations decorated its facing. But what held Brehan's fascination the most was a magnificent bluish crystal which crowned the mechanism. A pale, throbbing light moved within the heart of it.

"It's alive," she murmured.

"Mastric was designed to supervise the genetic reconstruction of the future race," Manak told her. When her green gaze swung to meet his, he added, "The crystal is indeed an entity, of a superior order than the Crou crystals in the Feeding Chamber."

"Manak," Barrit said chidingly.

"I see no harm in assuaging her curiosity."

"Be seated," a deep, authoritative voice commanded.

Without hesitation, the men returned to their chairs, leaving Brehan to ponder the familiarity of the voice. At the same instant it struck her that it was very much like that of the light entity she had struggled with on the beach, her gaze fell upon another figure approaching from the E wall.

A strange buzzing filled her ears. She recognized the face of the man she'd envisioned shortly before losing consciousness on the beach. The man who was supposedly to change her life forever. She took a precautionary step back when he came to stand directly in front of her. Her heart thundered so fiercely, blood seemed to pound within her ears, but she forced herself to look him straight in the eye.

He was a good foot taller than she was, and that, combined with the massive breadth of his chest and shoulders, dwarfed her. Black hair, layered rebelliously to his shoulders, fell back from his face. An enigmatic black band was visible across his brow, its center width oscillating with slow, rhythmic light pulses. Bronze-colored flesh covered his sharply defined features. His eyes were inhumanly the brightest blue she had ever beheld, so blue, she could almost swear a bluish glow was visible on his cheeks and brow. The upright collar of his black uniform—which nearly touched his distinct jawline—only partially covered his broad neck. His generous lips twisted in a mocking smile, showing to advantage a deep dimple to the right side of his mouth.

Numbness spread through her. She had mentally prepared herself to do battle with the *thing,* not this creature who was beautiful in a horrifying sense. His voice on the beach, she reasoned, must have been a transmission. He was certainly not the entity that had captured her. Nor did he possess the innocence or coloring of the other men. So if she were to keep thinking of *them* as angels, he could only be the devil . . .

"Christie was instructed to take you directly to the Counseling Chamber."

Brehan's first attempt to speak became lost in her throat. His tone was so deep, it vibrated in the air between them. Finally, she said, "She did. I left."

The giant haughtily arched a brow, staring down at her as if she was a petulant child.

"I will not submit to programming. I demand to be returned to my world!"

Erth heaved a sigh of impatience. "I haven't the inclination to stand here and argue with you. You will be escorted back to the Counseling Chamber, where you will begin—"

"You can't brainwash me into accepting any of this! I demand to be returned—*with* Lisa and Joy!"

The giant scowled. "You and your companions would have died without my intervention. The counseling data—"

"What gives you the right to . . . to abduct women as though they were no better than cattle?"

"The right of guardianship, little one. Your solar system is not protected by a galactic council of rights, or subject to the laws of the House of Sojan. Therefore, I have the authority to take whatever I need from your world to restore Syre."

Something akin to a laugh squeaked past the tightening in her throat. "Your arrogance is astounding!"

"No more so than your own," he volleyed dryly. "The matching will take place in fifteen days."

A breath whooshed from Brehan's lungs. "I will not submit to counseling, this mission . . . and certainly not to *you!*"

"Your sole purpose on this mission is to give life to a dying world."

Brehan closed her eyes and clenched her hands. She doubted her ability to contain her rage. It coiled tightly in her gut, building in tension, building upon her hatred of injustice. When she looked up at the giant's face, the intolerant gleam in his eyes made her lock her teeth against a retort.

"You may convince yourself that you are as independent as you like," he went on, "but you *will* conform to our needs, and you *will* obey the constitutions of this society."

"I'll fight you with everything I have!"

"To what end, little one? It is futile to oppose me. Your strengths bear no measure here."

The weight of his words caused her to sway. "If it takes the rest of my life, I'm going to make you choke on those words!"

"And you will learn, Brehan, that among us, a verbal lance draws no blood." Erth glanced at one of the men at the table. "Caenith, escort this woman to her quarters."

Humiliation scorched Brehan as the Syre man approached. Fueled by it, she swung a fist. The sidewinder slammed into the giant's jawline and glanced off. Pain cinched her wrist and shot up her arm, but she didn't regret venting her temper. For a moment, he appeared stunned by her action, then the headband's light pulsations rapidly increased, his eyes brightened ominously, and his facial muscles became taut.

"Katian?" Caenith stared at the woman in horror.

"Cancel that order," Erth bit out. Taking a tenacious hold on Brehan's wrist, he towed her back to the room she'd awakened in and shoved her onto the bed.

"Send me back!" she demanded, nursing her smarting wrist to her midriff.

"Tempting but time-consuming."

She eased up on her elbows, her breathing labored. "You can't force me to bear children!"

"It's not open to discussion. You will learn to obey me."

"Or what? You'll turn your resident light-thing on me again? Go ahead! I can take care of myself!"

"I am aware of your capabilities. I watched you empty a weapon into a man."

A mocking grin turned up one corner of his mouth in response to her stunned expression. "It was against my better judgment to interfere, but I could not accept a murderess aboard my ship. He lives."

"So much for justice!"

Leaning over, Erth planted his large hands atop the mattress to each side of her. "Listen to me, you obstinate, aggressive creature. Be very careful of what you say and do, or you shall know *my* anger."

"It was once said, 'a verbal lance draws no blood,' " Brehan mimicked scathingly.

A breath lodged in her throat. She beheld a degree of anger in his eyes which seemed to take on substance and curl around her neck, slowly tightening until she was on the verge of crying out.

His gaze lowered, then he rigidly straightened up.

Brehan looked down. The tear in her top gaped open, revealing a sizeable portion of one breast. Before she could cover herself, her abductor reached down with one hand, grasped the ridges of the tear into his fist, then pulled her off the bed. It was all she could do not to look away from his piercing, condemning eyes. As if relishing the idea of making her suffer his intimidating proximity a few tolling moments longer, he entwined the fingers of one hand through the tangled hair at the side of her head. She could feel her heart hammering against the hand at her breast, feel the weight of his other hand against her neck. Somehow, her gaze never veered from his. Instinct, pride, a history of abuse, wouldn't allow her to submit to him.

"Don't make me regret rescuing you, little one."

Brehan's response was to vehemently spit in his face. She'd hoped to make him recoil and release her. Instead, his arms swiftly enveloped her, molding her against his muscular-hard body. She cranked her head back, determined to equal his visual war, determined to prove she wasn't afraid of him.

For a sickening, horrifying moment, she thought he would kiss her. Instead, his deep tone vibrating through her, he issued, "Heed this warning, firehair: I am in no way tolerant of your species. If you pray, then pray *we* are not matched."

"Save your threats for someone of less spine."

The searing blue gaze caressed the contours of her face, meticulously as if to further brand his superior strength in her memory. Finally, he released her and headed for the exit.

"Heed *this*, you big bag of wind! You can't master *me!*"

He paused at the open threshold to level a measuring look on her. "You're out of your league this time. Don't ever underestimate me."

The wall closed after him, sealing Brehan within the strange surroundings of her assigned quarters. Her knees grew weak and she sank down on the bed. She wanted to cling to the hope this was all just another one of her very real nightmares, but her every nerve had been receptive to the giant's mere presence.

Throughout her life she had emotionally and physically battled against anyone who'd tried to dominate her. And now to be a prisoner of such a formidable male . . .

WHAT DO YOU THINK OF THE ENEMY?

Trembling violently, Brehan vowed, "His life is about to take a turn for the worse."

Chapter Three

Transition date: 00.17. Evening mode.

I've decided to keep a journal, if for no other reason than to alleviate some of my boredom.

Discovered a few interesting facts the past couple of days.

1. The ship's day-cycles are modes designed to condition us "lucky" captives for Syre's thirty-two hour days. Just what I always wanted; longer hours on a planet I wished never existed.

2. The personal computers initiate a red lighting mode when there is movement in a dark room. Nice touch. Makes it a little hard to sneak around, though.

3. There are no windows in the female quarters because his Royal-Pain-In-The-Neck believes our "conditioning" is best served with a sense of stability. I guess it's okay to know we're out in space, just detrimental to our primitive little minds to have a visual reminder.

4. Erth's headband. According to Manak, the big guy wears it to let his underlings know when he's displeased. I've yet to figure this one out. I'm certainly not aware he has a problem communicating his "displeasure."

I have managed to forestall the matching thus far, but I know my luck will soon run out. Erth watches me. I can't see him, but I sense him. I've been under locked security in my quarters four times, for various infractions. No one has yet figured out I actually have more freedom under these conditions. By the time this is discovered, it'll hopefully be too late for anyone to stop me.

All that keeps me reasonably sane are the ripples of unrest I've brought about. Deceit, regardless the motive, should be beneath me, but it's the only weapon available to me.

I mingle with the men and women to fill their heads with doubts, to make them—even if only subconsciously—question the right of anyone to enslave them. My main focus has been to turn them against the matching procedure. Without it, we would all have time to reflect on the rest of the so-called rules. If enough protest is generated, Erth will be forced to abolish the practice. Personally, I don't imagine his ego will withstand even a small defeat. Poor baby.

The best I've been able to accomplish is to convince the women to refuse to Barrit's workups, without which, I'm told, the matching can't proceed. But the men are a curious lot. Almost childlike. They're kind. Almost too sincere. But it disturbs me they don't seem to possess minds of their own. It's almost as if Erth has a fierce hold on their wills.

Joy and Lisa are still trying to convince me the counseling programs will help me shed the past. I prefer the reality of my childhood to programming. I revamped part of my comp console to stop the subliminal data, and have once again disabled the scan above my bed. I'm not sure of its purpose. Better safe than sorry.

One final note. Since my abduction, something has been different inside me. Although I haven't been able to overcome my anger over my abduction, the rage isn't present. I'm still trying to find a way to escape my future with the Syres, but I have somehow found a large measure of peace. I've tried to analyze this rationally. Yeah, right. Sometimes I get the strangest notion I'm exactly where I should be. Only sometimes, though. I think my curious nature is responsible for these slips.

END.

In the great domed Control Center positioned at the top of the ship, Erth shifted in his command chair, his thoughts darkly centered on Brehan. Since her arrival seventeen days ago, his meditation and intermittent monitoring had kept him apprised of her part in the unrest spreading among his charges.

She was proving to be a cunning adversary.

The women had a tendency to seek her out, to coax her among them. The men were drawn by the magnetism of her uncanny boldness, and yet, Erth reflected with deepening puzzlement, she kept herself emotionally distant from the others.

Brehan was a disturbing presence, an enigma to him. Without the others seemingly aware of it, she would be among them, watching, listening, seldom speaking unless directly spoken to, being in no way a willing participant in the socializing. When she did speak, it was to a captive audience. Her influence was undermining the programs which had been so effective in the past. Unless he put a stop to it soon . . .

He was so preoccupied with thoughts of her that he didn't hear the two who approached him. Startled from his reverie, he scowled into Barrit's face. "How are you faring on the reports?" he asked curtly, irked by the medix's cheerfulness.

"Faring. Minus one," Barrit informed, passing Erth an electronic data board.

"Brehan." Erth perfunctorily glanced over the reports, then peevishly looked at Barrit. "How much opposition can one woman give to a simple evaluation?"

Barrit made a face and replied, "She's adamantly opposed to it."

"You're intimidated by her."

"Wary," Barrit corrected on a sigh.

"Understandably so," Christie piped up, casting her husband, Barrit, an appreciative look. "We've both tried to penetrate her armor, but Brehan is strong-willed."

"What about her scan?" Erth asked huskily, having glimpsed the thought in Christie's mind.

"She-umm . . . put it out of commission. Again."

"How?"

Christie gave a bewildered shake of her head.

"No anatomical peculiarities showed up on the preparatory," Barrit spoke up, his light tone causing Erth to arch a censorious brow. "And I'm sure I can compile a psychological profile on her, without her cooperation."

"Then proceed." Erth glanced over the data again before testily handing the board back to Barrit. "We've already passed the designated matching date. I want this resolved."

"I can try—"

"*Do* it."

Resisting a notion to look at Christie for support, Barrit nodded in acknowledgment of the order. More than anyone aboard the *Stellar,* he was aware of his superior's restlessness since leaving Earth's orbit.

"Christie." Erth's oppressive gaze shifted to her. "I suggest you have a long talk with Brehan—at your earliest convenience."

"About anything in particular?"

"If she persists in her defiance, I will personally introduce her to the tranq-choker."

Barrit stiffened in shock at the insensitivity of Erth's threat. A look of anger flashed in his round eyes before he was able to veil his feelings.

"It will turn her brain to mush!" Christie exclaimed. "I lasted seven agonizing days with that thing, and she's far more headstrong than I was."

"I know of your dislike for this method, but it is effective."

"It's barbaric!" Christie paled beneath the giant's visual warning. "Even now, when my temper rises, I can feel those electrical shocks the choker fed into me," she said more calmly, although her posture was stiff.

"You gave me your word you wouldn't use it again unless all other options failed."

Erth shrugged. "She has not responded to direct orders, or the conditioning subliminals. I cannot allow her disruptive conduct to go unchastened."

"No, but—"

"She's testing my ability to command her."

"Maybe she is, but she has every intention of making this trip sheer hell—and she *can.* I'm telling you, Erth, she's physically and willfully stronger than any woman you have come up against. Threaten her, take action against her, and mark my words, she'll use it to *her* advantage."

"What do you suggest I do?"

"Be patient."

"I agree," Barrit stated. "I don't believe it's her intention to harm anyone. Her aggressive behavior is most prevalent when she feels she or someone else is being threatened. Under different circumstances, we might sit back and admire her spirit."

"That's highly questionable. She's a woman." Erth fixed his stormy gaze on the depths of space beyond the dome in front of him. "Aggressiveness is not acceptable in a female—certainly not tolerated under *my* command."

Looking over his left shoulder, he issued a sharp, "Manak!" When the man came immediately to his side, Erth instructed, "Repair the scan in Brehan's quarters."

"I have, but she keeps—"

"Do it! Then find her and escort her to her quarters. Inform her she is under security lock again for the next two days. On your return, cut off her communication unit."

"But *Katian*—"

Erth's steeled gaze arrested Manak's protest, and he hurriedly walked to the central lift.

"This is only going to deepen her resentment!" Christie asserted, ignoring the warning hand Barrit placed on her forearm.

"I'm growing weary of this conversation, Christie."

"Erth, she has a wonderfully imaginative brain—"

"Which she uses for disruptive purposes."

"What about *your* mate when she's chosen?" Christie persisted. "When you leave us, isn't *she* the one who will be ruling over the all-male consul? Imagination and backbone sounds like a necessary endowment to me."

"She will be conditioned by the time we reach Syre."

"Who is *she*, Erth?"

A look of spleen was leveled on Christie. "Get to the point."

"Who do you think Mastric is going to match with you? Poor, timid Karen? Or a bully like Kousta?"

"Christie—"

Erth lifted a hand to silence Barrit. "Let her finish."

Christie took a moment to carefully choose her words. "In sixty-five years of going back and forth between Syre and Earth, Mastric has not *logically* determined your mate. Maybe your expectations are too high, or maybe your genius matchmaker has been waiting for someone just like Brehan to come along.

"Leadership qualities, Erth," she went on. "Not only do I think Brehan can take on the responsibilities of a *Katiah*, but I also think she's not going to be all that crushed when the time comes for you to return to Haveth."

Erth's features took on a bored expression. "Are you unhappy with us?"

The query took Christie aback. "Not at all, but that doesn't mean I agree with your methods. Although I choose not to personally rebel against your laws, I do refuse to be placed in the middle anymore." Turning, she headed toward the lift. "You deliver your warnings to her. I'm abdicating my position as arbitrator."

By the time the lift returned from the second level, Barrit was beside her. They entered the cubicle together, the medix's expression guarded until the lift descended past Erth's probing gaze.

"Couldn't resist, could you?" he chided.

"He can be so *damn* infuriating at times!" A pang of regret cooled her temper, and she asked in a low tone, "Do you think I've made things worse?"

"It's hard to say. But it makes me nervous when you challenge him."

"Barrit—" Christie paused when the lift stopped at the second level and they stepped into the corridor together. "—the women have been talking about stopping the matching."

"I've heard the rumors." Barrit strolled to a stop in front of the Med Chamber and sighed as he draped his forearms on her shoulders. "Erth won't give in on this."

Wrapping her arms about his middle, Christie laid her brow to his chest. "Maybe. I keep thinking . . ."

Barrit tenderly placed a crooked finger beneath her chin and lifted her face. "What have you been thinking?"

Tears welled in Christie's blue eyes, and pain shadowed her delicate features. "If Brehan *could* pull this off, Barrit, maybe she could help with Adam."

Wrenching away from his appointed mate, Barrit entered the Med Chamber. Christie was quick to position herself in front of him. "I want my son back!" she cried. "I've begged and pleaded with all my heart, but he doesn't listen. Don't you see—" Her hands clutched the front of his jersey. "—changes are happening! Little changes, but they're there, Barrit. You've noticed Erth's restlessness. It's *her!* In ten years, I've scarcely seen him display emotion. Until now. He's *attracted* to her. Somehow, she has touched something in him and made him a little human. If we asked her—"

Barrit adamantly shook his head.

"Why? I want Adam back, dammit! Barrit, I ache for him."

She broke down into sobs and Barrit wound his arms

about her shoulders. "I know you do, but Brehan is close to stasis, herself. She just isn't aware of it yet."

"Sometimes, I hate him," she choked, pulling away from Barrit and turning away. "And I *hate* feeling helpless."

"When the matching is done, I promise to speak to Erth about Adam."

Christie despondently stared at him. "It won't do any good." Then, as if dismissing the subject, she walked to one of the consoles at the far end of the room. Barrit forlornly watched her. Unlike the previously matched couples who remained on Syre after each return, he, as high medix, had been duty-bound to make himself available to the new acquisitions during the remaining voyages. The trials and stress of space travel on the women had warranted *his* particular gifts. He'd trained two men on Syre to oversee his comp medical unit during his absence, men capable of handling routine medical problems. Christie had never once balked or complained about the additional treks, not until the problems with Adam had begun. He, too, resented their son's imposed stasis, but Erth *had* warned them not to conceive until the return of the last voyage. But Christie had so desperately wanted a child . . .

Two days later, the dawn mode was in effect when Erth put the ship on autopilot and left the Control Center. He carried an air of disquieting hostility about him as he descended to the second level and turned left in the corridor. The Meeting Chamber's E wall opened to admit him. Standing in different sections of the room, the men turned in his direction, and watched as he brusquely seated himself mid-table with his back to the wall.

"Be seated."

While the Syre men went to their designated chairs, Erth activated a console to roll up in front of him. One of many light-coded buttons was pushed. The far wall opened and Mastric hovered to a stop in the center of the room. Its base maintaining an altimeter hold of two feet, it waited for further instructions.

Erth looked up to check on the men's mini-consoles which had also rolled up. Barrit alone was not a participant this time, but he sat at the far end of the table, to Erth's left, a store of data crystals set up in front of him.

"You are all aware of what this procedure signifies," Erth spoke, casually studying the nervous elation in most of the men's expressions. "I expect you to conduct yourselves accordingly once you leave this room."

Resting his spine against the backrest of his chair, he impatiently gestured to Barrit. "Pass down my records."

Several of the crystals were removed from the case and placed upon a narrow conveyor belt. When they stopped within Erth's reach, he placed them into three slots within his console and transferred the information to Mastric's waiting memory banks.

A question mark appeared on his monitor.

A frown of impatience drawing down his black eyebrows, Erth tapped the appropriate light keys and waited again for the receiving signal to appear.

—I am waiting—appeared on his monitor.

"Manak, run a diagnostic on Mastric's intro-quartz."

Shortly, Manak curiously looked up at Erth. "The crystals are reading clear and receptive, *Katian.*"

Erth tried again to relay the information to Mastric, then demanded Barrit to pass the women's psychological files to him. But when these, too, failed to respond to the console's command, a flush darkened Erth's bronze face.

"What is it?" Barrit asked, rising from his chair and going to Erth's side.

"Something is interfering with the signals," Erth muttered. "Barrit, try your medical files."

Rising from the chair, Erth stepped aside to allow Barrit access to the main console. Baek passed down the remainder of the data crystals, while Manak used his own console to check on another possibility. Barrit inserted one of his own crystals, but Mastric's response was another question mark.

"There has to be a simple explanation," Barrit said. "We couldn't have both taken the wrong crystals."

"They've been tampered with," Erth said, but in a tone suggesting he couldn't accept the possibility. He noticed Manak paling. Walking around the table, Erth stood behind him, braced his hands on the back of Manak's chair, and peered over the man's shoulder at his mini-unit. "What have you uncovered?"

Manak cleared his throat and verbalized the data on his small monitor. "They've recently been erased. Yesterday morning, *Katian.* The master computer was instructed to erase all information pertaining to the women, including all backup files and personnel data relating to the matching procedure."

"Bring up the biological code."

"There wasn't one used, *Katian,*" Manak said weakly, his dark eyes seeming lost amidst his ashen face.

"That's impossible—" The information on the monitor blurred to Erth's vision as he stiffly straightened back.

Although he was acutely aware that his men were watching him, he allowed his outrage to surface. "Damn her!" he thundered, his hands balled at his sides, the oscillation of light pulses on his headband so swift they appeared as a single line. "This time she has gone too far!"

Barrit alone found the stamina to rise to his feet. "Who are you accusing?"

"Who else but that cunning she-devil!"

Manak broke from his stupor and stood to face his superior. "She's been under locked security."

"When did you last see her?"

Erth's belligerent tone unnerved Manak. "When I escorted her—*as ordered*—to her quarters, two days ago."

"Prior to that?"

"The previous evening, but it was only to finish instructing her on computer basics."

"Basics?" Erth asked caustically.

"I didn't breach security!" Manak protested. "She was curious about the structure of our systems, that's all. Besides, she couldn't have entered the master computer yesterday morning. It's impossible from her private system. And she couldn't have accessed from one of the four possible computers because she was confined!"

"Not to mention the impossibility of her body chemistry bypassing the BRS to gain access to the data," Stalan added from his chair.

Erth carefully regarded each man, his mind probing their thoughts, hoping to glean a clue to the truth. But his men were as perplexed as he, and this intensified his outrage.

"I know she is responsible!" he grated out. Then he clenched his teeth as a warning tremor coursed through him. He released a feral growl as his height began to increase. His jersey shredded and his pants split up the sides. When the distention satisfied his internal ignitions, he looked down at Manak's white face from his eight-foot-nine-inch height, his eyes fiercely brooding.

"Erth, there's no evidence—" Barrit swallowed his words when the brilliant blue of Erth's eyes turned on him.

"Return to your posts," Erth growled, then turned and stormed out of the room.

Barrit's bleak gaze focused on Manak's hand as it reached for the console. Swiftly, the medix reached across the table and took a firm hold on the outstretched wrist.

"She must be warned!"

Although Barrit agreed, he nonetheless gave a firm shake of his head. "We can't interfere."

Manak straightened back as if sickened by Barrit's words. "When are *we* going to take control of our lives?"

Sadly, Barrit regarded the other men's anxious

expressions before replying, "Diplomacy is crucial, Manak."

"But she's innocent of erasing the data!"

"For her sake, I hope so," Barrit murmured, then wearily sank onto the chair Erth had earlier occupied.

Unaware that Erth was on his way, Brehan restlessly paced in her quarters. Two factors were weighing heavily on her mind. The isolation imposed on her left her little choice but to listen to the educational holograms if she wanted to hear another voice, but even the droning of the mechanical vocals was grating on her nerves. The second matter was not knowing what was happening in the Meeting Chamber. She half expected to hear a *boom* at any time. Also expected to see Erth come stalking into her quarters, snorting flames through his nostrils.

So what if he did?

She stopped pacing and stared at the wall computer. In a nutshell, this machine produced everything except weapons and normal food.

A mischievous glint came into her eyes as she glanced in the direction of the archway. The facilities in her private bathroom remained a mystery to her. When she showered she wore the sweat suit. As she never removed it, it was the only way to keep it fresh. The dustlike particles which emerged from the showerhead, allowed one to cleanse oneself without getting wet.

One eyebrow arched as she thought about the commode, and the similar dust which floated in the basin like a diamond mist. No flushing required.

"Idle mind, idle hands," she said in a singsong manner, and walked to the vanity and picked up a jar of skin cream. Prancing into the bathroom, she theatrically held the jar over the basin, then released it. The container soundlessly entered the mist. Nothing indicated it had struck a solid bottom.

Her curiosity deepened, tingled along her nerves as she knelt in front of the basin. For a brief time, she playfully danced her fingertips along the surface of the mist. The possibility that the unknown substance could harm her skin was all that kept her at bay, but doubt soon crumbled to her compulsion to experiment.

At first she only plunged her hand in up to her wrist. A close inspection upon withdrawing it showed that her skin had not changed. Lowering her arm up to her elbow, she withdrew it to find that the lower sleeve of her sweat shirt had vanished. The fine hair on her arm was intact, the skin soft and dry, so she plunged her arm in as far as the seat permitted, and groped. Nothing. It was as if the basin possessed an infinite nothingness in all directions.

A blush of denial heightened the color in her cheeks. "No inner sides. No bottom. No logic whatsoever. Tell the john, Brehan, this is impossible." She dropped her voice an octave. "This is impossible, john."

Stymied, yet even more determined to understand the enigmatic dimensions, she painfully stretched her arm within the mist. It was then the imaginary red light went off in front of her mind's eye, and her gaze cut to the left, in the direction of the archway. Mortification scorched every part of her skin as she slowly withdrew her arm, her gaze fixed on Erth, who was leaning against the arch, his arms folded against his chest, a twisted smile on his lips. His jersey hung in shreds from his shoulders, and his split pants resembled a loincloth, exposing more of his thighs than she ever cared to see.

"If you're through playing with that facility, I wish to speak with you," he said with an uncharacteristic lazy drawl. Straightening away from the arch, he turned abruptly and walked into the bedroom.

It was long seconds later before Brehan felt steady enough to get to her feet. Although the right sleeve of her sweat suit was missing just below the shoulder seam, she made the motion of smoothing it in place before forcing herself to leave the room. She stepped through the second archway to see Erth removing the wisps of material from his powerful shoulders. When the last of his jersey was piled atop his leveled left hand, he closed his fingers over the pieces. For a split second, a blue glow appeared around the hand. When it vanished, Brehan was flabbergasted to see that the material had disintegrated. Ash was falling from between his spread fingers when he looked up to find her watching the pale cinders flutter to the floor. When her gaze finally met his, her expression was guarded, her posture hostile.

"I resent you barging into my quarters."

Erth crossed his arms against his chest. "You feel invasion of privacy is solely your prerogative?"

"I don't know what you're talking about."

With a sardonic grin, he said, "The Mastric files."

"The what?"

"How did you manage *this* coup?"

Brehan sighed with exaggerated impatience. "I don't find this talking in circles particularly amusing."

Erth's gaze lit upon the makeshift metal strip Brehan had fashioned into a pin to keep closed the rip in her top. "How did you manage to bypass the security lock on your quarters?"

"The what?"

A muscle began to tick along Erth's jaw. "How were you able to bypass the BRS and access the files?"

"BRS?"

"Biochemical response system," he replied tightly.

Brehan adeptly feigned a shrug of innocence. "Unless I'm a miracle worker . . ." She shrugged again.

His patience at its end, Erth moved closer to her, but stopped when she winced as though expecting him to strike her. Annoyance darkened his features and his intense blue eyes narrowed in contemplation. His mind reached out to breach the veils of her thoughts. To his further pique, his efforts met with an impenetrable mental shield.

"I have never struck a living creature," he said huskily, "but you may *yet* become the first."

"Are you threatening me?"

The belligerence of her delivery didn't quite camouflage the quiver in her tone.

"Have I reason to threaten you?"

Realizing he was toying with her again, Brehan set off to walk around the bed to put some distance between them. But as she passed him, his hand shot out and took hold of the long, thick braid trailing down her back. In the next instant, he wound it about his fist, slowly bringing her closer to him. A tug forced her to look up into his face, which was devoid of expression.

Something caught Brehan's notice. She'd glimpsed it before, but had not seriously questioned it until now. It was a red sheen that was sometimes visible over his eyes, depending on the movement of his head. A chatoyant sheen not unlike that in most animals' eyes when light reflected off the orbs. It was a disturbing characteristic, one which held her attention for several seconds. The spell of her pensiveness was broken when his lips twisted into a smile, and the deep dimple to the right of his mouth became noticeable again. Then, quite unconsciously, she studied the masculine contours of his mouth—until that infuriating smirk returned. Collecting her wits, she backhanded the inside of his wrist.

"Let go of me."

"You only escaped my anger earlier because I found it amusing to watch you play with the commode. You possess the curiosity of a child."

"I'm not a child!"

His gaze brazenly roamed over her flushed features. "Hardly a woman."

"Which I'm sure you'd like to remedy," she retorted, and slapped her palms to his chest to shove him away, only to hastily jerk back. "You're hot," she said dazedly, curling her fingers against her palms.

"My system is still cooling down."

Brehan eyed him speculatively. Deciding not to question his statement, she calmly demanded, "Take your oversized mitts off me."

"What were you trying to accomplish with the commode?"

His question took her by surprise. "Nothing."

Another length of her braid was wound about his fist, his eyes never wavering from her own.

"All right! I was curious about the dimensions."

"What about them?"

"There doesn't seem to be any insides to the basin."

A fist length of her hair was released. "The cassis mist diffuses elementary confines."

"Meaning what?"

Releasing her hair, Erth walked to the E wall, where he stopped and faced her once again. "Your world is stagnated by an embryonic form of science. But you're a fast learner, aren't you." It was a statement, sourly delivered. Before she could respond, he added, "Which brings us back to the reason for this visit. I don't know how you managed to sabotage the matching, but I will uncover the truth."

"Let me know what you find out. I'd like to personally thank the culprit—whoever she or . . . *he* may be."

"You have only delayed the inevitable."

Hostility flashed in Brehan's emerald eyes. "You're deluding yourself if you think I'm the only one opposed to this practice. It's degrading to have a machine decide something as personal as a . . . a . . ."

"Mate," he completed, his dry tone bordering comical.

"Yes!"

"Would you accept a mate of your own choosing?"

"When cows fly!"

"As I thought," he murmured. Activating the E wall, he paused to inform, "You will remain under locked security until I have my answers."

"Big surprise," she laughed, but as soon as the E wall

sealed him from sight, she sank onto the edge of her bed. Anger born of helplessness quaked through her. She didn't doubt he would keep digging until he could prove her responsible for the erased data. And it would be only a matter of time before he discovered her escape route.

As for the master computer . . .

She vaguely remembered going into Erth's quarters and sitting at his private console. Dimly remembered going through the motions. But she'd left his quarters with no idea as to how she'd actually accomplished erasing all the data pertinent to the matching procedure.

A soft buzz drew her troubled gaze to the E wall. Expecting to see Erth, she sighed with great relief at the sight of Manak standing demurely at the threshold.

"May I enter?"

Rising from the bed, she gave a stilted nod. Although she had not once felt threatened by any of the Syre men, she wasn't about to let her guard down.

Manak patiently waited until the E wall closed behind him before he approached her. Stopping several feet away from her, he stood with legs slightly apart and hands clasped at the small of his back.

"I waited until *Katian* returned to his quarters," he began, but his voice so faltered that he had to clear his throat. "We were concerned— Well . . . the way he stormed out of the Meeting Chamber, we thought . . ." Manak frowned at his inability to express his reasons for checking on her. The woman, he noted with unease, was staring at him through an unreadable expression, and calmer than anyone should be, under the circumstances.

"I take it this locked security doesn't prevent *you* from entering my quarters," she said matter-of-factly.

"Barrit alone has permission to visit you." When Brehan arched a haughty eyebrow, he added, "But I designed the system."

"You're violating orders?"

"I was—*we* were concerned. Yes . . . concerned."

"Alive and kicking."

Her singsong tone brought a smile to Manak's mouth. "You're not easily intimidated, are you?"

"Should I be?"

"Considering . . ."

Again, Brehan's right eyebrow arched up. "Considering I've been kidnapped, stuck on a spaceship going to parts unknown, and told by an egotistical windbag my sole worth is that of a baby factory?"

Manak's demeanor radiated his unease with the subject. "Yes, my lady, considering all that and . . . more."

"Piece of cake."

Manak remained thoughtfully silent for several seconds. He spoke gravely. "You are an enigma to us, my lady. I admire your ability to stand up for what you believe in, but I feel it necessary to warn you to curb your obstinacy—at least lower it to a roar."

"Careful, Manak, you're developing a sense of humor."

"I'm here—"

"To warn me, I know."

"You don't know what *Katian* is capable of."

"You do, and that's why you jump at his every word? *I'm* not the enigma here, Manak, you—"

The sound of the E wall opening startled Manak more so than Brehan. She looked up in the direction of the exit with a sigh of exasperation. Manak turned on his heel, the color draining from his face at the sight of Erth standing at the threshold. Noting the unnatural erectness of the blond man's posture, Brehan stepped to his side and inspected his profile askance. There was fear in his expression, further bringing home his statement that she didn't know what Erth was capable of.

Shifting her attention to Erth, she casually looked over his clothing, which now consisted of snug-looking black pants and a black shirt he'd tucked into the waistband, but had also left open down the front. His feet were bare. His mood— She seldom saw him without his formidable scowl.

The ensuing silence so filled the room, it seemed to possess weight. Brehan became keenly conscious of Manak's unease, the heat of tension emanating from his body. She also sensed his torn loyalty and it tugged at her conscience to spare him further discomfort. Forcing herself to keep her tone light, she quipped, "I would have brought out the champagne and caviar had I known this was going to turn into a party." As Erth's long strides closed the distance, she added, "But a little warning would be nice next time. I'm not exactly—"

"Be quiet."

"—dressed for socializing," she completed, crossing her arms against her chest and meeting the searing blue gaze.

Erth glared at Manak. "I'm waiting for an explanation."

"*Katian*—"

"Not here," Brehan interrupted, stiffening with defiance when Erth slanted a contemptuous look at her. "All this attention is simply going to my head."

"I will not tell you again to be quiet!"

"Blow it out your ear," she laughed.

"*Katian,*" Manak bit out, surprising Brehan further when he grabbed her arm and tugged her to stand behind him. "I came here out of concern."

"Concern for *her*?" Erth asked with heavy sarcasm, the light pulses on his headband increasing in rhythm. "If she *is* innocent of sabotaging the matching data, what has she to fear?"

"Only fear itself."

Brehan's statement brought Manak around to face her, and Erth's gaze to harden.

"These charges against you—"

"Manak, I can take care of myself."

"Then defend yourself against them!" he cried.

Brehan narrowed a contemplative look on Erth. "What is the punishment for ingenuity aboard this tub? Confinement? Oooh, lashings? Ah ... a soulful tête-à-tête with that delightful light creation that grabbed me outside my cabin. Right?"

Manak cast a furtive glance at Erth, then looked beseechingly into Brehan's eyes. "This is serious."

"No doubt." She met Erth's fuming look. "By the way, how *do* you deal with criminals?"

"I dare say you're about to find out, little one."

"You couldn't have bypassed the BRS," Manak said adamantly to Brehan.

"I am responsible for stopping the matching. *Solely,*" she added coldly, looking up at Erth, "in case you're entertaining the notion someone collaborated with me."

"Brehan, *I* designed the system."

Despite herself, Brehan felt a pang of sympathy for the blond male. "And *I* discovered a few kinks."

"What kind of kinks?" Erth demanded.

Brehan took several seconds to haughtily stare Erth straight in the eye. "Gee, they've slipped my mind."

"You're a smug, obstreperous little creature, aren't you?" Erth grumbled, darkly observing Manak move defensively to her side.

Brehan feigned to contemplate his words. "Smug ... maybe. Little ... no one's accused me of that before. Ob-Ob—" She wrinkled her nose expressively. "Oh well, if the shoe fits ... I'm a doer. People like doers. Only dictatorial, oversized windbags seem to have a problem with—"

"She couldn't have done it!" Manak interjected, his pleading gaze burning into Erth's. "There is no possibility she could have left this room, let alone bypass the intricate biochemical security shield on the feedboards!" His voice became husky and low as he added, "Unless you believe I'm a party to it, too?"

"Return to your post."

"*Katian*—"

"Stop talking around me!" With a sharp intake of breath, Brehan walked to the other side of the bed. "Manak, I'm sorry if my resourcefulness has put a crimp in your technology, but all these electronic gizmos aren't that hard to figure out."

In perfect time to verify her statement, a loud whisper came through the communication box on the computer. "Brehan? Brehan, you there?"

Walking to her console, Brehan depressed one of the buttons. "Not terrific timing, Joy. What's up?"

"Rumor is, the matching data is missing. Seems we've been given a reprieve."

"Imagine that," Brehan said cheerfully, a smug look riveted on Erth's stunned expression. "Later, kiddo. I'm in the middle of something almost interesting, here." She cut off the line and cocked an arrogant eyebrow as Erth quickly came toward her. He was about to say aloud that he had ordered her Com cut off, but having seen the button she used, he lifted a bemused gaze to her face after a quick inspection of the panel.

Manak came to stand alongside Erth. His interest was focused on the set of panels next to the feedboard. After a brief inspection of the crystals and works behind several of the plates, he released an abrupt laugh. "She's circumvented the Com with the educational terminals!" He looked up at Brehan, his eyes bright with admiration, and she told herself that she was definitely growing fond of this particular Syre male.

"Manak, return to your post," Erth repeated, the light pulsations on his headband almost a solid line.

"But *Katian,* her mastery of our technology is incredible! I couldn't have done a finer—"

"Manak!"

Manak issued Brehan a visual warning before he left the room. When the wall sealed behind him, Brehan cocked her head to one side and cheerfully regarded Erth's livid expression.

"I suppose you're going to take my computer now?" A flicker of something deadly flashed in his eyes.

"Go ahead," she challenged. "Do whatever you have to, to save your floundering ego. But it won't stop me from opposing your laws, and it certainly won't make your miserable life any easier."

For a time, Erth seemed at a loss as to how to proceed. A gamut of expressions played across his handsome face, but then his traditional scowl reasserted itself. "Tell me, firehair, are you really so confident that I have no means by which to end your petty rebellions?"

"Short of murder?" she chuckled. "How would that look to your people? And you do fancy yourself their savior, don't you?"

"It is not for you to question my rule."

"Hmm. I must have missed that particular ordinance. There's such an extensive list in the subliminals, the information tends to become muddled in my mind."

An oddly amused twist formed on Erth's generous mouth, but the light pulsations on his headband remained swift and erratic. "I will have my answers."

Brehan walked to the vanity and half-sat against its front edge. "You may know about a female's biological functions, but you don't know diddly about a female mind. Now . . . unless you're seriously contemplating doing a lobotomy on me, I suggest you go play elsewhere."

She had hoped her condescending manner would send him away, but he came toward her with a deliberate slowness she knew was meant to fragment her defiance. It wasn't working.

"Fear is one tool by which to alter behavioral patterns." He stopped directly in front of her, towering over her, the breadth of him casting her in shadow. "Your blusters are shallow, Brehan. These rebellions are not for the good of the women, but to shield something *you* fear. Once I have uncovered this secret, *then* your true education will begin.''

Brehan sighed, ''Are you threatening me again?''

Her nervous system went into a state of shock when one of his massive hands swiftly cupped her nape and brought her to her feet. The heat of his flesh branded her skin and set off throbbing pulses throughout her rigid body. His head dipped closer. His eyes were gleaming with a challenge for her to deny the havoc his proximity was rendering on her resistance.

''Don't mock me, woman,'' he said finally.

''Does repeating this same old song help you sleep?''

Erth abruptly released her. He turned and walked several feet away. When he faced her again, his countenance bore a savage look. Despite Brehan's attempts to appear unaffected by him, she paled and again leaned against the vanity.

''I don't require sleep . . . or food. I'm not human.''

''At least we agree on that,'' she retorted, but a tremor slipped out in her tone.

''My tolerance of your sedition has met its end. Tampering with the master computer could endanger the lives of all aboard this ship. Unlike you, *their* welfare is my first concern.

''Until further notice, you will remain isolated from the others. Your computer will be altered to serve you clothing and sustenance only. Nothing more. Anyone attempting to contact you will suffer the same penalty. So consider they may not have your penchant for confinement.''

''Is that all?''

Erth remained broodingly silent for a long second. ''You have not stopped the matching, Brehan, only postponed it. In the meantime, seriously think about confessing the means by which you gained access to the data.''

''Now why would I do that?''

Her lofty expression vanished to one of alarm when

he rushed at her, stopping at the same time his hands slapped the vanity to each side of her. He didn't reply right away. Instead, he leaned to and placed his face inches from her own. Brehan experienced a strange pulling sensation inside her head. She felt as if she were falling through one of his pupils, through a long dark tunnel of which she knew there was no hope of ever returning. Panic built inside her. On the verge of crying out, he pushed away and headed for the E wall.

"I will return in a few days for the information. Don't disappoint me."

The exit no sooner sealed behind him, Brehan picked up her hairbrush and flung it at the wall.

WE WON ONCE AGAIN.

Ignoring Di'me, Brehan turned to stare at her pale, taut reflection in the mirror. Her eyelids fluttered closed as she struggled to stop the trembling in her body. Fears. If Erth discovered her one true weakness . . .

HE WON'T.

Brehan looked dubiously at her reflection. "But what if I provoke him beyond words? There's no telling what he's really capable of."

HE USES INTIMIDATION TO CONTROL.

"No, I sense something about him . . ." Turning away from the mirror, she closed her eyes again. "Not human, he said. What is he? He cindered the material in his hand."

ONLY A MAN. A VULNERABLE, FRUSTRATED MAN, Di'me laughed without mirth.

"He's a male *something*, but he's not a man."

HE'S A MAN IN THE SENSE HE WANTS YOU. AS LONG AS YOU REMAIN OUT OF HIS REACH, HE WILL REMAIN EMOTIONALLY UNBALANCED. IN TIME, THIS WILL CRIPPLE HIS CONTROL.

Shivering, Brehan crossed her arms and rubbed them for warmth. "If you hadn't interfered, I'd be in lala land on the bottom of the ocean right now."

YOU STOPPED YOURSELF. THE PSYCHIC WALL WAS NOT OF MY MAKING.

"Have I told you lately what a royal pain in the ass you are?"

NO.

"Well, I'm telling you now. Go away."

Chapter Four

All slept but one. The tranquil, gentle hum of the engines was the only sound within the walls of the *Stellar*. Designed and built by the most distinguished thru-space craft architects in the galaxy, it was the vanguard of a people's future. But to Erth, her walls were a constant reminder of his disgrace.

He stood with feet apart and hands clasped behind him, staring off into the depths of space with a look of emptiness. When alone in the Control Center, he felt small and unburdened with the mission's future. Sometimes he needed to ignore his people and their plight. There were times he needed to wipe away the memories of another existence in order to endure his present station. But at least now he felt he had charge of his destiny.

Soon, one of the females would become his mate—for the duration necessary to produce and rear a son. This son would grow quickly, become strong and able to replace his father on Syre. It did not disturb Erth that his son's legacy would be one of bondage. To be free himself, he could not feel compassion for one yet unborn.

He pressed his palms against the dome as an unbidden memory of his long-past lover, Lanulee, filled his mind. Such time had passed since their parting. There had never been the shell of flesh to bind him in those days. The free spirit was the only form in his father's house.

Renewed resentment of his epidermal cage crept up on him.

He'd ignored his birthright of the Guardianship. His freedom and Lanulee was all that he'd ever wanted. Why should it have been put upon him to care for the inferior species scattered throughout the universe?

For two thousand years, since his ostracism from his father's house, his pride had maintained that freedom alone was his birthright. But it was a need for his own kind which induced the cold shroud his personality wore openly, and yet, loneliness was a condition he couldn't acknowledge or understand—as with love. These were conditionings he believed had no substance, no existence in reality.

Nothing within the time-space continuum equaled him. He was Erth. Son of Sojan. Birthed by Mythia. *Katian*—He Who Guides.

The face of his tormentor came into focus in his mind's eye and he straightened away from the dome. He had endured minimal defiance in the past from the procured females, but always, by the time the matching procedure came about, they had succumbed to his will. Only twice had he found it necessary to resort to using the tranq-choker. There had been Colullah on the second voyage, who had given in after two days. And Christie, who had lasted a week.

But Brehan Tucker was made from a different stuff than either of those women.

Sixty days had passed since leaving Earth's orbit. Sixty long, exasperating days, forty-five of which Brehan had been kept under the strictest security confinement in her quarters. Not that that had daunted her in the least. Much to Erth's vexation, she continually found a means of bypassing the lock on her E wall. She had taught the women how to disable their individual scans. Her coaching had steeled them against the physical and psychological profiles Barrit had striven to work up on them, until Erth had personally visited each one two days prior and threatened isolation for the remaining months of the journey.

Brehan alone had laughed in his face.

"Consider this, airhead! You kidnapped me and have imprisoned me in this room like some kind of—of criminal! You think if you bark long and loud enough, I'll turn into one of your subservient pups! Think again."

Prior to that confrontation, she had stated, *"Well, mister, you may know about a female's biological functions, but you don't know diddly about a female mind!"*

That was a gross understatement. He couldn't for the life of him understand anything about the woman. In his presence, she was fire and ice, her mood swings as fierce and rapid as an electrical storm on Canta Ke-Ro.

Her incredible outings had brought about another complication. The men and women had mingled too long. Erth was aware of them pairing off, of coupling going on right under his nose. It infuriated him that his men were succumbing to the female manipulations. Two of the women were pregnant. A Syre man would accept a child not his own, but Erth knew the women's emotions would strongly object to Mastric's decision should the fathers of their children not be chosen for them.

Twenty-three previous treks had not known such unrest. And all because of one devious, cunning she-devil, who was not only *not* intimidated by him, but also not *particularly* afraid of facing punishment for her actions. She had challenged his authority with such audacity at times, he'd found himself fantasizing about shoving her into a disposal chute and casting her off into outer space.

Erth released a long sigh.

But although she was antagonistic and disruptive he admired the vitality of her lifeforce. Her survival instinct was unlike anything he'd ever encountered. His first contact, first link with her had been just prior to the vehicle plunging from the cliff. Her determination to suppress her fear had amused and charged him, and he could not refrain from toying with her in the cabin. However, here in the heart of his people, her determination was not so amusing.

He would not have his authority usurped.

Confused by the feelings of guilt and uncertainty warring inside him, he lowered his head. Somehow he had to come to terms with his fundamental reasons for taking her.

In a few days, the matching would be done. Once Brehan became his mate, he would use *armai* to control her, use *armai* to purge himself of his inexplicable curiosity to experience physical coupling with her.

The completion of a dream awakened Brehan. Her eyes opened and she stared unseeingly into the dim red lighting. Something had reached out to her in her sleep. A voice. Weak. Desperate. Getting up, she took her secret route from the room, a while later emerging in the Med Chamber. The ship was cloaked in eerie quiet and stillness, making her edgy. All slept, unsuspecting. She hadn't encountered a soul, which suited her purpose, although what that was, she wasn't certain. For a time, she stood at the computer console, absently looking over the dials and levers. Then the voice—no!—*thought!* crept into her awareness again.

She passed through an open E wall into an area called the Surgical Chamber. At the rear, she went through another exit, and into a shadowed smaller chamber.

Everywhere she looked, there was complicated equipment. She was about to turn away when she caught sight of a bluish glow behind a partition. Walking around it, she stopped short and gasped in horror.

A tall cylindrical, glass tank stood before her, filled with a misty, bluish light. And within this, suspended in midair, was a boy of about fifteen. Brehan's gaze riveted on his features. His blond hair was curly, much like Christie's, but he bore a strong resemblance to Barrit.

"Adam," she whispered.

His eyes were closed. Brehan could not sense a pulse of life within him.

Her chest began to heave as she struggled to breathe. Then she was falling into darkness, welcoming it, for she could not immediately deal with her find.

Transition date: 00.63

I grow more confused and withdrawn every day. My thoughts never stray far from Adam. I don't know who he is. It's impossible he's Christie and Barrit's son. I don't know what brought about his imprisonment, but I can't think of Erth without my blood boiling.

In the beginning, I thought the Syre men incapable of emotions, or of taking a personal interest in their futures. Not so. Despite my attempts to resist linking with them, I have discovered their impassivity is not inherent, but rather the result of their upbringing. I hate this empathy I'm feeling toward them. I hate feeling for anyone. It hurts like hell. But it's hard to shut down. So hard to resist the dictates of my nature.

Adam.

His fate terrifies me. To exist with only thought . . .

Manak brought Joy to see me a few minutes ago. He somehow rigged the security monitor so she and I could talk in private. But I regretted her visit as soon as she began to speak. The matching is going to take place later this morning. The women will be holding a secret meeting to determine how to stop it. Joy pleaded with me to join them. I can't describe the hurt I read in her eyes when I refused. Here, I had instigated the rebellion, and was now declining to see it through. But I kept seeing Adam, trapped in a living death, and I couldn't agree.

I'm so tired of fighting the powers that be.

END

With great reluctance Brehan left her bed. Taking two food capsules from a compartment on the computer console, she washed them down with a glass of the bland protein drink, then returned the glass to a separate compartment to be cleansed and sterilized. Wearing her sweat suit still, she took a shower beneath the dry cassis mist, taking some into her mouth to clean her teeth.

Mastric.

She mechanically sat at the vanity and began to brush her hair with hard strokes. The friction caused static electricity to crackle along the strands. She had yet to figure out the motive force of Erth's mental structure, although her uncanny intuition told her that his refusal to bend on the matching was not out of spite toward Lisa and Jackie, or toward the men who had impregnated them.

Erth, for all his bluster and autocratic airs, was apparently intolerant—if not oblivious—to the basic drives between males and females.

Placing the hairbrush down, she slowly rose to her feet and looked up on the wall. Her face was devoid of expression, her eyes betraying none of the workings of her thoughts.

Last night, she had refused Joy's plea, but she'd awakened knowing she could not set herself apart from their stand. As a very small child, she had discovered pain and isolation were more bearable than hearing another child cry, or seeing anguish in another child's eyes. Lisa, Joy, and countless other children during those long years, had never felt the cut of the headmistress's whip, or suffered more than a day of hunger, or endured those endless hours locked within that dark, dank closet in Paula Pitts' office. Knowing she could tolerate more than the others, Brehan had taken responsibility for infractions not her own.

Her power to endure was needed once again.

As the E wall to Deboora's quarters opened, voices swelled over Brehan before an unsettling hush fell over the room. The wall sealed behind her, giving the quarters a sense of suffocating closeness. For several long moments, she silently observed the faces of the assembly and analyzed the psychic vibes emanating from their diversified emotional levels.

Lisa, Joy, Mindi and Karen were sitting on the bed. Kousta straddled the vanity chair. Dawn and Jackie sat crosslegged on the floor in front of the arch. Jamie and Deboora stood behind them.

Brehan's gaze flitted to Christie, who was standing by the computer wall. Brehan remained impassive, careful not to betray her annoyance at finding the medix's wife present. Christie's loyalty was doubtful, a fact which disturbed Brehan.

"Joy said—"

Brehan was quick to cut Mindi off. "I changed my mind." She again looked at Christie. "What's your stake in this?"

"She's on our side," Lisa defended, casting Christie an appreciative look.

Brehan arched a challenging brow as Christie walked up to her. It lifted higher at the blond woman's statement, "The procedure's already in progress."

"Does Barrit know you're in on this?"

Lowering her gaze but for a moment, Christie replied, "No. But this isn't about him, is it? I've resented Mastric for ten years. This time, I want to see *our* side win."

Brehan examined the expectant expressions of the

other women, then she took another long moment to stare Christie straight in the eye. "What's your plan?"

"We stand collectively and refuse to accept our imposed roles."

Sighing, Brehan gave a low shake of her head. "Refusing to accept the men won't change anything. You'll all wear down, given enough time. Our only hope is to put the machine, itself, out of commission."

After a second of stunned silence, Christie seated herself on the foot of the bed and looked up at Brehan. "I'm not sure how we could go about that, Brehan. Mastric is only part machine. Its brain is a highly evolved crystal used to apply deductive reasoning beyond the scope of a computer.

"According to Barrit," she went on, "Mastric's sole function is to formulate parents for a genetically superior species. After you destroyed the data, Brehan, Erth chose another means of obtaining a balance of information."

"What kind of balance?"

"With the women refusing to submit to new physicals, a DNA workup couldn't be done. So now Erth has opted for a psychological pairing. Barrit mentioned last night that Mastric has been visiting each of you when you've been asleep. It's been evaluating your dreams, gauging the density of your lifeforces."

"Charming," Brehan sighed irritably. "Instead of matching strengths against weaknesses in our DNAs, he plans to use the same principle to balance our emotional compatibilities."

"Basically, that's it."

"I'm confused," Deboora said with a frown, peering at Brehan and Christie between dark jagged bangs hanging in her gray eyes. Tiny metal rings ornated the rims of her protruding ears. "What's wrong with our children being better than us?"

Christie looked at Brehan, who readily replied, " 'Genetically' superior isn't the real issue here. Good, bad, or indifferent, the people on our world, and the men's ancestors, survived evolution without the benefit of a *machine* dictating parentage."

Brehan looked at Christie. "Who's Adam?"

The blonde reacted as though Brehan had struck her. "How could you know— He's my son. Mine and Barrit's."

"Why is he imprisoned in that chamber?"

Christie swallowed past a lump in her throat. "He became restless and . . . unmanageable. There were no other children around for him to relate to. Erth . . . placed him in stasis until we reach Syre."

"I thought you've only been aboard this tub for ten years."

Christie lowered her head. "He underwent an aging process." She looked up, tears misting her eyes. "I want my son back. If we can win this score with the matching . . ."

Low murmurs passed among the other women.

"We were abducted," Brehan addressed the assembly, contempt lacing her tone—"told what quarters to use, and when we could and could not be with our . . . *mate* . . . once the choice had been made for us." Brehan again searched the faces of the other occupants. "Where does it end? Erth is like an over-protective parent. One who is willing to suffocate us for our own . . . good? A genetically superior new generation at what cost, ladies?"

"The cost of what we are," Kousta said, getting to her feet and threading her fingers through her unruly hair. She pretended not to notice the look of suspicion shadowing Brehan's face as the green eyes watched her every move. "If we don't do something right *now*, we may not have the chance again."

A flicker of uncertainty was seen in Christie's eyes

when she tore her gaze away from Kousta and looked at Brehan. It was well known that animosity existed between the two women. But Christie decided that the two forceful personalities had one goal in sight, thus eliciting civility between them.

Finally, Christie spoke. "We have to interrupt that meeting and force Erth to listen to us."

"We have to let him know we will absolutely shun any decision Mastric makes," Kousta asserted.

Brehan tried to submerge her instinctual dislike for Kousta, and asked Christie, "The Meeting Chamber again?"

Christie nodded.

"I'll go."

"No!" Joy jumped from the bed and rushed to Brehan's side. "It's about time *we* took some of the risks!"

"Brehan's succeeded where we've failed in the past—"

"Shut up, Kousta!" Joy hissed. Fear blanching her face, she fixed a pleading look on Brehan's profile. A chill passed through her. Although Brehan was staring at Kousta through a deadpan expression, Joy sensed something ominous in her friend's bearing. "If we stand as one force—"

"I stand a better chance at taking him off guard."

"Bre—"

"Don't argue with me! Joy, if he sees all of us walking into the Meeting Chamber, he'll be watching our every move. Alone, he'll think I'm there out of sheer arrogance. He won't expect me to do something right under his nose." Brehan activated the E wall. "Besides, my butt's already in a sling. One more infraction won't make that much of a difference."

Joy's mouth gaped open when Brehan abruptly passed into the hall and signaled for the wall to seal. Then a flush of anger darkened her coffee coloring, and she released a guttural cry as she faced the other women. "We can't let her do this alone!"

"She has a plan," Karen said, excitement lending her plain features a glow.

"She's taking all the risks again!"

"Joy . . . Joy," Lisa said soothingly, coming to stand in front of the young woman. "You and I know Bre better than anyone. Don't you trust her judgment?"

Joy swallowed painfully.

"She's not stupid, Joy," Lisa went on. "She doesn't leap before she looks—" At Joy's dubious expression, Lisa gave a feeble shrug. "Okay, so she does . . . sometimes."

Numbed with doubts, Christie added, "Brehan's right about Erth not expecting her to pull something off under his nose. Maybe we should just leave this up to her."

"So she can get all the credit?" Kousta spat.

"This isn't about recognition," Christie said, anger coloring her cheeks. "But Brehan *has* single-handedly managed to cripple all Erth's attempts to enforce the matching."

"Yeah, Brehan this and Brehan that," Kousta sneered, turning in the direction of the exit. "She is not the only one here with backbone."

Kousta was no sooner beyond the threshold, Joy gestured for the others to follow. "She's gonna blow this whole plan," she charged, glaring after the woman.

"Not if we're there to stop her," Christie muttered, then led the others into the corridor.

There were no thoughts going through Brehan's mind when she calmly triggered the pyramidal wall device and entered the Meeting Chamber. Immediately, she saw the men grouped around the table. All eyes turned in her direction. The Syres were surprised to see her—Manak alone bore a look of alarm.

Erth, his expression darkening with vexation, rose to

his feet. "You were not invited to these proceedings. Return to your quarters."

Heads continued to turn as Brehan advanced into the room and came to stand a distance across from Erth. Although she had made no obvious effort to look over the machine now behind her, an image of it was branded on her mind. With a calm as unsettling as the silence in the room, she unwaveringly stared into the giant's eyes.

"Leave this room!" Erth ordered.

Brehan walked up to Niton, who was sitting directly across the table from Erth. She tapped him on the shoulder and gestured for him to move away. Without hesitation, Niton got up and walked to the far end of the table.

Standing behind the chair, Brehan curled her fingers over the backrest. "I'm here on behalf of the women, to demand you abolish this practice."

Erth's sole response was to glare through her, the oscillation of light pulses on his headband a solid line.

"I see. You're too shy to discuss a compromise, is that it? Or is it, Erth, you're just too *pigheaded* to listen to reason?"

Silence.

Brehan cast a speculative glance at each of the men. "Speak up, gentlemen. This is your life, too, he's puppeteering."

"Brehan, I'm warning you."

Green eyes swung around to clash with bright, condemning blue ones. "There are no strings attached to me, Erth. Nor the other women. There are qualities in both cultures which could benefit the future generations of Syre. You can't expect us to forget who and what we are!"

"This meeting will proceed," Erth growled, lowering himself onto his chair.

Brehan stopped herself from looking in the direction of the exit. In her mind's eye, she could see the other women quickly approaching. A smug grin ticking at one corner of her mouth, she looked at Erth. "Only half of the constituents are present, and our voices *will* be heard."

The exit opened. The remaining women stepped into the room and formed a shoulder-to-shoulder line in front of the sealing E wall.

Brehan's right eyebrow lifted with an undeniable air of superiority. *"Now* we're all present. Do we negotiate, Erth, or must we get ugly?"

His eyes fairly glowing with animosity, Erth slowly rose from his chair again. The women started toward Brehan, distracting him.

NOW! Di'me hissed.

Lifting the chair, Brehan whirled and bound the distance to Mastric. She swung the synthetic chair through the air with all the strength she could muster, plowing it through the crystal crown of the machine. A shower of crystal segments ensued amid a lowering whine at the computer's power loss. Sparks fountained. The machine, the last of its kind, crashed to the floor, a lifeless relic of a practice used for centuries on Syre.

Conscious only of the thundering of her heart, Brehan turned to find Erth standing close to her. She looked up and studied the incredulity carved into his features. The chair slipped from her hand. The sound of it hitting the floor causing her nerves to jump.

The others in the room were as motionless as statues.

Erth's gaze lowered, broodingly questioning Brehan's sanity. Then he glanced at what remained of Mastric, at the women, the men, and back to Brehan's upturned face.

"I suppose I'm confined again."

Quaking beneath her outer composure, Brehan didn't wait for Erth to summon up a response. She headed for the exit. The silence seemed to rob the room of air, but her gait bespoke of ease and confidence. Passing the stunned, gaping women, she gave a buoyant salute and intoned, "Ladies, I'll be in my quarters."

The corridor walls passed her in a blur. Her gratification at permanently stopping the matching was shadowed by the imminent repercussions she was to face.

As yet, she had not provoked Erth beyond words and confinement. But she had sensed his outrage, and somehow had come to realize he'd never before encountered sheer defiance. She had not only terminated the matching, but she had irrevocably lanced a part of Erth that was all male—his ego.

She heaved a sigh of relief when the E wall closed behind her in her quarters. Her pulse drummed at her temples. Queasiness frolicked within the pit of her stomach. Glancing about her quarters, she tried to focus through a dense mental haze.

Her bravado was quickly ebbing. Destroying the crystal had been a spontaneous action, one, had she given it *serious* forethought, she might have stopped herself.

A hand pressed against the sickening flutter inside her stomach, she contemplated reviving herself with the tasteless goop the computer offered. At the moment, she would have given anything to have a simple glass of water, to feel the cool liquid pass down her throat, to feel it splashed against her face to ease the heat of her skin.

She nearly cried out at the sound of the E wall opening. Whirling on a heel, she felt her heart rise up into her throat. Erth's formidable features filled her vision as he stepped into the room, but she refused to move a muscle, to show the slightest fear. To do so would take away what little ground she had won thus far.

"I thought you would like to know the outcome of your achievements."

Eyeing him warily, Brehan strove to remain outwardly calm.

"I have ordered the men and women to decide their matches within the next two days."

"How magnanimous of you."

"Let me finish," Erth said suavely, a glint in his eyes that readily devoured Brehan's flippancy. "I've saved the best part for last."

Brehan remained motionless when he came to stand directly in front of her. She had been expecting rage. Uncontrolled fury. *Threats abounding*. To her increasing unease, she read amusement in his mesmerizing eyes.

"I also decided," he went on, "to spare your indefatigable brain from having to deviate from its delirious machinations for something as *inconsequential* as procuring a mate."

"I don't want to hear this," she rasped, and would have turned away but for Erth's thumb and forefinger cinching her chin. He applied just enough pressure to keep her face turned up to him.

"I have claimed you."

Brehan tried to pull away.

"Why are you so surprised, Brehan?" Releasing her, he smugly studied her ashen face. "You're far too headstrong for a Syre to handle."

"And you think *you* can?"

"It's a challenge I hope will take the edge off my boredom."

A span of combative silence ensued. Neither would fold beneath the visual lock between them until Erth issued, "You have two days to come to terms with this match. Then I will return to claim my rights."

"Toss all the threats you like! It won't alter the disgust I feel for you!"

"You *will* accept my child."

The weight of his words lingered in the air after the E wall sealed behind him. Brehan stared at the exit through a pale gray haze before the full impact of his assertion penetrated the core of her consciousness. Something began to solidify deep within her, coil and stretch through every part of her. As icy-hot sensations passed rapidly beneath her skin, she forced herself to walk toward the bed. The room seemed to shrink, close in on her. She tried not to dwell on the terror mounting inside her.

Sucking in a hoarse breath, she staggered to a halt, pressed her arms to her abdomen, and gingerly bent over. Pain moved sleekly like a sharp razor, slicing at her inner torso, seemingly bent on releasing something vile unfolding within her. Cold perspiration broke out on her skin. Then a harsh whisper exploded within her skull, LET ME OUT! MY TIME HAS COME!

—Disfunctioning female—the computer announced.

—Appropriate personnel have been advised—

The presence yawned upward into Brehan's throat. Gagging, she clamped a hand over her mouth and steeled her determination to dispel the madness she was sure was trying to overtake her.

Di'me's voice was soft, seductive, WE'RE ONE. LET ME HELP YOU.

Leave me alone!

HE'S DOING THIS TO YOU. YOU WONDERED HIS POWER!

Falling to her knees, clutching her arms even tighter to her midriff, Brehan squeezed her eyes shut and fought with all her willpower to resist the words inside her skull.

LET GO. TRUST YOUR CARE TO ME.

"Why?" Brehan rasped, rivulets of perspiration trickling down her temples.

BECAUSE I AM THE POWER WITHIN YOU. YOUR LIFEFORCE.

"Go-a-way!"

NOT UNTIL—

Di'me cut off abruptly when the E wall opened. Her back to the exit, Brehan couldn't summon the energy to look over her shoulder. Coldness began to crawl beneath her skin, snake around her bones and tighten, tighten until she nearly cried out with fear that they would fragment. An extraneous voice fell on her ears, but was received as a faraway distortion. Panic filled her more completely as she found it impossible to focus. A foggy gray world appeared to stretch out before her. Nothingness was waiting in the distance to embrace her. She'd known this realm before, on the countless occasions she'd spent locked in the closet at the orphanage. Then, it had offered her a false sense of escape. But now it represented the void she'd always known she carried within her.

"Brehan. *Brehan!*"

Something warm and firm cinched her bare right arm. The outer world shook—or something within it was shaking her.

"My lady, I'll call for Barrit."

Brehan heard the medix's name spoken. The parameters of the grayness began to darken, gradually close in. She swallowed hard past the tightening in her throat. The inner pain was gone, but her stomach was churning in a decisively threatening manner.

"He's on his way."

Focusing on the voice, Brehan willed herself to soar above the darkness, escape it if she could. It seemed an endless battle until Manak's worried face began to materialize in front of her. He was kneeling. One of his warm hands, gentle and caring, came up to frame the left side of her face.

"Are you ill?"

The tip of her tongue moved along her parched lips. "No," she managed in a hoarse whisper.

"Why couldn't you have permitted the matching to finish?"

"Manak . . . it was wrong."

"But it would have worked for—" Dipping his head forward, he pressed his brow to Brehan's. "You had no way of knowing. It's too late now, but I want you to know I will always be here for you."

"What are you babbling about?" Brehan grumbled, beginning to feel more like herself. She was flustered by his proximity, his touch. His unwarranted kindness.

Manak went back on his haunches. "Is there anything I can do to make you more comfortable?"

"Leave me alone."

The *whoosh* of the E wall opening brought her head around. Locking her teeth, she made a feeble attempt to stand. Two pairs of hands anchored her with holds on her arms.

"Steady," Barrit cautioned, sinking to his knees beside Manak. "What happened?"

"I don't know. When I came in, I found her like this—actually worse. At least her color is returning."

"Brehan, look at me."

The green eyes lifted. "I'm fine."

"You look like you've seen better days."

Brehan flexed her stiff shoulders. "I'm tired. I haven't been sleeping well."

"I'd like to do a workup—"

NO!

"No."

Barrit cast Manak an exasperated look before slanting one of paternal impatience on Brehan. "It's fast, pain-less—"

NO!

"No."

"Why are you so stubborn?"

"It's part of my charm," Brehan sighed, getting to her feet. Barrit and Manak rose as well. "Go away," she added softly.

Manak withered in defeat and nudged Barrit to follow him. The medix hesitated before heading for the exit.

"Thanks . . . for your concern," she said, turning her head just enough to watch them pass the exit threshold.

"Comes with the job," Barrit said as the wall sealed.

For several seconds after, Brehan stared into space. Not since she was that child at the orphanage had she felt so alone.

Chapter Five

The synthetic voice droned on in unison with a holographic projection of the solar system the ship was currently passing through. At the conclusion, Brehan sat up on her bed and folded her legs beneath her. The silence in the room seemed almost an entity now, magnifying her restive mood.

Erth—at Barrit's request later the day of Mastric's demise—had restored part of her computer programming. She'd spent the past two days whiling away time going over the Syre history data and the astronomy lessons. But nothing she had viewed had tempered the bitter irony of what awaited her later this morning.

It had taken her eighteen years to turn her back on the orphanage and know freedom for the first time—only to have it taken away from her seven years later.

Adam entered her thoughts, but she forced his image back into a lesser plane of importance. How could she help him, when she couldn't help herself? She looked about the room in another attempt to find something by which to distract her sense of helplessness. She had come to terms with the fact that Lisa and Joy were content with their lot in Syre's future. A new life. Certainly an existence more promising and exciting than anything they could have had on Earth. But Brehan, no matter how hard she tried to sympathize with the mission's objective, could not find the peace within herself to accept the role of a breeder.

YOU NEED TO GAIN THE UPPER HAND.

"Don't tell me what I need."

THE MASTER COMPUTER.

Brehan looked up, as if the voice in her head were coming from the heavens. "What about the master computer?"

A moment of silence.

THINK!

"How can I think when you're always in my head!"

Silence followed, which Brehan felt was testing her stamina—to what end, she didn't know.

THE STAR MAPS.

Realization straightened back Brehan's shoulders.

NEED I TELL YOU WHAT TO DO, TOO?

No. Brehan didn't need further coaxing. The plan was so simple, excitement tingled through her. If she buried the star maps deep within another program, she could blackmail Erth into returning her to her world— her and anyone else who wanted to escape his control!

Leaving the bed, she dashed across the room to the highboy. Opening the doors and pulling out the drawers to resemble steps, she climbed to the air vent high on the wall above it. She tugged free the screen and dropped to the floor, then she climbed into the boxy passage and scuttled through the ventilation ducts. Keeping in mind the layout she'd memorized from other excursions, she crossed above the corridor and turned left. Cool air chilled her, but she went on, her determination growing stronger with each passing minute.

Nine rooms to go.

Erth's quarters was isolated from the others. She could gain access to the star maps through his console—

"I've had enough of your excuses!"

The shrill words filtered through a vent screen up ahead of Brehan. Slowing her pace until she reached it, she peered beyond the mesh. Three women were in the technologically advanced gym. Deboora and Joy were standing side-by-side on a floor mat. Kousta, dressed in a black leotard, was facing them, her livid profile angled to Brehan's view.

"You've had two days to pass on that message!"

"Lay off!" Joy warned, her body trembling with anger.

Kousta's hand shot out and shoved Joy to the mat. That in itself locked Brehan's teeth, but seeing the big-boned, larger woman swing out a foot and swipe Deboora's legs from beneath her, threw Brehan's caution to the wind. Hooking her fingers through the broad mesh, she planted her bare feet to it and gave a firm kick. When the screen freed she angled it into the passageway.

"I warned you, didn't I?" Kousta spat, jabbing a finger at Joy, who was shakily helping the other woman to her feet.

"No one is allowed to see her!" Joy bit out. "That includes Lisa and me! Even her com has been cut off!"

A malevolent gleam lit Kousta's eyes. "I want Tucker to know—"

"Then tell me yourself."

Kousta pivoted, her eyes widening at the sight of Brehan standing within arm's reach.

"Brehan! How did you—" Joy's dark-eyed gaze happened to spy the open vent on the far wall.

Kousta, too, noticed it. A slow, malicious smile marred her thin mouth as she searched Brehan's flushed face.

A pulse was drumming at her temples, as Brehan forced a semblance of calm. "Is there a reason you're assaulting my friends?"

"Erth!"

"The planet or King Kong?"

"He's mine!" Kousta hissed.

Brehan glanced at Joy and Deboora. "Kousta and I would like to talk alone."

Reluctantly, the smaller women headed toward the exit. Brehan watched them until the wall sealed behind them, then turned her fiery gaze on Kousta.

"I intend to have Erth! I'm the only one here who could satisfy a man like him!"

LET ME OUT!

Ignoring Di'me, Brehan casually stated, "I didn't ask to get stuck with that dictator."

"I've seen the way you look at him!"

A niggling compulsion to laugh was barely suppressed as Brehan took a moment to scan the room. But then her sixth sense picked up on a wash of vibes emanating from the other woman. Pictures flashed through her mind, too rapid to decipher. She was aware of something dark within Kousta, something which existed just beneath the surface of her personality. The woman was abusive, inclined to bully. Brehan had more than once sensed the woman's hatred directed toward her, but until now, had not understood the basis for it.

All her pent-up frustration with Erth finally found a second *deserving* receiver. "What do you want me to say, Kousta? Sure, he's got a nice bod. Nice tight buns. Broad shoulders. All that muscle . . . and pretty blue eyes to boot. Pity, though. He's a dud. The only thing he can get up is his temper."

Visibly shaken, Kousta's eyes protruded in her face. "Why should I believe you?"

"Actually, I don't care if you do or not. Bottom line is, I won't stand by and watch you push the others around. It ends right here. We're all stuck together on this tub. Either we strive to get along . . . or *somebody's* going to get hurt."

Deciding to let Kousta mull over her warning, Brehan turned in the direction of the exit. Now that her secret passage-traipsing was exposed—and she wouldn't put it past Kousta to be on the com the minute her back was turned—Brehan thought it best to return to her quarters via the corridor. But no sooner had she turned away, a sucker punch crashed into her right temple. Pain exploded within her head and she dropped to her knees. A vicious kick to the small of her back slapped her to the floor.

"I take orders from no one!" Kousta snarled, drawing back her foot to deliver another blow.

A swift sensation of falling swept Brehan into momentary blackness.

A dark blue hue crept into Kousta's angular face as she rammed the toe of one sandal to the right of Brehan's lower spine. Only a grunt was heard from Brehan. Then to Kousta's disbelief, the redhead rose to her feet.

"Stay down, you *tucca!*"

She was about to lunge at Brehan's back when the redhead swiftly turned. Kousta froze in a moment of stunned disbelief, her gaze riveted on the brilliant amber orbs glaring at her from her rival's livid face. She made a futile bid to turn away, but Brehan's hand shot up. A flash of energy emerged from the slender fingertips. The charge struck Kousta on the jaw, lifting her off the floor and dropping her in an unconscious heap.

Brehan experienced a sensation of soaring. As she broke through the darkness, a long gasp of gratification filled her lungs. It was several seconds before she realized she was still in the workout room. Stepping back, her expression oddly rapt, she peered down at Kousta with lofty bewilderment.

A sound caused her to sharply look over her shoulder. Her blood seemed to drain from her body at the sight of Erth and one of his men standing poised at the threshold.

Turning on a heel, Brehan fled in the direction of the vent. When she was close to the wall, she propelled herself up and grabbed the bottom edge of the opening. Her arms strained to draw her upward. The back of her toes worked against the smooth surface of the wall to give her leverage. She'd just managed to plant her elbows inside the vent when she was grabbed from behind, roughly swung away from the wall and dropped to the floor on her rump.

"Get Kousta to the Med Chamber!" Erth bellowed to Uhul.

Without hesitation, the Syre man lifted Kousta into his arms and quickly headed out of the room.

"Get up!"

At his imperious bark, Brehan seethingly peered up at Erth through her tangled hair. Mindless of later punishment for her actions, she brought her legs beneath her, then rocketed upward, throwing her weight against his torso. Both toppled over, Brehan landing on top of him with her elbows embedded in his chest. She jumped to her feet, pausing only long enough for Erth to begin to sit up. Dimly aware of the guttural sounds emanating from his throat, she pulled the back of his jersey up over his head and jerked the material down past his shoulders. Then, driven by fear and determination to escape him, she ran for the exit without looking back.

Flabbergasted by not only her cunning, agility and strength, but also the swiftness by which she had executed the attack, Erth took several seconds to regain his wits. Then the jersey flash-ignited and fell away from him in ash, in time for him to witness her dash into the corridor. He jumped to his feet in a fluid motion. His muscles bunched. His naked, glistening flesh twitched with the onslaught of his internal ignitions.

"Not this time, little one," he growled, and went in pursuit.

Brehan was running with all her steam when her counterpart again took over, plunging Brehan's consciousness back into the cradling darkness. Entering the central lift, Di'me's right hand came up. A brushlike discharge swept from the palm and swept along the panel of buttons. The lift descended past the first level of storage rooms, to a level forbidden to the women. When the lift came to a stop, Di'me stepped from it and walked into an enormous, circular room.

Then Brehan awakened as if from a nap.

The energy level in her body plummeted and, swaying, she grabbed onto something solid beside her to steady herself. She looked up, stunned to see that she was no longer in the corridor. Icy tentacles of fear wrapped around her hammering heart as her surroundings finally began to register. She was braced up by a massive computer console. Across from her was a row of six, tall, tubular encasements. The walls and domed ceiling of the room were embedded with thousands of multi-faceted crystals the size of grapefruits.

It was as if the room were a world unto itself, or a massive crystalline womb. She sensed an unknown life form thrumming around her, and in awe of it, she straightened away from the console and walked further into the room.

Above, Erth broke his run in the corridor when an image flared up in his mind—Brehan standing beneath a canopy of Crou crystals. He slowed to a stop at the central lift—telling himself she couldn't have possibly bypassed *all* the security measures preventing the women access to the Feeding Chamber—and peered down the shaft. The top of the lift was far below, below the permitted floor levels. He waited a few more moments, repeatedly jabbing the appropriate button, but the lift didn't ascend to its pre-programmed second level station.

Suspicion and incredulity gnawed at his insides until he was forced to give in to the impressions bombarding his mind. He detonated his system. Gone was the human likeness. A mass of turbulent glowing energy, he streaked down the shaft and filtered through the lift. The instant he entered the Feeding Chamber, he saw Brehan inspecting one of the teleporters.

BEHIND YOU!

Brehan turned to find a cyclone of energy bearing down on her, a similar creation to what had grabbed her at the cabin. Before she could react, it ingested her within its embodiment. Blinding light surrounded her as her arms and legs flailed within an otherwise nothingness. In the next instant, she found herself enclosed in one of the clear tubes she'd been looking over moments before.

The mass moved away to hover by the computer console. Clawlike fingers of lightning forked outward from the upper region of the *thing*, distending and moving upward toward the crystals embedded in the domed ceiling. A sporadic interplay of webbed lightning filled the room, the brightness of which forced Brehan to turn her head away and close her eyes. Mingled with her fear were impressions beyond the scope of her understanding. Impressions of light and heat and timelessness and life, all boundless and unbridled, defying clear definition.

When she looked up, the lightning display had ended. The crystals throughout the room glowed white-hot, and hummed with internal kinetic life.

The light mass moved in her direction. The door to her teleporter slid open and, nearly sick with fear, she pressed herself to the back of the encasement. But the light creation closed in and absorbed—vacuumed—her back into its main body. For the next several seconds, she was only aware of swift, stomach-dropping movement. Then sizzling and hissing. Next, she experienced a sensation of being . . . *coughed out*. Something hard lay beneath her. While there was a sense of security in her inertia, her heart continued to thunder and her senses reeled. Gradually, she realized she was folded over her bent legs, her brow pressed to the cool floor of her quarters. When she drew her painfully leaden arms closer to her body, she discovered she was naked, covered only by the thickness of her long, unbound hair.

A movement of light in her peripheral vision brought her head slowly around. Unfolding to a sitting position, she stared in horrified fascination at the mass, which was shifting and shrinking, seeming to fold within itself. A hazy human form began to take shape. At the first sight of a skeletal frame manifesting within the cloud, she scurried on her knees to her bed and yanked the top cover down across her. She sank onto her folded legs and trembled violently as she watched muscle and flesh materialize on the creature from its feet to its head.

When the last humanlike detail solidified, Erth's immense frame stood where the light mass had been. Stunned that the entity which had abducted her on the beach, and Erth, were one and the same, she gasped, "You!"

Deep breaths bellowed in and out of him with his attempt to bring under control his disgust at having to confine his true form. His large hands flexed by his sides. The flesh covering him felt restrictive, suffocating. His bright eyes came to light on Brehan's face, then lowered to the cover she clutched above her breasts. Had her gaze not dropped to the region of his bare thighs, and had her look of shock not crumbled to one of blatant disgust before she lowered her head, he would have taken pity on her and have dressed before questioning her.

"How did you bypass the biochemical response system?"

Silence, but for her hoarse, rapid breathing.

"Don't anger me, Brehan! The BRS is programmed to respond to the Syres acidotic metabolism. It should have denied you access to the Mastric data *and* the Feeding Chamber!"

Clenching and unclenching his fists at his sides, Erth happened to notice the gaping vent. A breath burst from him. He swung a harried, condemning gaze to Brehan's bent head. Struggling to control the churning within him, he closed the distance between them and bit out, "You used the air ducts to enter my quarters when you erased the Mastric files, didn't you? What was your objective *this* time?"

"I was out for a stroll."

Erth's patience snapped. Wrenching the cover from her hands, he flung it aside. Brehan released a cry and kicked at his shins, but the giant was quick to cinch her upper arms and pull her up onto her feet. It was then he glimpsed something in her mind. His outrage overruling any compassion he might have shown her, he charged, "You were after the star maps!"

Brehan's head shot up. Disbelief enlarged her eyes. "How could you—" She bit into the soft, inner tissue of her bottom lip. "Oh God, don't tell me you can read minds!"

Erth's response was a grim tightening of his lips.

The pulling in her mind she'd been experiencing since the cabin ordeal, was finally making sense. A suffocating sense of helplessness closed in around her at the thought that even her mind was open to his invasion. In a desperate attempt to break away from him, she lifted a knee to slam his groin, but he anticipated the move, and the blow landed against one of his corded thighs. With a low growl, he whirled them both around. Brehan released another cry as she found herself falling atop the bed, and Erth's powerful body canopying her. Her knees drew up to shove him away. One of his legs forced them back down.

"Get off me!" she screamed, driving a fist into his jawline. Immediately, her other hand came up to yank his hair. Shifting his weight onto a hip, he caught her wrists and with one hand, effortlessly pinned them to the pillow above her head. With a cry of frustration, Brehan bucked up in a futile attempt to throw him off balance. The light pulsations on his headband formed a solid line, as he planted his other hand on her hip and forced her to lie flat. Brehan's lips curled back from her clenched teeth. The palm and fingers resting on her hip seemed to brand her skin. Squirming, tears slipping from the corners of her eyes, she vowed, "I'll kill you!"

"Cease moving against my body."

The words, spoken in a guttural warning, froze Brehan in fear. She released a thready breath and stared into his radiant eyes, her own pleading with him to leave her alone.

Erth's gaze swept over the curve of her hip and waist, then came to dwell on her heaving breasts. An uncomfortable warmth spread through him at his body's response to her nude softness. He'd been in the company of humans for over two thousand years, and yet, this was the first time this condition had manifested in his humanoid framework.

He looked down at the rigid implement at his groin and scowled. His true form did not react in so obvious a manner, no matter how great his desire to couple.

"Get off me," Brehan pleaded in a strained whisper of a tone.

Erth found himself staring into large green eyes, filled with such fear it took him aback. He became conscious of her rigidity, the heat of her body, her stark vulnerability, and his expression softened. Slow, easy light pulses began to blip across the headband. Staring deeply into her eyes, he slid his hand along her thigh, then shifted her slightly onto her left hip and cupped one of her rounded buttocks. Although he sensed her seething anger, he was inwardly quieting, experiencing a kind of euphoria that was previously unknown to him. His body was taut, anxious with need, but his mind was drugged by the rush of imput her softness, curves and scent was transmitting through his external senses.

"You have no right to put me in this position!"

Her righteous tone brought a wry grin to his mouth. With a ruminative moan, he leaned over her, buried his face against her neck and deeply inhaled her briny scent. He was aware of the hostility sparking along her every nerve, but also conscious of her hardened nipples against his chest.

"Stop it!"

Lifting his head, Erth leaned back just enough to look down at her right breast—round and firm, the nipple inviting. There had been times when, during his meditations, he'd glimpsed couples in the throes of sexual heat. He'd wondered the significance of a grown man suckling like an infant at his mate's breast, but now found that his own mouth had gone dry with anticipation. Frowning at his deepening curiosity, he enclosed the enticing mound in one of his large hands, his thumb testing the firmness of the dark peak.

"Stop!" Brehan cried, then clenched her teeth when a spasm of pleasure gripped her. Her body quivered in restraint as his fingers moved languidly, exploringly over her collarbone and one side of her neck. Desire she refused to accept pummeled her unmercifully. Perspiration broke out on her feverish skin as she instinctively arched up. Erth's hand returned to her breast, kneading, stoking the ache of longing behind it, his thumb lazily rolling the nipple in sensual circles.

"Oh God," she moaned, her eyes squeezed shut, her breath passing her parted lips in spurts. Icy-hot pain throbbed beneath every part of her skin. She could think of nothing but the blaze of passion cocooning her.

Erth's lips descended around the nipple and tentatively suckled. Mindless of her actions, she arched higher, signaling him to suck harder, clear through her swollen breast if that's what it would take to end her torment. But he chose, instead, to rub his tongue back and forth over the top of the peak.

"Erth!" she gasped, tears slipping from beneath her lashes.

He suckled again, his hand kneading. Delirious, she wrenched a hand free and swiftly wove her fingers through his hair. She drew him closer, closer, wanting his mouth to surround her entire breast. Never in her wildest dreams did she ever imagine torture could be so sweet, so *consuming*.

STOP HIM!

Instantly responding to the belligerence of Di'me's command, Brehan slammed a fist against Erth's shoulder, then frantically tried to pull his hand away from her breast. At the same time he lifted his head and his glazed eyes met hers, her wrist was again imprisoned with the other.

A frown creased Erth's brow as he regarded the feral bewilderment in her eyes. She trembled beneath him, her softness prompting him to run his fingertips along her lips.

"You have a beautiful body," he said, his voice inordinately deep as his gaze traveled once more the length of her. "A breeder's body," he added, smoothing a palm across her abdomen.

It was a fierce struggle for Brehan to get beyond the strangulating grip of her mortification, especially in light of the fact she had acted so uncontrollably wanton moments ago. Watching Erth's fingers trail over her ribs, she realized he had never actually explored a woman's nudity. She was a curiosity, otherwise, he would have mounted her before her reasoning had returned in time to spare her the union.

Forcing humility into her tone, she implored, "Please don't submit me to any more of this."

Erth stared into her eyes for a long moment. This quieter side of her touched him in ways her fiery spirit had yet to brook. He was tempted to explore every plane of her body with his hands, but he decided to end her ordeal before her temper resurfaced. However, the instant he released her wrists, she slapped her palms to his chest and tried to push him away. Then, managing to free her right leg from beneath his left, she planted the knee to his hip and shoved. To no avail.

Forcing her leg down with a hand, he informed her, "Your actions brought us to this point."

"Get the hell *off* me!"

"Your squirming is arousing my flesh. I strongly suggest you stop—unless you would like to continue?"

"You're crushing my side!"

It was Erth's intention to shift her into a more comfortable position, but when his hand moved along the small of her back, he touched upon something. "What is this?"

Brehan's fist sailed toward his face.

Again, without effort, he caught her wrist in midair, but this time, he flipped her onto her front and placed a hand between her shoulder blades to anchor her.

"Damn you, you can't treat me like this!"

"Like what?" he asked absently, running his fingers along the raised scar tissue on her back, buttocks and thighs. "What caused these?"

Brehan released a feral cry and made every effort to kick and scratch some part of Erth's body. Managing to get onto her side, she put all her strength into ramming her elbow into his chest. Pain radiated throughout her arm on impact. A low grunt was all that came from Erth. Her arms and legs wildly scrambling, she nearly made it over the side of the bed when she found herself lifted and again flipped onto her back.

With a nonchalant air about him, Erth rested his left forearm on the mattress to the other side of her, caging her within the muscular power of his torso and arms. "What caused the scars?"

"None of your goddamn business!" she panted, squirming fiercely beneath him. "Get off me, you naked ape!"

She kicked, punched, bucked and released a stream of colorful invectives until the futility of her actions penetrated her reasoning. Breathing deeply, she forced herself to quiet, but the fiery hatred in her remained as she glared up into his face. She was profoundly conscious of his palm coming to rest again on her abdomen, but she suspected he was testing her, feeding her portions of his superior strength, and waiting to see how she fared with its ingestion.

One of Erth's eyebrows arched as he lazily contemplated her unexpected stillness. "I suspected you were untried, but now I sense there is more to your inhibitions than a reluctance to face the intimacies."

Staring up at him, she again glimpsed the puzzling red sheen in his eyes, the sheen that was even more unsettling than the unnatural, mesmerizing brightness of his blue irises.

"I don't know how I bypassed the BRS or got into the Feeding Chamber," she asserted, striving to keep her voice level despite the indignation quaking through her. "You're a mind reader! You must know I'm telling the truth!"

"Were you telling the truth when you implied to Kousta I was impotent?"

"N-no—so what! How could you have heard that?"

"Since your arrival, most of my meditation has been focused on your whereabouts. I could sense your movements, but I confess I never figured the air ducts as your avenue of escape."

"So now you know. *Get . . . off . . . me!*"

Erth's eyes softened further with something akin to compassion. "I need a son."

A brief caustic laugh burst from Brehan. "Fat chance you'll get one from me, you sorry bas—"

Erth curtly interjected, "There is a method of impregnating you which doesn't involve coupling. I will grant you this, to spare your shyness."

Shyness? She wanted to laugh—or spit—in his face, but he was offering her a chance to spare herself a physical union with him. "I'll take it! But I want your word you will never force yourself on me!"

"You have it, but there is a price, *te-ni-e.*"

Cold dread knotted her stomach.

"We are mates, Brehan, whether you choose to accept it or not. I am your superior, and as such, you must learn to obey me. Accept my judgment in all matters."

Brehan fiercely spat in his face, but to her amazement, Erth laughed. For a moment, she almost thought him human.

"You never fail to surprise me," he murmured, his eyes still unnaturally bright. "You and I will create leaders."

"Only in your wet dreams. Just what exactly is this *price* you're talking about?"

Erth searched her flushed features, as if re-committing them to his memory. "That you contain your displeasure of the mission's objective. It is one thing to vent your frustration on me, quite another to embroil the others in your schemes."

"I haven't—"

"Be quiet." Annoyance drew down his eyebrows. "You *will* bear me a son. How you conceive does not matter to me, but it must be soon."

"I don't want children!"

"One. My son."

Erth purposefully ran a hand along Brehan's side, his eyes never wavering from her own. "I would like to experience a physical union with you, Brehan."

Vehemently, Brehan slapped him in the face, but Erth captured her wrist and brushed the back of her fingers against his generous mouth. An exquisite tremor rocketed through her. To add insult to the treacherous betrayal of her hormones, the gleam in his eyes warned her that he was aware of her body's willingness to be touched by him again. As if to verify this, he forced the back of her hand to caress the cheek she'd struck.

Desperate to cut off the desire that was again swelling up inside her, she coldly stated, "My *mind* will never submit."

With startling agility for his size, Erth got up from the bed and walked to the intercom. His lack of modesty unnerved her, but so did the fact that she couldn't tear her gaze from his magnificent body—until, at the intercom, he unexpectedly looked at her. Shame burned through her. Tuning out what he was saying into the communication unit, she retrieved the cover from the floor and hastily wrapped it around her. She glanced up at the sound of the E wall opening. Lute stood at the threshold and passed a pair of black pants to Erth. Crimson colored Brehan's face as she caught the look of surprise in the young man's eyes when he glanced her way.

"Nothing happened!" she cried.

To add to her consternation, Barrit entered the room while Erth was still donning the pants.

"I want her examined, Barrit."

"Right now?"

Erth looked across the room through an unreadable expression. Brehan locked eyes with him. Her attempt to show contempt for what he'd put her through, melted as his physique once again commanded her full attention. Dressed only in the pants, his powerful build homed in on her sexual radar.

"Yes," Erth grumbled, finally breaking off eye contact with her. "And I want her psychologically prepped and conditioned to receive artificial insemination by the end of the week."

His magisterial tone banished Brehan's fleeting biological urge and reinforced the foundation of her defiance. She would never again forget his true motives, or the fact that he was not an actual man. He was only a being determined to break her spirit, a being prepared to use any means available to him to persuade her to accept childbearing.

Sensing Brehan's emotional withdrawal, Erth brusquely left the room.

Barrit waited until the E wall sealed behind his superior before focusing on Brehan. Whatever had gone down between the guardians, she was obviously distraught.

"Leave me alone," she said dully.

Although he was appalled at the thought of proceeding at this time, he rationalized that in her weakened state he might have one chance to try to understand her. "I have my orders."

Chapter Six

After requesting a jumpsuit and sandals from the computer, Barrit went to the bed and proffered the bundle.

Brehan churlishly snatched it from his hand and stormed into the bathroom, where she dropped the cover to the floor and stepped beneath the showerhead. The dry, diamondlike mist cascaded over her while she briskly scrubbed every part that Erth had touched. After a long time of indulging herself, she exited the shower and grudgingly slipped into the jumpsuit. Since she preferred to remain barefoot, she kicked aside the sandals, then rigidly turned to face a full-length wall mirror. The garment was of a simple design, the pale blue material similar to cotton-blend. It had a round neckline, and the sleeves barely covered the curve of her shoulders. The legs tapered to her ankles.

When she reentered the bedroom, she found Barrit patiently awaiting her by the bed.

"I won't take off my clothes."

A flicker of surprise danced across the medix's features before he stated, "It's not necessary."

Removing a small oblong instrument from an

encasement attached to a wide black belt around his waist, he strapped the implement to his left wrist. A sphere-shaped instrument was unclipped from his belt, then placed on the night table. With an adjustment of a dial on the oblong box, the sphere began to pulsate with tiny rhythmic lights. When the lights equaled in rhythm with the light pulses on his wrist instrument, he gave a casual gesture for Brehan to recline on the bed.

"I prefer to stand."

"This is a kilbrater," he explained, indicating the wrist instrument. "It registers any internal discrepancies my hi-icpathic sensors detect, and stores the information within the portable memory banks of this sphere. Now, unless my patient is horizontal and reasonably quiet, my sensors could relay inaccurate information."

"I'm perfectly healthy."

He gestured again. "I have my orders."

Muttering beneath her breath, a flush of anger heightening the color in her face, Brehan forced herself to go to the bed and stretch out on her back. Every muscle in her body was taut. When the medix seated himself alongside her, she could not bear to meet his gaze, and turned her head the other way.

"Try to relax. This won't hurt," he advised, and gently touched his fingertips to her skull. He paused to digest her cringing reaction to being touched, then made a slow descent along her body with his sensitized fingertips. Images flashed through his mind. Part of his gifted brain catalogued the information, while another part focused on other factors. He noted her tense muscle reaction to his light probing, the heat of her skin beneath her clothing, the aura of energy crackling around her.

"You have abnormal scar tissue along your back—" His fingers moved over her outer thighs again. "—and on the back of your thighs." Suppressing a stab of revulsion, he stated, "I can easily remove these."

Her piercing green eyes swung to his face. The depth

of her animosity startled Barrit. "Just get this mauling over with."

Despite the fey impressions tingling through him, Barrit chuckled and rose to his feet. "I like your spirit. It can be difficult to understand, but I admire it."

Warily watching him replace the instruments on his belt, she eased up into a sitting position. "That's it?"

Barrit looked down at her with a ghost of a smile. "That's it. You're a healthy specimen." He sat on the edge of the bed again. "Those scars . . ."

He saw a flicker of resentment in her eyes before she replied, "A leather strap in the hands of a madwoman."

Barrit gave a solemn nod. "I suspected as much. Joy and Lisa have told Christie some frightening stories about the Marson Estate, and the headmistress, Paula Pitts."

"I don't need or want your pity."

"Not pity. Compassion."

"I don't want that, either."

"What *do* you want, Brehan?"

"To be left alone. Is that so hard for any of you to understand?"

Barrit's dark eyes continued to observe her, his inner sense imbibing her reactions to his words, his very presence. "I mean no disrespect by prying. We have lived sheltered lives, Brehan. It's difficult to comprehend cruelty—especially to a child."

Brehan scooted back on the bed and braced her back against the nondescript headboard. Drawing up her knees, she linked her arms around them. "You never raised a hand or your voice to Adam?"

Barrit could not disguise his inner pain with the subject of his son. "No. When he was very young, my greatest pleasure was soothing his tempers in my arms. At his worst, he was still the best part of me."

"Why do you allow Erth to keep him in stasis?"

"It's not my place to object—"

"He's *your* son!"

Barrit nodded. "He is. Erth's methods may at times seem harsh, but his reasons are just. Adam ... was lonely. His need for other children—for attention—drove him to reckless measures. His pranks nearly caused the deaths of two of the women on the previous voyage. The safety of all had to be taken into consideration."

"Couldn't you have found something to occupy him, channel his energies?"

Barrit deeply sighed. "He refused instructions. We tried everything we could as parents and peers to get him to open his mind to learning, Brehan. Adam is headstrong. His lessons are transmitted to him during his stasis. Hopefully, by the time we reach Syre, he will be prepared to accept his role in society."

"The lessons aren't reaching him, Barrit. He's still lonely, and damn frustrated. He needs to be given the chance to prove himself aboard this tub."

"How do you know this?"

"Sometimes he talks to me."

Skepticism darkened Barrit's face. "He's in stasis."

"Yes, but his mind is very active. I'm usually sleeping when he communicates with me—although, not always. Either he's also telepathic, or I'm unusually receptive to his thoughts."

Barrit searched her face for a long time. "His mind is active," he murmured, paling.

"Yes. This stasis is a living death, Barrit."

"As *Katiah,* you could possibly convince Erth to end Adam's sentence."

"It's unlikely Erth will listen to me." At the deepening pain in Barrit's eyes, she added, "But I'll try to talk to him."

"Thank you. You have a good heart, Brehan. You will make a wonderful mother."

"I don't have the tolerance."

"You bear the scars."

Brehan grimaced. "For all the wrong reasons."

"I don't agree. You're a compassionate woman."

For a time, Brehan stared into the knowing eyes of the man across from her. She didn't want to discuss her past, or her ongoing conflict with the rage within her. Barrit was easygoing. All too likable. Like Manak, he seemed to know how to calm her, how to bring her gentler side to the surface.

"What's this hi-icpathic pulse you mentioned?"

Although he knew she was trying to sway him from the subject of her past, Barrit nonetheless replied, "It was once a gift my entire race possessed. It's a combination of sensitivity of touch and empathic-telepathy."

"What does it do?"

"When I touch someone for the purpose of screening their biological functions, I receive images ... very much like x-rays. My ancestors used this gift to monitor their own health, but it began to fade a few generations before the last Feydais attack."

"Why?"

Barrit shrugged. "Probably because so many centuries had passed without illness."

"Do any of the other men have this gift?"

"I was the last Crinlun to carry the gene. When Erth discovered it in me, he taught me the anatomy of the prospective races."

"How are you and I different?"

"Syres have two hearts. Our body chemistry is slightly different. And as you may have noticed, we share identical skin, hair and eye coloring."

"Even your ancestors?"

"We have always looked as we do now. But the hybrid offspring varies between parents."

"Why is it you call Erth by his given name, while the other men use his title?"

Barrit released a low laugh. "Arrogance, I guess, and partly because he allows me to. He and I worked closely together during my medical training, which was about the time I was entering my rebellious adolescence. I was filled with a sense of self-importance. Erth found me amusing and permitted me to drop his title."

"How old are you?"

"Using your terminology, two hundred thirty-one."

Comical disbelief glowed on Brehan's face. "You don't look much older than me. What's your life expectancy?"

"Previous generations lived approximately eleven hundred years—but they were breathing semi-polluted air."

"Oh . . . sure . . . polluted air."

"I would say our life expectancy now is about eighteen hundred years."

"I wouldn't want to live that long."

"Your body has already altered its aging process."

"I don't feel any different."

"You're not normally aware of aging, are you?"

"No, I guess not. What about this Crinlun thing you mentioned?"

"That's a bit more complicated. You see, my ancestors were more advanced than other civilizations. Their brains had become the center of their existence, and their craving for knowledge—" He grinned. "—not unlike your own—was insatiable. They hoped the Guardians would grant them the freedom to spread out among the other races in the universe as the Seekers had. During their training—which spanned centuries—reproduction was considered a hindrance."

"Wouldn't genocide have occurred in time?"

"There was never any danger of that. The Orthandite was designed to replace the mother until a time of nesting—placing of the infants into desired homes."

"It sounds like the babies weren't returned to their natural parents," Brehan said with a hint of disgust.

"My people didn't—still don't—value the tie of bloodlines as do cultures of your world."

"Then I think your ancestors evolved too far. Blood ties give a stronger sense of family. At least it seems important when you don't have ancestry to think back on."

His gaze shrewdly studying the enigma sitting across from him, Barrit casually crossed an ankle over the opposite knee. This more personable side of her intrigued him almost as much as her disruptive abilities.

"Why didn't any females survive the Feydais attack?"

Barrit hesitated before replying, "The females were nested first . . ." His throat constricted, and he lowered his eyes. "Feydais destroyed every living thing, except those of us who were protected by the Orthandite. We've never been able to determine why *we* survived."

"Erth survived," she said, a note a bitterness in her tone. "The history data says he removed the infants from the Orthandite and raised them."

"Yes, he did."

"Why do you call him *Katian?*"

"It's a title befitting his guardian status. The majority of his race lives beyond the universe as we know it."

"He really isn't human?"

Barrit shook his head.

"Then why does he make himself look human?"

"It's forbidden for any of the Guardians to exist in their energy form outside of Haveth."

"Why?"

"I'm not sure. It's not a subject Erth will readily discuss."

"How old is he?"

"Twenty-seven, twenty-eight—"

"Hundred years!"

Barrit laughed. "Thousand."

"Twenty-seven thousand years," Brehan muttered dazedly.

"He's relatively a child to his own kind. Over two thousand years of his life has been spent guiding my people. He's gone to great lengths to rebuild Syre. He was close to returning to his home when Feydais— Well, now he must endure an extended term."

"Anything *I* can do to help send him on his way?"

Barrit was thoughtfully quiet for a few moments. "Erth is a very powerful being, Brehan. The first of his kind was pure energy, a great mass which divided and subdivided into countless suns—life-giving suns. At one point, the nebula of the original mass developed a conscious will, and Sojan came to be.

"Erth's family are the gods written about in fables," Barrit went on, "but he has been separated from his kind for a long time. He can be understanding ... compassionate, but he is not accustomed to being crossed."

"Maybe it's about time someone stood up to him."

"Do you mind if I ask you about Kousta?"

Brehan shrugged noncommittally.

"What provoked the confrontation?"

A snort of air gushed from her nostrils before she could suppress it. "There's something about her that irks the hell out of me," she said testily. "She's a bully. Doesn't seem to have a conscience. I caught her pushing Joy and Deboora around."

"So you struck out at her."

"I think so. I know I warned her to lay off. Something happened, but my memory of it is hazy."

"You don't know how she received the burns on her jaw?"

"Burns?"

"I rejuvenated the damaged tissue, but a strange discoloring remains on her skin. I haven't been able to analyze it as yet."

"I don't know what could have happened," she said with puzzlement clouding her expression.

"She also mentioned your eyes became amber just before you struck her."

A nervous chuckle escaped Brehan. "Joy and Lisa have said the same thing on a few occasions. It's probably just a trick of the light."

Barrit stared deeply into her eyes. For several long

seconds, he tried to comprehend how such a vivid green could be mistaken for amber. When he finally noticed that she was staring at him with an eyebrow cocked peevishly, he withdrew his study. "You are most definitely a perplexing woman. Why do you keep yourself emotionally distant from the other women?"

"I have always preferred my own company."

A smile ticked at one corner of Barrit's mouth. "After so many years of taking care of Lisa and Joy, I find it hard to believe you can so easily shut yourself off from them."

"I know what I'm doing."

"Do you?" Barrit asked softly.

Sighing, Brehan ran the fingers of one hand through the crown of her hair. "My absence forces them to become stronger individuals. It seems whenever I'm around, the men and women alike want me to tell them what to do and how to do it."

"You're overly sensitive."

"Am I?" Crossing her legs, she rested her forearms on her thighs. "These gatherings, Barrit, have formed a strong bond between the men and women. All by their lonelies, they're working out their aspirations for Syre's future. Without Erth. Without me. The laws should be written by the people. Leaders should be chosen *by* the people."

"And if the people choose to honor your title?"

"Give it a rest, will you! You've spent your whole life under Erth's thumb. Do you really believe you need another ... *guardian* ... hovering over you?"

Barrit thought over her words for a time, then lifted his eyebrows in a gently mocking manner. "In many ways, Erth is our father."

"People outgrow their need for parental guidance."

"We're a little slow in that regard. He's security."

Brehan digested the information, then a question pushed to the fore of her mind. Unable—or perhaps unwilling—to stop herself from verbalizing it, she asked, "Why is it so important to him to have a son?"

"To watch over Syre."

"Because of Feydais?"

Barrit frowned. "Possibly. As I said, Erth had nearly brought my ancestors to a zenith in evolution when Feydais returned that last time. A son endowed with his abilities might prevent such a disaster from ever happening again."

"But Erth wasn't able to stop Feydais."

"He was on Vastra-Sha during the attack. You know, in your own way, you have been leading us down a specific path."

"Right," Brehan said snidely.

"Yes, I am right. Take the matching, for instance. Opposing it required drastic measures, and you triumphed. That single act alone gave the others the courage to question their right to free thinking.

"Lisa," he went on, "gave a little speech at one of the gatherings, regarding productive creativity. She credited *you* for that advice."

Brehan self-consciously twitched her shoulders.

"Lute and Karen created Decco, and now we have arts and crafts classes. Jackie is working on graphics to introduce video games. Lisa and Joy are creating infant paraphernalia. Jamie is designing clothing—"

"To *their* credit, not mine."

"And Erth has uncharacteristically stayed in the background and allowed them to progress on their own." Barrit fell silent, observing the flush in Brehan's cheeks. When he spoke again, his tone was soft. "Tell me again that you are in no part responsible for these changes."

"Maybe inadvertently," she said, to which Barrit chuckled.

But then he regarded her pensively. "Isn't it time you allowed us to help you?"

"Meaning what?"

"My empathic abilities permit me to experience your

emotional states, but I need to have a clearer understanding in order to help you."

"There's nothing you can do to help me."

"Not true, Brehan. There's a strong possibility a full psychological workup may convince Erth you need more than a few days to accept the role of motherhood."

NO! HE LIES! SEND HIM AWAY!

"I don't think he cares one way or the other."

"I've seen him express anger over you, *and* regret for your inability to accept this life we've imposed on you. Tap into his compassion, Brehan. Make it work for you."

GUARD YOUR MIND! DON'T LET ANYONE KNOW US!

Brehan frowned. *Us?* Di'me was getting out of hand.

"All right, Barrit. I'll do whatever it takes to keep Erth away from me."

YOU *FOOL!*

Noting that Brehan winced, Barrit asked, "Is something wrong?"

The word, "No," came out as a hoarse whisper. Pressing her fingertips to her temples, she tried to massage away the ache in them.

"You're pale, Brehan."

"I'm all right. Sometimes my conscience gets on my nerves."

"Your conscience?"

"The voice in my head."

A sinking feeling struck Barrit in the gut. "What is it telling you?"

"Not to trust you."

"Why?"

A wan grin touched Brehan's mouth. "Paranoia."

Barrit was quick to guard his deepening suspicions. "Does this . . . voice influence your outbursts?"

Lowering her hands to the bed, she said, *"Erth* influences them. Look, I keep trying to tell myself that Syre's future holds the key to all my dreams, but it's hard, Barrit."

"No one expects you to accept the unknown without reservations." Barrit reached out and took one of Brehan's hands into his own. She flinched, but to her credit, she didn't pull away from him. "It's human to fear what we don't understand, but you're a fighter. Syre *desperately* needs your strength and determination."

"Why do you think I need to forgive you?" she asked suddenly, her gaze seeming to bore into Barrit's brain.

The medix shrank back, startled by her ability to have read his underlying guilt at her predicament. For an almost unbearable time, he felt as if something were scanning his soul.

"Barrit?"

"What?"

"I understand the reasons for our abductions."

"Do you?"

Brehan nodded, the intensity remaining in her eyes. "Survival. The extinction of your race would have been a horrendous injustice."

Dispelling the chill within him, he asked, "Are you going to let me do the psychological workup?"

"What does it entail?"

"A simple mind-meld."

"You're going to try to get inside my head?"

"It'll give me a deeper understanding of what motivates you."

Brehan grimaced. "Have you ever done this before?"

"Twice. Brehan, once we discover what our darkest, deepest fears are, we can confront them. We would all like to believe that we have it within ourselves to cope with our problems. Truth is, as humans, we require the emotional oneness of those around us. We need understanding. We crave the reinforcement of our individual existences.

"In sharing your mind with me, you'll be freeing your fears and allowing the whole woman locked up within you to be released."

"The rage, Doc . . ."

"Stems from your childhood."

"I realize that, but I don't understand how rehashing it all is going to make me feel . . . *whole*."

Barrit took her hand again and placed it between his own warm clasp. "I suspect there is something deep within your subconscious that you have not confronted."

A dry laugh rattled in Brehan's throat. "What, something worse than what I *do* remember?"

"Possibly."

Sighing, she looked up to study the ceiling for but a moment. "Okay. Let's get it over with."

I'M WARNING YOU!

"I need you to slide down and recline. That's it. Relax, Brehan." The green eyes looked up at him trustingly as he positioned the fingertips of both hands to her temples. "Close your eyes. Good. Now listen to the sound of my voice. Feel yourself relaxing. More, Brehan. More. Slip through the grayness. Deeper. Deeper. Your body is becoming weightless. Look for a golden glow, Brehan. Tell me when you see it."

After several seconds, Brehan murmured, "I see it."

"Go to it. Bask in it, Brehan."

"It feels . . . good."

"Yes, it feels good."

"Safe."

Barrit closed his eyes. "Yes, it's safe there. I'm going to join you now, Brehan. I'm coming toward you. Can you see me?"

"Yes . . . yes I see you. You're . . . you're standing beside me. Holding my hand."

"We're going to soar now, Brehan. I need you to guide me through time, to that first day when you arrived at the orphanage."

Without hesitation, Brehan's image cast off. Tightly grasping Barrit's hand, she drew him through a tunnel of swirling colors. The physical couple remained motionless, like stone, while their metaphysical selves glided through the layers of memories, moving swiftly back through the pages of Brehan's history.

At the end of the tunnel, the two came to light in a small room, at the foot of a cot. The metaphysical Barrit felt Brehan release his hand and back away. He looked at her to see horror deeply carved on her face.

Confused because the orphanage files transferred to the ship had indicated that Brehan's parents were killed in an automobile wreck, Barrit concentrated on the woman thrashing and weeping on the cot. His gaze riveted on her bare protruding belly, distended and contorted with the active life inside it.

A painful drumming began in his chest, his temples. In hopes of diverting the intense pain building within him, he tried to shift his focus to the room's only other occupant—a wiry, gaunt woman, teeming with impatience. A sneer marring her angular face, she anchored the younger woman's shoulders to the bare mattress.

Barrit recoiled when he realized this second woman was Paula Pitts, the headmistress of the orphanage. Brehan's tormentor. Then something tugged on his awareness. He tried to glance over his shoulder to locate Brehan's metaphysical being, but as if compelled by some powerful hand, he was forced to look upon the swollen belly again.

He experienced falling—falling through nothingness while images relentlessly assaulted him. Battered by the sheer force of them, he could not summon the will to resist their urgency. People, places, situations became part of him—as he a part of them. He struggled to deny their existence, for these were not of Brehan's past, but of the woman's on the bed.

Rebecca Landers. Brehan's mother, who was in the throes of a difficult birth.

Then Barrit found himself alone in the golden glow, the room nowhere in sight. Shortly, new images began to flash all around him. His brain ablaze with a fervent obsession to learn all he could about his patient, he strained to gather every piece of information available to him.

Pieces of Brehan's childhood were revealed, the pain of which Barrit felt to the core of him.

The darkness of the closet.

Beatings.

Lashings.

Hunger.

Isolation.

Then came the relative years of freedom following her eighteenth birthday.

Her resolve to build lives for Joy and Lisa when they, too, reached the legal age to leave the orphanage.

Her encounters with Jakes.

The joys and frustrations of her short singing career.

The birth of her rage.

The shooting in Jakes' office—

A door appeared within the golden glow. Barrit stared at it long and hard, a pulse throbbing wildly through him. He had found what he believed to be the true cause of Brehan's turmoil—that which she consciously had not accepted. His hand went out to grasp the knob, but something searing lanced his gut and slowly sliced upward into his chest.

Pain as he'd never known paralyzed him. Something flexed within him before unfolding and squirming through to the very tips of his extremities. He tried to withdraw to his physical body, but some unknown intelligence beckoned him to open the door. His resistance met with increasing agony. He felt himself gliding closer to the image of the door, his fingers turning the knob of their own accord. A cry for help went off in his skull, further panicking him when he realized the voice was his own.

The door began to open. Impressions invaded Barrit's mind with ferocity that nearly drove him mad. Then, from beyond the door, he spied two brilliant amber orbs rushing toward him. A face began to materialize around them when Barrit sensed something beside him. A hand shot out from his left and slammed the door shut. The same hand pressed to his chest and shoved—

Brehan awakened and bolted into a sitting position in time to see Barrit fall to the floor several feet from the foot of the bed. With a cry of alarm, she rushed to his side, where she knelt and checked his vital signs. Barrit's pulse rate was unnaturally slow, his skin peculiarly cool.

"Barrit? Barrit, can you hear me?"

When no response came, Brehan glanced up at the computer. "Computer, advise Erth of Barrit's condition!"

—Disfunctioning male reported—

Brehan noted Barrit's sickly gray color. Guilt quaked through her. She told herself she couldn't have harmed him—not Barrit!—but there he lay, the proof. Her hands were poised above him. She had no idea how to help him, and this stirred wild thoughts of his injuries. She vaguely remembered something about a golden glow ... Something about a room ...

The void in her memory wrenched a cry of frustration from her. These gaps were becoming more frequent, the violent spells too swiftly following at the heels of each occurrence.

But to strike out at Barrit ... ?

What had he triggered in her subconscious?

When the E wall swept aside, Brehan sharply looked up to see Christie entering the room. Her face blanched with shock, she hastened to her husband's other side and went down on her knees.

"I swear, I don't know what happened, Christie!"

Brehan looked up again to see Erth crossing the threshold. Without sparing her a glance, he knelt by Barrit's head and held a palm over his face. A moment later, he looked up to search the anguish carved into Brehan's face.

"What happened?"

Brehan tried to swallow past a painful lump in her throat. "He said he was going t-to mind-meld with me."

"Did he?"

The husky calmness of Erth's tone caused a shiver to pass through Brehan. "I think s-so. I woke up and saw him h-hit the floor. It . . . it was as if something propelled him from the bed."

"Erth, why isn't he coming to?"

At the fear in Christie's voice, Erth looked at her. "He'll be fine."

A low moan came from Barrit. He opened his eyes moments later, bewildered to see the faces above him. Then he met Brehan's tearful eyes.

"Brehan, this was in no way your fault."

"What happened?" she whimpered.

"I'm not sure," he wheezed, struggling into a sitting position. His hands capped his thundering skull. "I need to evaluate my findings."

"The door."

Barrit noted Brehan's sickly pallor. "You pulled me out in time."

"What are you talking about?" Erth asked gruffly.

"In time," Barrit grunted, getting to his feet with Christie's help. He massaged the stiffness at the back of his neck as he turned to face Brehan and Erth. "Brehan, do you remember what was behind the door?"

"No," she rasped, quivering with an inner coldness she could not explain.

"Dammit, Barrit, you can hardly stand!"

"Christie, I'm just a little shaky. I need to lie down for a while."

"When you're up to it, I want a full report," Erth stated, stepping aside as Christie urged Barrit toward the exit.

Barrit merely nodded in response to Erth's directive. His lightheadedness wouldn't permit him to say anything more.

With the sealing of the E wall, Erth turned to face

Brehan, who was staring vacantly at the exit. He lifted a hand to her pallid cheek. She neither cringed nor issued him a warning look. It was as if the fight had gone completely out of her. "Brehan?"

She leveled a bleak, haunted look on Erth. "I'm worried about him."

"His faculties will be normal in a short time."

"I couldn't have pushed him hard enough to propel him like that," she murmured, staring dazedly off to one side. "He just . . . flew away from me."

"Brehan." Erth waited until her gaze turned up to him again. "What about the door you mentioned?"

"Something Barrit came across."

"Is that all you can tell me?"

At long last, a sign of the old Brehan came to life. A glint of resentment flashed in her eyes. "You would like to believe I deliberately hurt him!"

"To the contrary." Erth walked to the exit and cast her a cryptic look. "I suggest you rest."

"I would rather get the hell out of this room!"

Erth nodded. "Stay away from Kousta."

Stunned, disbelieving she had heard him correctly, she hugged herself and warily stared at him. When he impatiently cocked an eyebrow, she asked a bit hesitantly, "I'm free to visit with the others?"

He passed the vent on the wall a beguiling look, and sighed, "I haven't been able to stop you in the past." His gaze swung to meet Brehan's, which was shadowed with suspicion. "But I'll be watching you," he added solemnly, then left her quarters.

Chapter Seven

Transition date: 00.73. Early morning mode.

I don't know whether it's because of concern for Barrit the past ten days, or what, but my sleep has been plagued with new dreamings. Christie assures me Barrit has suffered no side effects from the mind-meld, but I have not seen him since. I suspect he's avoiding me. I'd rather not hazard a guess why.

Erth, too, has avoided me. I've pretty much been left alone, although in the back of my mind I know he is expecting me to submit to the artificial insemination soon. I try not to think about it.

Joy and Lisa have settled admirably into married life. Niton and Caenith are nice men. Eager to please their brides. I try to appear happy for them. In a way I am, but my own fate shadows any joy I might earnestly feel for them. I always feel like a fifth wheel around the couples, and tend to spend a lot of time alone.

I came across Kousta and her match, Uhul, in the corridor last night. I couldn't help but notice the purple discoloration on her jaw. We didn't exchange words, but I did pick up on the hatred within her. My sympathies lie with Uhul. Kousta will never love him, not as long as Erth is around. She's a strange woman. I've studied her culture through the data material, in hopes of getting a handle on what it is about her that eats away at me. Although her world is very similar to Earth, the social structure is more female-oriented. Women are revered as the leaders, which could feasibly explain her attitude. On the other hand, it could be as simple as she's a first-class bitch. Our personalities are too volatile a combination.

I'm restless. I've got to find something to occupy my time. I keep thinking about Adam. I've tried to work up the nerve to approach Erth about him, but something keeps stopping me. The right time is bound to crop up. Patience, I tell myself. Not exactly one of my virtues.

Christie suggested something to me yesterday that took me by surprise. Seems the Syre men have never been exposed to music. She suggested I think about teaching the subject on Syre. It definitely has appeal. I suppose pianos, violins and guitars could be produced on Syre. All my years of lessons could open up a new challenge for me. Perhaps, if I could prove worth other than that of a childbearer, it would be enough to dissuade Erth from forcing me into the role of motherhood. I must somehow convince him to leave me alone. I am willing to offer Syre my strength, endurance, and creativity. Anything that is asked of me, but that one horror I have dreaded most of my life.

One last note. There is something strange going on inside my computer. I must talk to Manak about it. Glitches of some sort. I know it sounds crazy, but sometimes I think I can sense fragments of intelligence when these occurrences are going on.
END

Later that morning, Brehan was mentally working on a melody as she walked down one of the corridors on the second level. She was dressed in one of Jamie's designs, a white, loose-fitting, jumpsuit with a dark green broad belt. Her springy gait suggested an unusual carefree mood. The tune in her mind had her so preoccupied, she bypassed the quarters area. She withdrew from her musings to discover herself standing in front of an arch and sealed E wall, a dark blue B centered against the pale gray background.

The A corridor was the living quarters. B and C were mentioned in the educational data, but Brehan couldn't recall their uses. She was about to turn away when the E wall unexpectedly opened. Startled, her heart seeming to rise into her throat, she stared wide-eyed into Manak's surprised expression.

"*Katiah,* what are you doing here?"

Brehan released a nervous laugh. "You startled me."

"Forgive me."

The reverence in his tone and manner drew down her eyebrows in a frown. "Knock it off. What's back there?"

Manak glanced over his shoulder. "The workshops." He looked at Brehan again. "Why do you ask?"

"What kind of workshops?"

"The repair labs, equipment testing facilities, and my private shop and lab."

"What do you do there?"

A mischievous gleam came into Manak's eyes as he beckoned her with an isolated finger. "See for yourself."

Brehan easily fell into step alongside him. Her gaze began to scan the vast difference in this section of corridor. Not only was it wider, it didn't possess the polish of the A section. The E wall areas were broader and set further apart.

"One of Jamie's designs?"

Manak's question drew her gaze down to her outfit. "Yes."

"It looks great on you. Dawn fancies the—what did Jamie call it?"

"Peasant look."

Manak nodded. "It's nice. I had no idea clothes could so alter one's appearance."

A sparkle of amusement danced in Brehan's eyes. "Then why are you still wearing this terrible uniform?"

With a wounded look, Manak tugged on the front of his jersey. "Terrible?"

"Absolutely heinous," Brehan replied with a mock shudder.

Pensively, Manak came to stop in front of one of the exits. "Dawn never said anything about—"

"Maybe she was trying to spare your feelings." Brehan clapped him on the back. "Trust me, a new wardrobe will make you feel like a million bucks."

"Like a million four-legged creatures with antlers?" he asked, seemingly aghast at the image. But he couldn't keep a straight face at Brehan's earnest reaction to his apparent ignorance. "I was pulling your leg."

"You were, huh?"

Manak's amusement youthened his handsome features. "Ready to see *the* shop?"

"Ready as I'll ever be."

Manak paused for effect, then signaled the wall to open. The instant the room was exposed, elation lit up Brehan's face.

The room was a massive conglomeration of computers and equipment. Gadgets of every imaginable size and shape littered long tables and were in countless heaps on sections of the floor. Brehan slowly ambled along haphazard pathways to the center area the room. Her gaze settled on a chemical laboratory set up against the far wall to her right, then lifted to observe the monitors, cables, and numerous unidentifiable objects dangling from the vast ceiling.

"Just what is it you do in here?"

Arriving at her side, Manak sighed, "Create."

"Create what?"

He grimaced comically. "I have yet to think of names for my inventions." Walking to one of the tables, he lifted a narrow implement. "Mostly I endeavor to modify ancient weapons—which we collected a lot of information on from your world and others along the treks. I alter existing mechanisms and try to improve their work force. Some things are just ... *things*. Like this." He picked up a crystal wand. "This projects holographic pictures, which change according to the heat of the hand, and the angle by which it's held. And this—" Putting down the wand, he picked up a small round object. "—flies around the room. It has its own G-stabilizer, but as yet, I haven't figured out what use it could have."

"Entertainment."

Manak pondered her suggestion. "How would it serve to be entertaining?"

"Ever seen tennis played?"

"No."

"Well, the object of the game is to whack a ball back and forth over a net. A hovering ball could prove to be a lot of fun."

"Hmmm. It's a type of sport?"

Brehan nodded.

"We viewed a little of one game—football—while we were in abeyance waiting for Erth to return."

"Football and baseball are probably two of the most revered sports in the U.S."

"All the running and slamming one another is fun?"

"The fans think so."

"What about the players?"

"I doubt if they would be participating if they didn't enjoy the challenge."

"Sports. We could have sports on Syre."

Again Brehan nodded. She was keenly watching the shifting expressions on Manak's face. She could almost hear the wheels of his brain turning as he mentally toyed with the endless possibilities. When she grew restless waiting for him to explain more of the wonders laid out about her, she walked to one of the tables and picked up an object shaped like a child's futuristic water gun. She peered down the narrow muzzle, then held it out sideways in front of her to inspect its smooth lines. Unintentionally, she squeezed an indiscernible trigger.

A cry of surprise rang out from her as a whooshing explosion came from the muzzle. Her gaze cut instinctively to follow the blazing trajectory beam which widened at the fore as it sailed across the room. It cleanly cut a hole through the wall adjacent the exit, then continued on beyond.

"*Katiah!*" Manak's outcry was followed by his snatching the weapon from her grasp.

Brehan gawked down at her emptied hand, then leveled a bewildered look on Manak's shock-blanched face. "What the hell is that?"

"A weapon—"

The sound of the E wall parting drew their attention. Manak dropped the gun to the floor as if it had suddenly become too hot. Grimacing, Brehan tried to think of something adequate to quip, but the sight of Erth at the threshold—his clothes smoldering, his expression deadpan—closed off her throat.

"*Katian,*" Manak wheezed. "I was merely showing her my creations . . ." He cast a sickly look in Brehan's direction.

"I didn't know it would do anything when I picked it up," Brehan said finally, minutely flinching when Erth came toward her. He stopped and held out his hand to Manak, who readily retrieved the gun and placed it on the extended palm.

After a brief inspection, Erth reached past Brehan and put the weapon down on the table. The strain of hiding his vexation was obvious, for the rhythm of light pulses on his headband was wildly erratic.

"By all means enlighten her on how to blow up the ship," Erth said dryly, his humorless gaze riveted on Manak.

"Don't be ridiculous."

At Brehan's haughty words, Erth's gaze shifted to her. "Is it ridiculous to expect the unexpectable from you?"

"*Katian,* she had no way of knowing—"

"Manak, I can speak for myself." Brehan stiffened

against the accusations she anticipated would be next to come. "Okay, so I triggered the damn thing! So sue me."

To her bewilderment, Erth abruptly headed for the exit. "I'll be sending for you later."

"Why?"

At the threshold, he looked over his shoulder and regarded her through the wisps of smoke curling up from his clothing. A massive hole was visible on the far wall beyond him.

"Because I yearn for your company," he delivered with the same dryness, grimaced, then disappeared down the corridor.

For a long moment, Manak could only stare at the sealed E wall.

"What do you think?"

Brehan's low tone brought Manak to look at her. "About what?"

"Taking me on to organize this mess," she replied, her gaze on the damaged wall across from her.

"I don't understand your request, *Katiah.*"

"Don't call me that, and I'm asking if I can name and catalog your inventions."

Manak's eyebrows arched at the thought. "I would welcome the help, but—"

"The big guy might object?"

A barely perceivable nod was his response.

"What if I clear it with him?"

"Then the job's all yours—once I've instructed you on the potential hazards of some of the pieces."

"No qualms?"

"About you being in my lab?" Manak grinned. "Not a one."

"You're okay for a spaceman," Brehan said evenly, but she was inwardly beaming that he trusted her so completely.

Then a thought struck her. "Manak, if I could convince Erth to release Adam, would you permit him to work in here with me?"

Manak's expression went blank.

"This could be just the kind of chore to give Adam pride in himself."

"Perhaps, but the risks—"

"I promise to watch him. Adam needs something to challenge him."

"Barrit told me of your telepathic link with him."

"Well?"

Sighing, Manak clasped his hands to the small of his back. "Adam's stasis disheartens me. If you're willing to take on the challenge of trying to focus his curiosities, I have no problem with him working in my lab or my workshop."

"You won't regret this, Manak."

"I'm due topside. Are you sure you want to—" His hands gestured expansively. "—take this on?"

"It'll definitely keep me busy."

"And hopefully, my lady, out of trouble."

As soon as the E wall sealed behind Lisa and Joy, Erth sat back in his chair and looked at Barrit, who was sitting across the table from him. "The more I learn about Brehan, the more perplexed I am."

Barrit nodded in agreement.

"Are you now prepared to explain what occurred during the mind-meld?"

"It's extraordinary, Erth," Barrit said quietly, his gaze unseeingly fixed on his clasped hands atop the table. "Even with the time you've allowed me to organize my findings . . ."

Erth released a great sigh of impatience.

"One of the things I discovered was, Brehan's parents did not die in a car wreck—at least not her mother," Barrit finally began. "The ruse was instigated by the Marson Estate to conceal Brehan's true parentage.

"When Rebecca Landers' mother discovered her daughter was pregnant, she paid the headmistress of the Marson Estate to keep Rebecca in seclusion until after the child was born. Rebecca was then to have returned home, leaving the infant in the charge of the headmistress. But there were complications which resulted in Rebecca dying two hours after the birth."

The frown which had appeared on Erth's face moments after Barrit had begun to speak, darkened.

"Brehan's subconscious knows the truth—dates, names, everything," Barrit went on. "While in her mother's womb, her mind served as a receptacle for every emotion and thought her mother experienced."

"That's impossible."

"No, Erth. Mother and daughter shared one mind. Brehan's psychic and empathic abilities matured prior to her birth, and certainly surpass anything I could accomplish in this field.

"There's a memory file in her brain which belongs exclusively to her mother. Tapping into it was directly proportionate to being inside Rebecca's mind. I felt every simplicity the woman treasured throughout her young life: every elation; every hope. Her death was an appalling waste."

Sitting forward and placing his elbows upon the table, Erth steepled his fingertips. "Is Brehan conscious of the circumstances of her mother's actual death?"

"It's deeply locked away. I had difficulty getting in. But it explains her androphobia. She's probably relived her mother's feelings of betrayal a thousand times, and has never consciously realized it. Brehan's father seduced Rebecca, then abandoned her when he learned of the pregnancy. There is overwhelming rage within her subconscious in regard to him. It has such substance, Erth, I feared it would consume me.

"There's another file locked behind a door in her mind. I started to touch upon it when Brehan's metaphysical being pulled me away."

"Conclusions?"

Barrit solemnly shook his head. "I've tried to analyze my impressions. It's what has taken so long for me to report. The only determination I can offer is that it's something dark and . . . *unprincipled.*

"We may be dealing with a split personality, Erth. It would certainly explain her blackouts, and this voice she hears inside her head."

Barrit's discovery had caused a shocking awareness in Erth's mind. Subconsciously, he was aware of the danger Brehan presented to his people's future, but he refused to allow the knowledge to surface fully. He could not accept the truth of Brehan's lineage, although his ostracism from Haveth should have taught him that one cannot forsake responsibility for the pleasures. He was recklessly traveling on the same path, this time guided by a feint in the guise of a mortal woman whose visage and spirit shackled his reasoning.

"Brehan requires a great deal of understanding and patience, Erth," Barrit added, his dark gaze studying the play of emotions which had passed over Erth's face during the briefing. "I beg of you to keep her relatively calm until I am able to delve a little deeper into her subconscious."

Lowering his hands to the table, Erth heaved a ponderous sigh. "I will do my best."

Sharp-winged butterflies fluttered in Brehan's stomach when she crossed the threshold of the Meeting Chamber. The man at her side, Uhul, placed a hand to the small of her back and gave her a gentle nudge, but her legs had locked at the sight of Erth and Barrit sitting across from each other at the table. A furtiveness in the air further unsettled her. She'd seen Joy and Lisa leave this room,and they'd barely spoken to her before hurrying off. Now Barrit was walking in her direction.

His smile was strained, his eyes shifting away from meeting her own until he stopped in front of her.

"What's going on?"

"Don't panic, Brehan. He only wants to talk to you."

Erth again steepled his fingers beneath his chin. Watching Brehan try to detain Barrit with questions, he mentally went over the information Barrit had given him. After a short time, Brehan reluctantly came toward him, her posture once again hostile. So as not to further incite her defensiveness, he casually watched Uhul and Barrit leave the room before lifting his gaze to her wan, taut face.

"Please, sit down."

Brehan tried to relieve her dry mouth, but she could not summon any saliva. "Why were you interrogating my friends?"

"It was not an interrogation. Please, sit down."

"If this is about the BRS—"

"It isn't." Erth sighed wearily. "Your chemistry slightly differs from that of the other women. That, and the fact Manak was working on my console earlier that morning—"

"Manak had nothing to do with it!"

Her heated defense of Manak stabbed at Erth. In a tone guarding his darkening mood, he continued, "Not intentionally. Barrit believes the oil from his fingertips may have been enough on the feedboard to permit you access."

"I want to help Manak organize his lab."

Taken aback by the demand, Erth cocked a questioning eyebrow.

"It'll give me something to do to pass the time," she rushed on, her tone defensive, cold. "I like to work with my hands—"

"The crafts—"

"I'm not into pretty trivials!"

Erth's eyebrows expressively betrayed his mounting exasperation. "Just deadly devices."

"Manak trusts me."

A hint of jealousy shadowed Erth's features. "He doesn't know you as well as I do."

"You're wrong. He probably understands me better than anyone on this damn tub!"

"Explain that statement."

Brehan felt her temper surfacing. "He has a creative imagination—not unlike my own. We just spent the better part of the morning brainstorming electronic devices. It was exhilarating, and he never once questioned my motives for wanting to understand how something worked."

"You could discuss such matters with me."

"You? Not if I were drowning in a bottomless, dark pit of desperation."

Erth lowered his head slightly to hide the fact that her words had deeply stung him.

"Manak has also graciously offered to allow Adam to assist me in the lab."

Erth's head shot up at Adam's name. "Adam is not your concern."

"He's constantly in my thoughts, dammit! I'm willing to work with him. It isn't fair to Christie or Barrit to deprive them of their son!"

"Their mental well-being *was* taken into consideration." Erth fell silent for a short time. "This ship was not designed to cater to the whims of an adolescent."

"How dare you sit there and pretend you give a damn about that boy! Adam's sentence is a farce. Do you really believe this stasis crap is going to curb his adolescent actions once he's released on Syre?"

"You have no understanding—"

"I understand more than you give me credit for!" Brehan exclaimed heatedly. "His mind is awake, Erth. You're psychologically scarring him!"

"The subject is closed."

"You're a monster," she said breathlessly, quaking with anger and disappointment. "You're an abomination," she charged on, using all of her willpower to lock eyes with him when he looked up. "You have no understanding of humans. But then how could you? You're that . . . that hideous *thing* that molested me at the cabin!"

"Hideous?" he repeated incredulously, stunned that anyone could consider his energy-self anything less than magnificent.

Split personality, Barrit had suggested. Was it possible he had only dealt with the darker side of this woman?

Erth's insides tightened as he wondered if this virulent side of Brehan was the better half.

"You're here to discuss the impregnation date."

"I refuse to submit to it."

"We made a bargain, Brehan. I have no intention of going back on my word, unless you deign me to—"

"In your dreams."

A smug grin twitched on his lips. "Should I believe your cutting words, Brehan, or the language of your body?"

She shivered in spite of her determination not to buckle to the fears gnawing at her nerves. But it was impossible to look at Erth and not recall how close she'd come to submitting to his naked power. It didn't even help to conjure up the image of his true form.

Suddenly weak-kneed, she pulled out the chair and sank onto it. "I'm tired of this threat hanging over my head."

"Kousta."

Brehan leveled a combative look on him. "She's trouble."

"You're not?"

She paled. "I have never struck out at anyone weaker than myself. The question is, why haven't *you* stopped her from harassing the other women?"

"I have spoken to her."

A bitter laugh burst past Brehan's lips. "I'm sure she's quaking in her boots."

"Brehan, our match has placed you in a position of authority."

"Oh, really?"

"Spare me the sarcasm. You are now the people's *Katiah*, including the future generations for the rest of your life. It is a position of reverence—"

"Blow it out your ear."

"One," Erth continued, ignoring her remark, "that requires a certain standard to be upheld. You have already set yourself apart, and you have won the respect of the men and women with your daring. Now it's time you set a better example for them. You must begin your conditioning."

"I will not submit to brainwashing."

"Brehan—"

She cut him off with a question from left field. "Since you're some kind of light thing, why do you use a human form?"

Erth knew she was resorting to evasive measures, but decided to see where the question would lead them. "How much do you know about me?"

"Your origin, family, your ostracism, and the history data relating to Syre."

"It is my father's will that, while in the company of humans, I release myself only under certain conditions."

"What did you do in that crystal room?"

"I directed my overload of energy into the crystals. Usually I prefer to use the Feeder relays, but the situation didn't permit me much time. My shell is much like your flesh, but it's just a containing pod. My race is of an energy form, and sometimes it's difficult to keep my source encased. Anger is an emotion which ignites my *pliyistical* molecular structure. My shell will expand to allow triggered ignitions the amplitude required to defuse, but this flesh has limitations." His eyes narrowed, as if to tell her the next part of his revelation was especially relevant to her. "It can only withstand a certain degree of distension before it gives way to my core's needs. This is called decomposing. And should I be out of control during this process, you and every living thing aboard this ship could be reduced to cinders."

"I don't recall you being in 'control' down there."

"Relative control. Although, had I not been further piqued at finding you in the Feeding Chamber after our wrestling match, I would have been able to transport us to your quarters without sacrificing our attire." He grinned unexpectedly, adding, "Not that I'm complaining. What followed proved to be a memorable experience."

"You're pathetic," she grumbled.

A spasm of alarm speared her when Erth abruptly stood and came around the table. He turned her chair to the right, then pulled out the one beside her and positioned it to face her. When he lowered himself onto the seat, with his knees to each side of her legs, it was all she could do to sit quietly.

"I understand your reasons for attacking Kousta, but you handled the situation in a manner unbefitting your new station. You must learn to control your temper."

One of his knees brushed against her thigh, bringing home the sensations he'd awakened in her nearly two weeks ago. Determined not to squirm, not to give him the satisfaction of knowing how completely aware she was of his masculinity, she met his gaze levelly.

"That act saved your precious star maps. And if I am in a position of authority, then I demand Adam's release."

Placing his hands on his thighs, Erth straightened back. "Joy and Lisa talked at great length about the Marson Estate." He sat still when Brehan bolted from the chair and walked around the table. Her face livid, her body trembling, she came to stand across from him.

"My past is none of your damned business!"

"To the contrary. No child could endure that kind

of abuse without it affecting them later on in life. I cannot allow you to harbor this anger. You must let go of the past."

Brehan screamed in sheer frustration, then slapped her palms on the table and leaned forward. "I'm fed up with your spying, your probing, and your insufferable attitude! Pitts' strap, the closet, the beatings—they were a cinch, mister, because I knew if I could survive until my eighteenth birthday, I would be *free* of it all! But what's my sentence here, huh? Ten, fifteen, fifty years— *life?*

"You're a part of the Syre race now."

"I'm talking about my sentence with *you,* you *ass!*"

Erth drew in a sharp breath, then slowly rose from the chair. "When my son is old enough to take my place, I intend to return to Haveth."

The word "return" harshly echoed in her mind. The knowledge that he would actually one day leave his people—leave *her,* slashed a very deep wound in her heart. It sickened her that she even cared they didn't really have a future together. Her eyes fiery with betrayal, she flung, "Why didn't you let me die in the crash? You had the other woman to take!"

Erth's core constricted within him.

Knowing her question had shocked him, Brehan straightened up, pale and unsteady on her feet. Turning her back to him, she leaned against the table for support. Pain stabbed at her temples. Her lungs ached. For some inexplicable reason, her mind drifted to another place—another time. She was sitting in history class at the orphanage school, drawing a beard on a glossy picture of Betsy Ross. Her teacher, Joseph Sheehan, had given her a start when he slapped a hand down on her desk. He took the book and scowled at her attempts to sabotage Betsy's youthful face.

"Someday, my girl, someone's going to have the strength to squash your irascible nature. I hope I'm around to see it."

She remembered staring up into his good-natured, Irish face with the uncanny feeling that his comment was actually a grim prophecy of her future.

"How long have you known?"

The words were low, husky, and startlingly close to her. Lifting her head, she peered up into Erth's face through a daze. A pale light was simmering in his eyes. His mouth was grimly set. The pulse on his headband was throbbing with an erratic tempo.

"I read all the files before I erased them. I replaced Danielle Simmons. But I don't understand why."

"I couldn't let you die."

"How many times since, have you regretted that moment's weakness?" she asked shakily.

Erth reached out to touch her unbound hair. When her hand lashed out and struck his aside, he turned and put some distance between them. He peered heavenward, his taut features lending him a look of vulnerability. "Surely my father has a hand in this mockery. To pit me against a creature so adverse to physical touch and childbearing!"

Turning, he glimpsed fear in her eyes before she lowered her head to hide her face beneath her hair. His system quieted, despite his inability to penetrate her stubbornness.

"You're a beautiful creature, Brehan, more vibrantly alive than any I have ever encountered. Since that first day, here in this room, you have known your defiance excites me. You have been testing my untried instincts to mate in this humanoid form. Dangerous ground for one so . . . mortal."

A terrible ache pounded in Brehan's chest.

"You sampled the pleasure—"

"Shut up!" she cried, flipping back her hair from her face.

"You're sorely trying my patience, woman."

"Th-that whole episode s-stemmed from your using

s-some kind of drugging t-telepathy on me! I don't like to be touched!''

Erth heaved a sigh of vexation and leveled a dark look on her. "You're only lying to yourself. Regardless, the sooner you accept the artificial insemination and bear my son, the sooner our bond will be severed. Only a child will free you of me."

Brehan pinched the bridge of her nose. "None of this is real. You don't exist, Erth. You're the product of a night out on the town, eating too much pizza and drinking too many beers. After the longest night of my life, I'll wake up in my cabin to find you were only a nightmare born of indigestion."

"Nothing lacking with your imagination."

An abrupt wash of weakness coursed through her. She squeezed her eyes shut. Her head lolled forward, the movement causing her hair to cascade into a curtain about her torso. She became aware of Erth's hands confining her waist. Pressing her palms to his chest, she tried to focus on his face, but couldn't. In her mind, he was slipping away, floating through a swirling tunnel of dull lights. Her arms were leaden, preventing her from reaching out to bring him back. Fear began to suffocate her—fear he would leave her alone in the darkness.

As an unbearable sense of loneliness closed in on her, she cried out Erth's name.

It was imperative she reach him in time. There was only death without him. Eternal nothingness awaited her.

Erth's insides were afire, his mind under assault by the chaotic patterns her mind was projecting. Drawing a deep breath into his pseudo-lungs, he placed a finger beneath her chin and tilted up her head. With his other hand, he gently brushed back the strands of hair in her face.

"Brehan, tell me what's wrong."

A shiver worked through her as she once again

glimpsed in his eyes the enigma that continued to puzzle her.

"Brehan?"

Her wariness of him always deepened whenever he spoke so softly. To shroud her weakness, she coldly stated, "I think I'm allergic to you."

Erth was distracted from commenting when his name came through the intercom on the table. Testily, he depressed one of the buttons. "What is it?"

"We're nearing a plenum belt, *Katian*," Stalan reported from the Control Center. "The demagnetic shields are fluctuating. Manak's in the Feeding Chamber trying to locate the problem."

"I'll meet you at the lift." Straightening up, he took Brehan by the elbow. "I'll take you to Barrit."

"I can take care of myself."

"There are times your defiance . . ." Erth's expression softened as he recalled Barrit's earlier digest of her life. Releasing her, he turned and headed for the exit. "We'll continue our talk, later."

"Be still my fluttering heart," Brehan muttered, sinking onto the nearest chair. She buried her face in her hands, ignoring the sound of the E wall closing behind Erth.

Her freedom lay in bearing a child. But how could she explain to anyone that her worst fear was to birth the demon of her nightmares? She knew it was waiting patiently inside her, waiting to be released into an unsuspecting world. She had discovered its presence shortly into her puberty, during one of the countless sessions she'd spent in the cramped, locked closet.

There had been times when she nearly visualized its entire countenance. Female. A resemblance to herself. An extension of herself. That dark part of her which remained elusive and secretive, robbing her of brief intervals of time.

Brehan locked her teeth against her despair. She could never risk having a child of her own, risk the chance of her nightmares manifesting into a thing of stark reality. And after this last conversation with Erth, she had finally given up hope of him leaving her alone. Which left her only one recourse.

Erth and Stalan arrived in the Feeding Chamber in time to witness Manak thrown to the floor by a bolt of electricity from the Feeder's console. With a gesture for Stalan to see to Manak, Erth rushed forward to switch the signals going into the problem panel to a backup crystalstat. Then he activated the red warning lights throughout the ship, signaling for everyone to proceed to the Safety Chamber.

"Into the teleporters!" he barked over his shoulder.

Without explaining to his men that it was too great a risk to rely on the crystalstat at this point, he waited with growing impatience as they hastened into separate teleporters, which would protect them against any heat he might inadvertently release. Then he stripped out of his clothing and boots, and swiftly decomposed.

He moved his fiery energy-self into the hull below the Feeding Chamber. The Defense Bay's lights came on. Through his telepathic command, the Bay's computers were instructed to discharge the laser banks in the ship's trajectory route. The coordinates' signal locked in, but his sensors detected the crystals were not accurately interpreting the interface.

Passing through one of the floor ports and down into the defense region of the ship, Erth bypassed the computers and discharged swells of his lifeforce through several silos. When he was satisfied the ship's pathway was clear of matter, he reascended into the Feeding Chamber, where he reluctantly began to reconstruct his humanlike canister. He was oblivious to Manak and Stalan leaving the teleporters and approaching him. By the time they reached his side, he had put on his pants and was flexing his shoulders.

"The energy levels on the crystals have been unstable since our departure from Earth," Manak said, a hand massaging his chest where he'd received the current. "Possibly, we overestimated their life span. Or there could be an energy surge moving through the system."

"I want a thorough diagnostic run on all the systems," Erth ordered, stooping and retrieving his jersey and boots. "If the crystals' sporadic complaints stem from a depletion fault, I may have to advance to Purlothal and replace them."

"There's a *loh* remaining in storage."

"Let's hope it's sufficient. Stalan, work with him through this. Once we have a readout on the diagnostic, we'll decide what more needs to be done."

"Katian," Stalan said, "some of the personal computers have been acting up."

Manak nodded. "Brehan mentioned her computer had a 'glitch' in it."

A disgruntled sigh passed Erth's lips before he headed for the lift. "Whatever the problem, I want an *absolute* determined."

Chapter Eight

It was the middle of the night when Erth entered Brehan's quarters. He had planned to give her the news in the morning, but had sensed her distress even before her computer transmitted her restlessness to the Med Chamber's monitors. At his entry, the computer cut the dim red lighting of the night mode and brightened the room. He seated himself on the edge of her bed, concern furrowing his brow as he observed the beads of perspiration on her face and neck. Drawing back the top sheet, he also noted her nightgown was soaked and plastered to her body. Her eyes were moving rapidly behind her closed eyelids, and her breathing was shallow. She was shivering, obviously in the throes of a nightmare. He attempted to probe her mind to analyze the dream, but again he found he couldn't penetrate her mental wall.

"Brehan," he said softly, brushing aside strands of hair clinging to her moist face. She moaned and tried to roll onto her side away from him, but he placed his hands on her shoulders to anchor her. "Brehan, wake up."

Her breathing took a laborious turn. The computer announced her increasing pulse rate, and the elevation of her body temperature. Uneasy with his sense of helplessness, Erth lifted her into his arms and carried her into the shower stall. The weight on the floor tiles initiated the spray. His frown seeming a permanent fixture, he observed the way the glistening Cassis mist played over her skin. Her restless movements quieted. The misery previously carved into her features, softened until she appeared angelic in her sleep.

Carrying her back into the main room, aware that she was beginning to come around, he gently placed her in the chair by the arch. He'd no sooner straightened up, than she awakened. The instant she saw him, she bolted out of the chair and pressed herself against the wall, staring at him with the wild distrust of a cornered animal.

"Was it dreams of Adam distressing you?"

Brehan shuddered. The dream had in fact been about Erth. Her last memory of it was that of his weight pressing her into the mattress as he ruthlessly consummated their match.

"Get out of my quarters," she rasped. "Get out!"

Erth lifted a hand in a gesture meant to calm her, but again she reacted violently, dashing to her left, shoving over the vanity and chair and pressing herself to the wall behind them.

"I came with news of Adam," Erth said calmly, although her reaction to his every movement was gnawing at him. "He's sleeping off the effects of the stasis, but has been instructed to report to you in the morning."

Brehan's brain struggled to comprehend what Erth was saying.

"Barrit and Christie have agreed to let you take charge of his education."

"Adam . . . ?"

"Is eager to work with you."

Tears sprang to Brehan's eyes as she tried to compose herself. "You-ah . . . you-ah . . . He's free?"

"For as long as he behaves himself. It is what you wanted, isn't it?"

Brehan stiltedly nodded. "Yes, but . . ."

"I'm trusting you to take this responsibility to heart."

For the first time, Brehan looked into Erth's eyes. Her breathing slowed. The wildness in her eyes waned beneath a look of sleepy, mild confusion. "Why have you changed your mind?"

Erth abruptly turned and headed for the exit. By the time the E wall parted and he was about to cross the threshold, Brehan ran halfway across the room and managed a hoarse, "Wait!" Erth turned and looked at her, careful to guard the chaos twisting through him at the sight she presented. It wasn't so much the clingy gown accentuating the curves of her body that aroused him. It was her hair—fiery, silken, and falling about her slender frame like a living cloak. Whenever he looked upon it unbound, his fingers ached to feel its texture.

"Why this change of heart?" she asked, with suspicion.

"For no other reason than to please you, *te-ni-e.*"

Brehan shook her head. "I know what's running through your devious little mind," she accused. "You'll threaten to return him to stasis if I don't obey you."

Long strides brought Erth to within arm's reach of her. "You really don't understand me, do you?" he challenged, his pained expression confusing her. "And yet you know me better than any living creature in this universe. In your heart—" He touched a finger between her breasts, then touched one of her temples. "—but not in your mind."

Brehan took several paces back away from him, her eyes wide as they searched his features. She couldn't accept that he was genuinely wounded by her words. It would mean he had feelings to hurt, which would require her to think of him in human terms. Yet, the desolation emanating from him, seemed very real.

"If you look long and hard enough into shadows, Brehan, you will undoubtedly find a monster lurking there."

With those words, he turned and left her quarters. When the E wall closed behind him, Brehan sank to her knees, then to her bottom. "I'm sorry," she murmured.

It was so much simpler to deal with him when she thought him a monster.

"What exactly am I supposed to be watching for?"

Brehan didn't respond to Manak's question right away. Her chin resting on her folded arms atop the bench, she patiently waited until another wisp of energy could be seen escaping the flow of current between the two experimentally rigged Crou crystals. When the phenomenon finally occurred again, she was quick to point it out.

"That," she said, straightening up on her seat. "I haven't noticed any particular pattern or time sequence when the divisions happen."

"She sits for hours waiting for a sign—of *something,*" Adam said with a smile. Leaving his chair at the far end of the workbench, he stood to Manak's left.

For the hundredth time, Manak glanced about the perfectly ordered room and sighed. True to her word, Brehan had diligently organized and categorized his gadgets, then recorded them into the computer. For nearly three weeks, Adam had worked at her side to accomplish the small wonder.

A fluctuation in the experimental beam of light prompted Brehan to say, "Watch this." Standing, she went around the workbench and carefully moved her hand through the air above the beam. Within seconds, a tiny starburst of energy affixed to her palm. Patient not to move too quickly, she brought her upturned palm down and waited until Manak and Adam stood in front of her.

Briefly, she observed the wonder in their faces. When Manak looked up, she offered him a crooked smile. "It's alive. As alive as the Crou crystals themselves."

The starburst began to dim until it was no longer visible.

"A very short life span, though," she sighed, absently running the fingers of her other hand over the tingling palm.

"You believe these are the glitches troubling the computers?"

"Pretty sure." With her palms flattened to the bench, she stared down at the red and gold beam of current flowing between the crystals. "Adam came up with an interesting idea."

Manak met the boy's pride-filled dark eyes. "It's possible the Crous are trying to reproduce."

Manak looked stunned for a moment. "Spontaneous reproduction?" Trying to collect his thoughts, he placed his hands on his hips and scowled down at the experiment. "Well . . . I suppose anything is possible. I'll have to come up with a way to contain them and hope the computer can provide an analysis of their particle structure."

"Wouldn't it be the same as the generated energy from the crystals?" Brehan asked Manak.

"Unlikely. The starburst shape, and the fact it responded to your body energy, dissociates it from the norm the crystals produce."

"It's weird to think these things are pinging around inside the computers," Adam commented.

Brehan nodded absently. "If more than one divides at a time and affixes to another, we may be facing energy surges capable of doing some serious damage to the mechanics of the ship."

"Charming thought," Manak murmured. His gaze swept the walls of labeled glassed-in cases serving as a home for his inventions, then he looked at Brehan, who was intently watching for another emission. "Have I told you recently, *Katiah,* you never cease to amaze me?"

Brehan slanted him a peeved look. "Call me by that title again . . ." She let the threat hang in the air, and ignored the laugh which caressed Adam's throat.

"What are you going to call your discovery?" Manak asked.

"Call them?" Brehan fell thoughtfully silent for a time. "Adam, what do you think?"

He shrugged. "They're your babies."

"Then . . . sprites."

Amusement danced in Manak's dark eyes. "Why sprites?"

Brehan turned to face him. "Because they remind me of something out of a fairy tale. Which, speaking of ogres, where's His Majesty been the past few days?"

"Miss him?"

"Like a hemorrhoid," she drawled. "It's been absolute heaven not to have him popping up every time I turn around."

"He's collecting samples from a new species of plant on Igeral."

"Plant, huh? Wouldn't be a mutation that sucks the life out of nuisance energy beings, would it?"

Brehan regretted her words when Adam laughed outright. There were times when she forgot he was an impressionable boy, especially when it came to civility with Erth.

"Actually," Manak went on, "the plant produces a form of vegetation that is highly nutritious. All of the vegetation on Syre and in the Garden Chamber comes from other worlds."

"The Garden Chamber. Joy was telling me about it."

"You haven't been there yet?"

"She spends all her time here," Adam quipped.

Brehan arched an eyebrow at him. "I believe it's long past your studies."

Adam grimaced. "Later."

"Now. If you don't present that essay on the Gahandra System to your parents on time, you're grounded from the lab and workshop. Savvy?"

"I hate astronomy," he groaned.

Brehan leveled a stern parental look on him. "Adam, we have an agreement."

"All I want is a little more time in here. What's the big deal?"

Folding his arms against his chest, Manak rolled his eyes and tried to suppress a smile.

"Adam, your studies."

"Yes, *Katiah,*" he conceded, spitefully emphasizing her title to rattle her. Like a petulant child, he stormed in the direction of the E wall. He paused at the threshold when Brehan called his name, and cast her a scowling look through his long, unruly bangs.

"When you're through with the essay, I would appreciate a short verse on the sociological value of a promise."

"Brehan!" he whined pleadingly.

"Don't return here without it."

"You're worse than my parents," he grumbled, but his defiance was quickly waning. When the E wall sealed behind him, Brehan released a breath of relief. She brushed a rebellious wisp of hair back from her brow and momentarily studied the grin trying to work its way out on Manak's mouth. "What's so funny?"

"You. I admire the way you handle him."

"He's no worse than most teenagers." She looked to the E wall and smiled crookedly. "He's a good kid. Thickheaded, but a good kid."

"See some of yourself in him?" Manak chuckled.

"Ha Ha. I'm getting punchy. Adam is right about me spending too much time in here."

"The Garden Chamber is a very calming place."

A glint of mischief brightened her eyes. "Is that a hint?"

"Only a suggestion."

"I'll check it out after—"

A chilling invisible wave crashed down on her. Paralyzed by its unexpectedness and coldness, Brehan opened her mouth to cry out, but no sound emerged. She was dimly aware of Manak's hands gripping her upper arms. With the roar in her ears, she could make out that he was asking her what was wrong. But she couldn't answer. She could only focus on whatever was trying to manifest within her. And it came within a few seconds.

A split scene stretched out in front of her, as clear as if she were there and not on the *Stellar*. To the right side was a stark world with a few scattered buildings. Two massive air ships were docked in the background. People were dodging laser fire emitted by flying metal globes, and hand weapons she didn't recognize. A magnificent serpent cried out a warning to someone named Echo. Brehan's focus trained on a beautiful towheaded woman running across the desert terrain in the direction of a tall, dark-haired man. Behind him, two men and a woman cowered on the ground, while he held up a brilliant crystal as if to ward off the advance of several uniformed men who were firing at him.

The serpent cried out again, but his warning fell short when the towheaded woman released a blood-curdling, "Kragan, above you!"

Brehan looked up to see a powerful being with ram horns standing atop a building a short distance behind the dark-haired man. A red ray blasted from a weapon in his hand. Brehan released a silent scream when it ripped through the man called Kragan.

To guard her sanity, Brehan trained her focus on the left side of the scene. An old Victorian house sitting on a rocky beach was under assault by numerous men with machinery. They were trying to penetrate something enveloping the building ... something unseen, but resisting their efforts to gain entrance to the place.

Brehan tried to pull herself out of the daydream. She had never felt so cold, so barren, so disconnected from the solidity of the real world. She glimpsed something moving from the right toward the left. The horned being, limping, a taloned hand clamped over a wound bleeding on his arm, appeared to step into a burst of light at the division of the scenes and vanish.

The towhead again came into Brehan's focus. She was kneeling by the dark-haired man, her hands covered with his blood, a look of stark grief masking her face. "You can't leave me," Brehan heard her whimper. "Not you, too! *Kragan!*"

When the towhead threw back her head and released a shrill wail of grief, Brehan felt herself slip from the clutches of the vision and thrust back into reality.

"*Katiah!* Snap out of it!"

Weak, her legs unable to support her, Brehan would have collapsed if Manak had not pulled her into his arms. He embraced her tightly for a time, planted a lingering kiss on her cheek, then held her out to search her pale face.

"What happened?" he asked, his voice gravelly with concern.

"I'm not sure."

"I've never been so scared in my life," he said unsteadily. "It was as if you had turned to stone, *Katiah*. Only your eyes moved . . . as if you were watching something happening that was frightening you. Then you . . . faded . . . in and out."

Collecting her wits, Brehan stepped out of his hold. "It was definitely a weird experience."

"Explain it."

"I don't know if I can. It had something to do with people I don't even know. Maybe something in the future. I don't know."

"Can I get you anything, *Katiah*? Do anything for you?"

Brehan regarded him for a time before offering him a wan smile. "Stop calling me *Katiah*."

Manak reached out and touched the back of his fingers to her cheek. "Are you all right?"

"Yes . . . yes, I am."

"Do you often see in your mind, things that are going to happen?"

"More than I care to," Brehan laughed a bit unsteadily. "But this was different, Manak. Very strange. These two people, Echo and Kragan, I could almost feel what they were feeling. I don't know them, but I strongly sensed that they were very important to . . ."

"To what?"

"Dammit, I'm not sure. Something to do with my world, I think."

"You're still shaken from this experience," Manak said. "Get some rest. If not for yourself, then for *my* peace of mind."

"What about the sprites?"

"I'll come up with something to confine them."

"Let me know."

Manak nodded.

Brehan started to turn away, then stopped to ask, "Where is the Garden Chamber?"

"To the left, just beyond the living quarters."

For the third day in a row, Brehan sought the Garden Chamber to purge herself of the daily tensions plaguing her since her resolve to surrender to her current dreamings. The room was an enormous forest of alien trees, shrubs and jeweled flowers, intermingled with plants she recognized from Earth. An electric blue and pale pink sky appeared to be overhead—liquidlike lightning of vibrant colors moving in and out of low, fluffy, diaphanous clouds.

Sedated by the extraordinary beauty of her surroundings, she followed one of the fluorescent red-tiled pathways to a raised area with a massive view window, beyond which, a horizonless, star-speckled space awarded her a visual definition of the word "infinite."

She had found a true home on the ship, a solitary world where nothing existed but beauty—a world minus the mission's quest.

Nearly an hour later, a faint sound rippled through the stillness. Brehan's head shot around and she caught her breath. Turning mechanically, she faced Erth as he came to a stop at the platform's step. The lighting lent an eerie bluish tone to their skin, but it also enabled her to fully see the chatoyant property in his eyes. Humanlike pupils stared at her from catlike orbs. Their unsettling luster held her fascination until Erth stated, "My return was greeted with a report on your success in the lab."

"I'm sure you were expecting mayhem," she said, and turned to stare out into space again.

"It crossed my mind. But then you always manage the unexpected."

In response, Brehan released a pettish sigh.

"The sprites are your discovery. I've authorized your heading the study on them."

"How very kind. But I suspect you *already* know everything about them."

Erth paused to quell his annoyance with her attitude toward him. "I will leave the progression of the mutation in your capable hands—and Manak's, as you both work so well together."

"Adam is a vital part of the team."

Erth nodded. "It pleases me that you are using your intelligence in this manner."

"Pleases *you?*" she echoed haughtily, sparing him a dark look over her shoulder. "I enjoy the lab because it gives me something challenging to do. Don't make anything more of it."

Erth heaved a breath. He looked upward with a silent plea for patience, but none was granted him. His system sparked, forcing him to willfully calm the ignitions. After more than three months of traveling together, he'd hoped to have gained more ground with her than what he had—which, apparently, was none at all.

"Don't you have something to do . . . *elsewhere?*"

A rueful grin twitched on Erth's mouth as he tried to resist her needling. "I understand you experienced a premonition."

A disgruntled breath was heard from Brehan.

"It concerned Manak enough to warrant his discussing it with me. Tell me about it."

"Quite frankly, it's none of your business."

"Then let's discuss something that is," Erth said with an edge to his tone. "How long are you going to stall the impregnation?"

"You're the omniscient one. Figure it out."

Her cutting tone lingered in the air as she turned the back of her head to him once again. Erth considered walking away before another unpleasant scene erupted between them. He regarded this room as a special place, a sanctuary to be alone with oneself. And perhaps he would have left, but there was a tantalizing challenge in the way she stood staring out into space: the rigidity of her body; the defiant thrust of her chin. Her body language dared him to pursue his questioning.

He stepped up on the platform, a portion of his concentration focused on keeping his system as calm as possible. Her goading wouldn't work on him this time, nor would her uncanny ability to avoid her responsibility to him. They were mates, and it was high time she afforded him the rights due him—even if it reduced her to the clinging, over-sexed type of woman the other women had become since the matching. He'd often wondered—when he'd come across one of his men yawning or looking dreamily off into space—if the men really felt sex was worth giving up sleep and peace of mind for. Not one had complained. Nor did they seem to mind their mates demanding all of their free time.

Frowning at Brehan's back, he wondered how he would fare if she clung to his arm, followed him around, and demanded he gratify her needs every night.

The real question was, would he ever find out?

"How long, Brehan?"

"You sound like a broken record."

"It's a simple enough question."

Turning to face him, she icily delivered, "From a simple enough mind."

"Your insults are wearing thin."

"No. My insults are driving you crazy. You can't control what I think, or what I say."

"I thought we'd gotten beyond the power play phase," he laughed mockingly. "Obviously not. We made a bargain. I *will* make you hold up your end of it."

A chill settled in the pit of Brehan's stomach. She'd known she was running out of time. The dreamings had forewarned her, had shown her the only out available to her. The promised release was a harsh finality to her dilemma, but it could prove swift—*almost painless*—if she could just push Erth over the edge of his control.

Taking several steps in his direction, she stated, "All I have to do is bide my time."

"To what end?"

"Your verbal threats don't bother me anymore. You can't *force* me to submit to artificial insemination."

"I can, and I will, physically master you, if you so *force* me," he said solemnly.

"Physically master me," she murmured thoughtfully, then arched a challenging eyebrow at him. "Don't waste your *valuable* time on someone who is repulsed by the very sight of you, Erth. There are too many other things simply crying out for your attention."

"Feel free to enlighten me."

"Let's see, there's the fact that you've been steadily losing control since my arrival. Your men are beginning to show contempt for your laws. Accept it, Erth, you're losing your influence and your authority over them. And all I've had to do was drop a few suggestions here and there, and show a little spine."

Compelled to push him to the brink, she closed the distance between them and clipped him beneath the chin with the knuckles of one hand. "Doesn't it just irk you that a *mere* woman has the testicle fortitude to defy you?"

"Your mouth," Erth exhaled. He took a moment to still the frolicking bursts of heat within him. "I have never considered you a *mere* anything," he chuckled unpleasantly. "My men and the women are adjusting relatively well—with the exception of you. I am, and always will be, in control of this ship and my people."

Brehan rolled her eyes. "May you drown in your delusions."

His gaze smoothly glanced over her features, and he asked himself for the hundredth time how anything so beautiful, could possess such a sting. "What exactly do you hope to gain by arousing my anger?"

"The people's emancipation from you, and your emasculation. But I'm not greedy. I'll settle for the latter."

"Quite an undertaking. Even for you."

She was beyond fearing the portent of the dreamings, beyond fearing death. A life of fear was no life at all, anyway. If this was her only chance to escape childbearing . . .

"Why don't you go to some dark, faraway corner of the universe, find a deserving, mentally deficient species who can appreciate your sadistic form of nurturing, and leave us the hell *alone!*"

"You have amazing lung power."

"I'm glad you find it so amusing."

"To the contrary," Erth said quietly. Turning, he stepped down from the platform and seated himself on the upper level. He looked up into Brehan's bemused face, his expression guarded, masking his urge to shake the arrogance out of her. "It disturbs me that we continually fail to communicate."

"It's my refusal to whore for the sake of a *mission* that disturbs you!"

"My kingdom for a bar of soap," he moaned, and ran his hands down his face. His insides were heating up. He realized there was no winning solution where she was concerned. Turning his head slightly, he looked up to regard her hostile stance, and again considered simply walking away. But damn! He was tired of offering compromises, only to have her spit them back in his face!

"Go away," she coldly demanded.

Before she could walk away from him, he reached out and grasped her wrist. He calmly yanked her down across his lap and secured her in place with a hand to the small of her back.

"You wouldn't dare!"

His nostrils flaring, Erth raised his right hand into the air. "You will wish *you* were in some dark, faraway corner of the universe before I'm through!"

Every muscle in her body tensed, but nothing could have prepared her for the shocking sting of the first blow. Each time his palm connected with her buttocks, she fought with every ounce of her will to keep from crying out. But when she was suddenly on her feet, and staring up into his stony face, she burst into tears.

To Erth's chagrin, her weeping turned into hysterical laughter. Mutely berating himself for having lost control, he gave her a sobering shake. "Dammit, Brehan, this has to end!"

"I dreamt you tried to beat me to death," she sniffed, her eyes glazed with tears. "And it turns out to be a spanking." Laughter bubbled from her as she added, "Damn you, you *fool*, I was ready to die!"

* * *

Barrit entered Erth's quarters to find him stretched out on a massive bed with his hands folded beneath his head. Erth's eyes were closed, but Barrit knew his presence was known. Being in no mood to stand patiently by and wait to be acknowledged, he accused, "You were unnecessarily rough on her."

"I don't recall asking for your opinion."

"*I* spent the better part of the night prying Brehan from a catatonic state! Regardless of the provocation, you have taught us corporal retaliation is barbaric. Is this conviction solely based on one's station?"

Erth rose from the bed. "She goaded me into that confrontation! She was expecting me to end her life!"

Barrit stiffened with shock.

"She mentioned a dream in which I tried to beat her to death. She believed I was capable of killing her— with my hands!"

"You are."

Erth incredulously stared at Barrit.

"She brings out a dark side of you I never knew existed," Barrit stated. "You lose all sense of reason when you're around her."

"I know," Erth murmured, raking the fingertips of his right hand across his bare chest. "And it disturbs me. I've never given in to such petty irritations. But there's something about her ... My mind tells me one thing, my instincts another. I have no wish to attain the distinction of being the first guardian to suffer a nervous breakdown."

"Her defiance stems from a childhood of abuse, Erth. There's no telling what further psychological scars your actions have caused. There must have been a malfunction in Mastric's initial psychological evaluation of her. She should have been denied on her obstinacy alone."

Here was Erth's chance to unburden his guilt. "She was never accepted by Mastric. I made the decision to take her, and I altered the records to make it appear otherwise."

"Only Lisa and Joy were to be taken?"

Erth inwardly cringed. He was feeling overwhelmed by an emotion he had never before experienced—shame. "The scenario was simple enough. I'd planned to cause a fire in the cabin after taking Joy and Lisa. As in the past, the parties remaining would accept the deaths and go on with their lives. But while I was waiting at the cabin for the women to return, I became aware of complications. The shooting at the office. The storm. The gunman on the road. And then I unintentionally mind-linked with Brehan moments before the lightning struck the road. She was having a hallucination of burnt corpses sitting beside her in the car."

Crossing the room, Erth hooked his thumbs into the waistband of his pants. "When I extricated Lisa and Joy from the falling vehicle, something within Brehan reached out for me. I couldn't ignore her will to live. After the vehicle had crashed, I set her down, and used the illusion of the burnt corpses in the car to convince her that her friends had died. But she saw herself as well, behind the wheel. It was then I realized she was indeed psychic, and she would never accept Joy and Lisa's deaths.

"I went to Jakes' office," he went on, "and minimally repaired his wounds. There was no going back to the original plan after that. When I returned to the cabin for her, I sensed she was waiting for me."

"Why the secrecy?"

"I had a decision to make, Barrit! I couldn't allow something that vitally alive to die, or face an attempted murder charge alone! What would *you* have done?"

"The very same, but I wouldn't have shown outrage at her every indiscretion! You were aware of her extraordinary gifts before you brought her aboard."

"To a certain degree. I certainly had no idea she

would prove to be such a complicated package. Barrit, I have never encountered a human of her caliber."

"You're not likely to again."

The room suddenly seemed to be closing in on Erth. "I can't begin to explain what I feel when I'm in her presence, or how she haunts me when we're separated."

"You're embarrassed because you feel you should be above physical needs," Barrit said unsympathetically. "Well you're down here with the rest of us emotional slaves. Either endeavor to override your love for the woman, or learn to grow with it."

A scowl darkened Erth's features. "This miserable quandary I'm in, is love?"

Barrit nodded.

Erth grimaced as if suddenly overwhelmed by a bitter taste in his mouth. "How do I begin to make her accept the mission?"

"You can't *make* her do anything. It's you, she's denying. When you're not around, she's calm and quite at ease with the men and women. She seems to regard you as the personification of every enemy and injustice she has had to deal with in her young life."

"Why?"

"You're an indestructible threat. She hasn't figured out how to control you."

"Control me, how?"

"With fear. As a child she learned to deal with it, and later, utilized it to protect herself and others."

"I'm no threat to her," Erth argued. "I gave her life!"

"In exchange for . . . ?"

"Bringing life to Syre."

"You gave her life, but in return for something which was not part of her existence on Earth."

"Childbearing? None of the women—"

"But most of them had lovers," Barrit interjected impatiently. "Brehan is strongly opposing the chemistry between you. It's new to her, and she doesn't give in easily to anything she doesn't understand. *You* should certainly understand what motivates her actions. You're as intimidated by sexuality as she is."

"Curiosity can hardly be construed as intimidation!"

"She also harbors a profound fear of childbearing. I haven't determined the why yet, but I intend to find out."

"And I'm telling you, Barrit, that woman isn't afraid of anything!"

Weary of trying to reason with Erth, Barrit abruptly turned and left the room.

Erth was confounded. Feeling as if the last vestige of his authority was being challenged, he stretched out on his bed and stared up at the ceiling.

The spanking had in fact left him despondent. There had been no satisfaction in besting the woman, only self-recrimination. Unwittingly, he had lowered himself to her level. How could he have forsaken the knowledge of the cruelties she'd suffered during her life at the orphanage, and the empathic implant of her mother's trauma?

"What motivates you, Brehan?" he mused aloud. "You're a mortal creature with no significance other than to bear children." He closed his eyes and her image appeared on the insides of his lids.

What was sexuality?

What exactly was this chemistry Barrit had spoken of?

Slowly opening his eyes, he tried to analyze the uncomfortable sensation twisting within his groin.

"I haven't known a moment's boredom since—"

He sat up suddenly and expelled a breath. "Now I'm talking to myself. I'm getting humanized!"

The night mode was in effect when Manak slipped into Brehan's quarters. Sitting on the edge of the bed, he stared down at her features, which were softened beneath the dim red lighting. It was some time before she began to stir in her sleep. When her eyelids fluttered open, he braced himself against the indignation he read in her eyes.

"What are you doing here?" she asked groggily, then sat up and scooted back against the headboard.

"Checking on you."

"I'm fine. Go away."

Manak solemnly watched her run the fingers of a hand through the crown of her hair. "Is it true you tried to provoke Erth to take your life?"

Brehan glanced at him briefly before looking away.

A tightness formed in Manak's chest. "It *is* true. When Adam told me—"

"Adam?" she gasped. "No!"

"He overheard Barrit and Christie discussing what happened. He's upset, to say the least. Not that I'm all that thrilled to hear it's true. Why, my lady? Are you so unhappy with us?"

"I can't explain my reasons."

Clasping one of her hands, Manak gave a tug to draw her gaze to him. She reluctantly complied, shame lending her features a gaunt appearance.

"I will always be here for you," he said huskily, his thumb massaging the back of her hand. "I won't try to pretend I understand your fears, Brehan, but I will tell you I can't imagine a future without you. I learn from you every day. I-I admire and respect you—"

"Please don't," Brehan sobbed, closing her eyes and dipping back her head.

Manak lowered his for a moment to will back the tears pressing at the back of his eyes. "Adam is confused. My lady, you must try to explain your reasons to him. He's impressionable. Likely to—"

"Don't say it!" Brehan looked at Manak. "I'll talk to him." Tears welled in her eyes. "Only I don't know what I'm going to say. I know it was wrong to . . ." The sentence ended when her voice broke with emotion.

"Take an easy out?" he suggested softly. When she

began to weep, he pulled her into his strong arms and held her. "Shhh, *Katiah.*"

"I hate to cry," she confessed against him, unable to stop her tears, or the trembling of her body.

Manak smiled in understanding and lovingly smoothed the hair at the back of her head. "Crying is a necessary release."

Something between a chuckle and a sob escaped her. Backing away from him, she briskly wiped a hand across the moisture on her cheeks. "It always gives me a walloping headache."

"Want me to fetch Barrit?"

"I don't want to face him right now."

With a thumb, Manak brushed away a tear which had slipped from the corner of her left eye. "Embarrassed?"

"Understatement of the year."

"You're a survivor," he grinned.

Brehan gave a gentle shake of her head. "You're a good friend, Manak. Sometimes . . . I think you know me better than I know myself."

"Next time you get it into your head to die, take a moment to reflect on what your absence would do to us. The boredom alone would be devastating."

A low laugh escaped Brehan. "I don't know about you."

"I know you don't. Now scoot down. You need your rest."

Manak stood while she settled beneath the top sheet, then he sat again, leaning over her, the fingers of his left hand tenderly caressing her brow. Brehan's heavy eyelids closed, and the tension in her body ebbed to his ministrations. When he was sure she was asleep, he planted a tremulous, lingering kiss on her cool brow.

"I love you," he whispered, pain lacing his tone. "If only you knew how much."

He left the room before his breaking hearts could betray him.

Chapter Nine

TRANSITION DATE: 00.112. Afternoon mode.

The feeling of being in limbo continues. It's almost as if I'm existing within the eye of a storm. Waiting, but for what, I don't know.

My foolish attempt to escape the mission has magnanimously been forgiven by all, except Kousta. She taunts me at every given opportunity, but I know she's ticked off because I didn't succeed in dying. Her obsession with Erth has only grown stronger since the matching. Poor Uhul. I can't help but wonder how this affects him. He's certainly a moody fellow. Quiet, and basically a loner.

To date, Manak has been unsuccessful in coming up with a means by which to confine the sprites. We have discovered, however, their life span increases minimally on a daily basis. Adam's interest in the new life form has also increased. He's very dedicated to learning all he can about the sprites. It keeps him out of trouble.

I have not laid eyes on Erth since the Garden Chamber incident. Oddly enough, I haven't even sensed him meditating on me. I hope against hope, my willingness to die to avoid motherhood, has impressed upon him how strongly I feel about the subject. I hate to presume to second guess him, though. He's very unpredictable. The one thing in my favor is that he is not human, and not governed by sexual drives as are the males of my species. If he were a human male, and prone to reacting to the chemistry between a man and woman, I doubt if I would have been able to put him off this long.

I can't imagine him as a lover, but then I have never been interested in sex. Whenever I'm around one of the pregnant women, I wonder if the conception of that child was at all pleasing. One of these days, I must work up the nerve to ask Joy or Lisa about the experience.

END

It was late when Brehan decided to quit. The sprite entries she'd been making in Manak's lab computer were swimming before her eyes, and the muscles in the back of her neck had long since grown knotted. Leaving the lab, she shuffled along the corridor, reflecting on how much she loved the quiet and stillness of the night mode.

She was nearly to the E wall to the A corridor when an exit to her right abruptly parted and exposed one of the storage rooms. Massaging the back of her neck, she squinted her tired eyes to see beyond the threshold. It was unusual for an E wall to open of its own accord. If someone had activated it from the other side, where were they?

Curiosity waylaid her intentions to go straight to her quarters. She entered the room, stopped, then moved on a little further. The distorting red lighting caused her eyes to burn and water as she strained to scan the shelves and cabinets within the large compartment.

Deciding another glitch of sorts had triggered the opening, she turned to leave, and nearly jumped out of her skin when the exit sealed.

A knot of fear tightened in her stomach. The hairs along the back of her neck began to creep along her sensitive skin. Then an overwhelming sense of danger arose, igniting her primordial survival instinct.

"I've been waiting for you."

Brehan spun around and narrowed her eyes on the man standing across from her. The red lighting accentuated the madness she read in his eyes.

"We're alone." He swayed on his feet, then steadied himself. "You and . . . me."

A terrible coldness seized Brehan's insides as she realized the incident in the Garden Chamber with Erth was not what the dreamings had forewarned. A swift blow from him would have ended her life quickly and painlessly. The threat of languishing pain confronted her now.

"What are you doing in here?"

A smile contorted his face. "Waiting for you."

"Why?"

"You know why," he slurred, teetering again.

"Tell me," Brehan urged, cautiously stepping back, a hand behind her ready to grope for the triangular mechanism on the wall.

"Once you are eliminated, *she* will have control."

"Erth will—"

"He can't stop me!" he snarled, raking a clawed hand downward through the air. "She taught me how to block my thoughts from his probing. He'll . . . never know." He stepped menacingly closer. "He'll *never* know."

"She's using you."

"Shut up!" he barked, swinging an arm out at her. Then he stretched out the same hand to touch her cheek as he stumbled forward, his face grotesquely contorted with rage. "I wanted *you*. You never looked at me. Never spoke to me."

"The sight of you disgusts me!" Brehan hissed, edging along the wall to avoid his touch.

"Pity," he slurred, "but I will have you *and* my dream."

He lunged at her, his fingers biting into her shoulders

until the pain wrenched a cry from her. Brehan attempted to ram a knee to his groin, but with a madman's strength, he flung her to the floor. Stunned and uncoordinated, she couldn't prevent his fist from slamming into her temple. Now, beyond pain, she was unaware of him straddling her, unaware of his fists rendering blow after blow to her head and face.

Her last thought before losing consciousness was, *damnation*.

In the Control Center, something within Erth surged and then plummeted, jarring him into straightening up from the master console. Disoriented by the unexpectedness of the experience, he looked dazedly about the massive, otherwise empty room and reached out with his sensors. But there was nothing he could pinpoint to explain the strange phenomena. Finally dispelling it and returning his concentration to the panel he was working on, he unknowingly allowed the presentiment of Brehan's danger to pass. Sometime later, the sound of the lift plied him from his musings. He looked up to see Christie and Barrit hastily approaching him. He rose from his command chair, his movements lethargic, his usual bright-eyed gaze dulled by a sinking suspicion that he was about to hear news of Brehan being on the rampage again. He had avoided her—even avoided meditating so as not to connect with the infuriating woman in any way.

Christie stopped short in front of Erth, her gaze riveted disconcertingly on his face. Barrit came to stand at her side, his face taut and ashen.

"Have you seen Brehan today?"

Christie's sharp tone dissolved Erth's stupor. "No."

"Don't you think that's a little odd . . . *considering?*"

"Considering what?" Erth asked impatiently.

"No one has seen or heard from her since yesterday," Barrit said. "She was supposed to meet Adam at the lab this morning, and never showed up. We've been searching for her all morning, but we can't find her anywhere."

Inexplicable coldness moved through Erth's system like a shockwave. He reached out with his inner sensors, strained to locate her, but it was as if she had vanished from the ship.

"Stalan, remain here! If you see or hear from Brehan, let me know immediately! Christie, organize the women and wait with them in the Meeting Chamber."

"If Brehan *is* hiding, she may listen to me."

Barrit agreed with his mate.

Erth gave a reluctant nod of consent. "Stalan, inform Rao to escort the women to the Meeting Chamber. And inform the rest of the men to come topside."

Manak left his post and came to Erth's side. "How are we to proceed, *Katian?*"

"Meticulously."

Hours later, mentally exhausted and heated with frustration, Erth pressed his palms to one of the walls of the Feeding Chamber and once again tried to feel out Brehan's location. But his sensors were cold. He couldn't shake the grim notion that if she'd been desperate enough to provoke him into taking her life, she might have decided—

Hearing his name through the intercom, he rushed over to it. "Yes, Barrit?"

"Maintenance-Supply Twelve has an escape hatch unlocked. She may have jettisoned from the ship."

Erth's system painfully constricted. He'd no sooner released the intercom switch when Manak's shrill voice boomed through it. "We've found her! B storage by the lab!"

During his ascent in the lift, many thoughts whirled in his mind. Manak's voice had held what? Horror? *Anguish?* When he arrived at his destination, he found

Manak and Christie waiting for him by an exposed exit. Their sickly gray-green pallor caused an eruption of alarm in him. This intensified when Niton staggered from the room, fell to his knees, then began to retch. Stepping over him, Erth entered the room, braced, he thought, for anything.

Barrit looked up from his kneeling position. "I don't know what to do!"

Erth knelt beside the body, staring dazedly at the vermillion mane fanned out on the floor. A sheet was drawn up to the back of her neck, a mere glimpse of her right profile showing through the tangled strands of hair. His hand touched the back of her skull. It came away with blood on it.

Easing his right arm beneath her, he gently turned her over, keeping the sheet secured about her naked body. He brushed aside a sticky mass of hair and was given a jolt. Her face was ridden with gashes, bruises and blood, her left eye purple and swollen shut, her lips mashed to a bloody pulp.

"Brehan," he rasped, torn with denial.

Rising to his feet, he protectively cradled her in his arms. Through a haze of surrealism, he found his way to the Med Chamber, where he placed her on the nearest bed. Barrit positioned himself on the opposite side of it, his face pale and ravaged by shock. He held out something to Erth. Seconds ticked by before Erth took the material into his hand, and it was still some time before he recognized it as the remains of a jumpsuit. He looked up to see Barrit gingerly probing Brehan's abdomen.

"She's dying. Severe hemorrhaging. Erth, it's gone beyond my ability to repair."

Erth savagely flung the material to the floor, then bent over Brehan with barely controlled rage. He wanted to shake her, to punish her for surfacing emotions in him that hurt so much. Passing his right hand over the length of her body, he straightened up with the fires of hell burning in his eyes. Without a word to Barrit, he left the room.

Panic seized Barrit. Believing Erth had abandoned the woman, he reached out to touch her arm. His fingers were inches from her skin when he felt a startling coldness emanate from her. A ragged sigh of relief escaped him. Erth had manifested a cryostate to arrest her deteriorating condition.

Manak and Niton solemnly followed Erth into the Meeting Chamber. They flanked their superior and stood at rigid attention—with legs slightly apart and hands clasped at the base of their spines. The boisterous speculation in the room wound down. All eyes riveted on Erth. His face was a mask of stone as he probed for the culprit, which proved futile. He was too incensed to concentrate on what lay behind their fear and anxiety.

He trained his attention on Adam's ashen face. Rao and Lute had restraining holds on the boy's arms. Then Erth focused on Lisa and Joy across the room. Their protruding bellies awakened his concern for the children they were carrying. Turning his head, he said to Niton, "Attend to your woman."

Erth numbly observed as the other couples huddled together. Adam stood alone, trembling, lost and vulnerable.

"Brehan?" Joy sobbed, holding tight to Caenith's arm.

"She's alive," Erth said in a monotone. "Barely alive," he amended, and raised a hand to quell the effervescent uproar of questions. "She was found in a storage unit, brutally beaten and left to die." When wails rang out, he bellowed, "Be still!" He waited until he was awarded their silence, taking this time to analyze the intensity of emotions permeating the room.

"Step forward, violator," he ordered, his gaze scanning each male face before him.

The ensuing silence was deafening.

"Have the courage to bear the penalty for this iniquity you have perpetrated!"

Silence.

It took all of Erth's willpower to retard the swelling of his core, his flesh tingling in anticipation. The miscreant's ability to shield his guilt could not—and would not—withstand Erth's obsession to pluck him out once the emotional levels de-escalated. Confident of this, he gestured for Joy and Lisa to come forward. When they complied, he said to them, "Come with me into the corridor. The rest of you remain here until we're through."

Adam rushed forward and took a firm hold on Erth's arm. "What can I do to help?"

"Remain here until I have spoken with Joy and Lisa."

"I need to—"

"Adam!" Erth drew in a steadying breath. "When I am through talking to these women, I want you to go to the lab and proceed with the tests Brehan had scheduled on the sprites."

"I don't give a damn about the sprites!" he wailed.

"Brehan is counting on you to carry on with the experiment until she's able to return to the lab."

Adam quieted. "All right. I won't disappoint her."

When the E wall sealed them off from the others, Erth asked the two women, "Has any man shown an inordinate interest in Brehan?"

"Inordinate? N-no," Joy replied. "I don't think so."

"There's an awful hatred between her and Kousta," said Lisa.

"A man attacked her."

"How can you be—" Joy braced her back against the wall to keep herself up. "Rape?"

"She didn't volunteer it!" Chagrined by his outburst, Erth murmured a feeble apology.

"We want to see her," Lisa insisted.

"Not as she is. I want you both to return to your

quarters with your men, and stay there. Instruct the others to do the same. Joy?"

She was hugging herself and staring off into space. "It just occurred to me, one of the women is with a maniac."

Erth's brow furrowed. "Niton, Stalan and Manak were with me in the Control Center. Barrit—"

"I know Caenith didn't do it!" Joy protested.

"Was he with you?"

"No, but I know he isn't capable of such a thing!"

"Be safe with that conviction," Erth said dryly. "In the meantime, until I know the identity of the assailant, I want you to keep in close communication with the other women. Anything suspicious, I want to hear of it immediately."

Erth left for the Med Chamber. Lisa and Joy went back into the Meeting Chamber, where Joy informed the group of Erth's orders. Adam left immediately for the lab. After a time of circulating conjectures, the couples began to leave. Joy and Lisa remained beside Niton and Caenith, watching the faces of all who passed them, in hopes of gleaning a clue. As Kousta and Uhul walked by, Joy's hand shot out and stayed the woman.

"You had something to do with Brehan's attack," Joy accused in a low voice. "I can feel it in my gut."

Kousta's mouth twisted contemptuously. "You've been hanging around Brehan too long. Her quirks are rubbing off on you."

"I'm sorry about your friend," Uhul said. "*Katian* will keep her safe."

"Yes," Joy said, her voice stilted with disgust. Then an eerie calm fell across her features. "I almost feel sorry for whoever attacked her."

The four left, leaving Uhul and Kousta staring after them. When Kousta was sure no one could hear, she struck Uhul across the face. "Fool! Can't you do anything right?"

Feeling the heat of shame sweep through him, Uhul lowered his head. "I don't remember too much."

"All you had to do was kill her!" Kousta fumed, her fist clenched and held menacingly beneath his nose, her face contorted with rage.

Uhul's eyes slowly lifted and impaled her face. Kousta caught her breath and lowered her fist to her side. For the first time, she questioned the extent of her control over him.

Sensuously she caressed his smarting cheek with the back of her hand. She cooed, "You do love candy, don't you?"

Hunger shadowed his eyes. With an evil smile playing on her lips, she took his hand and led him from the room.

Barrit glanced up, his anxiety at the point of eruption. "How long can you keep her stabilized like this?"

Removing the hibernation force, Erth gently lifted Brehan into his arms. He carried her to the center of the room, where he stopped and stared up at the ceiling as though looking beyond it.

Arrogance and pride had ostracized him from his father's house, and pride had prevented him from calling to his father after the Feydais attack. But he had matured and grown wiser since those days. A single life mattered now, and occluded his desire to shun his father's overshadowing omniscience.

"Father!"

Silence followed, and the frightening realization that his woman's life was dependent upon a tenuous will to live.

"Father! Hear me!" he implored, the cords in his neck straining against his bronze flesh. "Grant me my full inheritance!"

Silence.

He closed his eyes. Ignitions were beginning in his

core, radiating throughout his system. He unwittingly gazed down at Brehan's mutilated face, and his imagination conjured up and magnified the horrors she had suffered during the attack.

"This woman should not die!" he cried, glaring up at the ceiling. "My wrath shall see no equal! And my wrath shall first fall on the House of Sojan!"

Barrit cried out when blinding light replaced the ceiling. Covering his face with a lifted arm, he cowered against the wall. Erth winced and closed his eyes until the aftermath glare had dimmed, then he peered upward into blackness. Thunder rolled within it. Infinity yawned above him like a gaping mandible.

"You have yet to understand humility," came a feminine voice from within the subsiding thunder.

"Where is Father?"

"Vastly occupied. Fortunate he did not hear your rash threat to exact vengeance upon his house."

"It was no rash threat, Mother. This woman is dying. I need Father's help."

There was a tense stretch of silence. "You have no need of your father. Your powers are within you."

"I would know—"

"Had you the wisdom to perceive them! You assumed your father had stripped your full powers. Not so, Erth. It was your guilt that curbed your abilities, and it disheartens me to know it took such a passage of time and this violent act to supplant your pride."

"Tell me what to do!"

"Only *Cahfu* can save her."

Erth swayed on his feet. "You cannot expect me to make such a sacrifice!"

"The choice is yours. Desire alone will not give you the strength you need to restore her. It has poorly served you in the past, Erth. Search your *nai-ohua*. I must detach. Your father grows impatient with my absence."

The blackness rolled away until the ceiling was once again normal. Paralyzed with indecision, Erth wretchedly stared into Brehan's face. The powers necessary to restore her would have to be summoned from the core of his source. *Cahfu*—the communion of souls—would couple them for her life span. Once bonded, he could morally take no other mate. No other would be accepted by the House of Sojan.

To be a captive of the flesh for such an inferior creature as she, would surely be insanity. To accept, irrevocably, a mate so in loathing of procreation, would be condemning himself to Syre for centuries.

His grim thoughts became lost to memories of sensations he'd experienced when in her company. She did offer a promise of obliterating his accursed boredom. Her fiery spirit relentlessly challenged him to venture into the mysteries of her mind.

Inferior though she was, he had somehow grown attached to her.

No! Not attached! Not even . . . *fond!* He knew its true name now, and denying its existence didn't make it so. Somehow, Erth, son of Sojan and Mythia, Light Lord and guardian of the Syre race, had fallen into the abysmal depths of . . . love.

But if I tire of you? he mutely asked Brehan.

Barrit sagged against the wall. He saw Erth's indecision and was suddenly afraid that Brehan meant too little to him to warrant tapping into the unknown. "Dammit, Erth, you have the power!"

Erth glowered at Barrit, but the medix's plea had touched upon Erth's reasoning.

Relegating his doubts and fears to the back of his mind, Erth's consciousness inverted until it was one with his *nai-ohua*—his soul. Once he mentally invoked his dormant heritage to the surface, a golden aura formed about him and the near-lifeless form in his arms. The aura began to pulsate. Erth threw back his head, teeth bared and clenched against the pain unmercifully ripping through him. Light began to seep through holes manifesting in his flesh. He sank unsteadily to one knee as a struggle between his mind and his source raged through him, the latter determined to reject the alien consciousness it was being willed to unify with. Doubled over, he strengthened his resistance against the agony, although he felt it would consume him before his core relented to his command. The streams of light poking through the holes in his flesh became luminous snakes, twisting and snapping in the air before completely cocooning him and the woman. He was conscious of lifting into the air, then of being confounded by sensations as his system merged with hers. He experienced the complexity of the human body as if it were his own, then at last, touched upon her soul.

Barrit took a step forward and braced himself against the side of the bed. He watched in awe as the gyration of lights decreased, the appendages slowly receded into Erth's body, and the holes in his flesh gradually sealed.

Erth lowered to his feet. Exhausted from the ordeal, he sank to his knees. For a time he rocked to and fro, possessively cradling Brehan's form against him, as if to let go was to lose a part of himself. At last he got to his feet. He carried her back to the bed and laid her down. Straightening up, he languidly searched her features. Her skin was smooth, with neither a bruise nor a scar to testify to her ordeal. Thick dark eyelashes were curled upon the blush in her cheeks. She sighed in her sleep, drawing his attention to the contours of her lips. He tentatively touched her mouth with his fingertips, but she sighed again and startled him. Self-conscious, at odds with himself, he met Barrit's venerating gaze.

"I heard *Ni-Katiah's* voice," Barrit breathed. He released an abrupt, hysterical laugh, his gaze sweeping Brehan's length. "I witnessed a miracle!"

Erth was disoriented and weakened by his experience, but he refused to allow himself to give in to it.

"Giving in to the communion of souls couldn't have been an easy decision. For a time, I feared you would let her die."

"Centuries, Barrit," Erth groaned low. "My father's mirth must be thundering the boundaries of Haveth."

"She has served to entertain you thus far," Barrit said. Mindless of the annoyance shadowing Erth's face, he deftly ran his fingertips along Brehan's form, imbibing the results of the miracle.

"Where is Christie?"

Barrit looked up. "She insisted on rechecking the area in hopes of finding a clue."

"I'll be in my quarters," Erth said, turning abruptly. "Brehan will sleep until tomorrow. I want her well guarded."

"Who better than you?" Barrit challenged, his tone staying Erth at the threshold of the exit.

"If I am to detect the assailant, I must clear my mind." His gaze dropped to Brehan's face and he felt his system surge. "I have to know who did this. My meditation is not to be disrupted unless it is urgent—or related to her."

"I'll stay with her," Barrit said, an edge to his tone, "and I'll endeavor not to disturb you."

"Barrit, I *do* care about this woman."

"Do you? Then be here by her side when she wakes up. Let her know that you regard her as more than a possession."

Erth left the room.

Manak / Dawn Husset   Niton / Lisa Donner
Caenith / Joy Lowery   Stalan / Karen Stanberg
Rao / Deboora   Joea / Mindi Fargo
Baek / Jamie DelRea   Lute / Jackie Shaw
Uhul / Kousta

Erth leaned back in his chair and scanned the computer entry several times before realizing that he had neglected to include his own match. Adding the data, he switched off his unit and locked his fingers on his chest. He remained this way for several hours, staring off into space while his mind repeatedly recreated the storage-room scene. When he could no longer bear the images, he called to mind the time he had lain naked beside her, exploring her own nudity. He had never given much thought to the texture of flesh prior to that day. However, it occupied his thoughts too often, since. His own was merely a canister, a shell. But hers ... It was warm and soft. Curvaceous. It breathed, and it glistened with perspiration. It even had its own intoxicating scent.

An image flashed through his mind, startling him. He wearily rubbed the back of his neck, ignoring it as one might ignore a nightmare. But the same image reared up again, and he ran from the room, just missing the call from Barrit through the intercom. When he arrived at the Med Chamber, he stopped short near a group of men and women. Kousta was sitting on the floor, sobbing, rubbing her right ankle. Barrit left her side and approached Erth.

"What happened?"

"We left the room when we heard Kousta cry out. The wall sealed immediately after us. Manak's at the main control switch, but he's obviously not able to get the entrance to open."

Delivering Kousta a dark look, Erth turned and pressed his palms to the E wall. His flesh began to tingle. His brain became inflamed.

"Stand back!" he ordered the observers. In his mind's eye he saw Brehan dragging herself along the floor, gasping for air that was no longer being supplied into the room. A growl rumbled deep within his throat. The cords in his neck strained against his flesh as he focused his concentration. Within seconds, his hands became enveloped by a fiery glow. His arched fingers gouged into the metal-like fabric of the wall and, when he had a firm hold, he gave one mighty jerk and disjointed the E wall. Then, lifting the massive piece, he turned and discarded it upon the corridor floor.

Brehan gulped in the sudden rush of air. When someone stopped and lifted her, fear induced her to wrap her arms tightly about his neck. She didn't care who had rescued her, only that the agony of being denied oxygen, had passed.

Erth swung around and stepped into the corridor, raking a look of distrust over the group. "Repair this unit," he ordered, his eyes fixed on Baek's stricken face. "Barrit, Christie, come with me."

Brehan remained docile until Erth stepped into her quarters, where, much to his surprise, her fists began to assault his face and neck. Although he didn't feel pain as did mortals, the idea of being struck instinctively made him defensive. He hurriedly crossed the room, dropped the struggling woman upon the bed, then knelt on one knee. Brehan sprang up, again taking him by surprise. Her right hand shot out and ripped the headband from his brow, while the other drew back in a fist to strike him again.

"Brehan!"

Mindless of all but the rage prompting her actions, she drove the fist forward. Erth took the blow to his cheekbone before capturing her wrists. She cried out, wildly jerking back and forth in an effort to free herself.

"You're safe, *te-ni-e.*"

Came her acidic cry, "Not as long as you live!"

Her words struck a sensitive chord and Erth inhaled sharply. He fleetingly tried to surface the knowledge dancing just out of the reach of his consciousness, but his attention became focused on the heat her skin radiated. Releasing her, he stood and backed away, all the while feeling as though her eyes were dissecting him, shredding his existence. Christie and Barrit circled behind him and stood off to one side, their silence induced by Brehan's savage demeanor.

"Who is he?" Erth asked impatiently.

Puzzlement replaced the anger in Brehan's eyes. Her gaze hesitantly lowered to her right arm, her left, then to the short robe she was wearing. Her face, scantily seen through her lioness mass of hair, turned up.

"We found you in one of the storage rooms," Christie said, finding the tension in the room unbearable.

"I had this dream . . . "

"It was very real," Erth stated. "I want his name!"

His emotion-ridden tone cut through Brehan's stupor. She drew in a shaky breath, her chin quivering as shame blanketed her. "Leave me alone."

"Identify him."

"This has to be another nightmare," she moaned, but then something fell shockingly into place and hope faded into the shadows of fear. It *had* happened. And there was a frightening sense of rightness about her predicament. But what could possibly be right about the vicious attack she'd endured?

"Identify him," Erth pleaded.

Brehan looked up at him, her eyes bright with unshed tears. "The right to revenge is mine. I damn well earned it!"

Barrit started to speak, then clamped his mouth shut. Christie pressed closer to him, tears misting her eyes.

Brehan held her breath. Erth's bleak expression filled her with a sense of guilt. She sensed that something within him was trying to reach out to her. He was desperate to comfort her, but she couldn't ever let him get that close. Why, though? God, she needed *something* to get her through this! Why couldn't she bring herself to accept his kindness, accept the security of his arms, if only for a little while?

His sudden movement gave her a start of alarm. He raised his right arm and formed a fist. She watched him, growing more apprehensive when he closed his eyes briefly, then opened them with an enigmatic gaze fixed on her face. She felt an odd tingling sensation on the third finger of her left hand. Lifting it, she saw that a band of some unknown crystal had appeared. Numbed by its appearance, she studied the intricate symbols on the band—symbols appearing to be made of liquid fire.

"The Omeres believe the firestone has a spiritual healing property," Erth began in a dull tone. "It's given as a symbol of friendship. If I have learned anything from your species, it is that friendship must exist in any relationship."

She eyed him cynically, warily. When she tried to slip it from her finger, she found she couldn't budge it. "Take it back! I don't want it!"

"It's one more thing you will learn to accept," he said huskily, and left the room.

"Get out!" she screamed at Christie and Barrit.

After the wall sealed behind them, her emotions erupted. She flung herself across the bed and buried her face into the pillow. She wanted no one to see the tears welling from her sense of shame, or hear the weeping of a strong-willed woman reduced to a fragment of what she had been.

It came upon her in the middle of the night, a madness evoked by the rage leaving the confines of her subconscious. Drenched in cold sweat and panting, she sprang up and crouched in a savage, feline manner. Her movement activated the ceiling lights into a dim, precautionary mode.

Her clawed hands raked downward and effortlessly lacerated the bottom sheet and mattress. She repeatedly vented her rage in this manner until the contents of the mattress were strewn about the room. The pillow was shredded by her fingers as easily as if by razors, then she turned on the top sheet and quilt, mutilating them into strips of material.

She bolted from the bed, her fingers craving the solidity of anything to serve as a victim. Her wild-eyed gaze fixed on the nightstand. Yanking out one of the drawers, she wielded it like a club and launched an attack on the wall art.

—Disfunctioning female—

"Belay that!" she shrilled, crossing the room to the computer. Her red vision hungrily scanned the levers, dials and keyboard. The first blow was relatively ineffective. Each that followed became more inhumanly powerful, until the wall was a mass of mutilated metal and sizzling wires.

The madness began to ebb. Trembling, she dropped the drawer and stumbled backward across the room. She sank onto the vanity seat, panting, the room's shadows feeding a terrible coldness in the pit of her stomach.

"You bastard," she wept, "what have you done to me?"

Her head snapped up and she glared at her assailant's face superimposing her own in the vanity mirror. Her fingers curled, flexed, then raked down the glass in a slow, purposeful manner.

KILL HIM! RIP OUT HIS HEART!

Brehan straightened back as if she had been struck.

TERMINATE THE VIOLATOR!

"I . . . "

WHAT? YOU *CAN'T*? WE BOTH KNOW YOU LIVE TO OVERPOWER!

Brehan painfully gulped. "You're wrong. You make me sound evil!"

The legacy stretched its controlling fibers through Brehan's nervous system. The power yawned, testing the levels of the human consciousness. Then, having inadvertently allowed a fragment of information to slip out onto the conscious plane of the human part of Brehan's mind, it quickly retracted.

It was suddenly Erth's image superimposing Brehan's in the mirror. Feeling as if she were being squeezed between two inexorable forces, she shot to her feet. Her eyes widened in horror as the image faded. Her own ravaged expression stared back at her as a truth filled her mind so forcefully that her legs threatened to buckle beneath her.

Even as a child, she had known of Erth's existence! HE'LL USE YOU UP. YOU'LL BEAR HIS BROOD AND BE LEFT TO WITHER INTO AN OLD WOMAN. THINK! HE HAS BUT ONE USE FOR YOU! LIKE THE OTHER, HE WILL VIOLATE YOUR BODY AND SOUL!

Brehan hugged herself, weeping, fearful of the isolation enveloping her. She sank to her knees. The light held fear. The shadows held uncertainty. Life held despair and pain.

"Someone help me!" she cried, sinking to her buttocks and folding over.

The exit opened to admit Manak, who rushed to her and lowered himself next to her. Urging her into his arms, he said, "You're safe. The rage will pass, my lady. I'll stay as long as you need me."

In one of the other living quarters, Uhul's eyes shot open. Fear throbbed within his hearts. He was unable to move. Psychological weights crushed down on every part of him.

Kousta's warm, naked body was stretched out alongside him, her breathing regular, her sleep undaunted.

The craving was surfacing, so strong that he feared it worse than death. In a corralled corner of his mind, he was vaguely conscious of his crime, but the craving was all dominant, poisoning his conscience.

Soon he would wake Kousta. He was never able to fight the craving for the "candy" very long.

Chapter Ten

Erth was pacing in his quarters when a mental image reared up of Brehan turning on her computer. Expelling a breath, he stood perfectly still and slipped into a deep meditative state. Shortly, the screen of Brehan's monitor formed in front of his mind's eye. Under any other circumstances, he would never violate the privacy of her journals. But since the attack, his fervent hope had been that she would expose her assailant through an update. This was the first time she'd opened the file.

TRANSITION DATE: 00.135.
Three weeks ago, I nearly lost my sanity. Ironic that it took a brutal rape to make me cling so tightly to life. I have not left my quarters. Not because I fear a replay, but because I fear I will lose what little control I possess. My body has forgotten the assault. My mind can't. I have spent hours in the shower, but the violation clings to my skin. Vile and dirty. Although I wasn't conscious at the time, my mind plays a phantom enactment of what took place. I understand death. I understand his motives. I do not understand the sex part. I have never

understood the sex part. What pleasure could he have gained using my body as he did?

Joy and Christie and Lisa want me to talk about it. What do I say? I know what physically took place? I'm dealing with it? They don't want to hear I'm lost. They don't want me to admit I've faced my mortality, and I'm as vulnerable as they are.

The nightmares grow worse. Last night I wept myself to sleep in Manak's arms. He offers his strength, but I can't bring myself to reach out. The pity in his eyes makes me inwardly shrivel. He has even suggested I try to talk to Erth about what happened.

Erth! The mere idea of facing him makes me physically sick. I know the shame is not mine to bear, but it weighs heavily on me nonetheless. It would be so like him to lay the blame on me. The old Brehan would have thrown it back in his face. This one weeps within.

I must force myself to carry on my investigation. Perhaps an answer will free me.

END

Erth drew in a ragged breath as he opened his eyes. Pain was etched deeply in his face. His eyes mirrored the turmoil twisting inside him as he wondered, the answer to *what,* did she hope would free her?

Sitting on the edge of his bed, he braced his forearms atop his thighs, and leaned to. She had fallen asleep in Manak's arms again.

Manak. It was always *Manak.*

Jealousy lodged within Erth's chest. His arms ached to hold his woman, to comfort her, but he couldn't approach her without her mental barriers going up against him, and her ire cutting lose. He had long ago tired of patience. What more could he say, what more could he do to convince her they belonged together?

He wanted his mate to fall asleep in *his* arms!

"Not likely, unless she learns to trust me," he murmured disparagingly, and lowered his face into his upturned hands.

Erth straightened from the console when Manak came to stand beside him. "Why were you in Brehan's quarters last night?"

"I was monitoring her room—as ordered. I witnessed her having another nightmare and responded to her distress." Peeved with the suspicion he read in his superior's eyes, Manak went on, "I suspect there is more going on than what is readily apparent. I found something wedged between the terminals in the Relay Chamber. I'm sure it was left to divert suspicion."

"Give it to me."

Manak dropped a gold chain into Erth's leveled palm. "Joy gave it to Caenith some weeks ago. He's always wearing it, but as you can see, the clasp is broken."

Erth's abrupt walk toward the lift startled Manak. Realizing Erth's conclusion, he shouted, "It couldn't have been Caenith!"

Glimpsing the savagery in Erth's expression before the lift descended, Manak tapped out the code to Brehan's quarters and shouted her name several times into the intercom. When she drowsily responded, he informed her of his incriminating find and Erth's reaction to it.

Erth stormed into Joy's quarters, startling the couple who were idly stretched out on the bed. Caenith bolted upright, his surprise escalating to indignation as he left the bed and took a stand across from Erth. Joy was paralyzed, her eyes transfixed on the erratic pulse of Erth's headband.

"Explain this!" Erth spat, flinging the chain at Caenith.

"I've looked everywhere for this."

"Not everywhere." Erth advanced into the room.

"The clasp broke when you were shutting down the air duct to Brehan's quarters!"

Caenith backed against a wall. "You accuse *me?*"

Erth lunged forward and caught Caenith by the throat. When the smaller man began to struggle in fear of his life, Erth lifted him from the floor and pinned him to the wall.

Joy's inability to move was broken when, through a flood of tears, she stared at Caenith's red-purple face and protruding eyes. She jumped from the bed, her fists targeting Erth's back. A death rattle filled the air, shocking her insensible. At the moment of feeling that nothing would deter Erth's blind rage, hands gripped her shoulders from behind and swung her onto the bed.

"Stay put," Brehan warned Joy, then turned toward Erth. "Let him go!" She yanked on his arm. "You're killing him!"

Erth's head jerked around. It took a moment before his eyes lost their glazed look. Breathing heavily, he dropped Caenith, then clenched his fists and released a guttural cry. His insides expanded, increasing his height. His jersey burst apart from his chest and arms, and his pants split until they resembled a loin cloth on his immense frame. While he fought with all his will to quell his internal turbulence, Joy rushed to Caenith's side.

"Tell him, Brehan," she wept, glaring up from her kneeling position, "before he kills an innocent man!"

"Do you really believe I'd allow one of my friends to be with a potential killer?" Brehan asked Erth in a surprisingly quiet tone. "Have you lost your mind?"

"Yes! As well as my patience!" His height began to slowly ease back to normal. "This was found—" He bent and retrieved the chain from the floor where Caenith had dropped it. "—near the air duct controls!"

Brehan took the piece of jewelry from him and spared

it a cursory glance. "Your brain isn't capable of juggling all the input going through it. This means nothing."

"Tell him!" Joy pleaded, helping Caenith to his feet.

Brehan noticed the welts on Caenith's throat and felt a bitter-cold wind of remorse sweep through her. She walked up to him and placed the chain in his palm. "I'm sorry this happened."

Erth's face was a study in guilt. With a slight bow of his head, he said to Caenith, "Forgive me."

"I understand," Caenith rasped, gingerly touching his throat.

"The suspicions are driving us all insane!"

Brehan stiffened. "I'm sorry, Joy. I wish—" Unable to deal with her unbalanced emotions before an audience, she turned and swept from the room. She kept her fiery anguish bottled up until she was sealed in her quarters, then succumbed to another weeping bout as had frequented her since her attack. But she was not allowed the time to fully release her emotions. The exit opened and Erth walked into the room. Too mentally exhausted to deal with another confrontation, she collapsed onto her vanity chair and buried her face into her hands.

Erth surveyed the room in shock. A little voice in his head comically observed that he was fortunate not to have been around her during this particular temper tantrum. When his gaze fell to where she sat, a strange buzzing began in his ears. He slowly made his way across the room and stopped behind her. A sob escaped her controlled facade, its sound knifing his reserve.

"Only once during the other voyages did I tear my clothing. I'll need something that stretches, Brehan, unless we end our confrontations."

Brehan rose from the chair and, kicking aside debris, walked to the foot of the bed. There, she heaved a wavering sigh to give respite to her shattered nerves.

Erth watched her movements with fascination: the way her slender body moved beneath a blue, full-length nightgown; the way her single braid swayed against her partially exposed back. He tucked his thumbs into the waistband of what had been his pants, and tried to analyze what it was he was feeling. Nervousness seemed the only emotion he could pinpoint. But he noted with relief that she was also uneasy, shifting her weight from foot to foot while she kept her back to him.

"It was cruel of you to attack Caenith." She turned and faced him, her paleness telling him that it was all she could do to bring herself to face him. "You reacted to a false lead like a wired adolescent, Erth," she said, her soft tone causing a rippling sensation along his flesh. "He violated *my* rights, not *yours*. Although I'm sure your ego has taken a bruising since the man had the audacity to perpetrate a crime practically under your nose. But my right to consent is the issue, here, Erth, not your damn pride."

Erth appraised her graceful poise with deepening curiosity. "You have changed, *te-ni-e.*"

"You expected me to fly into one of my rages, seek him out, and draw my pound of flesh?" She forlornly looked about the room. "Maybe it was memory of him that provoked me into doing all this. I don't know."

"I'll help you clean—"

"No," she cut him off. "You're wasting your time here. I have no intention of discussing what happened, with you."

"You may be content to wait, but how do I placate my rage while this man is free?" he asked harshly.

"You're not my concern."

The cold apathy in her tone ripped through him. He walked up to her in three determined strides. Ignoring the way she cringed away from him, he forced her left arm forward and held the ring hand before her face. "Even without this ring, I am your legitimate mate."

"Words."

"Are you trying to provoke me into amending that?"

"Why, are you in the mood for rape?" she volleyed,

in a tone so devoid of emotion, he immediately dropped her hand. His stricken look stabbed at her conscience, and by way of an apology, she offered, "I had no right to say that."

Erth made a gesture of futility. "We are neither patient, nor guiltless of wanting to control the other." He laughed, like a neurotic on the verge of a breakdown. "I'll never understand you," he went on. "You are two people, Brehan. One who loves easily, and one who loves not at all."

"I'm surprised you didn't fall on your lips saying that word."

"Love? What is *your* definition of it?"

"Reduced to its lowest term . . . need."

"What need are you referring to?"

"Need of companionship. Something you have never desired, have you?"

A smile ticked at one corner of his mouth. "There are moments. We are very much alike in some ways, Brehan. We have both been thrust into leadership roles not of our making."

Brehan sighed deeply as she folded her arms against her chest. "But I'm not an unbendable prig when it comes to stepping aside and letting the next guy take the reins."

Erth humorously arched an eyebrow at her words. "Why is it so important to you to keep your subordinates naive? Are you afraid they'll outgrow their need for you?"

The question took Erth aback, but he was quick to collect his wits and reply, "This mission has been the one constant of my existence."

"Maybe so, but like any parent, you must let go."

Unwilling to deal with this subject, he started for the exit. Brehan ran to him and, placing a hand on his arm, stopped him. He slowly turned to face her, an incredulous look fixed on her hand. It was the first time she had touched him in such a gentle manner.

"How were you able to find women with no families?"

"In my true form, I have the ability to scan and lock onto the memory files within most life forms. The required specifications were transmitted to Mastric. Out of the 2,976,431 females I located, Mastric chose the acquisitions."

"The burned bodies I saw in my car?"

"Illusion."

"I saw them. I smelled their burnt flesh."

"A very real illusion. The police, coroner, and even the mortician believed they were real."

Brehan's skeptical expression prompted Erth to make a gesture with his right hand. An acrid stench of smoke filled her nostrils before she glanced over her shoulder. The sight of her transformed quarters wrenched a squeal from her throat. She unwittingly turned and jumped back into Erth's arms, the back of her head pressed against his collarbone. Her eyes wide with disbelief, she gaped at an exact replica of the crash scene on the beach. The smoking car and the burnt corpses behind the shattered windshield. The morning sky above. The sound and salty smell of the ocean behind her . . .

With another gesture of his hand, Erth dissolved the illusion.

"Your existence on Earth had to be finalized," he said quietly, watching her stagger several paces away from him.

"You should have never taken me," she stated shakily.

"But I did. And I have rightfully claimed you."

His words shocked her, then incensed her. She resisted a strong urge to scream that she was no one's possession, but the insidious voice in her head said otherwise.

YOU ARE HIS TILL DEATH DO YOU PART.

Mindless of his infraction, Erth remained motionless

while Brehan backed further away, contempt reddening her face.

"Possession! That's all you understand, isn't it?"

His words fell on deaf ears. Erth was preoccupied with a piece of information her closeness had relayed to him.

Feeling as though his lifeforce had been drained from him, he left the room.

Her nightmare resumed itself in the guise of *a two-legged snake stalking her through the corridors of the ship. She ran on and on, her legs so heavy it was difficult to keep herself up on her feet. When a wall opened, she dashed recklessly into pitch-blackness, then stopped. Slow steady breathing was filling the air and closing in around her.*

"Go away!" she wailed, fearing the snakeman was in the room with her. "This is only a dream. You can't touch me!"

Light flooded the room. When it dimmed, she saw Erth stretched out atop a massive bed, his bronze-nakedness beckoning her, compelling her toward him, and she mechanically went to his bedside.

She was staring down into his face when a movement was caught in her peripheral vision. Too scared not to investigate it, she swung her gaze to the right. A leering snake slowly uncoiled from Erth's loin, its tongue lashing out, touching her naked abdomen.

"This is only a dream," she whimpered, closing her eyes and swaying with the tides trying to beach her reasoning. Then Erth was drawing her down into his powerful arms, his warm mouth possessively making demands on hers.

The need was at last surfacing—

She screamed from the depths of her soul.

It was not Erth stimulating her need but the snake. Its

massive head was between her thighs and it was pressing to enter her body.

Brehan woke from the nightmare screaming and thrashing, until she felt herself being drawn into the warm security of powerful arms.

"You're safe, *te-ni-e*," someone said softly above her.

Panting, she blinked rapidly as she tried to digest the fact that she was not in her bed, but somehow in the Garden Chamber. Pain gripped the pit of her stomach. Her limbs felt like ice, too heavy to move now.

A movement at her back drew her attention to who was holding her practically in his lap. She looked up into Erth's bright eyes, but her state of mind did not permit her to fathom the stark concern etched deeply in his features. The horror of the dream returned, twisting through her with maddening swiftness. Screaming, she reached up with her right hand and tried to rake Erth's face with her fingernails, but he gently warded off her attempt with the back of an arm. Then she began to struggle wildly, using her fists and elbows to extract herself from his hold, animal sounds gurgling in her throat.

It was this scene that greeted Manak when he entered the room. He ran to the platform where Erth was trying to subdue Brehan. Without thought, the blond man took hold of one of her arms and jerked her up onto her feet. She began to strike out at him, but Manak determinedly pinned her within his embrace. "It's all right, my lady," he rasped by her ear. "It was only another nightmare."

Erth remained sitting on the platform, staring in numbed silence as someone else quieted and comforted his woman. When jealousy began to penetrate his stupor, he slowly rose to his feet and made a valiant, although vain, attempt to hide his emotional wounds.

"I'll take her back to her quarters," Manak said, his defensive tone chafing Erth's tolerance.

"Keep him away from me, Manak," Brehan whimpered, refusing to look at Erth.

Manak and Erth's eyes locked in a warring challenge.

Unbefitting his nature, Erth was the one to concede, and left before Manak was finally able to convince Brehan to return to her quarters.

"The approach graphics on the Lyiany Belt are up on the sextant screen," Stalan reported.

Standing at the dome, Erth ordered, "Thrusters on full depulsion. Manak, place yellow alert. Niton, monitor our approach factor."

The sound of the lift brought Erth's head around. A frown of annoyance creased his brow when Brehan stepped into the room. Pointedly, he fixed his attention on the Lyiany Belt, a system of thirty worlds linked by a rainbow display of gases. When he was aware of Brehan coming to a stop directly behind him, he clipped, "I left specific orders you were not to go anywhere unescorted."

"Barrit is waiting below for me. I need to talk to you."

"You have been silent for weeks." Erth fractionally turned his head, but he did not look at her. "Now is not the time to plague me."

"It's important!"

"I'm listening."

The suction of Brehan's own breath roared in her ears. Her heart pounded so fiercely, she was sure everyone in the room could hear it. "I'm pregnant."

Erth turned to face her. Taken aback by his apathetic demeanor, Brehan asked breathlessly, "Did you hear me?"

"Yes."

"Is that all you have to say?"

"Congratulations."

The color drained from her face as a poignant feeling of betrayal lanced her. "How long have you known?"

"Track beam on sextant screen," Manak announced.

Erth's head shot around and he looked out at a blue and purple gaseous cloud. Ignoring Brehan, he went to the console and positioned himself between Stalan and Manak.

Two spherical displays appeared on the elongated monitor in front of him. One represented the absolute map sphere, the other the ship's legitimate course. When the spheres began to overlap, Erth worked the sextant console until the map and course were in synchrony.

"Niton, at reading of *marc-eintha,* relieve comp-pilot."

"Comp-pilot relieved. Manual override is locked in."

A triangular red light, representing the ship, showed the *Stellar*'s steady approach to green ladder-lights designating the track beam. The ship jarred slightly as it connected with the magnetic field of the track beam. The ladder-lights became a solid green line; the red triangular shape moved toward a brightly lit area symbolizing the aperture.

"Niton, cut depulsion," Erth commanded.

"Depulsion cut. Track beam is maintaining our momentum."

"Stalan, maximum shield efficiency."

"Shields are holding at peak level."

"Manak, take over the sextant."

As Erth stepped aside to allow Manak access to the console, he glanced at Brehan, who was staring dazedly at her surroundings. It occurred to him it was her first time in the Control Center. He walked up behind her, placed his hands on her shoulders, and urged her closer to the dome.

"Brehan, you're about to see a wonder of technology. The cloud we're approaching conceals the aperture, UK-ONT. It's one of thousands in this galaxy, created to allow travelers to cover parsecs of space within minutes. Without them, our journey to Syre would take one hundred and five years, instead of nine and a half months."

"Do all advanced civilizations use these?" she asked, her anger with him temporarily forgotten.

"Not all. There are rigid regulations imposed by a galactic council to prevent warmongers accessibility to them. Each portal requires a specific code to activate its attending track beam."

"What does the track beam do?"

"It navigates the vessel through the opening. Without it, the aperture remains sealed."

"Who created them?"

"A race called the Seekers. They existed over a billion years ago, garnering knowledge from every corner of the universe. In their beginnings, it took generations to travel from one galaxy to the next, so they created these portals to reduce the time and space involved in voyaging. There isn't a solar system in existence that doesn't have at least one."

"How many more of these before we reach Syre?"

"Three."

The instant the ship entered the cloud, darting fingers of light enshrouded the exterior of the dome. Brehan instinctively pressed closer to Erth when the lights intensified. She turned the side of her face to his chest, but he propped up her chin and insisted, "Watch, *te-ni-e.*"

She squinted and peered at the spectacular colors bursting beyond the dome. Her blood began to race wildly through her veins. Her mind ignited with sheer delight. She had never felt so alive. Every nerve in her body was charged with excitement.

Erth unintentionally became sensitized to her emotional rapture. A magmalike fluid seemed to pass beneath his flesh. This time he was careful to meld with her mind. Wanting to experience all of her reactions, he focused his attention on their empathic coupling. But, too soon, the ship sailed through the last of the aperture and passed into another realm of starry space. He first felt her withdrawal mentally, then physically as she extricated herself from his hold.

"Now we discuss my problem," she demanded, turning and looking up at him.

"Your refusal to impart the attacker's name has closed the issue." With a harried look, he added, "Go to your quarters," then he directed to Niton, "Engage comp-pilot." To Manak, "Verify route to UK-KET. Stalan, full depulsion status."

"Comp-pilot engaged."

"Route locked in."

"Full depulsion. Shield status?"

"Lower it to .25 factor. Turn the monitoring over to the scan's directory."

".25 factor . . . done. Scan directory in acknowledgement."

"Erth!" Brehan's sharp tone brought Erth around to face her. "I want this thing out of me!"

The vehemence of her words straightened back Erth's shoulders. "We are in the business of producing life, not wasting it!" Abruptly seating himself in his command chair, he barked, "Manak, see your *Katiah* to her quarters!"

Manak gently took Brehan's arm and walked her toward the lift. Midway, she wrested free. With a belligerent gesture warning him to keep his distance, she turned and stared beyond the dome to where a ball of light was shooting past the ship.

"Matter configuration, *Katian?*" Stalan asked.

The abrupt, "No," incited further curiosity among the men.

Brehan knew what was happening. She walked up to the command chair, her head thundering with foreign sounds. "It's a ship. They're calling for help."

Erth looked at her as if she had struck him dumb with her knowledge. "A Varc ship," he said finally.

"Why aren't you doing something to help them?"

"They're not my concern."

"You heartless bastard!"

Erth cried her name in a roar, then he was suddenly

consumed by his internal force. He instantaneously imploded and transported himself from the ship. Brehan, compelled back several paces by an unseen force, gaped at the emptiness where Erth had been a moment before.

"There, *Katiah*," Manak said, pointing.

A massive cloudlike apparition, Erth sped through space in pursuit of the troubled ship. Brehan crossed to the dome and pressed her brow to its clear surface in time to witness Erth's source envelope the vessel, his lifeforce as bright as any star.

"Katiah!"

Manak's cry startled her. She turned to deliver him a reprimanding look when something caught her attention. Turning fully around, she ignored the men as they protectively gathered beside her. Six unexpected visitors were leaning against the far wall, their drab, grimy robes emitting wisps of smoke. When Brehan attempted to step forward, Manak's grip restrained her, and he issued in a low tone, "No, *Katiah*."

Calmly disengaging her arm from Manak's grasp, she crossed the room and stopped several feet away from the strangers. By human standards, they were hideous-looking, but there was a vulnerability about them that touched her. They were less than five feet tall, with humanlike arms and legs, their hands oversized with distorted, thick fingers. Their hairless heads were strangely deformed, slits for eyes, pinched flat noses, and mouths that were invisible when compressed. Wrinkled, gray flesh hung in flaps from their cheekbones and jawlines.

"Don't get too close," Niton warned from behind her.

Brehan was too curious to be afraid. "They may be thirsty." She took another step in the aliens direction. "Erth wouldn't have—How did they get here?"

"He transported them," Manak replied.

"Well, he wouldn't have if they were dangerous."

Manak shrugged noncommittally at her reasoning. "How do we communicate with them? I know neither their origin, nor their language."

"Would you like something to drink?" Brehan asked, walking directly up to the visitors. She received no response. To demonstrate her question, she cupped one hand and brought it up to her lips. For a moment, the aliens remained as they were, then one stepped forward and spoke to her in a language which widened her eyes with defeat. She made the gesture again, displaying a bit of temper, and was rewarded with a crack of a smile from the one who had spoken.

"Stalan, order up some drinks," she called over her shoulder. "Scotch on the rocks," and sighed at his blank look. "Yeah, I know, that goop is the only drink on the menu." She smiled wryly at the one alien guest. "Hope your taste buds don't take offense to this stuff, but it's all we have."

Stalan programmed the computer with haste. Seconds later, six slender glasses rose on a tray from the console. Brehan's intervention stopped him from passing the tray to the visitors. Taking it, she handed a glass to each of the six in turn. The diminutive beings held the glasses a few inches from their mouths. Long, strawlike tongues flicked into the liquids. They drank noisily, then jagged smiles appeared on each face as they returned the glasses to the tray.

"More?" she asked.

The nearest alien graciously declined his head.

Brehan passed the tray back to Stalan. She was beginning to grow uneasy with the unabashed scrutiny of the beady black eyes floating in the deep slots, but she couldn't let the Syre men know just how nervous she was.

The alien leader unexpectedly captured her wrist. She stifled a cry and, before the men could react, she made a quick gesture of complacence. "Stay as you are," she warned the men. Although the alien's touch was cold and repulsive, she managed to cloak herself with an outer calm. The beady eyes studied her flushed face with open curiosity. She attempted to smile when the being began to inspect her fingernails, but her facial muscles were uncooperative.

"Katiah?"

"He's just curious, Manak."

"He has no right to touch you!"

Brehan kept perfectly still as her hand was raised to the alien's nose. Revulsion formed a knot in her throat when the being began to sniff at her fingers. To her further dismay, he forced the back of her hand to his brow, which began to glow with a blue inner light.

The sound of the lift snapped her head around. Relief washed through her at the sight of Erth stepping into the room. Re-attired in an all-black outfit, he casually walked to her side. The alien holding her wrist began to talk rapidly, his speech ending with his holding her hand out to Erth. Erth entwined his fingers through Brehan's and clasped her hand to his side. The alien nodded his approval, then began to talk excitedly, gesturing to Brehan. Erth responded in the strange language. The alien again nodded before placing a finger between Brehan's breasts.

Brehan scowled down at the imprudently placed finger. "What's he saying?"

"He was telling me what a gracious hostess you have been," Erth replied, his tone laced with mirth. "Olu's curious about the warmth of your flesh. The color of your hair has him convinced you're a fire spirit."

"Olu?"

Erth introduced the Varcs in turn. "Olu, Laq, Bje, Lun, Cre, and Blif. They were entering the opposite end of the aperture precisely at our entry. The *Stellar*'s superior size caused a vacuum which propelled their ship backward at a speed it wasn't equipped to handle."

"What about their ship?"

"It's been repaired."

"Such magnanimity."

"I have my moments," Erth parried sweetly.

Olu began to talk again. When he stopped and tapped his chest, Erth gave a gracious nod of approval. The Varc leader's fingers pulled up on a chain that was half concealed beneath his robe. As he drew it up over his head, an amulet came into view. The large flat sapphire and chain was passed to Erth, who in turn placed it over Brehan's head.

"I-I can't accept this," she said to Olu, her fingers caressing the stone and its intricately scrolled frame.

"Olu wishes to honor you with the Companion," Erth told her. "To return it would be an insult."

Brehan swung an indecisive look at Olu before bowing her head in respect. Pleased with himself, Olu smiled, then cocked his head questioningly at Erth. Erth spoke briefly in the Varc language. Then, after an enigmatic gesture with his left hand, the Varcs vanished. To convince herself her eyes were not playing a trick, Brehan passed her hand through the space where Olu had been standing.

"I've returned them to their ship."

After a moment to collect her wits, Brehan issued, "Now you're free to discuss my pregnancy."

Erth's lighthearted expression crumbled beneath a darkening scowl.

Backing away, Brehan choked, "You monster."

He watched her until she had descended in the lift. Although her words had made him flinch, he presented a mask of stone to his men.

Chapter Eleven

Simulated night cloaked the interior of the *Stellar*. Alone in the Control Center, Erth bleakly dwelled on thoughts of Brehan and the child she was carrying.

"Dammit!" he growled. Her reticence was driving him crazy. "How does he block my probing?" He leaned over the back of his command chair, his core dangerously close to bursting. "He nearly has substance in my mind. Sometimes, I'm so close to knowing—"

He happened a glance at the monitor to Brehan's room. Not seeing her, he experienced a stab of alarm. Then his sensors homed in on her whereabouts.

On the second level, he entered the Garden Chamber unnoticed and slipped into the shadows of a willowy tree. She was across the room, humming to herself, her fingers caressing the petals of a purple, *Timra* wildflower. His core drummed within its confines as his gaze moved down the length of her unbound hair, which fell to just below her buttocks.

Her humming stopped and she stiffened. Realizing she sensed his presence, he stepped from the shadows and moved toward her.

"You're waiting for him to kill you," he stated, coming to a stop directly behind her. When she continued to ignore him, he forced her to turn around. The fear in her eyes waned to an arctic expression.

His, "Why?" lifted her chin fractionally, defiantly. Goaded, Erth caught her chin between his thumb and forefinger, and repeated savagely, *"Why?"*

"Take your hands off me."

"Would you prefer *his* hands on you?"

"Yes."

"Damn you!" Releasing her, he testily looked down at the bare midriff exposed by her two-piece gown, then lower to the slits fashioned in the front of the full-length skirt. "Provocative attire. What is the purpose of exposing your legs? For *his* benefit?"

Her green eyes flashed in warning before the cold shroud encompassed her once again. "Jamie designed it for me. She thought it might lift my spirits." Reading the blatant skepticism on his face, she added, "And not that it's any of *your* business, but I was not expecting *him* tonight."

"Your appearance says otherwise."

"I indulged in a whim."

Sparks of energy going off inside him, he spat, "As he indulged in having you?"

Brehan paled and faltered back a step while, sorrier than he could ever express for having said what he had, Erth raised a hand and clenched it. His mind made a bid to apologize, but the words would not come out. The distance between them that had so frustrated him during the past months, seemed to be growing, extending beyond his reach and beyond his comprehension. What *would* it take to breach her anger? Her determination to shun him and everything he represented?

Watching her quake with barely controlled fury, her face flushed, her eyes such a vibrant green they reminded him of the fire emeralds on Baltrok, he vowed this day—this *moment*—he would prove to her their match was a gift of Haveth, and not the curse of the Darklands she seemed to believe it to be. But before he could say a word, the dam of her anger broke.

"You're the victim!" she cried, her right hand lifted in warning for him to stay back. "He as good as raped *you!*"

Erth's nostrils flared. His insides churned and heated. "How can you know what I felt when I held your dying body in my arms? I should have foreseen the attack!" Erth's hand shot out and gripped her upper arm, defeating her attempt to walk away from him. "I am not an insensitive monster, Brehan! I feel your anger and your pain as my own!"

"You should have let me die!"

"Stop struggling! Brehan, I want him out of our lives. I want this behind us!" He quieted unexpectedly, and it seemed as if time itself came to a complete halt. Energy crackled in the air around them, air thick and charged with emotion. "I want, just once," he said achingly, "for you to look at me without that damnable, baiting hatred in your eyes."

"I can't help how I feel."

"You feed your hate and fears. You refuse to accept me as a man, because that would make me touchable, wouldn't it? *Wouldn't* it!"

Confusion enlarged her eyes. "You're not a man. You have no blood, no heart, no real emotions beyond anger."

"I have showed you more patience than any other living creature in this universe, but you are relentless in pushing me away! Why do you punish *me* for what you suffered as a child?"

"I *don't!*"

"No? Then why is it you can accept comfort and security in someone else's arms, and not mine?"

"I don't know what you're talking about!" she cried, struggling to break his hold.

"Manak."

The name quieted her immediately. "What?"

Erth studied her bewilderment for a long moment. "You don't cringe when *he* touches you."

"He's flesh and blood!"

Dropping his hands away, Erth tapped his chest. "Touch me. No heart, no blood, but my flesh is warm. I have a pulse of life inside me."

Brehan stepped back and nearly stumbled over the lower step of the platform. Cautiously, she stepped up on it, making herself eye level with his chin. As her fevered thoughts sought a way to escape the room, she glimpsed an enigmatic light in his eyes and knew he had tapped into her mind.

"Touch me!" Grasping her wrist, he pressed her clenched fist to his chest. "I'm not metal! I'm not wood!"

"You're not human!"

"You're using that as an excuse!" he exclaimed heatedly, then lowered his voice, his tone ridden with despair. "Stubborn little fool. I know you're frightened. I don't understand these feelings any more than you do."

Releasing her wrist, he solemnly searched her features for a sign that he was reaching her, but there was only fear and mistrust. "The hurting has to stop, Brehan." Placing his hands around her waist, he gently drew her against him. Her body stiffened in protest and she downcast her eyes to avoid his. "Look at me, *te-ni-e.*"

"I'm not feeling well. I want to go to my quarters."

"You have asked me why I didn't let you die on your world." His soft tone brought her gaze up to meet his. "Ask me again."

Brehan was torn with indecision. She wanted to run, but she also wanted to understand his reasons for not unburdening himself of her. When she finally asked, "Why?" it was little more than a whisper. She didn't flinch when his hands came up and tenderly framed her face. It was a curious moment, laden with something she couldn't quite comprehend.

"Because, Brehan, you have been a part of me since our first contact. The fibers of our existences have somehow entwined. I never quite feel whole unless we're in the same room."

"Stop it—"

"You know what I'm saying is true. Deep within you, you sense that we are inseparable. It's what we fear, you and I. It's unknown. Powerful. Almost all-consuming, and we have struggled to resist it. It's something greater and more precious than what the others share, Brehan, and I know of no name for it. But it is there. Between us. Waiting to offer us happiness instead of pain, if only we let it.

"Brehan, I can't bear to deny its presence any longer. I can't allow the wall between us to exist another day."

A chill traveled the length of Brehan's body when the blue of his eyes began to glow, and the luminance left the confines of his irises. It came to bathe her face. Warm. Caressing. Offering tranquility. Although something deep within her subconscious warned her that the moment she'd dreaded was closing in on her, she couldn't bring herself to summon up even a modicum of resistance. When his hands threaded through the thickness of her hair, she remained perfectly still, somnolent, her gaze locked with his. She stood dreamlike when he drew two handfuls of her hair forward and buried his face in the strands, a gesture which inwardly delighted her.

Erth straightened up, his eyes glassy, unsettling, the glow ever-present and more vibrant. Impatience gnawed at him. He felt as though he should say something appropriate, but the tightness in his throat intimidated him. In a gentle, testing manner, he drew Brehan against him again. His inner sense locked onto the reawakening of her rage. It was impossible for her to resist the *armai* he was projecting, and yet her beautiful features were becoming masked with sheer contempt as she savagely gripped the front of his jersey.

"I'm warning you," she rasped, her guttural tone taking him aback.

Something rose up into Erth's throat and lodged there. Once again, he felt as though he were dealing with a completely different woman, and he thought back to Barrit's words in the Meeting Chamber. Was it possible for one human to possess two personalities? Could her darker side be a configuration created to protect her against the horrors she'd endured at the orphanage? And if it were true that she possessed even a part of her mother's memories, was it Rebecca keeping the real Brehan out of his reach?

"Back off!" she warned, lowering her hands to her sides. "You know I hate to be touched!"

Erth's fingers twitched against her waistline. "I've waited long enough. To save your life after the attack, I was forced to use *Cahfu*. Our match is unbreakable. For as long as you live, I may not accept another mate."

"Tough—" The words died in her throat as Erth strengthened the dose of *armai*. The blue glow brightened still and formed a cloud around their heads. Brehan jerked against his hold, but her struggle was weak. She couldn't look away. The glow brightened again, mistlike shrouding them entirely. With its progression, the calming influence of it strengthened, buckling her resistance, her inhibitions, and drawing her into a haze of sexual awareness.

"Don't . . . do this," she pleaded in a whisper.

"You leave me no choice, *te-ni-e*. I warned you I had ways by which to control you. Until you come to accept me, I will resort to *armai*."

Brehan felt strangely buoyant as Erth's left arm crossed her back and drew her tightly against him. She was vitally conscious of the muscular contours of his chest and arms. Of the corded muscles in his thighs.

Of his devastatingly handsome face. Of the undeniably raw chemistry existing between them.

"I've been conscious of what the other couples do during their private times, and it has nearly driven me to madness. I must know this intimacy with you." His voice growing huskier with every word, Erth slowly lowered his head. "From the depths of my soul, I want to please you."

The moment his mouth covered Brehan's, a spasm of shock detonated within her. Any hope she ever possessed of being repulsed by a kiss from him, became swept away on a tide of aching need. His lips were warm, experimental in their probing, yet masterful. She closed her eyes and leaned into him. The kiss became more demanding, and her hands—as if possessing a mind of their own—slid around to his back.

Erth's core heated and surged. There was an almost overwhelming need in him to surround and devour her with his lifeforce, but he retained enough sense to know this would kill her. Unlike Lanulee, this lover would never be one with his true self, but then, unlike Lanulee, this woman filled his mind with new and wondrous delights, and a promise of such physical gratification, he could barely contain his desire to experience it. But he promised himself he would hold back. Even if it became agony to go no further than the kiss, he would hold dear this moment. The treasures of her body would be all the sweeter if she offered them to him of her own free will.

Unconsciously, lost within the blissful folds of passion, he retracted the *armai*.

Brehan's mind was unable to analyze this virginal intimacy with Erth. With *armai's* balming influence, primitive lust felled her inhibitions and she slipped her hands beneath his jersey to explore the warmth and musculature of him. His bare flesh caused her fingers to tingle and ache for more than mere touching could grant her. She wanted him to surround and fill her completely with his naked flesh. Wanted every part of her body to become his possession, and his, hers. She couldn't understand why she'd been so afraid of giving herself to him, not when it felt so good to be in his embrace, and kissed in the slow, sensual manner he was kissing her. It could be so easy to love him—

YOU DISAPPOINT ME. YOU HAVE ALLOWED HIM TO MASTER YOU—ALLOWED HIM TO BELIEVE HE CAN *CONTROL* US!

BREHAN, BREHAN, WHERE ARE YOU? WHO IS THIS SLUT IN YOUR PLACE?

Wrenching herself free of the hypnotic state, Brehan bewilderingly stared into Erth's eyes, which were now absent of the glow. Fever throbbed throughout her body. The aftereffects of the *armai* continued to tingle along her skin, left her feeling weak and lightheaded. But her indignation of his ploy soon began to stoke her fiery spirit.

"This stunt was low, even for you," she charged huskily, clenching her fists at her sides.

"*Armai* is merely a sedative."

"You were using your powers to seduce me!"

"You returned the kiss of your own free will."

Reflexly, Brehan's open hand shot out and dealt Erth a blow to the side of his face. His head turned minutely at the impact, but his gaze remained locked with her own. When she swung again, this time with her hand balled into a fist, he caught her wrist in midair and calmly enclosed the hand within his fingers.

"Enough, Brehan," he warned softly, pressing the underside of her wrist to his chest. "I need you."

"You only want his name!"

Releasing her, Erth absently placed a hand beneath the hair at his nape. "His identity never crossed my mind after I—" Suddenly self-conscious about what had transpired, he lowered his hand and straightened back. "You can't seriously believe that I ..." Scowling, he shifted as his core stirred restlessly inside him. ". . . that I kissed you to get his name."

"You will stoop to any measures to get your own way!"

"I have wanted you all these months, but I have been patient, haven't I?"

Confusion warred behind Brehan's breast. "Why can't you just leave me alone?"

An image flashed through his mind, causing him to sharply dispel a breath. Brehan stared at him, a sickening sensation turning over in her stomach. "You sense this thing in me, don't you?"

He hesitated, then nodded.

"What . . . what is it?"

"Female."

Erth's hands came up quickly as Brehan swayed. Gripping her upper arms, he steadied her. "I have forsaken my principles in the past for you, woman. Again you test me." He paused, then issued, "Will it and the child will abort."

Stunned, Brehan could say nothing.

"Do it before I change my mind!"

The full impact of what he was offering hit her. But now that her chance to rid herself of the unwanted child was laid bare, only revulsion filled her. "I-I can't!" she choked, her face as white as a sheet.

Immense relief washed through Erth. "In the morning, I'll instruct Barrit to transfer the fetus to the Orthandite."

Brehan numbly pushed away from him.

"You will survive this."

"You don't understand!"

Placing a bent finger beneath her chin, he lifted her face to his perusal. "Explain to me why you are so fearful of child-bearing."

"I can't."

"You won't. Trust me to help you—"

"*Trust* you?" she snapped, staring at him as if he had

sprouted horns and a tail. "You're the louse who just tried to seduce me!"

"I didn't try, I *succeeded,*" he retorted dryly. "Look, Brehan, we could stay in this room all night, arguing. I'm perfectly willing to prove to you that I don't need *armai* to elicit a response from you."

"Your ego would love to believe that, you sorry snake."

Before she could anticipate his move, his right hand was cupping her nape and drawing her against him. A gasp passed her lips before his generous mouth closed over them. Her eyes defiantly open, the heel of her hands jabbing at his constructed rib cage, she released guttural sounds in protest. Then his eyes opened to watch her reactions, and his powerful arms cradled her tighter against him. A chuckle rattled deep in his throat, causing her to blush furiously. She pinched his back, to no avail. Erth slightly lifted his head, only to dip it to the other side before taking possession of her mouth again. And it was then Brehan felt a lethargic warmth sweep through her. Maddening sensations frolicked low in her abdomen and around her heart. Her eyelashes lowering to her cheeks, she shuddered. A whimper of protest rose within her, but never surfaced. When he broke the kiss and ran his smooth chin along her brow, a quiver of excitement passed through her.

"You are so incredibly soft," he murmured, brushing a cheek across her brow. "And so incredible to hold."

Although Brehan found it difficult to concentrate on anything but the sensual touch of his face, she managed, "I need more time."

"How much?" he asked, pressing his brow to her own.

Trying to bring her irregular breathing under control, she quipped, "A millennium . . . or two."

With an unexpected burst of laughter, Erth swept her up into his arms.

"Put me down!"

"It's getting late and you need your rest," he said matter-of-factly, swinging around and heading in the direction of the E wall.

Brehan soon questioned her decision to keep quiet when, instead of taking her to her quarters, he carried her into his own. She was feeling numb by the time he placed her on her feet. Numb and rattled to the point of being disoriented. It was one thing to let down her defenses in the Garden Chamber, quite another to find herself alone with him in an area that was solely *his* turf. She stared at his massive bed as if terrified it would come alive and devour her.

"I'll have your belongings moved here tomorrow. Do you sleep with a spare on?"

"Spare what?" she asked, glowering at him.

"Attire. Or do you sleep naturally?"

"N-naturally what?" Her face reddened. "Yes!"

"To which?"

"With something on!"

"Put on one of my jerseys for now." He turned toward a large clothing receptacle.

"I'll wear this."

He shook his head, a gleam of mischief in his eyes. "Not if you expect me to behave myself. The gown is too provocative. And the exit is locked in case you're entertaining any notions of escape."

Dumbfounded, she watched him lay out a navy blue jersey on the foot of the bed, then walk to an archway and stop at the threshold. "I'll be in my sitting room. Should you need help getting out of that gown, please feel free to call me." Grinning like an adolescent fool, he disappeared into the next room.

"Insufferable beast," she grumbled. She turned to the exit and tried in vain to prompt the wall mechanism, then leaned against the wall, glaring at the jersey.

It occurred to her that she would have to change clothing, or risk his using the gown as an excuse to further his love-making. Pulling the jersey over her head, she fumbled with the two sections of her gown until both had dropped to the floor. An angry kick sent them across the room, then she slipped her arms into the sleeves of the jersey.

Glancing down at herself, her exasperation was released on a sigh. The jersey fit badly, like an oversized nightdress, falling just below her knees.

A chuckle startled her. She glared at Erth, who was leaning lazily against the arch, a devilish grin lighting up his face, his thumbs hooked casually into the waistband of a new pair of black pants. He was shirtless, making her all too conscious of the incredible breadth of his chest and shoulders, and the narrowness of his waist and hips. Fluttering sensations played through her abdomen as he came toward her, and an inexplicable ache gripped that part of her anatomy about which she understood so little.

"I suppose I should be grateful you're allowing me to wear anything at all. Or does a woman wearing your clothes give you a sick thrill?"

Erth stopped, and laughed scoffingly. "You have the most infuriating ability to take an innocent situation and distort it until it reeks of indecency."

She eyed him warily, peevishly. "There's nothing innocent about what's on your mind."

"Did I perform the kiss correctly?"

Crimson flooded her face. "I'm c-certainly no expert on the subject."

"It's an invigorating exchange between two . . . people." Erth was relieved when she didn't correct his use of the word "people" in regard to himself. "Brehan—" He shifted his weight. "I know we need time to understand—" He frowned and completed, "love-making. That is correct, isn't it? Love-making?"

"I wouldn't know," came out of her sounding like a croak.

"Aren't you curious about conceptual mating?"

"Certainly not!"

His chest heaved. "Liar. What happened between us in the Garden Chamber was stimulating."

"Maybe for *you.*"

With a low chuckle mocking her fib, he covered the space between them in two easy strides. "Believe it or not, *te-ni-e,* I'm not ready to consummate our union. Tonight, I'm only going to hold you."

She cringed when he leaned over and tried to kiss her again on her lips. She turned her head away, claiming scathingly, "I'm not your possession!"

The blue glow again emanated from his eyes as his hands gripped her upper arms and drew her possessively against him. "There will come a time when you will come to me willingly."

"Never," she denied, but it was weak, unconvincing.

"Until then," he murmured, then kissed her with the intent of suppressing her resistance.

And it came all too quickly for Brehan. Her toes ached as she was coaxed to stand on the balls of her bare feet. Her breasts, although flattened against his chest, seemed to swell and harden of their own accord. His arms enfolded her, and his deep, lingering kiss basked her in blissful forgetfulness.

Reluctantly ending the kiss, Erth held her away and mutely questioned his resolve not to rush her beyond this point. Before his desires could take control of his options, he lifted her into his arms, carried her to the bed and gently laid her down. He stretched out alongside her rigid body. Easing his arm beneath her, he coaxed her to lay her cheek against his shoulder. Brehan was at first stiff and unresponsive. But the trembling in her body began to yield to the narcotic warmth emanating from him. As drowsiness settled over her, she reasoned that she would have to trust him this night, for she had neither the will nor the strength to fight him. She succumbed to her weariness. Closing her eyes, she unconsciously nestled closer.

Once he was sure she was asleep, Erth relaxed the

arm cradling her torso. He smiled wistfully up at the ceiling. In time, he was sure, she would come to forgive his use of *armai* to coax her sexual awareness. In time, she would come to love him. Meanwhile, he was determined to strengthen his patience, and grasp every nuance of the emotional planes he had just so recently been introduced to. If owning of human frailties were the key to her heart, then he would become a master locksmith.

His meditation tuned in to words and scenes belonging to the not-so-distant past. His once imperious regard for the laws that he, himself, had reared the men to obey, had become threadbare and insignificant.

Dipping his chin just enough to brush it against the crown of her head, he savored the overall rightness of holding her against him. If these feelings he was experiencing were a companion to love, then it was little wonder his men had fallen victim to its spell.

"You have always belonged to me, *te-ni-e,*" he whispered, and kissed the top of her head.

She stirred slightly in her sleep. Her hand slid across the ridged muscular plane of his midriff until her arm was draped across him. Erth felt overcome by the most tranquil feeling he had ever known—a sense of completeness. At this moment he felt as if he possessed a heart, and it was soaring. Soaring through the heavens. Through infinity.

How long he had waited to feel alive again!

Brehan awakened in the middle of the night. For a time, she didn't move, only absorbed the fact that she was alone in the massive bed. Her inner senses told her Erth was not anywhere in the quarters, which she questioned the significance of as she sat up and stretched out her arms. In part she resented his use of the *armai* to sedate her, but she had to admit that she hadn't slept better since the abduction. She wondered why he hadn't taken advantage of her—why he hadn't *forced* her to have sex. Perhaps he *wasn't* after quick gratification, and a son to replace him. What more did he want of her?

A cold, invisible hand seemed to suddenly clutch her heart. It paralyzed her momentarily, until an image of Christie flashed across her mind's eye. She dashed from the bed, the quarters, and ran barefoot down the corridor. She stopped only to wait for the E wall of the B corridor to open, then rushed on. Before she reached the opened entry wall to the lab, she heard voices raised in anger.

"Damn straight I have some say!" Adam bellowed. "This is *my* life! I'm an adult!"

"Adam, lower your voice."

"Give me one good reason why I should? Because of this big bastard, Mom? Is that it, huh?"

Brehan entered the lab in time to witness Adam stepping up to Erth and jabbing him in the chest with an isolated finger.

"You can't touch me," the boy sneered. "Brehan will stand up for me. *She* understands me." He cast a scathing look at his parents. "Which is more than I can say for either of you!"

"Adam."

Brehan's tone was soft, yet authoritative as she came to stand within arm's reach of him. She ignored his arrogant appraisal of the oversized jersey she wore. His expression changed to a look of condemning accusation. He glared at Erth, then scowled at her, his unspoken question demanding to know how she came to be wearing something of Erth's. Although she was aware of the rapid pulsation of Erth's headband, her immediate concern was for Christie and Barrit's sickly pallor.

"What's going on?" she asked the couple.

Barrit glanced at his wife, then lowered his head and gave it a solemn shake.

"Aw, c'mon, Pops. Tell Brehan what this is all about!"

"Adam." When his gaze returned to her, Brehan went on, "Don't interrupt again."

"But—"

Brehan stiffened. Adam looked away, his mouth compressed in a fine of defiance.

"He's been ignoring his curfew time," Christie said in a tremulous tone.

"Big deal—" Adam began snidely, but when he happened to glance at Brehan's bright eyes, he quickly murmured an apology.

"It's more serious than mere curfew violations," Barrit said, his tone throbbing with reluctance to speak against his son. "He's been—"

"I didn't really damage anything, did I?" Adam exclaimed with a laugh. He turned to Brehan, nervous elation heightening the color in his cheeks. "Certainly nothing as daring as some of the stunts *you've* pulled off!"

A chill coursed through Brehan. She walked around Adam and stood alongside Christie. "What kind of stunts, Adam?"

The boy stared at her through a mixture of uncertainty and chagrin. "Brehan, I was just experimenting a little."

Brehan met Erth's furious gaze, then arched a brow at Adam. "I hardly think your parents and Erth would be this upset about a *little* experimenting."

Adam tried to smile off the seriousness of the charges, but his facial muscles were growing more taut by the second. "Trust me. It was no big deal. I won't mess with the laser slims again."

Stepping up to him, Brehan gasped, "What? You know you're not supposed to touch any of the weapons unless an adult is with you."

"Yeah, but—"

"What did you do, Adam?"

The boy cast a furtive look up at Erth's livid face,

then meekly met Brehan's fiery gaze. "I was-ah, testing the density. I accidentally cut into the leads."

Brehan paled significantly. "To the master computer?"

Adam nodded.

"Where exactly were you when this *accident* took place?"

Again he looked at Erth, then bitterly confessed, "In the Control Center."

Brehan jerked back as if his words had delivered her a blow. "You're not allowed in the Control Center, are you?"

"No."

"Then why the master console, Adam?"

He looked downward to avoid the anger in her eyes. "I was pissed, okay?" He looked up, his boyish expression betraying that he was close to tears. "You wouldn't come out of your quarters. You wouldn't talk to me! I-I could have offered you comfort, you know. But you wouldn't let me near you!"

Brehan gulped. When she spoke, her words were strained, husky. "So you thought you would spite me by endangering the lives of everyone aboard this ship?"

"It was okay for you to—"

"No!" she spat, pointing a finger in Adam's face. "Contrary to what you may think, I knew *exactly* what I was doing, and it never involved risking the lives of innocent people!"

Tears welled up in the boy's eyes. "You neglected me."

"Adam," Christie sobbed, "she was emotionally suffering from the attack!"

"What about *me!*" Adam cried.

"What about you?" Brehan asked in a deadly quiet tone.

"Huh?" He looked into her eyes, his own pleading to understand her sudden coldness toward him.

"I thought Erth was barbaric to subject you to stasis.

Now I'm beginning to understand his motives. Your parents love you, Adam, but you don't seem to appreciate what you have in them."

"They allowed—" He belligerently jabbed a thumb in Erth's direction. "—*him* to put me in stasis. That tells me how much they love me, Brehan!"

"They love you enough to stop you from destroying yourself and everyone around you."

Adam's gaze pinged off the faces around him. "All right, I'll obey the damn rules!" he said to Brehan. "Are you satisfied now?"

Her voice barely above a whisper, she replied, "It's not up to me."

Brehan walked to one of the tables and kept her back to the group. This time, she vowed, she would not interfere, no matter how great the burning in her chest became.

"I love you, Brehan," she heard Adam sob. "You can't let them confine me again. I love you!"

Squeezing her eyes shut, Brehan clamped her hands over her ears. She had no way of knowing how long she remained this way. But when her stomach threatened to heave, she bent over the table and pressed her brow to its cool surface. She couldn't stop herself from shivering and, although she felt a strong need to weep, no tears came to relieve her. She wanted to sleep her pain away. Embrace oblivion.

A hand came to rest between her shoulder blades and gently massaged the knotted muscles. When she thought she could almost fall asleep beneath the ministration, she straightened up and turned. Erth's chest filled her vision. Unwilling to look into his eyes and see the accusation she believed they would betray, she gripped the front of his jersey and pressed her face into the material.

Sighing deeply, Erth wrapped his arms around her trembling shoulders. "You're not to blame," he said softly. "Barrit explained how human hormones affect teenagers."

"I feel sick."

"With concern for Adam?"

Brehan forced herself to look up at him. "Partly. His release gave Christie and Barrit hope. Because of my damn interference, they're going to have suffer all over again."

Another sigh escaped Erth as he released her and stepped back two paces. "You were not aware of his infatuation with you?"

Color stained Brehan's cheeks. "No. How could I? He's just a boy."

"You have this affect on males, *te-ni-e.*"

Shamed by his statement, Brehan turned away. She crossed her arms against her chest and tried to swallow past the tightness in her throat. Several seconds passed before she could bring herself to ask, "Will you return him to stasis?"

"The decision is yours."

"Mine?" Brehan turned sharply and stared at him with disbelief. *"Mine?* I agree his actions deserve some kind of punishment, but you don't have any understanding of how horrible stasis is! It can't be the only solution to this problem, Erth. It's terrifying. The mind remains active."

"Then what do you suggest?"

Her hands moved in a gesture of futility. "I don't know. Maybe . . . confinement."

"It worked wonders with you," he dryly quipped.

"Then seal the vent grill! Confinement may force him to rely on his studies. Isn't it worth a try?"

She stiffened when he came to stand close to her. Despite her unease with his proximity, she looked into the enigmatic depths of his eyes. She couldn't determine his mood. He appeared uncharacteristically calm, and it occurred to her that he was expecting something more—what, she didn't know.

"As you wish," he said finally.

On a sigh of relief, she murmured, "Thank you."

Erth lifted a hand and brushed the back of the fingers along her jawline. "You have a good heart, Brehan," he said softly, aware that she was barely tolerant of his touch. Lowering the hand to his side, he gestured for her to walk with him to the exit. She fell into step beside him, her head lowered to avoid his gaze. When they entered the corridor, he said in a calm but strained tone, "I want you to remain with me tonight."

Brehan faltered a step. "I would prefer to go to my own quarters."

They walked the remainder of the B corridor in silence. But when they entered the A section, Erth said quietly, "It is little to ask. I won't molest you."

She stopped in her tracks, Erth, too, halting, his bright eyes studying her face through a pained expression. A shout of refusal played within her mind, but to her surprise, something quite different passed her lips. "Will you hold me while I sleep?"

Utter pleasure glowed on Erth's handsome features as he gave a single nod.

A sense of peace washed through Brehan, and from left field, she asked, "Why?"

"Why am I willing to hold you in my arms while you sleep?"

"No. Why are you willing to listen to me now?"

There was a long stretch of silence, during which she got the distinct impression that he was carefully thinking over his response. She wasn't sure what she was expecting to hear him say. It certainly wasn't, "Because I love you."

The color drained from her face, and a look of incredulity flashed in her eyes. He'd spoken the words calmly and with such conviction, they continued to echo in her mind. She was beginning to cringe away from him when he pulled her into his arms and held her tightly against him.

"Don't be afraid of it," he cautioned.

Trembling against him, her hands clutching the material at the sides of his jersey, she mentally groped for a scathing remark. But none would formulate. He was no more capable of loving than was she, and yet he had somehow convinced himself that his desire to bed her was . . . love? It was so ridiculous, she almost wanted to laugh.

"There is nothing ridiculous about how I feel toward you," he chuckled, reminding her that he was sometimes able to penetrate her thoughts.

Mortified, she buried her face into his left shoulder.

"In time you will come to trust me . . . and love me, Brehan." He held her out, then propped up her chin with his left hand and stared deeply into her troubled eyes. "I don't profess to understand the complexity of human emotions, but I do feel this love for you. It is sometimes tormenting, other times, more rewarding than anything I've ever experienced."

"Erth—"

"Give *us* a chance."

Brehan stared up at him, conflicting emotions warring within her mind and heart. She wanted to throw herself into his arms and lose the specters of her past, but her inhibitions still retained too firm a hold on her. He'd proven he could keep his word, even when she'd been at her worst. He'd even compromised on Adam.

Deciding he deserved more than a flat refusal to meet him halfway, she said, "Maybe in time . . ."

"A millennium or two?"

A low laugh caressed her throat, and a delicate blush tinted her cheeks. "Maybe not *quite* that long."

Grinning, Erth set their stride for his quarters. "That's the first even remotely optimistic response I've heard from you."

"Patience has its rewards."

His response was a ruminative moan.

Chapter Twelve

The next morning, Erth stepped into the Control Center to find Stalan and Lute standing transfixed by his command chair. The object of their preoccupation was a giant blue star, its portentous tendrils of gases seeming to reach out as if to embrace the ship.

"*Katian,* what procedure do we follow?" Stalan asked.

"Check for a possible deviation factor."

As Stalan departed to the sextant console, Lute asked Erth, "What will happen to this system after the *hasenda?*"

"Absolute destruction. I hadn't anticipated a starburst this soon. No telling how the pulsations have affected the aperture."

"Do we re-route to the next aperture?"

"Not unless we want to spend the next seventeen years en route."

"*Katian,*" Stalan called, gesturing Erth to come to the sextant console.

"What's the problem?"

Stalan moved aside to allow Erth access to the monitor. "AM is in default of this region's charts."

After several attempts to pull up the charts in the computer, Erth straightened up with a savage look. "We've lost access to the file. Stalan, join Manak in the Feeding Chamber and help him trace the problem. Get back here as soon as you're through."

Stalan left to execute the order.

Muttering to himself, Erth sat at the master console and initiated the discharge of a thermo probe from the Defense Bay. He watched it speed toward the sun until the light indicator for the shields flickered, signifying the ship's power was fluctuating. Tension crackled within him as he jabbed the intercom control for the Feeding Chamber.

"Manak, shut down all addenda!"

"In the process."

The probe transmitted the temperature readings and the degree of increasing pulsations. However, it was incapable of determining the time element of the sun's destruction.

"*Katian*, addenda down. Relay default corrected," Manak reported through the intercom. "I also bypassed the defense terminals. We have full shield power."

"Stay below and watch the terminals. Niton—" He turned to the man. "—ready thrusters, but hold our present momentum until I signal otherwise. Initiate alert for standby."

"Our time factor?"

"Not noteworthy." Standing, Erth began to remove his boots. "We can't risk reaching the aperture and finding it closed. I'm going ahead. Track me. If you see me flare up, channel all power to full depulsion."

"But the code sequence—"

"If the aperture is undamaged, I'll open the track relay. But if I don't flare up seconds after I'm within the cloud, immediately re-route to Hoorturi."

"*Katian . . . ?*"

Erth glanced downward. "I just broke in this pair," he explained, then imploded and instantaneously transported from the ship. Before Niton could regain his wits, Joea ran from the lift and stopped when he found Niton alone in the room.

"Where is—?"

"Out there," Niton said. He fixed a worried gaze on Erth's energy form as it rapidly sped toward the cloud concealing the aperture, then he switched on the red alert system and announced that all crew members were on emergency standby. He then channeled through to Manak and explained the situation. When he looked out the dome, he saw Erth fuse with the cloud. At the sign of the flare-up, he initiated the comp command for maximum depulsion status. But to his consternation, a flashing red light appeared on the console. Switching through to the Feeding Chamber, he barked, "Manak! Insufficient power!"

"I know! I know! The relays are aborting the command!"

"Get up here!" Niton ordered shrilly, then quickly amended in a calmer tone, "Manak, I need you up here."

"On my way. Try interfacing the relays through the blue key system."

When Manak's end of the intercom clicked off, Niton did as he had suggested, but to no avail. He cast Joea a fearful look. "We don't have enough channeled power to clear the aperture."

Manak and Stalan stepped from the lift and ran across the room.

"Where is the power channeling to?" Manak grumbled, his gaze flitting over the erratic flash of lights across the master console. Nudging Stalan aside, he seated himself at one of the monitors. He began a systematic scan of the ship's mechanical graphics, then of the electrical nervous system. Finally locating the problem, he shot up to return to the Feeding Chamber. It was then the consoles lit to full capacity. Activating the intercom to the Feeding Chamber, he probed, *"Katian?"*

"I'm hooked into direct feed. Get to the Safety Chamber. I'll take over from here."

In the Surgical Chamber, Barrit's steady hand guided the slim encasement of the restoration ray along Brehan's abdomen, sealing the last remnant of the incision he'd made earlier. As he had been for more than an hour, he was engrossed in his work. The sterilization lights built into the ceiling provided a bacteria-free working environment, allowing him—unlike doctors on Earth—to perform surgical procedures without protective coverings on his person.

Fully awake during the entire procedure, Brehan had not experienced pain or discomfort—other than from her conscience. She had averted her eyes to block out the sight of the Crinlun tube being connected to the fetus end of the umbilical chord while still inside her, but watched as the tiny being was lifted free of her body, carefully removed from its sack, and placed into the thick liquid within the clear encasement of the Orthandite. Christie had stayed by her side throughout the ordeal. Clasping Brehan's hand. Softly offering words of encouragement. And although Brehan had lived most of her life never needing or expecting comfort from anyone, she doubted she could have made it through the surgery without the blonde's emotional support.

When Barrit began to put away the equipment, Brehan realized it was at last over. A sudden, deep-rooted sense of emptiness filled her. It wasn't guilt, for she knew she wasn't emotionally stable enough to carry the child full term. The emptiness was something she couldn't define.

"You haven't done this before have you?" she asked Barrit when he came to stand beside her.

"No." He inspected the smooth unblemished skin where the incision had been, and his eyebrows lifted in approval. "Is the area tender?" he asked, probing with his fingertips.

"No. Not at all."

It disturbed Brehan that the last time he had made eye contact with her was when she'd first arrived at the Surgical Chamber. She didn't have to be psychic to pick up on his too-cordial manner when he did talk, or his uncharacteristic remoteness during the procedure. At first she attributed it to a "doctor thing," a means of distancing himself from the patient during surgery in order to keep his mind focused. Not so. It hadn't taken her long to figure out that he was peeved with her. His remoteness was his way of stopping himself from saying something he knew she didn't want to hear.

He turned back to the comp console. Brehan glanced at Christie, who flashed her a sympathetic although wan smile. Sitting up and swinging her legs off the side of the bed, Brehan said collectively to the couple, "I'm sorry I put you through this."

Before Christie could respond, Barrit, his back to Brehan, said curtly, "You have nothing to be sorry for."

Brehan shot the fetus a hopeless look. Something toyed with her reason as she stared at it, but her ignorance of normal gestation blinded her to the fact that her child was several months advanced. "It's so tiny."

"She," Barrit corrected. He met Brehan's gaze, then quickly turned to shield his annoyance with her. Brehan glanced at Christie's somber expression, then at the back of Barrit's head, and finally glimpsed the reason for his mood.

"I've had my reasons for keeping silent."

Barrit stiffened his spine. "To infuriate Erth."

"No, Barrit, that's not it at all."

After a moment, he turned to face her, his expression grim. "Then why?"

"I was waiting to obtain the proof I needed."

Anger heightened Barrit's color. "Proof of what?"

"A mind-altering drug was made out of two of the plants in the Garden Chamber. Now that I have a copy of the formula in my computer, I intend to go to Erth with the information."

A cynical look masked the medix's face. "The only drug we use is a pain retardant."

"I know. This is something totally different."

"My God," Christie said in a barely audible tone. Her eyes widened on Brehan. "You're talking about Uhul, aren't you?"

Barrit stared at his mate for a long moment, then looked at Brehan through a frown. "I don't understand."

"Kousta invented a drug," Christie said dully, numbed by her deductions.

"Yes, she did," Brehan sighed, "and has cunningly been manipulating Uhul with it."

"Whatever Uhul's reasons, Erth should have been told!"

"Barrit, I haven't been protecting Uhul! But I felt the extenuating circumstances warranted investigation. Do you realize there isn't a single written law to deal with this situation?"

Barrit threw his hands up in exasperation. "To hell with laws! There is only right and wrong!"

"Nothing's that simple. The gray areas are also an intricate part of our lives."

Barrit eyed Brehan speculatively beneath the flush of his vexation. "Considering what has happened, your sense of justice astounds me."

"I just didn't want Kousta worming her way out of her part in it. And now that I have possession of the proof . . ." Brehan slipped down from the bed. "I need to change and face Erth with this."

To Barrit and Christie's amazement, she hurried off into the corridor.

"Shouldn't we have made her stay here?"

Barrit leveled a dubious look on his wife. "Once her mind is made up . . ." His expression became grim as he looked at the fetus across from him. "What do you make of the baby?"

Christie looked at the Orthandite, and sighed. "She had to have been almost five months along."

"I know for a fact she wasn't pregnant prior to the attack. It's just one more mys—"

His name came through the intercom, cutting him off. With impatient strides to the unit, he depressed one of the buttons. "What is it?"

"Code red," Joea replied. "We're facing a forced entry through the aperture."

Barrit switched off the intercom and turned to Christie. "We'd better secure the Orthandite."

After changing into a gray jumpsuit and braiding her hair, Brehan paced within her quarters, trying to work up the nerve to broach the subject of her attack with Erth. She'd known Uhul wasn't himself that night—*known* she had to get to the truth before her rage left her tenuous control and targeted him.

"Or did you just want to handle him yourself . . . in your own time . . . and in your own way, just to spite Erth?"

Damn insufferable pride! she scolded herself, then happened to notice a red light flashing above the intercom.

"Now what?"

"It appears to be a warning of some sort, Mistress."

Alarmed, Brehan turned a full 360 degrees, her face running the spectrum from white to crimson. Her intercom was turned off. It couldn't have come through that—not to mention the voice wasn't even remotely familiar. And she couldn't see anyone else in the room. Breathing unsteadily, she muttered, "Now I'm hearing things."

"Not at all, Mistress. I'm on this table."

Once the psychological sensation of her heart leaving her throat, passed, she hesitantly approached the vanity and glanced over the odds and ends atop it.

"When my master presented me to you, you found me qu–ite pleasing." As the voice—tenor with a slight echoing quality—spoke, a tiny pale light flickered within the heart of the amulet's sapphire. "I can see you are wary of me, Mistress. I am called Samitan. I am companion to the fortunate possessor of the amulet."

Her curiosity overshadowing her initial fright, Brehan picked up the amulet and carefully studied it.

"I am within the stone, Mistress. Foul play dealt me this fate, although I should not complain."

Ignoring the absurdity of conversing with a gem, Brehan asked, "Foul play?" and slowly sank onto the chair.

"We were a perfect order, Mistress. It is a great relief to know I am now under the protection of the Light Lord."

"The what?"

"The Light Lord, Mistress. Why, he boasted to Olu, you were his woman."

"Erth?"

"Of course."

Brehan chewed thoughtfully on the inside of her cheek. A thousand questions were vying to roll off her tongue. "Why do you refer to Erth as a Light Lord?"

"Indeed, Mistress, I know who he is! I just wish I had not the misfortune to meet his half brother Zynus-Rye."

"I listened to some of the data on him. Lord of the Darklands."

"The epitome of evil, Mistress! You see, my planet, Yolania, bordered the feuding line between Zynus-Rye, and his twin, Zanus-Roul. We were a neutral people, Mistress, practicing the faith *Kiotihwo*—a faith of peace. When Zynus-Rye demanded we do battle with him against his brother, we, of course, declined. We knew he would take vengeance on us, but there was little we could do.

"On the second day after our refusal to join him, a black haze permeated our cities. My people turned to stone. There were five of us that I know of who transformed into the Tyhe stone—what you call a sapphire. When Yolania exploded, I was thrown helplessly out into space. I drifted many, many years, Mistress, before I crashed on a desolate, absolutely dreadful, uncharted world. Olu found me and had me shaped into this amulet before he discovered I was trapped inside this stone. And it was he who dubbed me the *Companion.*"

"How is it you speak my language?"

He released an indignant snort. "All civilized colonies pride themselves in knowing the languages of our galaxy, Mistress. Great wage has been gained by enterprising agents traveling our systems."

"Language merchants?" she chuckled.

"Of course. I pride myself on several other languages of your world—Spanish, French, and Latin."

Brehan unconsciously rubbed her thumb along the surface of the stone, and was unnerved when it sighed.

"I am endowed with sense perception, Mistress: video, audio, olfactory, and touch sensors. Your skin is very soft."

"Can you be restored to your former self?"

"Only Zynus-Rye could undo this macabre metamorphosis, but there is little chance he would even consider it. No matter. I am happy in my own way. It is an honor to be companion to the woman of Erth—and I see you are wearing an Omerean firestone! Mistress, a particularly fine specimen, I must say!"

The sound of the E wall opening distracted Brehan. Seeing Barrit and Manak rush toward her, she placed the amulet on the vanity and rose to her feet.

"Katiah," Manak panted, "we've been trying to contact you."

Brehan glanced at the flashing disc. "I turned my intercom off. Why?"

"Everyone's in the Safety Chamber," Barrit informed. "There's an entry problem with the aperture. We haven't much time."

"Where's Erth?"

"In the Control Center," Manak replied. "This is serious, *Katiah*. Please come with us—*Katiah!*" he bit out when she abruptly started toward the exit.

Stopping at the threshold, she turned a look of determination on the men that they knew only too well. "Go, I'll be along shortly." Then she lit into a run down the corridor.

"Maybe she's going to the Control Center."

"Damn if I know. Come on, Manak. Let's make sure everyone else is secured."

Manak and Barrit jogged down the corridor, unaware, as they passed the Med Chamber that Brehan was inside the connecting surgical room, checking on the Orthandite. They entered the Safety Chamber. The others were already seated and secured on the padded bench which hugged three quarters of the room's walls. Manak seated himself beside Dawn and depressed a button by his right thigh. A padded breastplate emerged from the wall above his head and began to lower in front of him. He was about to offer Dawn a reassuring smile when he looked at Barrit. The medix was standing in the center of the room, his face alarmingly pale.

"Barrit?"

The medix's pain-filled eyes swung to Manak. "Uhul!"

Manak made a quick survey of the others in the room. "Kousta's missing, too."

Panic solidifying within his chest, Barrit sprinted to the E wall. When it failed to activate, he reached for the intercom. It, too, had been disabled.

"Damn him!" he bellowed, frantically searching the faces of those who stared at him as if he had lost his mind. "The intercom's been cut off—the exit won't open! Brehan's out there with *them!*"

Realization speared Manak's hearts. He glanced up at the flashing red light above the intercom. It was too late. The breastplates would not disengage until the emergency was over.

"Secure yourself, Barrit!" Manak ordered. *"Now!"*

Satisfied with the computer's evaluation that the Orthandite was in no pending danger given the worst scenario of entering the aperture, Brehan planted her palms on the glasslike casing and watched the tiny being float contentedly in the protective fluid.

There was already a cap of white hair visible on the baby's head. The features were defined. Although she remained emotionally detached, she was fascinated by the creation. She had no "maternal" feelings toward it, she believed. Curiosity. Perhaps even fascination. But certainly no pride. Certainly no inner glow or feeling of accomplishment. She was contentedly . . . disconnected.

A reflection on the glass rose something fierce and primal within her. Turning her back to the Orthandite, she glared at the man who was standing across from her.

"My daughter," Uhul said thickly, his dark eyes dull and vacant as they stared beyond Brehan.

"She is no part of you!" Brehan hissed, taking a step forward, her fists clenched at her sides. Although she had tried to forgive him for what the drug had induced him to become, the fact that he was within the same room as her daughter, infuriated her.

Uhul took a stiff, unsteady step forward. "Move away from the Orthandite."

"I'll rip your heart out, you bastard! Turn around and get out of here!"

"My daughter—"

"Get out, Uhul! I've given you every opportunity to

go to Erth and make amends for your crimes! If you were a *true* Syre—any kind of *man* at all, you would resist the drug Kousta's been giving you, and do what's right!''

"Shut up and . . . move . . . away."

The instant he took another step forward, Brehan flung herself at him. This time, she didn't give him the chance to raise a fist to her. One of her own sailed through the air and slammed into his jawline. A cry of pain escaped him as he staggered back. She let go with another, then another, forcing him to back up toward the Surgical E wall. When it opened, she jumped up with both feet and kicked him soundly in the chest. The impact sent him reeling back, and he struck the floor with the length of his body. She landed on her side. Ignoring the pain radiating through her hip, she scrambled back up onto her feet.

"Stay down!" she spat, seeing him drunkenly falter to his feet. "I'll kill you before I let you anywhere near that baby!"

"You don't . . ." Breathing sparingly, Uhul forced himself to straighten up. ". . . understand."

"Don't I? You're a weak, sorry, sonofabitch!"

"Kousta—"

"Shut up! This is your last chance to turn yourself over to Erth. Because I swear to God, I'm going to—"

Pressure slammed Brehan between her shoulder blades, the pain of which robbed her of breath. Disoriented by the unexpectedness and severity of it, she made a half turn and dimly focused on someone a few feet away inside the room.

"You won't survive this time," Kousta sneered, her face a hideous mask of sheer hatred.

Not pressure, she realized. In her mind's eye she could see a piece of metal protruding from her back. Her energy was swiftly draining from her body. She spent some of it trying to remove the object, but it was too deeply embedded. The room began to spin, faster and faster. Struggling to resist the darkness closing in around her, she clumsily stumbled to the far side of the Orthandite. With each second that passed, her vision grew hazier. She could barely make out the couple standing side-by-side, watching her, waiting for her life to drain out of her. Rage sparked within her, but she didn't possess the physical stamina to let it work for her. The darkness continued to shrink her world, suffocating her. Her blood felt on fire, and yet she was colder than she'd ever been in her life. Her legs buckled beneath her. In a futile attempt to keep herself upright, she placed a bloodied hand on the machine, which slid down the glassing as she slowly sank to the floor. Through the beckoning unconsciousness, she clearly heard a shrill, "Kill that bastard! Uhul, do as I tell you!"

The baby. The child she had never wanted was in danger. But Brehan was dying and unable to do anything.

Deep within her, Di'me coiled and seethed. Not only was it possible her host might abandon her prematurely, but she had come to know and relate to the being that had been carried in the shared womb.

Without the body, *she* was also helpless.

And this enkindled her furies.

Erth sat rigid and still in his command chair. His empyrean consciousness was in communion with the control workings of the *Stellar*'s master computer and the external conditions threatening a safe entry into the aperture UK-TETH. In his natural form, he had physically opened the aperture, but without the code signal to activate the track beam, the entry route was another unstable factor. A smaller part of his consciousness was homed in on the alarming distension of the blue giant star, and its increasing magnetic pull on several nearby planets.

With the aid of his telekinetic powers, he maneuvered

the *Stellar* through the rapidly cluttering space, a timer in his mind counting down what he'd guesstimated to be the final minutes of the star's existence. The *Stellar* entered the gaseous cloud, but the explosion of the star caught the ship in the heart of the aperture. A horrendous solar wind jettisoned the ship through the portal, as well as a chunk of rock of nearly the same size. The boulder plowed into the hull. Erth swiftly decomposed as the ship ricocheted and sped helplessly toward the fourth world from the sun. Moments before impact, he merged his source with the minimally damaged propellant system at the base of the ship, and forced the gear back up into the Defense Bay Chamber.

The *Stellar*'s hull struck the planet's surface with thunderous force, its speed driving it fourteen feet into the ground and gouging a high-walled trench through hard rocky soil for nearly eleven miles. Erth remained in the Feeding Chamber, surrounded by showering sparks from shorting crystals, fires shooting up from the console and teleporters, and thickening acidic fumes.

Within seconds after the ship became stationary, Manak was out of his seat and trying to activate the exit. The others in the room were nearly hysterical—not only because it appeared they were trapped, but because of Barrit's allegations that Brehan was in grave danger at the hands of Kousta and Uhul.

The air in the room unexpectedly thickened. Niton unwittingly vocalized his belief that the air ducts had closed off. Panic ensued. Manak frantically pulled apart the triangular disc on the wall and hot-wired the E wall to open. When it slid aside, he raced into the corridor.

Barrit was about to follow when Christie lightheadedly sank to her knees. Crouching beside her, he looked up to see that only Joy and Lisa had lagged behind. "Find Erth!" he ordered. As soon as they were gone, he said to Christie, "I want you to rest while—"

Against Barrit's protest, Christie got back up onto

her feet. "I'm okay now. We've got to check on the Orthandite."

"Do you feel steady enough to walk?"

"Yes. Let's go."

Entering the corridor, the couple stopped in midstride. A foul, cloying stench was mingled in the wisps of smoke hovering in the air. Gagging, Christie clamped a hand over her mouth and urged Barrit to hurry. When they neared the Med Chamber, they were shocked to see an enormous hole in the outer curve of the corridor just beyond the Surgical Chamber.

"Breathe sparingly," Barrit cautioned and, taking Christie's hand, led her into the Med Chamber. The room was a shambles. Barrit guided her through the debris. The entrance wall to the Surgical Chamber was aslant, forcing them to squeeze through the opening. The sight of the Orthandite's base lights and the fetus squirming within the protective liquid, lessened their anxiety.

"Is someone here?" someone called out.

Stepping past Christie, Barrit walked around the artificial womb. At the same instant he spied Manak, he saw Brehan. His stomach heaved, then crashed against the sensitized lining. A hand clamped over his mouth, he observed a wide smear of blood trailing down one side of the Orthandite, ending at Brehan's outstretched hand.

Barrit dropped to his knees beside her, only half-conscious of Manak scooting back out of the way. Horror lanced his reasoning. He was kneeling in congealed blood. *Her* blood. His gaze dimly focused on a piece of metal protruding from between her shoulder blades, but the artifact didn't register in his mind.

"Barrit!" Manak cried, jerking on the man's arm. "She's dying! How do we stop the bleeding?"

Manak's hysteria finally elicited a reaction from the medix. "I'm not trained in this area. I might kill her if I attempt to remove this."

"It has to come out," Christie stated. Kneeling, she nudged Barrit to give her more room. "As soon as I remove this, apply pressure to the wound." She took a firm hold on the handlelike protrusion, then closed her eyes momentarily as a wave of nausea threatened her. Regaining a portion of her composure, she steadily eased the implement upward. Brehan groaned. Startled, Christie dropped the makeshift weapon to the floor.

"Brehan!" Erth's voice boomed.

"Over here!" Manak called.

Manak, Barrit and Christie quickly moved out of the way. Erth sank to his knees, his outstretched hand staying in the air just short of touching Brehan. A look of unbridled savagery contorted his face as he hooked his fingers into the neckline of Brehan's jumpsuit and ripped the material open to her waist. The sight of the gash took him aback for a moment, then he hovered a hand above it. Within seconds, the lesion transfused to his palm. Once his system absorbed the wound, he lifted Brehan into his arms and rose to his feet. He stormed across the room, the others following close behind. The tightness of the jammed exit elicited a growl from him, and kicking outward, he catapulted the E wall to the far wall of the outer room.

Barrit dodged around his superior and went to the sole bed that remained standing. The instant Erth laid Brehan down, the medix checked her vital signs.

"What happened?" Erth barked.

Barrit gushed, "By the time we realized Brehan, Kousta and Uhul were not in the Safety Chamber, we discovered the exit had been jimmied and the intercom put out of commission."

Uhul . . .

A memory surfaced in Erth's mind.

"Do you really believe I'd allow one of my friends to be with a potential killer?" whispered within his skull.

How could I not have known? Erth berated himself, his balled hands resting on the bed beside Brehan. His pain-filled, searingly bright eyes searched Barrit's face. The animosity between Kousta and Brehan had existed from their first meeting. Of all the women aboard the *Stellar*, Kousta alone would not have gotten sympathy or concern from his woman.

Christie positioned herself alongside Barrit. Tersely, she explained to Erth what Brehan had told them after the surgery that morning.

Drugs and conspiracy?

Pulling himself up through the strangling fibers of his despair, Erth brusquely moved a hand above Brehan's length. "This cryo-state will keep her sedated until my return."

A pulse throbbed wildly at his temples as he looked down at his woman again. The cords in his neck distended. Looking at Manak, he forced himself to focus on the matters relevant to the ship. "The atmosphere outside the ship is already beginning to corrode the exterior, and the crystals are deteriorating at a dangerous rate. I must transport to Arlanio for more."

"What about Kousta and Uhul?" Barrit asked angrily.

"I doubt if either *manoru* will attempt to return, but if they should, isolate and secure them. You're in charge during my absence, Barrit. Manak, detail a repair unit and restore the ship's functions as best you can. This chamber, the Control Center, and four living quarters are the only rooms we can spare full power to. Bypass and seal all remaining areas. Limit everyone's mobility. The manufactured oxygen must be used sparingly."

"I'll see to it," Manak said.

"No one is to leave this ship for any reason. There are questionable life forms on this planet. I don't want our paths to cross."

"Understood," Barrit confirmed.

Erth's gaze swept his woman's inanimate features. A look of hellish savagery darkened his face, then he vanished.

Chapter Thirteen

Brehan's eyes fluttered open, and for the fifth time that morning, she attempted to focus. This time she fought for consciousness with every ounce of willpower she possessed, until she finally broke through the cloudy veil curtaining her mind. But to her dismay, she discovered her arms and legs were strapped securely to one of the beds in the Med Chamber. The haphazard rearrangement of the room further served to feed her anxiety. She craned her neck to see into the Surgical Chamber, but the partially closed wall blocked off her view.

"Barrit!" From the corner of her eye she spied movement. "Barrit, are you deaf?"

"I will be if you don't lower your voice," Barrit said as he ambled to her bedside, Manak and Christie behind him. Brehan raked an annoyed look over their faces as they calmly looked down at her. When she fixed an accusatory look on Barrit, he arched an eyebrow.

"Take these off me!" she ordered, emphasizing her words with hard jerks against the straps.

"I was given orders—"

"Where is he?"

"Obtaining new crystals," said Barrit. "Our energy supply is dangerously low."

"How long has he been gone?"

"Four days."

"Unstrap me!"

"If I release you, you'll attempt to find Kousta and Uhul. Sorry. Your system has suffered enough shocks—"

"The baby!"

"She's fine, but *you* need to remain calm and rest—"

"Dammit, Barrit, unstrap me!"

"We haven't the authority to go against *Katiah's* wishes."

Manak's statement brought a scowl to Barrit's face. "Whose side are you on?"

"She is *Katiah*," Manak asserted.

Muttering to himself, Barrit reluctantly removed the straps.

Brehan sat up too quickly and experienced a sickening sensation of vertigo. "I'm all right!" she snapped when Christie reached out to offer her a hand. In a low, contrite tone, she added, "At least I will be once the room stops spinning."

"Was it Kousta or Uhul who attacked you?" Christie asked.

Straightening up, Brehan flexed her stiff shoulders. "I was having a confrontation with Uhul when Kousta snuck up behind me. If I ever get my hands on that bitch ..." She allowed her threat to trail off as she met Manak's eyes. "How much longer will the auxiliary power be operative?"

"A few days. *Katian* should return at any time."

Barrit's shrewd gaze searched Brehan's chalk-colored face. "I can't begin to understand how you broke through the cryo-state, but you're obviously suffering aftereffects."

"I need to go to my quarters."

"You need *rest*. You haven't an ounce of strength to spare."

"He's right," said Christie.

"There's too much to do." Brehan slipped from the bed to stand on her bare feet. "Barrit, I would appreciate it if you would ask everyone to meet me in the Control Center . . . in about fifteen minutes."

"Why?"

Brehan attempted to take a step and faltered.

"If you insist on ignoring my advice," Barrit scolded, "then at least have the good sense to allow Manak to assist you to your quarters!"

Accepting Manak's proffered arm, Brehan reminded Barrit, "Fifteen minutes."

"As you wish," he conceded, but his body language bespoke of his frustration with her stubbornness. He watched her leave on Manak's arm, then said to Christie. "I don't like this."

"Neither do I." Christie fell thoughtfully silent for a moment. "Can't say as I blame her for wanting to lay her hands on Kousta."

"I know," Barrit murmured.

Manak kept his arm firmly about Brehan's waist until he had safely seated her on the bed in her quarters. Along the way, he had been overly conscious of her pique with requiring his help, but he'd grown accustomed—and fond—of her pigheadedness. He admired her strength and fortitude, her intelligence, and her ability to spit in the face of fear. So it surprised and unsettled him when she released a strangled sob and lowered her face into her hands. He waited for several long seconds. Although she appeared to have gotten her emotions under control, her head remained lowered.

"*Katiah?*"

"Manak, how many times . . . ?"

"Forgive me."

She looked up, then lowered her head again to avoid his eyes. "I've really made a mess of things."

"It was not you who gave Kousta a corrupt nature, or Uhul his weakness for the drug she concocted. You cannot carry the burdens of all on your shoulders. A woman shouldn't suffer as you have."

"A woman is no different than a man," she said bitterly. Getting to her feet, she slowly walked past him and braced herself against the edge of the vanity table. "I hate being weak!"

Manak was wryly amused by her declaration. "Your weakness shames my strength."

A sigh shuddered through her as she straightened around to face him. "I should have exposed them right after Uhul . . . attacked me. But I was too damned bent on not flying off the handle again! I wanted to give him the chance to pull himself up out of her clutches—

"No, that's pure crap!" she went on. "I needed to prove to myself that I could forgive a wrong done to me! That's what it was all about. Me! Not Uhul. Not Kousta. Not anyone else aboard this goddamn ship . . . but *me!*"

"I don't understand."

"You couldn't understand, Manak. You've never known the kind of rage I've lived with most of my life, and I hope you never experience it even for a second. It's ugly. It eats you up inside until you begin to doubt whether you're even human anymore."

"You have these doubts about yourself?"

She cast him a look of impatience. "Haven't you wondered about me on occasion?"

"Never whether you were human or not."

"You're too kind, Manak," she said out of one corner of her mouth.

"No. But you are too hard on yourself, my lady."

"Oh, really?"

Her sarcastic tone brought a smile to Manak's mouth. "What about all that you share with others?"

"Oh God, don't spout off a list, pl-ease!"

"Your strength, your heartfelt convictions—"

"Manak! I'm going to throw up if you don't stop!"

The blond man feigned a comical grimace. "Someone has to remind you of your virtues."

In spite of herself, Brehan released what almost sounded like a laugh. "I give up. You, my friend, are simply blinded to my faults. I could clip you upside the head, and you wouldn't question what provoked me."

"I would never presume to question your reasons."

"Ah. My point, exactly." Brehan became sullenly still for a time. "Manak, is there any possibility the Orthandite could lose its power before Erth returns?"

"Unlikely."

"I couldn't handle it if anything happened to Misty now," she said tremulously.

"Misty?"

"My daughter. How I could let a machine replace me?"

"It doesn't matter who or what bears her into this life, but who loves and guides her during it."

"The Orthandite isn't flesh and blood!"

"The end result isn't something out of a nightmare, my lady," he said quietly.

A delicate blush tinted her cheeks. "Sorry, Manak. I'd forgotten it had parented you. Look, I think I've spent my self-pity. Please, would you wait in the corridor while I change my clothes?"

With a bow of his head, Manak started to turn away, then corrected himself and studied her for a moment. "Brehan, I must say one more thing."

Sighing, she asked, "What?"

"Syres have always been a people in need of purpose. Guidance."

"Manak—"

"Please allow me to finish," he said, his tone so husky and serious, Brehan frowned. "Our future consisted of rebuilding and repopulating our cities, and perhaps one day attaining the state of perfected bodies and minds our people had mastered prior to the last Feydais attack. Not to slight Erth's nurturing of us, but he did lead us to believe that was all we could expect of ourselves. Then *you* came into our fold.''

He paused, nervously clearing his throat. ''Do you know what a lodestar is?''

For reasons she couldn't begin to understand at the moment, Brehan was overwhelmed with emotions. Tears pressed at the backs of her eyes and seemed to fill her throat. When Manak continued to stare at her expectantly, waiting for her response, she could do no more than give a weak shake of her head.

''It shows travelers the way,'' he said, speaking unnaturally slow, the intensity in his eyes further unsettling her. ''It's a brilliance that, without a word, without a gesture, whatever your route, it gives you a point of reference. You—'' His voice cracked with emotion and he took a moment to compose himself. ''You are *our* one bright star, my lady. Whatever our mistakes or triumphs, whatever straight or crooked path we follow, we have only to look at you and know that we are going in the right direction.''

He closed the distance between them and, sweeping up her right hand, bestowed a reverent kiss on her upturned palm. Brehan held her breath as he straightened up. A tear fell unchecked down her pale cheek. She couldn't move and was too choked up to speak. It seemed to her that staring into the passionate depths of his dark eyes was equivalent to being swept into a whirlpool. She felt as if she were spinning out of control, being drawn into the heart of the unknown. When he backed away two paces, his chest heaving with each labored breath he drew, she tried to think back on what it was she could have said or done since returning to her quarters that had warranted his heartfelt speech.

''I know it displeases you to be called a guardian,'' he went on, his tone surprisingly level considering his rigid posture, ''but you are. I thank the gods for delivering you to us, my lady, and will till my dying breath.''

Finally, Brehan found her voice. "Manak . . . I don't understand where this is coming from."

He heaved a deep sigh. "The next time you heedlessly place yourself in danger—and yes, I *am* referring to Kousta and Uhul—I will personally put you in stasis until we reach Syre."

A strangled laugh escaped her, but she quickly sobered when he scowled at her. He was very much a man at that moment, a man determined to save her from herself, and it surprised her that she found comfort and security in his protectiveness. Nevertheless she said, "I have to go after them."

After a tense moment, he drew in a deep breath through his nostrils, then gave a nod. "I know." Then he left the room and posted himself in the corridor.

No sooner did the E wall seal, than a wistful voice emanated from the sapphire. "He's a nice fellow, this Manak."

Brehan turned and looked down at the amulet. "I forgot about you," brusquely wiping away the wetness on her cheek.

"I'm used to being ignored."

"I've got something important to take care of, Sami," she said distractedly.

"Can I be of help?"

She didn't reply, but stared at her reflection in the mirror for a time, analyzing a foreboding feeling simmering deep within her mind. Unbeknown to her, her counterpart hovered at the horizon of her consciousness, patiently waiting.

Waiting . . .

Dressed in a white jumpsuit and sandals, her hair carelessly fastened atop her head, Brehan absently surveyed the fog bound contours of the alien terrain beyond the dome. Although she felt the crew's eyes watching and urging her to answer their unspoken questions, she needed time to compose herself. She knew they would try to stop her from leaving the ship. In a sense, she wanted them to. She was rational enough to be afraid of venturing out into the fog, but the voice in her head continued to insist that *she* capture Kousta and Uhul. Not to do it, meant disgrace. Disgrace before whom or what, she wasn't sure, but the voice was impossible to ignore.

"Brehan, what's going on?"

She turned and faced Barrit, her expression unreadable. "I'm going after Kousta and Uhul." Protests rang out. With a raised hand pleading silence, she added, "I know what I'm doing."

"You're placing me in an awkward position. Erth left me in charge."

"Unless I'm mistaken, Barrit, *I* have the authority to relieve you of that responsibility."

"They could be waiting out there to ambush you!"

"They think I'm dead." Brehan searched the anxious faces. "Where's Manak?"

"He said he'd be right back," Dawn replied.

"Look at it out there!" Lisa cried. "They could be anywhere!"

"I dreamt of caves. That's where I'll find them."

"And do what?" asked Jackie.

"They could kill you this time!" Deboora exclaimed.

Turning her back to the group, Brehan pinched the bridge of her nose. Pain stabbed at her temples. A crackling sensation behind her eyes made her close her eyelids.

Joy stepped forward, her expression taut with determination. "This is one time you're not going to get your way. It's insanity to go out there after them!"

"My mind's made up. You can't stop me."

"You're going to have a helluva time getting past us!" Joy warned.

Unexpectedly, Brehan plunged into darkness.

Turning slowly around, Di'me said in a husky voice, "I said . . . *you* . . . *can't* . . . *stop* . . . *me.*"

The sight of bright amber eyes in Brehan's face paralyzed the group with shock. The alien consciousness inwardly laughed. Screening the emotional levels of the humans was sport for her—especially in light of the fact that slipping through the fibers of Brehan's restraint was becoming less challenging. In the past, she'd had to rely on the rage of the human consciousness to allow her to surface.

YOU LOOK AT ME AND DO NOT RECOGNIZE ME, Di'me thought as she regarded the humans. BUT THE TIME GROWS NEAR WHEN YOUR LAST BREATH WILL BE SPENT CRYING OUT MY NAME, FOR I AM THE BEGINNING OF YOUR END.

Di'me focused on a female who stepped forward.

"We're only concerned for—" Christie began, but she fell back a step when the inhuman eyes gave her the feeling that they were dissecting her soul.

"Save your concern for *those* who are in need of it."

"You intend to kill them," Barrit accused.

Brehan's eyelids closed. Deciding to conserve her energies for what lay ahead, Di'me receded. Brehan heaved a breath. Releasing it slowly, she opened her eyes.

Barrit gulped. The eyes questioning him were green. They swung to regard Christie, then again shifted to him.

"I suggest you worry about your wife, and not me," Brehan said calmly. "She's carrying your child."

After a stunned moment, Barrit went to Christie and flattened a palm to her abdomen.

"Barrit, is it true?" Christie asked shakily.

"Yes," he murmured, his gaze riveted on Brehan.

The strangeness of the moment was dispelled as the lift came to a stop, and Manak rushed to Brehan. Panting, his face flushed from his hasty flight to his lab and back, he took Brehan's right hand and placed something into it.

"What is this?"

"Protection."

Brehan released a light, scoffing chuckle. "You've designed brass knuckles out of one of the Crous?"

"It's designed to fit between the knuckles and the large finger joints. I've been working on it since your first attack."

Brehan slipped the weapon into place on her right hand.

"The crystals will increase the powers within your brain one thousandfold," Manak went on. "The degree of energy it will discharge is controlled through your will. I borrowed your brain wave patterns from Barrit's files and implanted the pulse signals into the crystals. Nothing can harm you as long as this weapon is in your possession."

Holding up the piece, Brehan watched tiny electrical pulses throb within it.

"It sounds dangerous," said Lute, his gaze warily fixed on Brehan's bemused face. Like the others who had witnessed her brief mutation, he was anxious about her having access to any more power than she already possessed.

The tension in Lute's voice made Brehan aware of the distance the others were maintaining. Quite naturally, she misread their strained expressions as being concern for her safety. Before she could voice further assurance as to her ability to bring back Kousta and Uhul, Manak declared, "I'm going with you."

"And I," said Caenith, stepping to Manak's side.

"And I," echoed Niton, stepping to Caenith's side.

"The three of you are staying put."

"Let them go with you," Joy pleaded.

Dawn readily agreed. "It certainly makes more sense than you going out there alone."

Brehan was appraising the men's steadfast determination through a frown when Adam elbowed his way to her. "You're not leaving me behind."

"Adam—" Barrit began sternly, but his son raised a hand to silence him.

"You're not to leave this ship," Brehan warned the boy in her most authoritative tone. "Manak, Stalan, and Niton are certainly enough."

Adam's youthful expression hardened. "Stop treating me like a child!"

"You are," Christie intervened. Taking her son by the arm, she marched him toward the lift.

Barrit placed a heavy hand on Brehan's arm. "Just remember, you're responsible for whatever happens out there."

Annoyance flashed in Brehan's eyes. "Thanks for the vote of confidence."

"I just don't think you've logically weighed the consequences of venturing off this ship."

"I have, Barrit. Make sure no one else follows us out. And keep an eye on Adam. He's headstrong enough to try to follow us."

With an impatient gesture for the three men to follow her, Brehan headed toward the lift.

The escape hatches were jammed by rock and dirt, forcing the team to use one of the disposal chutes. Caenith and Niton ventured down first, then Manak and Brehan. Thick, sweltering air greeted them. Drenched in cold sweat and nauseated from the pull of the heavy gravity on her already weakened body, Brehan staggered alongside the men. Some one hundred yards later, she looked back in wonder at the massive exterior of the ship. Shadowy figures could be discerned standing behind the dome of the Control Center.

Without thinking, she heaved a sigh. The acrid air seared her lungs, causing her to choke. Once she brought the moment's panic under control, she was chagrined to note that the men were less affected by the air and gravity.

The team went on, their hearts and minds united as one in their determination to capture Kousta and Uhul. But the fog, so thick in places that it was impossible to see more than a few inches in front of them hampered their progress, and forced them to hold hands and guide one another. Brehan maintained the lead. She seemed to have a recondite intuition as to what direction to go, miraculously steering the men clear of rocks and boulders they wouldn't have otherwise seen until they were nearly on top of them. She led them along narrow stone pathways which stretched between seemingly bottomless chasms on the mountainous terrain.

After hours of climbing and descending the rough ground, she finally crumbled to her knees. The air weighed heavily in her lungs, leaving a bitter, dry feeling in her throat and mouth. Beyond exhaustion, she was barely conscious of being maneuvered to the ground. The one clarity in her mind was that it was growing darker, but little did she know that she alone thought so. Finally, her head resting atop her folded arms, she drifted into sleep.

"Her health is poor," observed Niton as he crouched beside Manak. He picked up the crystal weapon Brehan had dropped and tucked it into one of the pockets of his pants.

"We should return to the ship," Caenith said.

"Don't think I haven't considered it." But Manak knew Brehan would only undertake the search again.

For better than two hours, the men sat in silence, listening to nothingness, keeping their doubts and fears to themselves, until Niton, the most restless, rose to his feet and stretched his back. "I'm going to scout around."

"Don't go too far," Manak cautioned.

Caenith watched Niton fade into the gray-green fog

before he seated himself on the ground across from Manak. "We could carry her back to the ship. *Katian* may return before she has the strength to—"

"Shh. She's coming around."

Brehan released a long groan.

"You're not well, *Katiah*. You're pale—"

"Stop nagging me," she grumbled, cranking herself up into a sitting position. "The caves have to be close. I swear I can feel them in my mind."

In lieu of responding to her statement, Manak observed, "The air's lighter, but the stench is terrible."

"This humidity's no picnic, either." Brehan began to massage the back of her stiff neck, then noticed that her weapon was missing. "Where's Annie?" The men's expressions went blank. "The weapon."

Removing it from his pocket, Caenith placed it onto her upturned palm. "You named a weapon Annie?"

"It makes me feel like Annie Oakley. You know ... Queen of the Wild West?" She sighed sparingly. "Forget it."

Something touched upon her senses and she listened to something the men didn't hear. "Over here, Niton," she called out.

Niton stumbled across the rugged ground and flopped down beside Caenith. He was drenched with sweat and panting, but his eyes were lit with excitement.

"You found the caves."

"Yes, *Katiah*, and I located an entrance!"

"How far away?" Manak asked.

"Alio."

Manak glanced at Brehan and translated, "About two hundred yards."

Brehan was instantly up on her feet. "Let's go."

Niton brought them directly to the entrance. Manak placed a restraining hand on Brehan's arm and gestured for the others to enter the cave first. Once inside, she wormed free of his grasp.

The air inside the cave was cold, clean and easier

to breathe. Shivering, she rubbed her upper arms for warmth. The men didn't seem affected by the drop in temperature. She watched them walk about the spacious room, as curious as children with their new surroundings.

Her attention was drawn to the nearest wall. A glowing yellowish-green mineral deposit speckled the black rock, providing sufficient visibility within the cavern. Reaching out to touch the substance, she happened a glance in Manak's direction.

A cry lodged in her throat.

The entire wall across from him was perforated with holes roughly two feet in diameter. Manak's arm, clear to his shoulder, was within one of these compartments.

Before Brehan could react, Manak released a wail. A flutter of musical chattering and scurrying followed in its wake.

Staggering back into Caenith and Niton, Manak clutched his wounded hand to his midriff. As he began to lose consciousness, the two men managed to hold him up on his feet while Brehan inspected the wound.

"It looks like teeth marks," she observed, gingerly touching the angry-looking welts surrounding the punctures. "We'd better move deeper into the cave and let him rest for a while."

Carrying Manak between them, Caenith and Niton followed her to a smaller cavern, where she gestured for them to place Manak on the ground. All three went down on their knees beside their shipmate. His hand trembling, Niton pressed his fingers to the base of Manak's neck.

"His pulse is very weak. *Katiah,* he's feverish."

Brehan again inspected the wound. "The bleeding's stopped, but his entire hand is inflamed. We've got to get him back to the ship."

Shrill cries rent the air. After the initial breathrobbing shock, Brehan and the men covered their ears, but nothing could dull the piercing sounds. Then an acrid, putrid stench permeated the air. Brehan whirled on her haunches, a thumb and forefinger pinching her nostrils shut.

Slushing and gurgling sounds mingled with enigmatic musical cries.

"Caenith, stay with Manak. Niton, come with me."

Niton rose to his feet. Although his expression was misgiving, he dutifully followed her back toward the mouth of the cave. They came around the last bend and stopped in their tracks at the sight of a huge creature blocking the entrance. Its great bulk of fatty, milk-white flesh quivered as it moved along the perforated wall. A dozen twisted tendrils invaded the compartments, removing tiny balls of fur and promptly sucking them into its enormous mouth. The creature gurgled and slurped, then captured more of the tiny creatures.

Brehan raised her arm level with her shoulder and determinedly aimed Annie, but a sensation of vertigo made her sway on her feet. In the next instant, she found herself mesmerized by the creature's numerous eyes. Her weapon-arm dropped to her side. She was conscious of the monstrosity steadily closing in on her, but she could not move.

Something stepped directly in front of her, blocking the beast from her view. Almost immediately, the creature's influence over her began to ebb. She became even more aware of the smell the being emitted and its gastric percolation while digesting its meal. Her eyes focused on the back of Niton's head—

Dropping to the ground on her front, she aimed the crystal piece up between Niton's parted legs. A broadening yellow beam flowed from the weapon. The creature shrieked—drowning out Niton's cry as he threw himself sideways against the wall—and thrashed within the cocooning energy. At the instant the alien disintegrated, the crystal bypassed Brehan's mental firing command and shut down.

Niton groaned, prompting Brehan to help him into a sitting position.

"Are you all right?"

"The ray only startled me," Niton gasped.

"I heard you hit the wall."

He managed a sickly grin. "I'm all right, *Katiah.*"

"God, I hate that title," she grumbled, pulling him to his feet.

"It suits you."

"How would you like to hit the wall again?" she asked testily.

"I'd rather not."

Manak was still unconscious when they returned. Brehan sat beside him and was sickened to discover that now his hand and forearm were swollen and discolored. Niton tersely explained to Caenith what had happened in the outer cave. Brehan absently listened until Niton had finished, then asked, "What should we do about Manak? I'm afraid to move him, and I'm afraid to wait."

"His immune system should start to respond to the infection. I think we should stay here and rest. There could be other dangers lurking in the fog." Caenith paused, then asked with adoration, "Weren't you afraid of the creature, *Katiah?*"

"Terrified. Look . . . what is it going to take to get you guys to call me by my given name?"

Caenith and Niton exchanged a smile.

"I'm serious."

"We know you are," said Niton, "but it would be disrespectful."

"Forget it," Brehan dismissed wearily.

"What about the little creatures?" Niton asked, easing himself to the ground as if his joints were rusted.

Caenith, too, sat, his attention riveted on Brehan as she tested her immediate surroundings with her inner perception. "I don't feel threatened by them," she said, then gently touched Manak's cheek. "He's sweating, but his skin is like ice."

"We would know if Manak were in real physical danger," said Niton.

"You would?"

Caenith nodded. "A link exists among us."

Niton's expression became grave. "We were all aware that something was not right with Uhul, but he has always been a loner. If we had—"

"You're not responsible for his actions," Brehan said curtly.

"No," Caenith murmured, "but perhaps we could have helped him before it was too late."

"How can a drug change one so?"

Brehan sadly shook her head. "My world is plagued with victims of drug use, Niton. It's something we can't let happen on Syre."

"You will see to that," said Caenith.

"Me?"

His smile boasted of his pride in her. "I used to fear the day when *Katian* would leave us."

"Why, Caenith? You're not a child. You don't need someone to watch over you."

"It's different for you, *Katiah,*" Niton said. "You know who you are. You know your strengths."

A tired laugh escaped her. "Sometimes I wonder about you guys."

"You're a survivor, *Katiah.*"

"Dammit, so are you, Caenith!" Brehan said with exasperation. Then it struck her. She regarded each man—each boy trapped in a man's body—and she suddenly felt centuries old. The hardships in her life had matured her beyond the men's years. Only Barrit and Manak had actually graduated into manhood.

The thought caused a tightness around her heart, and it was with difficulty she uttered, "We're very different, aren't we?"

"Male and female," Niton said in earnest.

"I mean . . ." She took a moment to further ponder

their innocence and simplicity. "I mean how we were brought up. Our cultures."

"Very different," Caenith agreed. "*Katiah* . . . You have never spoken to us in this manner before."

"It's quite nice," Niton grinned tiredly. "This venture is bonding us, right?"

"Right," she murmured through a ghost of a smile. "Let's get some rest. It's a long way back to the ship."

"Are you abandoning the search?"

"Only temporarily," she said to Niton as she stretched out alongside Manak.

"*Katiah?*"

"What, Niton?"

"I'm glad you permitted us to come with you."

"So am I," she said sleepily.

Luminous eyes curiously watched the strange beings settle down into sleeping positions on the ground. Hushed sounds, like soft music, were interchanged. Some time later, when it was determined the strangers were fast asleep, they scurried from their hiding places and organized.

Chapter Fourteen

The moment Brehan's eyelids lifted, her blurred vision filled with a surrealistic scene of eyes staring at her. Gulping down a swell of panic, she snugged Annie within her clammy grasp. Her focus sharpened to reveal that beneath the countless eyes was a blanket of fur covering and surrounding her.

"They kept us warm while we slept," Niton explained. He waited for some of the creatures to scurry out of his path, then eased himself to the ground to Brehan's right. "Manak's wound is completely healed."

Brehan looked up. Manak, leaning against the wall across from her, offered a lopsided grin.

"Good morning, my lady. Our little friends are mighty curious about you."

Her, "Why?" sounded like a hiccup.

"You destroyed the Dolenduc creature," he said, kneeling to her other side.

Easing herself up on her elbows, Brehan frowned at the creatures remaining atop her torso. "I hope they're housebroken."

By the time she was positioned with her legs drawn

beneath her, the creatures were clustered in front of her. One of the hundreds came closer, chirping excitedly. She lowered her hand and it jumped eagerly onto it. The roundness of its body was just larger than her palm, its fur a mute shade of gray and as soft as mink to the touch. The creature's eyes fascinated her. They flapped up from the top of its body, arch-shaped, with heavy lids and long thick eyelashes that fanned when it blinked. Its left eye was white, the right, pink. She glanced at the others. Their eyes varied in color, but none seemed to share the heterochromatic distinction of the one she held.

To steady itself, the palmed creature wrapped its protracting, segmented tail about her wrist. It chirped, then scratched its belly with the end of its sole appendage.

"They're adorable," Brehan laughed.

"Unless you poke a finger at them," said Manak. The creature in Brehan's hand directed a scolding at him. "My apologies, Pip. It was inconsiderate of me to invade your dwelling."

Pip puffed himself up before looking up at Brehan with a question in his expressive eyes.

Brehan looked at Manak.

"He's frustrated because you don't understand him."

"You do?"

"Yes. They speak a simple language." Reaching out, Manak playfully stroked Pip's belly with a bent finger. "You're holding Pip, the leader of the Alories."

"They really are adorable," Brehan crooned, hesitantly petting the creature's side. "They live in these caves?"

"What's left of his race."

Brehan's eyes brightened. The tip of Pip's tail was tickling the inside of her wrist, but the mischief gleaming in his eyes struck her as funny. Isolating a forefinger, she ran it over the creature's round belly. Pip sighed and rolled his eyes in appreciation.

"I wish we could take them with us," she sighed.

"Earlier, they expressed a desire to come to Syre with us, *Katiah*," said Niton, his arms filled with a number of the Alories.

"Really?" Brehan looked at Manak. "But would it be wise to take them from their world?"

"This planet has been undergoing catastrophic changes since the destruction of one of its moons a few months ago. The Alories are forced to live in these caves to survive. I don't see the harm in taking them with us."

Pip began to chirp. As if on cue, the other creatures followed suit. The acoustics of the cave lent an eerie quality to their musical cheers.

"Manak." Caenith's expression became grim. "You should tell her."

Brehan looked from Caenith to Manak. "Tell me what?"

Manak leveled a peeved look on his shipmate. He had been struggling with indecision most of the morning. Now, he had no choice but to tell Brehan the news. "Pip told us that a human female killed five of his people three days ago. The Alories ran her—and her male companion—out of the cave."

Brehan's features grew hard with anger. "Three days. They could be anywhere by now."

"One of Pip's scouts followed them," Niton explained. "He saw them captured by other aliens occupying this planet."

"What kind of 'other' aliens?"

"Pirithians, *Katiah*," Manak said, an edge to his tone. "Their ship crashed on this world nearly a century ago. Since, they've been systematically annihilating the indigenous species. The Alories are all that remain."

"How do we find these Pirithians?"

Manak replied, "The remains of an underground city about a half mile from here."

Pip cut in with a long-winded speech, the tip of his tail jabbing the air to punctuate his words. Manak translated, "Pip stresses his concern with our venturing there, my lady. And I agree with him—at least as far as you are concerned."

"The *four* of us will go after them, Manak."

Pip spoke to Manak, who in turn said to Brehan, "The Alories wish to guide us."

"No." She looked down at Pip. "Don't get involved in this. We'll come back for you when it's over."

Pip searched Brehan's face for a long moment, stunning her with the depth of emotion his eyes betrayed. He chirped in a flat tone, and somehow she knew that although he wasn't happy with the decision, he would do as she wished.

By the time the team reached the great, black archway of stone which led to the underground city of the Pirithians, Brehan's impatience to find Kousta and Uhul was at its end. Despite the men's repeated protests she held the lead and, passing through the archway, began to descend a wide, steep, granite staircase. The way was lit by flaming torches mounted approximately every twenty feet apart on the walls to each side. From the bottom of the stairwell, they crossed a long hall to another wider and steeper staircase. A stench of decay mingled with the dampness in this lower region. The rock steps were dry, but the luminous walls were splattered with a red, viscous growth.

The substance on the walls piquing their curiosity, the men unwittingly lagged behind. Brehan heedlessly descended until, from out of nowhere, a skeletal-like hand shot out and cinched her neck. Annie slipped from her grasp and clattered down the staircase. The creature's grip lifted her off her feet and gave her a jolting shake. Just as quickly, she found herself dropped on the steps. A razor-tipped spear was pressed to her throat to keep her at a disadvantage. She strained a look in the direction of the Syre men. They were frozen in place a landing away, staring at the creature in a spell of horror. Swinging her gaze back to the alien threatening her, she grimaced. White-pupiled, red eyes raked over her from its eight-foot height. It snarled, then one taloned hand shot out, gripped her hair, and yanked her up on her feet.

Brehan held her breath when the creature pressed its flat, broad, cleft nose to her brow and sniffed her. Its mouth was nearly as wide as her face, the upper lip thin, the lower lip so thick it curled outward. Baring its yellow teeth, it spilled a hot, fetid breath into her face.

The alien's hold tightened. Brehan looked down at the five taloned fingers clutching the spear. The yellow-ish, shriveled flesh was imbued with countless fissures. She forced herself to look into its face again. Every bone could be discerned through its taut, translucent flesh.

"Mon awaits your arrival," the alien slurred, spittle oozing from the corners of its mouth. Its eyes narrowed on the men. "Follow, *ahhsss*, not closely!"

Brehan tried to wrench free of the creature's hold. For her effort, she was given a vicious shake.

"Obey, *ahhsss!*"

With all the strength she could muster, she drove a fist up into the creature's midriff. A shriek of pain reverberated within the granite walls, a shriek so cutting she thought her eardrums would burst before it ended. She was abruptly dropped. The alien sank to its knees, its taloned fingers reaching out to gouge her leg. Before she could react, Manak was beside her, driving a fist up under the alien's chin. A sickening crunch was heard before the alien tumbled down the stairs.

Although less eager than the men to inspect the alien's condition, Brehan joined them at the bottom of the stairwell. The alien's midriff was caved in where her fist had struck it. Manak's blow had accordioned the jaw up into the being's face.

Dread knotted her stomach. Her companions appeared oddly unaffected by the sight. Then Manak looked at her, and as if reading her thoughts, he declared, "He had no right to touch you!"

"You're carrying this loyalty bit too far—"

A scream rang out, turning Brehan's blood to ice.

"It's Uhul!" Niton exclaimed.

The scream became screams, mingled with curious bursts of raucous laughter. Manak in the lead, the team followed the sounds, a route which directed them to the end of one of the tunnels, where an archway opened into a brightly lit area. The room beyond was sunken approximately ten feet from where they stood, spacious and filled with equipment. Six aliens, identical to the one they had killed, were behind an elongated computer console. The object of their shrill laughter was a man being subjected to laser beam torture within an enclosed glass cubicle a few yards from their platform.

"I don't see Kousta anywhere," Manak whispered to Brehan.

Brehan made a quick evaluation of the situation, then said in a low tone to the men, "If we're going to pull this off, we have to take those goons by surprise."

Caenith asked, "*Katiah,* where's your weapon?"

"We'll go back for it later. Ready?"

The men nodded in turn as her gaze questioned them, then she jumped into the room below and they immediately followed. The aliens were caught off guard. Brehan reached out for the nearest one and slammed him against the console. When he tried to straighten up, she kicked him in the back of his thigh. The area of contact fell away like parchment paper as the creature whirled, its taloned claws lifting to target her. Reflexly, she slammed the back of a hand to the being's throat. The head ripped from the neck and flew off to one side, while the rest of the body crumbled to the floor in powdery segments. When she turned around to take on another, she found that her companions had already made short work of the remaining Pirithians.

"I have never seen anything like this," Niton said,

coming to stand by Brehan. He drew her attention to the grayish powdery substance on his hands. "They fall apart, *Katiah*."

"That doesn't make them any less dangerous."

A sound pivoted them in its direction. Uhul's glass confines separated. Tumbling from the cubicle, he collapsed to the floor.

Rushing to Uhul's side, Manak went down on his knees and turned the injured man onto his back. "By the stars!" he gasped, looking away for several seconds. Uhul's face was a collage of raw flesh, his roving bloodshot eyes sunken in his skull.

Uhul's garbled attempt to speak before he lost consciousness, brought a mist of tears to Manak's eyes. He looked up at Brehan. Reading her hesitancy to approach, he held out his hand to her. "He can't last much longer."

"Maybe Barrit—"

"Nothing can help him now," Manak interjected, shivering with contempt for the helplessness he was experiencing. He gave his extended hand a shake to coax her closer. When she refused to move, he stated, "You must find it within your heart to forgive him his weaknesses."

Brehan's face drained of color, and she stared at Manak as though he had heinously betrayed her. "Forgive him!" Her gaze dropped to Uhul's ravaged face. She recoiled in revulsion, but as if her legs had a mind of their own, she found herself standing alongside Manak. When his strong fingers closed over her hand and gave a tug, she rigidly went down on her knees.

"The forgiveness is to heal *your* emotional wounds, my lady," Manak said gently, his warm fingers kneading her cold hand.

Memory of the events in the storage room leading up to the rape sliced through her control. She balled her free hand into a fist above Uhul's face, then froze. Whatever was preventing her from driving it downward, she was sure it wasn't compassion—not when there was a part of her savoring the fact that he was suffering. She was aware of Manak's gaze on her profile, of his silent plea for her to stop the rage within her before it brought her more sorrow.

Uhul's eyes shot open. Brehan's raised fist trembled violently, the muscles in the arm ached. She finally lowered the fist to her lap, to rest beside the other hand, which was also clenched.

"*Katiah,*" Uhul thinly breathed, "beware of Kousta."

Brehan's fists tightened until the knuckles were bloodless.

"I went to stop her . . . from hurting our . . . daughter. Couldn't stop her from . . . attacking . . . you." Tears slipped from the corners of his eyes, burning his raw skin. "Sorry." He arched up in a spasm of pain. "Couldn't stop my . . . self. For . . . give me. *Please!*"

Brehan trembled with such force, her brain felt as if it were slamming the interior walls of her skull, but not from anger or rage. Compassion unmercifully shredded her resolve to hate him, shredded her *need* to vent the emotional wounds still raw and festering. She looked upward, unshed tears straining for release, her teeth tightly clenched to prevent a cry from escaping her. She didn't want to feel *sorry* for him! She didn't want to feel anything at all!

"The baby . . . *Katiah,*" Uhul pleaded, his voice growing raspier, more hollow. "Her-her name?" After a moment, he repeated, "Her name!"

She looked down into the desperation betrayed by Uhul's dark eyes, and made another bid for the rage to spare her from forgiving him anything. But it wouldn't come. Barren, perplexed by the grief his suffering was causing her, she released a strangled sob. Then, "Misty," she said finally, her voice little more than a hoarse whisper.

"M-Mis . . . ty." A shroud of serenity fell across Uhul's features. The fear and anguish vanished from him, and it was through a fey calm that he looked up into Brehan's face. "Protect her. Stop Kou ... sta. Stop—" He valiantly tried to complete the warning, but his body arched up again in a spasm of agony. Fleetingly, he cast a fearful look up at his shipmates. Then the calm befell him again, and his body went limp with death.

For a long moment, the chamber was poignantly still.

Manak shuddered and harshly stated, "Forget Kousta! We must return to the ship."

"She'll burn for all the pain she's brought down on us," Brehan vowed.

"Another time. I'm returning you to the safety of—"

Seven spear-wielding Pirithians charged into the room. Brehan's misted vision filled with knob-kneed legs, hideously hanging beneath carelessly draped loincloths. Manak rose to his feet, hauling Brehan up on her own. One of his hands possessively gripped her arm to keep her close to his side.

"Don't move," she ordered, casting each of the men an added warning.

One alien viciously kicked at Uhul's body. Brehan jerked on Manak's arm to keep him from retaliating. "That's an order, Manak!" she hissed low.

Another soldier, a sneer the width of his face, prodded Niton with the razor-sharp tip of his spear.

"It isn't necessary to hurt them." Brehan issued the order coldly. The alien swung the spear tip to within an inch of her nose. Manak's hand shot out and wrenched the weapon from the taloned grasp. The remaining soldiers closed in, their intent to impale the blond intruder, unmistakable. Before that could happen, she snatched the weapon from Manak and threw it to the floor, then gripped the front of his jersey and gave him a firm shake. "I'm not telling you again!"

Manak's darting gaze surveyed the fury in the soldiers' faces before he lowered his head in deference. Brehan harriedly glanced at Niton and Caenith, who lowered their heads submissively.

"Come!" one of the other soldiers hissed.

Hastened through several corridors, Brehan and the men were ushered into an enormous room furnished with glorious draperies, tapestries, urns of jewels, and wood and stone artifacts. The floor was a colorful mosaic masterpiece of unfamiliar symbols. Centered in the room, reddish water gurgled and cascaded in a eleven-foot-high crusted fountain.

Atop a dais across the room another Pirithian sat upon a granite throne. A theatrical gesture of his hand prompted the soldiers to bring the captives forward. Brehan and the men were roughly shoved to the base of the dais, where two guards restrained her in place, while the Syre men were herded off to the side. The Pirithian leader stood and paraded its imagined grandeur, its loincloth and full-length cape a patchwork of Alorie hides. Tiny bones had been fused together to decorate the alien's neck and ankles.

The leader made another affected gesture and Brehan was roughly forced to her knees.

"*Ahhsss,* the Earth woman I have heard so much about."

At Brehan's attempt to get to her feet, taloned fingers bit into her shoulders. Her heart seeming to pound within her throat, she glared up at the leader, the green of her eyes inhumanly vibrant. "I demand our release."

The leader was at first astonished, then released a spurt of laughter. "*Ahhsss,* spirit!" He moved closer to the edge of the dais and squatted. Moving his head from side to side in narrow-eyed scrutiny of her, he reached out to smooth a talon along her jawline.

"Don't touch her!" Manak bellowed, and received a vicious jab to his ribs from the wood end of a spear. Straightening up, he stubbornly exclaimed, "She is the woman of the Light Lord!" His effort was met with a stunning blow to the back of his neck, dropping him to his knees. Spears were pressed in warning to Niton and Caenith's throats.

"Leave them alone!" Brehan demanded.

"Ahhsss, I have warriors dead because of you!"

Contempt flashed in her eyes. "You're all walking corpses, anyway."

The leader, Mon, clenched his fists. A furious snarl exposed sharp yellow teeth. *"Ahhsss,* a genetic disorder left my race as we are, but we are still the mightiest warriors in the universe!"

The proclamation induced a look of utter loathing on Brehan's face. A spastic tick began in Mon's right cheek. "Mock not Mon! Subsequent generations will become stronger until our bodies are powerful once again—ahhsss, especially now that we have a means to reproduce."

A hellish gleam lit the red, white-pupiled eyes when he saw suspicion cloud the woman's face. "Our females were the curse we bore, but they served us well as food after we crashed on this world. It is, *ahhsss,* a pity I have lost my taste for flesh. I believe, *ahhsss,* I would like the taste of you."

"Drop dead, you maggot."

His expression became comically rueful. "Your tone suggests you again, *ahhsss,* mock me." He glanced briefly at the Syre men. "I shall order their flesh stripped from their bodies unless you bow before me and press your insulting mouth to my feet! You will do this to prove you are humbled, *ahhsss,* and grateful for my tolerance."

Brehan turned deathly pale, but her body language bespoke of steeled determination.

"They shall die in agony before your eyes," Mon purred.

"No *Katiah!"* Niton cried, and received a blow to his chest with the blunt end of a spear.

"Katiah?" Mon guffawed, its sound echoing throughout the room. *"She Who Guides?"* He laughed louder. "What, *ahhsss,* travesty be this?" he roared tauntingly.

"Just one shot," Brehan muttered beneath her breath.

Mon's dementedly sparkling eyes looked down at her. "Threaten Mon?"

"Of course not," she lied smoothly. "I have no quarrel with you, Mon." *Only an urge to rip your heart out, you bony sack of shit.* "Spare the men from harm and I'll do whatever you ask of me."

Smiling in his hideously broad way, Mon gave an imperious toss of his head. *"Ahhsss,* now this pleases Mon. Proceed."

Many things flashed through Brehan's mind as she was jerked to her feet and left untouched by the soldiers to comply with their leader's wishes. Guarding the extent of her anger, she calmly contemplated the six taloned toes on each of Mon's gnarled feet. Forcing herself to shut out the men's protests, she lowered her head and pressed her lips to the right foot. The coldness and coarse texture of his flesh nearly made her gag. She was barely able to contain her deepening revulsion when Mon released an ecstatic sigh and it loosed her fiery temper. Without thought to the consequences, she deeply sank her teeth into the largest toe.

A bellow sirened. Two soldiers took hold of her arms and dragged her several feet back from the dais, but she was impassive as she observed Mon's wild thrashing, the pale green foam spewing from his mouth, and the thick, milky matter gushing from the punctures her teeth had inflicted.

"I knew you would need me," said a familiar voice to her left.

Brehan's head shot around. A hush fell over the room as Adam became the center of attention. Standing some fifty feet away, a laser pistol leveled in Mon's direction, he smiled with the arrogance of youth. "I think this changes the odds," he laughed, bobbing his weapon hand. "Order your . . ." He frowned at the two creatures subduing Brehan's arms. ". . . servants to release her," he completed.

The hands on Brehan tightened. Looking up at Mon's wrathful features, she felt a chill work through her body.

"Brehan," Adam went on, his tone jubilant, his face glowing with elation. "I love you enough to risk even my life. I'm more of a man than you thought, isn't that right?"

Before she could say a word, Manak shouted Adam's name, the raw fear in his tone shocking her. Her gaze shifted beyond the boy to see a blur of movement close in to his right. She, too, cried out a warning to him, but the words never left the confines of her mind. Kousta swung back with the clublike weapon in her hands. Adam turned his head to see what had stepped into peripheral vision. He never saw his end coming. The sharpened bone affixed to the tip of the club, impacted between his eyes and went on into his brain. Kousta released the club the instant of the blow. Stepping aside as the boy keeled over dead, she looked directly at Brehan with a malicious smile accentuating the sharp angles of her face.

"Destroy her, Mon! That was our bargain!" she called out triumphantly.

Brehan's horror-induced shock relented to a moment of poignant denial. Not Adam! Oh God, not the *boy!* Her insides heated, and heated until all-consuming rage ignited within her. A feral wail erupted from her. Using her fists, elbows and knees, she plowed through the converging soldiers attempting to block her path from Kousta. Spearheads punctured her arms and legs, her back. Blindly, fiercely, she smashed through bodies. One soldier made an attempt to tackle her, but she kicked out a foot and rammed one of his calves. The leg broke away at the knee joint, flew up into the air, and landed in her waiting hand. With the same swiftness, she slammed the leg upside his head, snapping off the lower jaw. She was pumping her feet into another run toward Kousta when an urn crashed down on the back of her head. Her legs buckled beneath her. Caught up in a gray daze, she struggled to regain her equilibrium and pick herself up off the floor. But talons raked and gouged every part of her body, causing her to jerk like a rag doll.

Sounds boomed, crescendoing in her head as she felt herself slapped onto her back.

Material ripped away at her chest. Then something clamped almost completely around one of her breasts, and she screamed in agony. Taloned hands pinned her wrists to the cold floor. Lifting her head, she blearily focused. Her left breast filled Mon's mouth. His teeth were slowly puncturing deeper into her as he drew her blood into his throat.

A scream of rage erupted from her. Endowed with a spurt of strength, she bucked upward. Mon's head flew back and a howl gurgled from him. Part of his lower gum and teeth remained embedded in Brehan's breast, ripped out by the force of her motion. With a spittle-flying snarl, he arched toward her neck. She bucked again, this time throwing him off balance and pitching him sideways off her.

Racked with pain and weakening beneath its intensity, Brehan rolled onto her front. She tried with all her might to move away from Mon, but her arms and legs were leaden. Explosions of pain within her skull threatened to render her unconscious. She could hear the men battling the Pirithians—spears clacking, cries of aggression, and shrieks of pain from both sides. Her vision was too blurred to make them out, but she knew the men were fighting valiantly for their lives.

Leaning on her right side, she gingerly dislodged the extraneous matter from the underside of her wounded breast. One yellow fang fell into her palm. Unconsciously, her fingers closed over it and kept it like a token within her grasp.

A new sound invaded the room.

Unsteadily propping herself up on an elbow, she strained to see more clearly Mon's retreating figure. She made a bid to get up, collapsed, and cursed in sheer frustration. Then she spied a swarm of Alories rushing into the room. The tiny creatures swept across the floor, taking the Pirithians by surprise by relentlessly attacking their feet and legs with mouths incongruously large for their size.

As if compelled, Brehan's gaze fell upon Adam. Blood covered his face, pooled beneath his head. His eyes remained open, his vacant stare locked onto her face, questioning how she could have allowed his life to have ended in this hellish place. Guilt, as hot and dense as lava, swelled up inside her, strangling her until she finally wrenched her gaze away from him. She spied Pip, his tail snaking him across the room in her direction. As he drew closer, she saw that Annie was clenched between his teeth.

Eyes bright and feral, Pip slipped the weapon over her fingers. The instant Annie glided into place, the crystal came to life, and Brehan became the heart of an explosion. Pip rolled across the floor, righted himself on his tail, and wide-eyed watched as a cloud of energy galed around Brehan. She rose to her feet and the forces swirling around her vanished, leaving her standing unscathed and enkindled with the alien power of Di'me, into which she had unknowingly tapped.

She raised the weapon above her head like an avenging sword, her concentration trained on saving her shipmates. Yellow beams of energy flowed from the Crou crystal, dispersing completely throughout the room. She could feel power coursing through her and feeding through the weapon—the sensation was feeding the core of her existence. Pirithian cries rang out, dimming as the soldiers' count steadily dwindled beneath the disintegrating rays she projected. When the last cry became swallowed up within silence, she lowered her arm and bellowed, "Kooou-sta!"

Something touched her shoulder and she whirled, her weapon hand fine-tuned for immediate action. But it was a solemn Manak standing next to her. Keeping his eyes trained on her face, he draped Mon's cape over her shoulders. Breathing heavily, she thought to decline it, but realized her breasts were exposed. Resigning herself to the immediate necessity of wearing the Alorie hides, she poked her hands through the wide armholes.

"Where did they go?"

Manak was too rattled to speak right away. He had seen the extent of her wounds, yet there was no blood. "Into the catacombs across from us," he said finally. "Caenith and Niton are pursuing them."

Brehan cast Adam a remorseful look before surveying the dead Alories littering the room. "Pip, gather your people and wait by the city's entrance."

Pip looked from Brehan to Manak, then scurried off, issuing orders for the Alories to retreat.

"Brehan—"

"Not now!"

She preceded Manak to a lower level of catacombs, running with a speed that indicated she knew exactly where she was going. In the bowels of the ancient city, the imaginary red light in her mind warned her of imminent danger. She moved quickly, leaving Manak no time to counteract her forceful shove. He struck the gray stone wall a moment before a thick web dropped from the ceiling and completely covered her.

"Don't touch it!" she cried.

Manak froze.

The adhesive web tightened. Losing her balance, she thumped to the floor on her back, Annie stuck fast out of her reach. "Go after Kousta!"

"I can't leave you here!"

Brehan swore beneath her breath. "I'll get out of this! Don't let Kousta get away!"

Manak's indecision made him angry and he kicked

at the wall. Brehan's, "That's an order!" broke him into a run down the corridor.

As soon as he was out of sight, she struggled within the mucilaginous resin of the web to reach Annie. She flipped onto her front, the gelatinous fibers making crude sucking sounds with the movement. A stream of curses rattled from her throat when the web suddenly hardened, and continued to until she was sure her bones would crush beneath the excruciating pressure. In the next instant, the webbing began to crystalize and break apart. Clutching Annie, she rolled onto her back—

Erth loomed above her, his livid expression momentarily robbing her of breath.

"The men are in danger!" she exhaled, scrambling to her feet. "C'mon! There's no time to waste!"

Erth's intended verbal thrashing caught in his throat at the sight of the wounds on her partially exposed breast. Wrenching free of his stupor, he gripped her arm and pulled her down the hall in the direction in which Manak had gone. From around one of the bends, a warrior came charging at them, its spear raised, its eyes grotesquely protruding, froth effervescing from its mouth. Brehan was about to activate Annie when Erth clamped a hand over her wrist and forced her arm down. She glanced up to see that his eyes were incandescent, their blue glow eerily bathing his face.

"*Armai?*" she wailed, on the verge of hysteria. "You want to *bed* that creature?"

The glow brightened then shot out like a laser beam, hitting the warrior and reeling it backward through the air. It crashed into the far wall at the bend in the corridor. No sooner had it fallen in a heap, its flesh turned to the color of blue-gray parchment. Millions of fractures appeared before the being dissolved into powder.

Around the next bend, Erth pulled a shocky Brehan into a large cavernous room. On the wall across from them, Kousta and Mon stood atop a broad ledge of stone, dodging Caenith and Niton's prodding spearheads. Manak stood armed on the steps to the ledge, barring the couple's escape.

"Drop your weapons!" Erth thundered at his men.

They turned in his direction before obeying his order.

Kousta broke into histrionics. "Erth, help me! Uhul abducted me—then this . . . this *creature* took me hostage!"

"You lying bitch!"

Erth glared down at Brehan in warning for her to be silent. "I'll handle this." Releasing her, he crossed the room in angry strides. "Kousta—"

Brehan barked Erth's name, her voice harshly echoing in the chamber. Looking over his shoulder, Erth stiffened at the sight of her weapon trained on him.

"This is *my* fight!" she cried furiously.

Turning to face her, his expression and posture formidable, he ordered, "Put down that weapon!"

"She *murdered* Adam!"

"I know," he growled, his anger with her conduct overshadowing his grief. "Know your place, woman, and lower that weapon!"

Brehan flexed her fingers within Annie's grip. Every fiber of her being wanted to end Kousta's life. She wanted it so desperately, it was like acid burning at the back of her throat. But at the same time, she knew Erth was right. In her frame of mind, she wasn't fit to judge what should be done with the hideous duo. She was about to lower her weapon hand when the vehemence of the inner voice overpowered her.

DESTROY HIM, YOU COWARD!

A burning sensation in her arm drew down her gaze. Her eyes widened at the sight of liquid fire passing beneath her skin, passing down her arm and into her hand. Against her will, her hand lifted and Annie discharged. A brilliant yellow blaze traversed the room and fed into Erth's chest, but he took the charge without a tremor. Stunned, incredulous that the weapon had gone off, she jerked her arm to her side and fell back a step.

She could not focus on anything but the emotional devastation she read in Erth's eyes. It penetrated her heart and mind, twisting inside her like a rabid serpent looking to escape its torment.

Erth turned to face the prisoners. "Mon, your warriors have been transported to Utular, where you will only have each other to destroy. Kousta, you will be banished to—"

NOW!

"To *hell!*" Brehan cried, simultaneously firing Annie. A violet beam blazed across the room and enveloped Kousta, a moment later, devouring her into nothingness. Brehan was vaguely conscious of Erth running toward her. Before he was able to reach her, she willed the weapon to fire again. Four incendiary blue rays targeted Mon. A shriek galed from his lungs as the rays amputated his hands and feet. He fell from the shelf and struck the ground, where he lay writhing in agony.

Erth's fingers painfully clamped around her weapon hand, causing her to cry out. For a brief second, she glimpsed a questioning wounded look in his eyes, then they grew hard and condemning. He dragged her to Mon and shoved her to the floor beside the leader. She stared into the red pools of Mon's eyes, her hatred of him nullifying all sense of guilt.

"This—" She gestured to his cauterized stumps. "—is but a token of my appreciation." Plucking the fang from her left palm, she flung it into his face. "For your generous hospitality."

Erth could not deal with his revulsion. With a swipe of his hand, he transported Mon to Utular where his own kind would tend to him.

Feeling the heat of Erth's gaze on the back of her head, Brehan stood and forced herself to face him. "And where am I to be banished to?"

Rage stormed within Erth's eyes before his face became devoid of expression. Looking at the men to his right, he said, "The ship's in orbit. Stand by with the Alories at the city entrance."

His head swung around. Bright, fierce eyes impaled Brehan's face. *"Your* hell will best be served at my side!"

Chapter Fifteen

It was nearly two weeks after the ship's departure from Carica before Barrit worked up the nerve to approach Erth. But his resolve nearly abandoned him when he stepped from the lift and found his superior alone in the Control Center. Alone, which meant the giant wouldn't be overly conscious of controlling his temper if Barrit were to say the wrong thing.

Crossing the room, he was greeted with a monotone, "What is it?" before he'd come to a stop beside Erth.

"What have you decided concerning the men?"

A muscle ticked along Erth's jawline as he continued to stare out into space. "My mind wagered your first concern would be Brehan's punishment."

Barrit gave a rueful shake of his head. "This attitude of yours is irritating. I prefer your anger to your moping."

"There is no release for what I'm feeling. The betrayal of values transcends anger."

"The men defended their lives, and that of their *Katiah*."

"Taking a life is forbidden."

"I keep forgetting," Barrit said sarcastically, "we have *you* to raise the almighty hand against our enemies."

Erth's narrowed gaze swung to the medix. "Mind your tone, Barrit!"

Barrit looked affronted. "The men have very little to do with what you're feeling. You would only punish them to punish her."

The light pulse of Erth's headband raced. "Don't preach to *me!* Her actions brought about the death of your son! And had I been less than what I am, she would have destroyed me!"

"Let it go, Erth."

Erth gave an adamant shake of his head. "I close my eyes and my mind re-enacts her turning that weapon on me." Despondently, he went on, "I believed in her—until I witnessed her mutilate Mon. She's ruthless. She has no conscience. No mercy."

"Why do you love her?"

Erth instantly corrected, *"Want* her," to which Barrit's expression turned to one of sour cynicism.

"It's beneath your station to condemn her without the facts. Give her a chance to explain her actions."

Bright, searing eyes searched Barrit's face. "How can *you* stand there and defend her?"

Although Barrit paled, his tone and demeanor were calm. "She was in no way responsible for Adam's death. *He* chose to disobey orders and set out after her. His loss has affected her just as deeply as it has Christie and me."

Erth's head lowered. When he spoke again, his tone was husky and strained. "We all regret Adam's loss." He abruptly rose to his feet and started toward the lift. "I need to be alone with my thoughts. Inform the crew I'm not to be disturbed."

As soon as Erth descended, Barrit went to the intercom and tapped in the code to Niton's quarters. "He's gone below."

* * *

Brehan lowered her face into her hands, but found there were still no tears to shed. Isolated in her quarters, she grieved alone for Adam, whose body was being held in stasis until a funeral could be arranged once the ship docked on Syre.

Wondering what had happened to Niton, Manak, and Caenith also haunted her sleep and shadowed her waking hours. She knew Erth was capable of anything, and the thought of the men suffering left an unshakable coldness inside her.

"Mistress, I wish I could comfort you in some small way."

"You do, Sami."

"You have not smiled. Come to think of it, I have never seen a smile grace your face."

"Just call me pickle-puss."

"What is a pickle-puss?"

Sighing, she murmured, "Me."

"Perhaps you should work on your journal?"

"No, Sami, I don't feel up to it. Besides, there's nothing left to say, is there?"

"Oh woe, Mistress, it pains me to hear you so glum."

She glanced down at the ring Erth had given her, which lay on the vanity in front of her. When she had been escorted to her old quarters twelve days earlier, it had slipped from her finger, as if signifying the dissolution of their union. Clinging to the hope of eventual forgiveness, she picked up the ring and shakily placed it on the third finger of her left hand.

It was still so loose that it easily slipped off again.

"Time is a wise healer, Mistress."

Dropping the ring onto the vanity alongside the amulet, she quipped, "It's certainly done wonders for you."

"Ouch."

"Brehan."

Startled by the whispering voice behind her, Brehan

turned in the chair. The sight of Lisa, Niton, Joy and Caenith standing a few feet away caused her heart to skip a beat. "He hasn't hurt you?" she asked, stiltedly rising from her seat.

"*Katian* has not even spoken to us," said Niton.

"Does he know you're here?"

"We waited until he went into his quarters to meditate," said Caenith. "We're safe. His mind is too preoccupied to probe our whereabouts."

"I don't know. The slightest indiscretion could—"

"Forget him," Lisa dismissed airily. "We've been timing him. Whenever he goes into his quarters to meditate, he doesn't come out for hours." Lisa peered around Brehan with a frown on her face. "What were you talking to?"

"Sami."

"Who?"

"The amulet. It-umm . . . never mind for now."

Niton stepped forward. "We have secured the Garden Chamber. The intercom has been temporarily disabled, and Manak is topside watching the monitors."

"We discussed this, *Katiah*," Caenith stated. "Although we dare not outright oppose *Katian* confining you, we can offer you some intervals of freedom."

"I can't ask you to take the risk! If he ever—"

Joy took Brehan's hand, turned it over and pressed something into the palm.

"What's this?"

"Manak rigged Erth's exit mechanism. This disc will flash red when he leaves his quarters."

"Made especially for this occasion," Caenith grinned.

"I don't know . . . "

Brehan protested all the way to the Garden Chamber. However, once inside, the beauty and serenity of the room swept away her fears, and she walked away from her four escorts.

"Remember, *Katiah*, when the disc flashes red, return immediately to your quarters," Niton warned.

"Make each moment count," Caenith added. "Our thoughts shall be with you."

When the couples stepped into the corridor and the E wall sealed, Brehan experienced a moment of panic. If Erth suspected . . .

Her gaze lifted to drink in the fabulous view of the manufactured sky and the liquid lightning frolicking within and between the clouds. The spell of indecision broke. Her spirits soared as she followed one of the paths to the platform across the room. It felt good to be free again—even if temporarily. The star-graced space beyond made her blood race. From this vantage point, life seemed as forever and as full as the frontier which stretched out as far as the eye could see.

She had been told by Barrit that the Alories were now residing in this room. For a fleeting moment, she thought to call out to them, but it was late, and as they hadn't greeted her, she could only surmise they were sleeping.

But if only she could sit with them for a while—

A sense of intrusion changed the air in the room. Brehan forced herself to turn in the direction of the exit, where Erth stepped from the shadows of drape-limbed trees. Heartsick and lightheaded, she looked down at the disc in her hand. There was no red light. And the Alories, she reasoned, were probably hiding from the big guy's wrath.

Erth closed the distance between them too quickly for her to react. Prying the disc from her hand, he flung it away.

"Undress."

His single word held the impact of a stinging slap. She remained frozen in shock, her gaze lowered to spare herself looking him in the eye. But after a moment of a stressful silence, she looked up to see a glint of malice flicker in his eyes. There was no doubt in her mind that his anger hadn't cooled during the past two weeks. If anything, the vibes she was picking up from him, warned her that his temper had been dangerously simmering. She flinched and downcast her eyes when his hands came up and moved sensuously over the contours of her neck and shoulders—as if testing her stamina not to run away from him. With almost punishing slowness, he slipped the gown down to her waist, exposing her full breasts. She could feel his heated gaze sweeping over her, and her mortification promised to incinerate her if he continued much longer.

Abruptly, he whisked his jersey over his head and tossed it aside. She looked into his eyes, despising his ability to appear so damnable calm.

"Erth—"

He pressed a finger to her lips to silence her. Through a blur, she watched him step closer. He gently gripped her upper arms and drew her against him, then prompted her to strain on the balls of her feet to allow him easier access to her mouth. His head lowered in a tauntingly slow manner. His mouth covered hers in a hard, demanding kiss, his arms molding her against his feverish body. Brehan forced herself to endure. The emotional discomfort of his embrace held a promise of forgiveness, if not for herself, at least for the men. But if she'd hoped to remain impassive in his arms, she soon discovered she couldn't. His kiss penetrated her mental resistance, probing, finding, and forcing her needs to surface—and without the *armai* to sedate her. Her fears and inhibitions melted of their own accord. She wound her arms about his middle and returned the kiss with a passion she couldn't believe existed in her. It felt so natural to be in his arms, sharing his warmth, exploring the magical wonders of something as ageless as a kiss. Nothing from the past intruded into her mind. There was only the moment, this empyrean exchange, and the promise of fulfillment to bask in, which was more than she had ever hoped for in her previous life.

A tingling, burning sensation manifested in her left breast, then rapidly spread across her skin. It became so distracting, she forced herself to shove away from Erth and turned her back to him. The discomfort intensified, unsettling her until she noticed that the scars on her breast left from Mon's assault, were fading. Shortly, the tingling appeared in other places, and she realized all the scar tissue on her body was disappearing.

Perplexed by the magnanimity of Erth's gift, she prudently righted the gown and turned to face him. There was an electric moment of silence between them before he abruptly turned and walked from the room. Fear gripped her. Something in his carriage set off a warning in her brain. She caught up with him in the corridor and, placing herself in front of him, she pressed her palms to his bare chest.

"You're going to punish me through the men, aren't you?" she asked, terrified of his disquieting calm. He merely frowned at the placement of her hands, and a whimper caught in her throat. "No, Erth, *please!* Leave them alone! Take your anger out on me!"

"In bed?"

She felt as if he had struck her across the face. "You sanctimonious ass!" she cried, tears welling up and streaming down her face. "You *knew* they were going to sneak me into the Garden Chamber!" Despite the knots forming in her stomach and the fire coursing through her veins, she told herself she was not dealing with a rational individual, and needed to calm down before their emotions got out of hand. In a softer, beseeching tone, she said, "Punishing the men isn't going to change anything that happened."

"And punishing you?"

His coldness sent renewed slivers of fear through her. "I don't expect to be let off easily."

"Is that why you tolerated my kiss without the *armai?*"

Brehan's posture stiffened, mistakenly verifying his suspicion. He swiftly pinned her to the wall and placed a restraining hand around her throat. "Your shallowness disgusts me!'' Then he released her as if he were ridding himself of a contaminant.

"I have the right to know what you're planning for the men!"

"I'm taking their sight."

"Why?" she gasped.

"Because I want to hurt you. I want you to know what hell responsibility is!"

"Then blind *me!* I'm solely responsible. I-I couldn't stop myself!"

A thought popped into her mind and she used it as a groping measure. "You killed a Pirithian warrior in the corridor, remember? What makes you right and us wrong?"

"My birthright."

"No, that's not good enough."

"*I* would not have permitted a boy to die."

The icily delivered words squeezed Brehan's heart. Her open hand flew up, but she stopped herself from striking him. After several seconds of the hand trembling in the air, she defeatedly dropped it to her side and lowered her head to hide the depths of her misery.

"Don't torment me with his death."

Erth roughly swept her into his arms. She expected his kiss to be savage, punishing, but instead its passion weakened her knees with desire. Realizing he had changed tactics to further test her, she pushed back her anger and willed herself to return the kiss with fervor. Her intention had been to placate him, cajole him into forgetting his threat, but again she found herself swept into a realm of blissful, aching contentment.

"Blind you *te-ni-e?*" he murmured against her lips.

Brehan's glazed eyes looked up at him as he straightened away from her. His features hard, his eyes holding flames of contempt, he issued, "I want you to witness what you have sown."

A hand to the base of her throat, she staggered back until the wall stopped her.

"I'll return their sight when you have birthed me a son."

"You bastard," she breathed.

A sardonic smile twisted his mouth. "A bastard who puts fire in your blood."

"That just shows how easy I am!" she cried.

Erth cruelly laughed at her feeble attempt to deny his power over her. Walking away, he reminded silkily, "The longer you refuse my bed, the longer your cohorts will endure a sightless existence."

Manak rubbed his closed eyelids with a thumb and forefinger before he again looked down at the monitor surveying the Garden Chamber. Although Brehan seemed to be enjoying her visit, wandering through the plant life and humming to herself, a prickly sensation teased the back of his neck, as if warning him that something wasn't quite right. He glanced at Stalan, who was running a diagnostic on the scan console, oblivious to the foreboding pressing in on Manak. Telling himself that he was letting his nerves get the better of him, he deeply sighed and forced himself to again focus on the monitor in front of him.

The sound of the lift brought his head around. To his astonishment, Brehan stepped into the room. He glared at the monitor, the subterfuge stunning him. He had been monitoring an illusion of her in the Garden Chamber all along!

"Manak, I have to warn you!" she cried, coming to a stop as Manak rose to his feet and turned to face her. Painful heart sensations disorienting her, she lowered her head.

"Has Erth threatened you?"

She guiltily looked into his dark eyes. "It's you, Niton

and Caenith he threatens. To punish me, he's going to punish the three of you.''

"What did he say?"

Needing a moment to pull herself together, she stepped around Manak and braced herself against the console. "When I threatened to kill him in the cave, I saw something in him snap. But I couldn't stop myself, Manak. The weapon just . . . went off."

"What was his threat?"

Painfully swallowing, she turned her head to look at him. "He's taking your sight."

Despite the shock her words had dealt him, Manak managed to keep his voice level. "I suppose there are less merciful punishments than being blinded."

A shuddering sigh coursed through Brehan as she turned to face him. Ordinarily, she would have rebuked him for his fatalistic passivity, but her raw emotions occluded her defiant nature.

"Did he say for how long?" Manak asked, a slight quaver in his tone betraying his brave front.

"Until I've given him a son," she murmured.

Manak's face mottled with anger. "Don't give in to his damned threats!"

"Manak—"

"Listen to me," he went on, reaching out for her, then pulling back. He knew if he touched her, he would hold dearly onto her and never let go. "Don't submit to emotional blackmail. He *wants* you, Brehan! Obviously, he will use any means at his disposal to—" Manak bit back the rest of the sentence when he became aware of Stalan intently listening. Deciding to ignore him, he stared deeply into Brehan's eyes. "We can bear up to whatever he does to us. We have a lot more stamina than you give us credit for."

Brehan lifted a trembling hand and tenderly touched her fingertips to his cheek. "I can't do it, Manak. I can't be *that* selfish."

"You *can,*" he bit out, clasping her raised arm with

his hands. "You are my *Katiah*—the people's *Katiah!* Let nothing sway you from your principles!"

"What principles?" she exclaimed. Turning back to the console, she slapped down her palms on the hard surface and squeezed her eyes shut. "I don't belong here—certainly don't belong among any of you!"

Opening her eyes, she gave release to the tears welling up from the sea of her despair. "You're already blind, Manak. You mistake fear for principles, fits of temper for bravery, emptiness for a strong constitution! Why do I even give a damn! It hurts like hell!"

A current of energy sparked beneath her palms. Crying out, she tried to break the hold the electrified field above the console had on her, but it held her fast. In an attempt to pull her free, Manak touched her shoulders, only to have an unseen force propel him backward to the floor. Several feet away, Stalan stood paralyzed with shock and fear.

Brehan's eyes widened in terror. From beneath her hands, a brushlike discharge of white-hot energy swept like wildfire over the console. More horrifying was the realization that the energy was coming from within *her*.

"Brehan!" Manak cried, nursing his burned hands to his midriff as he struggled to his feet.

A small explosion ripped through the interior of the computer. Brehan was catapulted backward, landing a short distance away from Manak. The ship surged, its velocity imprisoning them all on the floor with its gravitational force.

"We'll . . . burn . . . up!" Manak warned, his voice out of synchrony with the movement of his mouth. Face down, he used his elbows to inch forward toward the master console.

Brehan's fingers raked the floor in a futile attempt to anchor her against the invisible force pulling her toward Stalan, who was flattened against the wall beside the master console.

Erth stepped from the lift. Impervious to the G-force,

he ran across the room in the direction of the master controls. He reached out to shut down the hyperspeed momentum, but stopped when a kaleidoscopic tunnel of lights appeared around the ship. The *Stellar* was drawn into the swirling mass, swiftly vacuumed into the unknown.

Amid the smoldering and sparking remains of the console, Erth managed to default the Control Center's life support and artificial gravity functions to the secondary console across the room. The *Stellar* jettisoned into blackness. Its speed decreased. Before Erth could regulate the gravity stabilizer, the suddenness of deceleration threw Stalan forward. Manak flipped in the air and slapped the floor by Erth's feet. Brehan cowered to the floor.

Opening the intercom, Erth ordered, "Barrit, report!"

"As far as I know, the crew is only shaken."

Erth glared at Manak. "What happened?"

The quaking of his body wreaking havoc with his equilibrium, Manak could only shake his head.

"Stalan, are you injured?"

"No . . . *Katian*, I'm all right."

Erth swung his gaze to Brehan, who was unsteadily getting to her feet. "What do you know of this?"

"I-I didn't mean to—"

Barrit stepped from the lift in time to see Manak stagger to position himself between his two guardians, the rage in his expression equal to that of Erth's.

"Back off!" Manak hissed at his superior.

Erth imploded and instantly transported himself into outer space, where his unbridled furies caused a succession of explosions that were clearly visible through the dome. Manak turned to Brehan, his hands automatically going out to rest on her shoulders. Ignoring the pain in his raw palms and fingers, he searched her lifeless eyes as she watched Erth vent his rage in the distance. Her face was taut and pale, but a puzzling factor caught

Manak's attention. Although the front of her clothing bore signs of scorching, there was no indication that her hair had been singed, or that her skin had been touched. Taking her hands into his own, he turned her palms up to inspect them.

No burns.

He looked up to find her staring from his hands to her own. "*Katiah*, how is this possible?"

Brehan's eyes rolled up into her head. Her legs gave out from beneath her. Catching her up into his arms, Manak headed toward the lift.

Barrit was quick to stop him from entering it. "I'll take her to the Med Chamber."

"She doesn't require your attention. She must heal herself."

"Give her to me. Your hands need attending."

"No! I've trusted her safety to others for the last time."

Barrit gripped one of Manak's arms. "Listen to what you're saying! She's Erth's woman!"

"She is no one's property!" Manak exclaimed. Wrenching his arm free, he stepped into the lift.

The absolute map remained inactive. Niton worked continuously at the controls, even long after he'd realized there was nothing in the computer's files to indicate their position. His fingers were stiff. His back ached.

The sound of the lift brought his head around. Erth and Barrit entered the room. Niton glanced at Manak, who was on his back trying to restore an underpart section of the console. The expression on Manak's face as he gazed Erth's way, boded trouble—as if there hadn't been enough tension building up the past three days!

Erth lowered himself into his command chair, his face a stony mask as he surveyed the unfamiliar territory beyond the dome. Barrit, standing to Erth's right, sent Manak a mute appeal to restrain his temper.

"We couldn't have deviated far from our course," Barrit said, forcing optimism into his tone. All eyes turned on him solemnly, and he added, "At least we're alive."

"No thanks to that *hibasha*," Erth remarked.

Erth's head shot around at the clangor of instruments. He looked at Manak as the man rose to his feet and crossed half the distance. "Return to your post. And do strive to be seen and not heard."

Manak's defiant straightening of his shoulders goaded Erth to his feet. "I gave you an order, Manak."

"To hell with you!"

Manak stood his ground. Niton, Stalan and Lute hastily retreated to the far side of the room, while Barrit planted himself between Manak and Erth, his hands stayed in the air in a refereeing gesture.

"Go below, Barrit!" Erth ordered. When Barrit didn't respond, Erth shoved past him, and said to Manak, "I don't like your attitude."

"My attitude isn't the issue. Brehan is."

"Keep her out of this," Erth growled.

"Or what?"

Erth straightened back sharply when an impression struck home. A deadly glint brightened his eyes. "You covet my woman and expect me to ignore it!"

Barrit forced himself to intervene. "It isn't what you think, Erth!" When the giant glared down at him, he rushed on, "Manak is a brother to her. Nothing more!"

Erth's gaze cut to Manak. "What do you feel for Brehan?"

"We share a bond of friendship and mutual respect," Manak replied, quaking with anger. "Anything else is pure conjecture on your part."

"It had better be nothing more."

Manak's left eye twitched, matching a muscle along

his clenched jaw. "More threats, *Katian?* Shouldn't you carry through with one before issuing another?"

"I wouldn't push the issue if I were you," Erth growled.

Breathing heavily, Manak took a step closer. "Why not? Is there some dark, isolated world waiting for me if I dare to criticize your infinite wisdom? We were forced to defend our lives on Carica. Brehan did not kill Uhul. The Pirithians tortured him. He was barely alive when we found him." He drew in a deep breath to help quell his anger. "Brehan wasn't responsible for her actions when she turned the weapon on you. It didn't signify hatred on her part, rather desperation born of the humiliation and pain she suffered at Kousta and Mon's hands. If you weren't so damned absorbed in self-pity, you would see what all this has done to *her!*"

Erth abruptly turned and rigidly sat in his command chair. Feeling that he had triumphed in some small way—especially since he was breathing and in one piece—Manak returned to his post.

Barrit remained silent for a time, studying Erth's profile. Tension knotted his stomach. His throat was painfully dry. But he had to admire Manak's defense of Brehan. It was long overdue. If only he wasn't so damned sure that Manak was hopelessly in love with her. He had known all along that there was a special bond between them, something Brehan could never know with her mate. Trust was the foundation, and loyalty. But she belonged to Erth.

Casting a forlorn look at the back of Manak's head, Barrit tried to remember those lazy, peaceful days on Syre before the first voyage had begun. But they were gone, and so was Manak's adolescence, Barrit realized. The man Manak had become would ferociously fight for Brehan's heart. Even if it meant hurting Dawn. Even if it meant Manak's death.

Deciding to spend some time alone in the Garden Chamber, Barrit headed for the lift.

* * *

A hand lowering upon her brow drew Brehan up from the depths of a deep sleep. Opening her eyes, she dimly made out a face above her. As her grogginess waned, she focused on Christie's strangely elated face, and heard her ask, "How are you feeling?"

"Mmmm. Kinda numb."

Brehan's awakening awareness told her something was going on—something that certainly pleased the medix's wife.

"Barrit wanted me to wait until morning, but I was sure you would want to know as soon as possible."

Moistening her dry lips with the tip of her tongue, Brehan scooted up into a sitting position. "What have I done now?" she asked dully.

"Nothing, Brehan," Christie chuckled. "Except maybe co-created one of the most beautiful babies I've ever seen!"

The words struck Brehan funny and she laughed low within her throat. "I must be dreaming—"

"No. Misty's out of the Orthandite. She's beauti—"

"What?"

Anger shadowed Brehan's face. "What?" she repeated, more sharply than before.

"She reached her time about an hour ago."

"It's only been a few weeks," Brehan said thickly, a chill crawling across the skin of her arms.

"Well, it's . . . ummm." Christie's happiness became lost to unease. "I meant to explain about the progeria process . . . "

"Progeria? What the hell are you talking about?"

"It's, ah, an aging practice Erth's been using since he became the sole guardian of the infants after the last Feydais attack. It's for the children's protection— Brehan!" she cried when the redhead bolted from the bed and stormed in the direction of the E wall. By the time Brehan was crossing the threshold, Christie was at her side and matching the long strides in the direction of the Med Chamber.

"It's perfectly harmless."

"Accelerating a child's age certainly is *not* harmless in *my* book!"

"Barrit can explain—"

Brehan came to an abrupt halt and swung around to face the smaller woman. "Damn, Erth! He's not happy unless he's controlling or manipulating *something!*"

"Don't get yourself all worked up."

"Why the hell not!" Brimming with anger, Brehan resumed her pace. She cast Christie a heated look and asked, "Afraid I'll blow up the ship this time?"

"Don't be ridiculous," Christie said, looking aside to avoid Brehan's eyes.

"Ridiculous, huh?" Brehan released an undignified snort. "For the past five weeks, we've been in abeyance in God knows where. Everyone's on edge, and my blackouts are increasing. Ridiculous, Christie? This progeria crap is the last straw!"

"Brehan—"

"Damn Erth's hide!" she spat, and stormed into the Med Chamber.

The scene which greeted her instantly doused her temper. Everyone but Erth was present. Those with their backs to her moved aside to reveal a beaming Barrit cradling a bundle in his arms. Brehan's vision zoomed in on the tiny pink face visible within the lightweight blanket. She wasn't aware of the others eagerly awaiting her reaction. Wasn't conscious of Christie's hand on her arm. There was only the contentedly sleeping child.

She took a step forward, but stopped again when something invisible slammed her hard in the abdomen. Nausea filled her. A thunderous pounding at her temples disoriented her. Heat suffused her body.

HOLD HER. I NEED TO—

Shut up!

SHE IS *OUR* CREATION!

It was through tunneled vision that Brehan saw Barrit coming toward her, his arms lifting the infant for her to take.

AN HEIR, Di'me crooned.

Revulsion lodged within Brehan's throat. She stepped back, shaking her head wildly in denial.

"Brehan." Manak's voice drew her blurring gaze to his troubled features. "Your daughter needs you."

Needs you . . . needs you . . .

"No." Brehan backed up another step, her right hand uplifted in a warning for no one to approach her. "I can't . . . I can't be responsible for her."

"My lady—"

"Take her away!" Brehan demanded, then with a strangled sob, ran into the corridor. Hot tears blinding her, she forged on until strong arms came out of the grayness and embraced her.

"My lady," Manak whispered huskily by her ear, holding her tightly against him. "Tell me what's wrong."

"Me. I'm wrong," she wept.

"She's a part of you." Framing one side of her pallid face with a hand, he planted a kiss on her brow. "Forget Uhul."

"It's not about him," she choked. "It's *me*. I can't be a mother to her. Never! Do you understand? *Never!*"

"You're distraught."

"I'm evil!"

Although her words were scarcely more than a whisper, they had the impact of a blow on Manak. "I don't ever want to hear you talk such nonsense again. You are not evil, *Katiah*. Look at me. *Look* at me!" When her gaze finally met his, he added gently, "No one holds you responsible for our present location. Erth will soon pinpoint our station."

"Limbo, Manak."

Searching her features, he smiled. "Misty, like her mother, is magnificent. Come. Hold her. She is such a wonder."

A dark calm befell Brehan as she backed away. "The less I have to do with her, the better off she'll be," she said in a monotone. "Don't try to convince me otherwise."

Stunned, Manak watched her walk away in the direction of her quarters. When he finally found his voice again, she was disappearing around the bend in the corridor. He ran after her, beyond her, and was waiting at the E wall to her old quarters when she lethargically came to a stop in front of him.

"Where is all this coming from, Brehan?" When she didn't respond, he heatedly asked, "Guilt? Are you harboring some ridiculous—"

"Drop it, Manak."

"—notion that what happened in the—"

"Step aside."

"—Control Center was *your* fault?"

Resentment flashed in her eyes.

"For all we know, the sprites could have been responsible for the panels shorting out!"

"You don't understand."

"Then enlighten me!" he exclaimed with exasperation.

"That electricity came from within *me.*"

"Brehan—"

Manak choked back his skepticism when her right hand lifted off to her side and a multi-appendaged flash of lightning burst from her fingertips. It struck the panel, cascading sparks forcing Manak to back away. Then the E wall opened, further startling him.

"It grows stronger every day," she said as she walked into her quarters.

Manak stood rooted, staring in disbelief at a reddish residual play of static on the panel. When it faded, he numbly turned to see Brehan stretching out on her back atop the bed.

"Don't question me again, Manak."

The E wall closed. Manak gave in to a shudder, then raked the fingers of a hand through his thick hair.

During the past three weeks, he had noticed subtle changes in her, changes he couldn't quite put his finger on. She had been spending an inordinate time in the lab these days, testing and retesting the sporadic materializations of the sprites. He'd known she was deliberately keeping herself detached from him, from the others.

Until now, he hadn't known why.

His hearts constricted almost painfully as he glanced at the panel again. He had never seen anyone display spontaneous electrical discharge—except Erth. But Erth was a guardian, a divine creation of the living energy of suns.

Baffled and too wired to think clearly, he shuffled back in the direction of the Med Chamber.

He should have known she wouldn't have turned away from her child without good reason. Power. It was within Brehan. Growing. Frightening her. He couldn't for the life of him fathom how she had come to possess it, but he was determined to solve this mystery. Brehan's right to happiness depended on it, and in his heart of hearts, her well-being and happiness were all that mattered.

When he came to the threshold of the opened E wall to the Med Chamber, he stopped and solemnly regarded the cooing group. The baby was their sole focus. Temporarily forgotten was the mother's reaction, but Manak had long since realized that the others had a tendency to ignore Brehan's moods, accept each strange occurrence in stride and go on as if she had not affected them in any way.

Turning into the corridor and bracing his shoulders against the wall, he fought to hold back the emotions threatening to shatter his hearts.

Misty could have been his child if Brehan had not abolished the matching.

The thought sliced through him.

Where was Erth?

Did he realize Brehan's distress?

Did he care?

Hardness crept along Manak's features as he pushed away from the wall and headed for his quarters.

Power.

If only he possessed the power to protect her from herself.

If only . . . she loved him more than just as a trusted friend.

Chapter Sixteen

Late in the night, Manak entered his lab to find Brehan sitting at one of the work tables in the center of the room. She was so engrossed in her work she didn't hear his approach, and wasn't aware when he came to stand behind her. Looking over her shoulder, he watched as she patiently adjusted dials on the control panel in front of her.

"Computer, what's the time elapse now?"

—Eleven Point Three Seconds—

"Tell me when the next flare-up begins. And make sure you run a full spectrum scan."

—Affirmative—

Brehan studiously observed the three-foot-long, red energy flow between the two mounted crystals. As the seconds dragged into minutes, she began to squirm in her seat. The low whine of the energy flow was the only sound in the room, mesmerizing, drawing on her fatigue. She began to flex her stiff back when a hand settled on her left shoulder. Startled, she turned sharply on the seat and looked up into Manak's somewhat apologetic expression.

"Are you trying to scare the hell out of me?"

"The Darklands couldn't accomplish that," Manak chuckled as he stepped up to the table alongside her. "Still trying to evaluate our little friends?"

Sighing deeply, she relaxed against the back of her chair. "Their life span has been minutely increasing. They're up to a walloping twenty-nine seconds now."

"Interesting."

"That's not all. I got this queer impression during the last occurrence."

"Oh?"

"It's hard to explain. It was as if . . . for just a fragment of a second . . . something reached out to contact me."

"An intelligence?"

"I'm not sure. It could be wishful thinking. It didn't occur to me to have the computer monitor the flare-ups until the last one. I'm hoping a spectrum scan will reveal something significant."

"Why a spectrum scan?"

"As the Crous existence is based on concentrated light, I thought I'd try a long shot and increase the intensity."

"Better than a long shot." Taking a chair from the nearest end of the table, Manak placed it beside Brehan's. "But an intelligence capable of reaching the human consciousness is highly unlikely." He looked at Brehan's profile and frowned. "But then you are highly receptive to telepathic transmissions, aren't you?"

"Sometimes. But with the sprites, I see flashes of colors. I've also got the computer working on a chronological graph of the glitches throughout the ship. Maybe a visual on the color variables will trigger some answers."

"You've been busy."

Brehan smiled wanly. "It keeps me out of trouble."

"And away from Misty."

Avoiding Manak's probing gaze, she managed a calm, "Joy and Lisa don't seem to mind looking after her."

Manak drew in a slow breath before responding. "You

have no idea what you're missing. Each day she changes."

"How much can a child change in ten days?"

"She's sitting up on her own." At Brehan's startled look, he stared deeply into her troubled eyes. "You're not only cheating yourself, you're cheating her."

"Don't preach to me, Manak."

"You know I'm right. Alienating yourself from the people who love you—"

"Swell word, *alienate.*"

"Dammit, *Katiah!*"

"No, *damn you,* Manak! Let it go!"

—Fluctuation In Pulse—the computer announced, temporarily defusing the heated exchange between the couple.

Within seconds, minute white starbursts could be seen within the red stream.

"Computer," Brehan began, excitement swelling within her, "lock onto the first neonate and maintain a probe throughout its life span."

—Affirmative—

"Neonate?" Manak asked, his gaze never wavering from the sporadic bursts of light struggling to escape the energy stream.

"Newborns. I thought it an appropriate term for the initial divisions—" The words caught in her throat as five of the seven broke from the stream and frolicked in front of her face. Twinkling entities romping merrily within a specified space.

Manak intensely watched her elated response to the sprites.

"Tell me!" she gasped, then closed her eyes but for a moment. "Purpose? You need . . . purpose?"

The sprites faded away.

—Spectrum Scan Completed—

"Computer, give me an analysis," Brehan demanded.

—Disordered Spectrum Recorded—

"Meaning what?"

Manak intervened, "Computer, explain 'disordered spectrum.'"

—Abnormal Color Sequence Responsible For Instability—

Brehan put forth the next question. "Computer, were you able to determine if the neonates possessed intelligence?"

—Microscopic Simplex Lobes Determine An Inchoate Form Of Intelligence—

—Evolution Factor Indeterminable Until Further Data Can Be Obtained—

"Computer, have you compiled the graph I requested?"

—Memory Banks In Default—

For a time, Brehan closed her eyes and deeply pondered the information. Her heart was doing crazy things within her chest, in cadence to her memory of the sprites lively pulsations. Two colors flashed across her mindscreen. "Blue and purple. They're the unstable factors." She massaged her throbbing temples for a moment, then sighed. "I think."

"You've been right all along," Manak said dazedly. "The Crous *are* trying to produce offspring."

Pushing back her chair and standing, Brehan flipped her unbound hair behind her. "They need purpose, Manak. That's *your* department."

His jaw went slack as he watched her head for the E wall. "Where are you going?" he asked before she crossed the threshold.

"To bed. I'm getting punchy."

Blue and violet. His thoughts in overdrive, Manak shut down the Crous and waited until he felt reasonably sure Brehan was in her quarters. He entered the corridor with hurried strides, then broke into a full run once he passed the threshold to the A corridor. Arriving in the Med Chamber, he went immediately to the main console and lowered himself onto the chair.

"Is there a particular reason you're here?" asked Barrit as he left the Surgical Chamber and approached Manak.

Startled, Manak replied testily, "I'm initiating a new scan on Brehan."

Positioning himself behind Manak's left shoulder, Barrit read the instructions appearing on the monitor and wrinkled his brow in disapproval. "I think you need rest. Lots . . . of rest." When Manak didn't respond, Barrit asked, "Is she aware—"

"Of course not!"

Barrit cynically rolled his eyes. "What brought this on? Or is that a secret, too?"

"No secret." Anxiously completing the schematic alterations on the bio-scan connected to Brehan's quarters, he looked up into Barrit's face. "Every time we've attempted to scan her to update her medical and psychological files, we've run into problems, right?"

Bewildered, Barrit nodded.

"Not once have we gotten an accurate reading on her, right?"

Exhausted and teeming with impatience, Barrit scowled. "You're killing my brain cells with this."

"Barrit, on her world, red is used as a warning color. We assumed that the reason we haven't been able to accurately scan her, was due to her somehow altering the mechanism in her room, or the commands through the comp, right?"

Barrit wearily bobbed his head in acknowledgement.

A glow of pride softened the lines of fatigue on Manak's face.

"I finally figured out the problem, tonight, Barrit. She isn't physically altering anything. She doesn't have to, her mind is the barrier."

"So she's *willing* our equipment to fail?" Barrit asked sarcastically.

"Yes, only I believe she's doing it unconsciously. It's some kind of . . . protective biological mechanism in her brain. You see, Barrit, something she said tonight reminded me of the events on Carica. Annie's beams."

"Annie?"

"That's what she calls the Crou weapon I designed for her. Don't ask why . . . please. Anyway, when I created the weapon for her, I altered the intensity levels of the crystal. I was concerned that anything above yellow would be too much for her to handle. Too unstable.

"Twice I witnessed the yellow beams on Carica. She used it against most of the Pirithians, and when she turned the weapon on Erth. But it was a *violet* ray she triggered on Kousta, and a *blue* that amputated Mon. Barrit, that degree of power *couldn't* have come from the weapon. It came from *her* and merely channeled through the Crou."

"By the gods," Barrit murmured sickly.

"I can't believe I didn't think of it at the time. So much was happening . . .

"When I arrived at the lab tonight, she was in the process of trying to run a spectrum scan to determine why the sprites' lifecycle is so short. Before she left, Barrit, she mentioned 'blue and purple.' That's when I remembered altering the weapon's intensity."

"What do you hope a new scan will determine?"

"By changing the intensity to violet, I'm hoping to bypass her psychic shield. If it works, we should have a complete physical, neurological and psychological graphic."

Clapping Manak on the shoulder, Barrit wearily ambled toward the exit. "I'm going to bed. My brain can't take much more input. Let me know if this brainstorm of yours works."

"Yeah . . . good night."

The instant the monitor signaled that Brehan was asleep and the scan was beginning, he said tremulously, "Come on, Brehan. Give me something to work with."

* * *

Brehan's sleep was fitful. Again she dreamed of the girl who had haunted her for as long as she could remember. *She was slender to the point of frailness, a pale face with enormous green eyes. Brehan, and yet not Brehan. There were women in stonelike masks looming over her. A tiny room with a small table and a single chair. A cot with a thin mattress. Excruciating pain—*

She bolted up in bed, shivering and oblivious to the violet beam of light sweeping over her. A parasitic rage clamped its fangs onto her reasoning, but this time she willed the rage back, back into its metaphorical sheath, away from her consciousness.

The scan ended. The beam retracted into the ceiling unit.

A dull ache drummed at her temples. Striving to lessen her racing pulse, she glanced down at her clenched hands. Her nightgown was bunched in her right fist. But within those few seconds of having lost control, the fingernails of her left hand had ripped through the sheeting and mattress.

Physically and emotionally spent, she left the bed and walked to the vanity, where she sat and stared forlornly at her reflection. She needed a distraction to keep herself from dwelling on the dream. Picking up the hairbrush in front of her, she began to run it through her hair, harder and harder, until something rippled across the face of the mirror.

Brehan dropped the brush, ignoring Sami's grunt as it struck his stone. She first attributed the glass's hazy distortion to her state of mind, but then she realized she was staring into a face only resembling her own. The girl in the reflection wore a pale yellow blouse. Her hair was plaited. She was young, possessing an innocence which Brehan had never seen in herself.

Unexpectedly, Brehan's mother's file opened within

her mind. Images assaulted her. Words thundered inside her skull.

"Garth, don't leave me! It's your child, too!"

A wad of money was flung in the sobbing girl's face.

"Get rid of it, Becky. I'm not going to ruin my chances for a political future because of that bastard. Call me when it's over . . . over . . . over . . ."

After a moment of shock, Brehan pressed her fingertips to the cool surface of the mirror.

The image wavered and began to fade.

"No! Don't go!" Brehan released a tortured sob as her own reflection overpowered the dimming image. "You can't leave me again! I need you!

"Damn you, Garth Walker! *Damn you!*"

Aching for that which she had been denied, she spread her fingertips against the glass. Her head drooped between her outstretched arms. A feeling of permanence to her isolation threatened her tenuous hold on sanity.

"Mistress, do you wish to talk?"

Sitting back, Brehan forced herself to calm. A sparkle from the liquid fire within the ring caught her attention. Lifting it, she planted her elbows on the table and bleakly regarded the symbolic band.

"Sami, were your people emotionally . . . complicated?"

"Rightly so." The sapphire sighed. "Your distress pains me, Mistress."

Brehan glanced down at the amulet. "I have a name."

"Of course, Mistress."

A hopeless grin broke through her strained features, then despair became finely etched once again as her gaze came to light on the ring. On impulse, she pressed the crystal band to her lips. It felt cool and impersonal, a sorry substitute for the warmth of Erth's mouth.

"Are you missing him, Mistress?"

Frowning at the amulet, she chewed on the inner lining of her lower lip for a time. "He confuses me."

"In what way, Mistress?"

"If you must call me that, could you at least drop it out of a sentence now and then?"

"If you wish, Mis—Mmmm. It shall require practice, I'm afraid. But in what way does Master Erth confuse you, Mistress?"

"If I had the answer to that, my friend, I could get him out of my system, couldn't I?"

"Hard to say. Now you have me confused."

"Very good, Sami. You *can* talk to me without that irritating tag."

"I'm glad you're pleased, Mistress. Mistress?"

With a resigned shake of her head, she sighed, "What?"

"When will I meet your daughter?"

"Maybe tomorrow. Or the next day. I'm not sure."

"What is it like to be a parent?"

"I wouldn't know."

"I only asked because I was never given the opportunity to father a child."

"I'm sorry, Sami, but I don't want to talk about this right now."

Getting up from the chair, she cast a disheartened look at the bed. Unconsciously, she slipped the ring on the third finger of her left hand, and was unaware that it once again fit snugly in place.

"Go to sleep, Sami."

"As you wish . . . Mistress," he added smugly.

Crossing to the computer, she requested a new bottom sheet and carried it to the bed. After a quick inspection of the tears in the mattress, she placed the thin bundle down, and began to work the stuffing back into the slits.

The E wall opened. Taken aback by the unexpectedness of a visitor, Brehan sat heavily upon the mattress and looked up.

Her heart rose into her throat.

Erth stood at the threshold. There was no indication

of anger in him—not the telltale tightening of his jaw-line, or his frequent scowl. Casting the rips in the mattress behind her a furtive glance, she inched her bottom back until the tears were concealed. Then she calmly folded her hands on her lap and watched Erth come to a stop a few feet across from her.

"The b-bed needed changing," she said lamely, his disheveled state further unsettling her.

The headband was absent. It was the first time she'd seen him without it. His navy shirt was wrinkled and left open down the front. He was uncharacteristically barefoot. His hair was tousled, as if he had just awakened from a long restless sleep.

Erth bent over to pick up something on the floor. When he straightened, a remnant of mattress stuffing lay in his palm. His gaze swerved to Brehan's guilt-reddened face. "From where do you derive such destructive energy? Such physical fortitude would be best served in the Feeding Chamber."

"What do you want?"

Erth casually brushed his hands together. The remnant vanished. "I would like to understand why you would kiss something as cold and inanimate as the ring."

Automatically, she looked accusingly at the camera monitor set above the intercom system. Erth glanced that way, then swung his gaze back to her and shook his head. "I felt the kiss against my palm," he said, unconsciously rubbing it across his bare midriff. "Why, Brehan?"

"It seemed like a nice, safe, irrational thing to do at the time," she replied defensively, then looked down and realized the ring had once again conformed to her finger.

Erth gave an absent nod of his head. Brehan thought she determined a struggle within him to say more, but to her confusion, he lethargically strolled from the room. She stared at the open exit, torn by a mixture of feelings—disappointment the visit had been so brief, and vexation that even a simple whim, like kissing a ring in the privacy of her room, was open to his critical regard.

She caught up with him in the corridor. Unaware that his scowl was induced by the exquisite image she presented, she pleaded, "We have to talk."

Needing a moment's respite to quell the turbulence within him, Erth rolled his eyes upward. Talk? The silk-like fabric of her nightgown sensuously accentuated the curves of her body. Talk? And her hair . . . He mentally moaned. His resistance was always at its lowest when she wore it loose.

"Come with me," he said brusquely.

Brehan submissively followed him to his quarters. When the E wall sealed behind them, he remained by the exit while she nervously walked to the foot of the bed and kept her back to him.

"You wanted to talk," he said quietly.

"I appreciate you reneging on your threat to blind the men."

"Face me."

The gentleness of his tone gave her the strength to comply. But his next words caused her knees to weaken. "Does a chemistry exist between you and Manak?"

"He's my friend."

"And I am your enemy."

"It's an old subject, one I thought was settled."

"Define the relationship."

Uneasy with the questioning, Brehan peered off to one side. "He's like a brother to me. Barrit and I are very close, and yet you've made no objections to my confiding in him." She looked at him again. "Why Manak?"

"I *have* been envious of your friendship with Barrit," Erth admitted begrudgingly. "Envious of every pleasantry you have shared with anyone else."

"Erth . . ." She swallowed hard, unsure as to how to begin. "Something weird happened in my room. I saw my mother—her image in the mirror. And I remember things. Weird things.''

"Your psychic and empathic abilities were developed before your birth."

"How long have you known about this?"

"Barrit's mind-meld with you revealed it."

"I see," she said, bitterness lacing her tone. "I suppose enlightenment is better late than never. Like the progeria practice."

Erth's right eyebrow lazily arched up. "I was informed of your disapproval."

"Disapproval is putting it mildly. I want it stopped."

"Is that why you have ignored the child?"

Pain flashed in Brehan's eyes, but her back stiffened. "My reasons are my own. Where do you get off believing you have the moral right to interfere with a child's normal development?"

"The issue is not about morals, but survival, *te-ni-e.*"

"Don't call me that."

"What?" Erth laughed softly. *"Te-ni-e?* I have called you far worse than 'precious spirit.' "

"I don't like it." It was a lie. *Precious spirit.* Even saying it to herself, a thrill of delight fluttered through her. And here, all along, she'd believe he was calling her something that would translate into . . . *shrew* or *bitch.* Never would she have thought him capable of using such a heart-warming endearment.

Erth solemnly appraised her for a time longer. "I'm tired of waiting for you to openly accept me, Brehan. Weary of longing for you."

Crimson washed upward from Brehan's neck to her hairline. The old Brehan jumped to the fore, the Brehan afraid to let down her guard. "Then maybe it's time you started *accepting* the fact, I will never willingly be your wife."

A ghost of a smile ticked at one corner of his mouth. "The ring betrayed you. It wouldn't have remained on your finger had you not, at least subconsciously, acknowledged to caring for me."

Brehan tried in vain to remove the ring from her hand. She was frightened, feeling boxed in, although she could not understand why. "I know how I f-feel!" she stammered, lowering her hands to her sides and clenching them into fists. "Only *you* could interpret something as simple as tolerating your presence as a . . . a sign of giving a damn!"

She experienced a frightening headiness as she watched Erth peel out of his shirt and toss it aside, then remove his pants and drop them to the floor. Bold, towering and as naked as the day she was born, he waited for her to make the next move.

"No. Oh, no!," she fumed, unwaveringly staring into his eyes. "A romp in bed isn't the answer to our problems! I won't let you use me like this!"

Erth stepped toward her, his expression giving her no indication as to his mood. "What are you afraid of, Brehan?"

"Certainly not *you!*" she clipped, backing up as far as the foot of the bed would allow her.

"Commitment frightens you. You're afraid to love or be loved—"

"Damn you, Erth, leave me the hell alone!"

"Why you fear loving me, I don't know, but I can't let it go on."

Brehan held her breath when he went down on one knee in front of her, his large hands lighting possessively upon her hips. Despite her nervousness, her pulse quickened. Her blood began to grow hot within her veins. Looking down into his upturned face, she read desire in his eyes before he buried his face between her breasts. An exquisite sensation, like the trilling of birds, burst inside her lower abdomen and rapidly traveled throughout her body. She trembled when he palmed her buttocks and drew her closer.

Suddenly, aversion filled her completely. Unbeknown

to her, Di'me's influence was again trying to take over. Brehan slapped her hands to Erth's shoulders and fiercely tried to shove him away. He looked up. Before she could issue him a guttural warning to leave her alone, the blue glow of *armai* began to emanate from his eyes. Di'me retreated, returning the reins to the human counterpart.

Nearly entrapped by the sedative, Brehan threw back her head and cried, "No, Erth! Not this way!" She looked down to see that the glow was no longer visible, only a plea in Erth's eyes to understand her. He waited for her to speak, his hands moving absently over the base of her spine and down the back of her thighs. Words rose up in her throat, but she gulped them down. Her hands trembling, she slipped her fingers through his hair and slowly brought his face to rest against her heaving breasts. She looked heavenward, a threat of tears pressuring the backs of her eyes. Closing them, she choked, "Promise me you will never use *armai* on me again." Peering down at the top of his head, she went on, "Promise me, Erth, and I will promise to overcome my fears."

Erth nestled his face between her breasts for a time, then looked up and searched her face for an eternity of time. His hands moved to her back and, lowering his head, he brushed his mouth over the silken material between her breasts again. "You have my word," rippled against her skin, heating her blood once more.

"You have mine," she said breathlessly.

He looked up again, a sad smile playing on his lips. "How long must I wait to consummate our union?"

Brehan closed her eyes briefly, then rasped, "Do it now, before I lose my nerve."

Without hesitation, Erth languorously stroked his hands along the back of her, readily sensitizing every nerve in her body. With each second that passed, the fever in her skin pitched higher, higher, threatening to consume her in fires manifested of desires she had for so long tried to ignore. The warmth of his gentle caressing penetrated deeper, deeper, anesthetizing her fears, anesthetizing her programming to shun him. Caught up in a tide of sensuality, her fingers curled within his thick mane. Her dark lashes fluttered against her flushed cheeks as he slipped her gown to her waist. A moment later, it pooled at her feet, causing anticipation to rob her of breath.

Erth's gaze moved over the firm mounds of her breasts, the perfection of the skin covering her ribs and taut abdomen, and the patch of dark red curly hair at the junction of her thighs. Images flashed through his mind—segments of the men and women during various stages of lovemaking, actions, words and emotions he'd unintentionally touched upon during his meditations.

He'd thought their foreplay primitive, then.

Grazing his hands along the sides of her small waist, he took a moment longer to watch the labored rise and fall of her breasts. "Tell me what you want me to do," he said, his voice thick with passion.

"Touch me. Just . . . touch me."

He reached up, his fingertips featherlike as they traced the contours of her face and neck. A moan rattled in her throat, came again when his fingers stroked downward, over her breasts, her ribs. Gripping her hips, he brought her closer, his tongue gliding over the underside of one breast. Then he gave into temptation and gently enclosed one nipple within his warm mouth.

Brehan gasped, "Oh, God, yes!"

His hands once again palmed her buttocks, kneading the firmness as his tongue made a slow trail to the other nipple. He suckled longer, with more intensity, and felt a tremor course through her.

Searing pulses moved through every part of Brehan's body. Her fingers straining at the back of his head, she silently urged him to suck harder. Pleasure upon pleasure vied for her concentration. For hands as large as his, they possessed the most maddening gentleness.

They caressed every inch of her body, except the one area throbbing for attention. When at last his fingers smoothly glided along the inside of her thighs, her legs nearly gave out from beneath her.

Needing to touch him, she kicked the gown aside and went down on her knees, one hand clutching the muscular thigh of his raised leg. The feel of his bare, hot flesh prompted her to explore the muscular planes of his back, shoulders, and chest, while his mouth made a path of burning kisses along the hollow of her throat. Her fears were buried deep beneath an horizon of ecstasy, and she vowed to herself she would never let them return.

"Te-ni-e," he murmured thickly, staring into her passion-glazed eyes. His gaze lowered to her mouth, his expressive black eyebrows betraying his inner torment.

Sliding her fingers to the back of his neck, Brehan pulled him closer. His mouth took possession of hers, masterfully probing, eliciting her return kiss. When his arms encircled her, molded her against his rock-hard body, she clung to him, wanting their flesh to become one. She could feel the fingers of one of his hands moving through her hair, bunching it up into a fist before he lifted his head and looked deeply into her eyes.

"I am inexperienced with human females."

"Can't prove it by me," she whispered, her fingers flexing at the back of his neck.

In one fluid motion, Erth swooped her up into his arms and rose to his feet. Cradling her against him, he kissed her long and deeply, slowly making his way to the bed. He lowered himself alongside her, the kiss unbroken, his hands caressing her length, until he yielded to a need to satiate his visual sense.

The seductive glow on her features caused a whirlwind of sensations to build within his chest. Her eyes were clear and bright and inviting, her perfect mouth slightly swollen from his kisses. Her hair, more fiery than he ever recalled, shamed Syre's magnificent sunsets.

Brehan pondered his stillness. She could feel his arousal pressing against her outer thigh, a searing thing of throbbing need. She wanted to be impaled, surrounded and kissed until the tormenting fires within her were extinguished. But to her bewilderment, he seemed content at the moment to stare into her eyes.

"I love you," he said finally, then nuzzled her neck before lifting his head again. "You don't believe I'm capable of such feeling, but it exists in me, Brehan. It's powerful. More powerful than anything I have ever encountered."

Brehan unwittingly held her breath.

He brushed his lips against hers, then lifted his head and studied her face again. "You fill a void in me that has existed for as long as I have memory. I wish I were selfless enough to be satisfied with visual gratification, but there is such an unrelenting need in me to hold you—to know the intimacies alien to my kind."

Winding her arms about his neck, Brehan drew herself up and boldly kissed him. "Are you going to talk all night, or make love to me?"

Erth's hopes soared higher. His hand cupped at the back of her head, he kissed her, a slow, plundering-of-her-senses kiss. Brehan's patience crested on the tide of shivers swelling within her. Eager to proceed to the next culminating step, she luxuriously stretched a leg and caressed it along his flesh. The sheer masculine feel of him sent shivers anew skittering down her spine, and a deep sense of belonging as she'd never known before, filled the region of her heart she'd always closely guarded.

"I love you," he repeated, his lips trailing from her earlobe, along her throat, to the hollow in her shoulder. She moaned, arching against him, his admission of love as sensual as his caresses and kisses.

Erth could wait no longer. Their fingers locked

together above her head, he positioned himself between her thighs. He hesitated a moment, questioning the burning desire urging him toward gratification. If she truly wasn't ready . . . ?

His doubts sinking beneath the weight of his desire, he slowly pressed into her. Amidst the erotic sensations exploding throughout him, he watched her clench her teeth and arch up with a strange mixture of pain and bliss combined. He released her hands and stroked her body and kissed her deeply. His movements within her were as slow as he could manage until she unexpectedly thrust her hips up, taking him completely into the warm, moist cavity of her body. Her fingers threaded his hair, then clamped over his bulging biceps.

Their bodies moved in synchronous rhythm, feverishly working to bring them to mutual gratification. A moment before climaxing, Erth surrounded her in his arms and buried his face in her hair. Together, they soared beyond the realm of space and time, to a place between ecstasy and madness. Brehan cried out, her fingernails digging into his biceps as the most incredible sensations detonated within every part of her body. Before Erth lowered his face into her hair, she glimpsed a ravaged expression of blissful pain and disbelief. Seconds passed in stillness and silence. Breathing in short spurts, she dazedly stared up at the ceiling. She felt oddly as one with Erth. Sliding her hands to his back, she instinctually kissed the powerful shoulder by her cheek. The gesture lifted Erth's head. His eyes alight with tenderness, he kissed her, then gazed with satisfaction upon the raw contentment glowing on her face.

"How could I have ever been afraid of this?" she murmured breathlessly.

With a growl of approval, Erth nuzzled her neck, then kissed her again long and deeply until, separating their lips, he gave an incredulous shake of his head. "You're so incredibly beautiful."

"And easy," she quipped.

A startled expression flashed across his face. Easy? How could she— Seeing humor dance in her eyes, he laughed and nipped her on the neck.

"Erth?"

The humor in her had abruptly faded, replaced by a breathy solemnity that immediately sobered him. He met her gaze with a shadow of apprehension in his. But words of regret did not follow as he'd anticipated. Instead, she reached up and lightly trailed her fingertips across his lips.

"Being your wife has its moments," she smiled shyly.

He had longed to hear her voice her love for him, but even this admission lifted a great weight from his pseudo heart. Lowering his mouth to hers, he murmured, "You're home, *te-ni-e*. Home in my arms."

"IT'S APPROACHING DAWN!"

The sound of Barrit's thick voice nearly caused Manak to jump out of his skin. Lifting his face from the cradle of his palms, he swung his gaze up. Shadows underscored his eyes. Misery lined his handsome face.

"Enough is enough," Barrit chided, reaching out and turning off the monitor. "You're obsessed with—"

Manak turned the monitor back on. "Take a look."

Barrit released an impatient snort, but the instant he glimpsed what was on the screen, he felt his sleepiness instantly dissolve. "What the . . . ?"

Rubbing his bloodshot eyes with the heel of his hands, Manak released a sigh and focused blearily on the monitor. "I've done every analysis known to us. The results are accurate, Barrit. I've gone through the data three times and nothing changes."

"Impossible," Barrit murmured. Nudging Manak to stand, he sat in front of the monitor and reread the information.

"The violet scan bypassed the psychic mesh she uses as a body shield. See this?" He pointed to a specific notation on the monitor. "She uses eighty-three percent of her brain—and look. The graphs? They indicate that at least two consciousnesses are at work. Not a split personality as you first believed. These are interwoven, as if one can't exist without the other."

"The physiological workup is . . . astounding." Barrit pressed a forefinger to the screen and carefully went over the information once again.

"Those pulsations of energy recorded remind me of her sprites," Manak said almost wistfully, staring at the spontaneous bursts of lights appearing on the computer imagery of Brehan's body.

"It looks like some kind of—" Barrit looked away from the screen, a frown creasing his brow. "Metamorphosis?"

"Something. The density of her vital organs is decreasing. At least we're aware it's happening. Now we have to figure out the why."

Enlightenment cast a shadow across Barrit's face. "Two entities sharing one body. The voice Brehan spoke of in her head . . ." He looked up at Manak. "Her eyes. The amber irises."

"Joy told Dawn there were instances of that prior to Brehan's acquisition. I can't begin to understand any of it."

"Nor I. Erth—"

"No!"

Barrit swung a harried look up at Manak, prompting the latter to explain, "Brehan trusts us, Barrit. Not Erth. We can do more for her if we keep this between *us*."

"Don't you think *she* should be let in on this?"

Looking at the monitor, Manak gave an adamant shake of his head. "Not yet. I think it'll terrify her to know she's going through some kind of biological change. And if she finds out we're monitoring her again, her brain may just produce a shield we won't be able to penetrate.

"I was hoping to delve a little deeper, but the experiment was interrupted."

At the hardness that crept into Manak's tone, Barrit arched a questioning brow.

"She awoke from another nightmare," Manak said tightly. "Erth paid her a visit, and she left with him."

"I see."

"I'm only thinking of her well-being."

A wry grin touched Barrit's mouth. "And the ache in your hearts," he said sagely. "Get some sleep, Manak."

"What about you?"

"I couldn't close my eyes now if my life depended on it."

Brehan was disappointed to again awaken alone in Erth's quarters. Standing beneath the cassis mist in his shower stall, her hands absently moved over her breasts and abdomen as she allowed the memories of their lovemaking to warm her heart.

Never in her wildest dreams had she imagined the act could have been so pleasurable. She felt reborn. Freed from the mental scars of her past. It was time to go forward, with Erth and her daughter. He had proven to her, again and again during the night, that she possessed the purest ability to love and be loved. The old fears held no place in her future.

Lifting her face into the mist, she began to say, "I love—" when a vision blared in front of her mind's eye. Her arms tautly straightened out in front of her, her palms flattened to the tiles, she let herself fully enter the dreaming. The split scene that had visited her once before in the lab, was again stretched out in front of her. It played exactly as it had before, until toward the end. This time when the horned being was about to step into the division of the scenes, it stopped and swung a furiously incredulous look to its left, directly at her.

The sight of the yellow eyes glaring at her caused her

to jump back. A pulse drummed throughout her body. Although she vividly recognized the being, she was positive she had never encountered anything like it.

And it had recognized her, its vile hatred extending beyond the vision and into her reality, to solidify like a lance between her breasts. As quickly as it had appeared, the dreaming faded, but the aftermath lingered. This time, she could not deny that she would one day be a participant in that battle. The couple, Kragan and Echo, had to belong to Syre's future, but what a grim future the vision portrayed.

The Lian soldier dragged his twisted left foot along the stone floor of the corridor. His narrow, green-pupiled eyes glowed in the dim lighting. The broad nostrils at the end of his short nose flared and gushed hot air. He was eager to reach the Master. Since the injury to his foot on the botched mission to annihilate the Bahi colonies, he was desperate to regain the favors of his lord.

Vraus growled within his thick neck and moved faster along the corridor. His small brain burned within his five-inch thick skull as memory reared up to torment him once again. The Bahis had anticipated the attack. They were ready and waiting when the five-ship unit had arrived. Vraus's ship had barely managed to escape, but the landing gear had been damaged when his ship crashed just short of the landing docks on Pergasius. He alone had survived, but his left foot had been crushed beneath the burning control deck. The agony he had suffered while waiting to be rescued was minor compared to the wrath of the Master on his report of the squad's failure to complete the mission. Vraus was made to wait—forced to stand on his mangled, raw foot— while the Master, himself, saw to the destruction of the colonies.

Entering a large room, Vraus edged his way through

a crowd of performers entertaining the Master. Nude figures, sleek with sweat, squirmed and writhed on the floor in a provocative ritual praising their lord and this abode of pandemonium. The macabre antics brought hysterical shrieks of joy from the Grey Lord. Vraus elbowed his way through the bodies. When his injured foot was struck, his screech elicited ecstatic groans from the dancers.

Seated on his throne, Zanus-Roul eyed the Lian's approach with increasing annoyance. His catlike pupils dilated within their yellow irises. He dismissed the performers with a curt gesture of his hand as the Lian crowhopped on his good foot up the two stone steps of the dais.

Kneeling, Vraus reverently kissed each cloven hoof.

"Why have you left the pits?"

Vraus stood and winced when he leaned too heavily on his injured foot. "I have completed my term, Master."

"Unfortunate," Zanus-Roul snorted.

The olive coloring of the Lian's face paled. "I bring you news! Intruders, Master!"

The words gushed out of the Lian when the Grey Lord rose menacingly from his throne. Vraus timorously gazed up the mighty height, for Vraus' head barely reached the Grey Lord's waist. He was shoved aside as the Master leaped from the dais and stood on the cobblestone floor.

"Where?"

"In the Blorou sector, Master. They arrived a *mwio* ago, but I thought it wise to withhold this information until the identity of the vessel was determined."

"And?"

"It was a matter of waiting, Master. A great dome on the ship enabled me to view some of the occupants." Vraus' eyes narrowed gleefully. *"Syres,* my lord! No mistaking *them."*

"Only Syres?"

Vraus was caught in the hypnotic intensity of the Master's eyes. "Male Syres. One fire-haired female."

Zanus-Roul sprinted about the room. Vraus watched, not fully understanding the Master's reaction, and not daring to speak further. When the antics came to an abrupt halt, the Master stood before Vraus with eyes wildly aglow.

"Who is guardian of the Syres? My *brother* you low wit! Erth . . . in my possession," he said, sensuously rolling the words over his tongue.

He began to pace, his taloned fingers kneading the fine white fur covering his abdomen. "How my brother comes to trespass within my realm is not important. By all the laws of Sojan, what is within that ship belongs to me! Including that dull-faced, pampered curse Mythia bore. I have loathed him since the dawn of his existence! At long last I have the opportunity to show him the depths of my brotherly devotion."

Vraus crow-hopped down the two steps and looked up at Zanus-Roul with an evil gleam in his eyes. "Give the word, Master, and I will lead a squad to force the ship to dock."

The Grey Lord rolled his eyes up into his head. The yellow orbs glowed fiercely, forcing Vraus to avert his face.

"Ahhh, yes," Zanus-Roul moaned. "He knows! He feels my presence. He is no doubt frantic now that he realizes whose hands he has fallen prey to. I shall wait. I want him to squirm." His narrow, pointed tongue flicked from his mouth. He knew that for every moment his brother was made to suffer, he, too, would suffer.

An evil smile bared his teeth. "My pristine-prig brother shall hang in effigy before his cursed people. That almighty martyr shall kneel before me and show Sojan once and for all, who deserves the Guardianship. *"Erth!"* He contemptuously spat the name of his brother. "You have broken the oldest law of Haveth! You are guilty! Guilty and punishable by *me!*"

The anger dwindled and laughter boomed from his throat. "I shall show no mercy! *Thou shall not trespass thy brother's realm!*"

Erth had earlier dismissed Lute and Rao from their posts. Now alone, he stood with his hands clasped behind his back, and scanned the planets of the solar system with his inner senses. A small part of his consciousness contemplated two of his least favorite half brothers. The twins.

Zanus-Roul, the Grey Lord of the Underworld, was more like a bad child. He believed in his own greatness more than any other living being, with the exception of his disciples, which Erth knew to be of little intelligence. And Zynus-Rye, the very essence of evil. Lord of the Darklands—where only the Medusian relics of once-intellectual species who gave into the dark powers, remained imprisoned.

For good there must be evil. For light there must be darkness. That was the balance unto which creation began. From extreme opposites came the mediums, the variations of nature. Zanus-Roul was one of these mediums, shadowed by the darkness of his twin, and the lightness of Erth.

The women aboard the *Stellar* would attract Zanus-Roul. It seemed an incredible blow from fate to discover that his people were stranded in this particular region of the galaxy. Especially since the routes had been charted so very far from these boundaries. Unless his half brother's hand had been in on the unaccountable factors that had jettisoned the ship through the displacement warp . . . ?

Erth turned at the sound of the lift. Brehan stepped into the room. Dressed in one of his dark jerseys, her hair unbound, she walked up to him and wrapped her arms about his middle.

"I expected you to sleep later," he said, planting a kiss on the crown of her head.

Brehan stared into his eyes for several moments before she frowned. "You know where we are."

Once again her keen perception took him aback. "This is Zanus-Roul's domain."

"If I recall, you and your brothers are not on the best of terms."

"Half brother," he corrected with an edge of impatience. "Our position is in violation of boundary law."

"An accident doesn't take law into consideration," she chuckled, although uneasy with his solemn mood.

"There are standard regulations regarding the domain of a lord, Brehan, which even my father cannot make exception to. In this case, I'm not sure what rights are mine, or what rights are my brother's. But I can promise you, Zanus-Roul will make the most of our predicament."

"I'll explain to him—"

Swiftly, Erth grasped her upper arms and gave her a shake. "If he comes aboard, you are to stay out of sight!"

Too stunned to speak, Brehan merely stared up at him.

"You will have to trust my judgment on this," he said, releasing her and turning to face the dome again.

Erth's anxiety deepened as his imagination dwelled on his brother's reaction to Brehan. He was only too aware that she was his vital weakness. And she was one lure Zanus-Roul would not be able to resist.

As if coming out of a daze, he saw something in Brehan's reflection on the doom which caused a spasm of shock to stab at his mind. Piercing amber eyes glowed in her face. Turning back to Brehan, he found bewildered green eyes watching him. Desperate to deny what he'd seen—although he didn't understand why—he pulled her into his arms and held her tightly, a cheek brushing across her crown. "I love you, woman."

For the second time in a matter of moments, Brehan felt herself plummeting into darkness.

Di'me again surfaced. Burying her face against Erth's chest, she hid the smug, self-satisfied smile marring her lips.

She knew the first trial was almost upon her.

Fingers curled against her palms, she savored a mental image of the battle to come. The mere thought of pitting brother against brother engorged her self-admiration! The ultimate power beckoned, taunted her from the top of a seemingly endless, steep, ascending stairway. But until that time when the human consciousness expired, Di'me would have be content with amusing herself. The love-thing which had developed between Erth and her counterpart was going to prove a magnificent weapon. She could secretly wallow in the pleasures with him, while counting the lessening days to his demise.

Patience had its rewards.

The excitement has only just begun! Soon Brehan's adventures continue in Mickee Madden's *Written In The Stars*. We hope you will enjoy this preview of the second book in the "Katiah" series. . . .

Written in the Stars

by

Mickee Madden

"I'm the epitome of patience these days." Brehan's words were tested when she remained poised within Erth's quarters for some time, contemplating his statuesque stance across the room. His back was to her. She knew that he was aware of her, but also knew that, for one reason or another, he was determined not to see or speak to her.

Something hanging on the wall by the entry caught her notice. Stepping up to the oblong sheet of paperlike material, she studied an intricate drawing of the Garden Chamber. Scrawled at the bottom right corner was her daughter's name. Not only was she taken aback by her child's burgeoning talent, but the fact that Erth had chosen to display it.

Turning, she stared at her husband in bewilderment. He was more Misty's parent than she could ever hope to be. A doting father-figure. She could accept the 'scowling, brooding Erth'. The Erth who had abducted her. The Erth whose anger challenged her every waking moment. But the tender being, the man-thing determined to make her love him, frightened her more than anything she'd ever encountered.

Air escaped her parted lips as her gaze took in his magnificent build. His black jersey was stretched tautly across the powerful breadth of his shoulders, and tucked into the slim waistband of his dark, snug-fitting pants.

Memories surfaced. Disturbing memories of the pleasure she'd derived from the touch of him. Longing stirred deep within her abdomen. Her lips tingled, but she could not help but wonder if the *armai* had not super-sensitized her responses to his kisses, his lovemaking. The doubts, she feared, would always haunt her.

She shivered and crossed her arms against her chest. Closing her eyes, she forced back the treacherous emotions weakening her purpose. She hadn't come to make love, or be held, or kissed. Now was the time to put the horrors of Romnl behind them.

When she opened her eyes, she was startled to find Erth's vivid blue gaze on her.

"What do you want?" he asked coldly.

"I'm worried about you—so is everyone else."

His shoulders straightened back with an air of hostility.

"Well?"

His black eyebrows drew down in a scowl. "Do you expect me to applaud your . . . concern?"

Again Brehan closed her eyes, but for a moment. Straining to control herself, she ambled up to him, leaving an arm's distance between them. For a time, she studied his face. The hardness in his eyes. The formidable thrust of his jaw. The grim set of his mouth.

Although she had counseled herself not to let her temper get the better of her, the wrong words nonetheless came tumbling past her lips. "You really are a piece of work. You know, Erth, I like the idea of you being mortal. Maybe real flesh and blood will knock these arrogant, superior airs of yours to hell!"

With a swipe of his hand, Erth tore open the front of

his jersey. Brehan snorted, misunderstanding his action until she noticed the unmarred bronze flesh covering his broad chest.

Forgotten was her belief that she preferred him mortal. With a cry of joy, she rested her palms against the smooth perfection of his pectorals. But the moment was shattered when he shoved her back two paces and leveled an isolated finger in warning for her not to approach him again.

Stricken by his reaction, she could do nothing but stare into his anger-brightened eyes.

"Now leave," he ordered, and turned his back to her.

Brehan started to turn to the exit, then stopped herself and stared at the back of his head. "Why are you angry with me?"

Infuriating silence.

"Dammit, Erth!"

Silence.

"What about the men? You could at least have the decency to let them know you're all right!"

With the agility of lightning, Erth spun around and haughtily snapped his fingers in front of her face. "How solicitous you are of others," he sneered. "And how kind of you to remind me of *my* moral obligations!"

His hand shot out and stopped her from wheeling away. Brehan refused to struggle, but every nerve in her body was as tight as a spring.

"What do you want of me?" he asked, in a tone barely more than a whisper.

She peevishly looked up at him, his soft voice making her as defensive as his previous caustic one. "Is this about Manak kissing me?"

Rage flashed momentarily across his features before he could suppress it. "No. But it had better not happen again."

Brehan stiffened. "Is that another threat?"

His eyes strayed to her mouth and lingered for a time. "You belong to me, woman. Your body . . . your soul."

"I should have nailed your hide when I had the chance!"

Erth's gaze flitted over her flushed face. The voice of his conscience goaded him to spill the truth behind his anger, but he could not. He was wiser to the mysteries surrounding her—at least wiser to a certain degree. There were still many questions taunting him—especially regarding the sameness in composition they now shared. Their bond was unbreakable and he berated himself for not having meditated on his suspicions when her adjustment to her new life had not proceeded within the usual parameters. He had been so blinded by the allure of her beauty, her spirit.

He'd fallen prey to a being of his own kind. Worse still, he'd been blindly leading his people into the heart of a macabre plan to not only end the mission, but to terminate his existence. And his wife remained the irresistible bait by which to entrap him.

Yes, that much he'd learn after undergoing grueling hours of meditation during the night. The who and the why were still unknown, but he would unveil the answers before long. In the meantime, he had to force himself to detach from her emotional reign over him. He knew he was incapable of starving his sexual drives, but he could possess her, satiate his needs, and walk away with a modicum of willpower.

"Why didn't you?" he asked finally, his tone soft, almost mesmerizing.

A dull ache played at Brehan's temples. Something was dying inside her, giving birth to a void. She was still unaware that the aching behind her eyes was due to the fact she could no longer cry. "Why didn't I what?" she countered bleakly.

"Destroy me when you had the chance."

Trembling, aghast, she stared into his eyes as if questioning his sanity. "It n-never crossed my mind."

She walked a few steps away, her fingers absently trying to comb through the snarls of her hair. "I didn't have any control over my actions after we entered your brother's realm." She heaved a ragged breath before continuing, "Pitithurus was manipulating my mood swings . . . the blackouts. I'm sorry, but I didn't know what was happening to me."

"You are never responsible for your actions."

His chilling tone made her flinch. Facing him, she inwardly struggled to lessen the painful throbbing behind her breast. "What more do you want me to say?"

That you love me, Brehan. "And I suppose you're going to claim it was Pitithurus' influence which prompted you to make love to me?" he challenged, his tone devoid of emotion.

Crimson stole up Brehan's face. A spasm of nerves jolted her when he unexpectedly closed the distance and captured her chin between a thumb and forefinger. His mouth captured hers in a brief, punishing kiss. A kiss meant to strip the fire from her soul. When he lifted his head and looked down into her glazed eyes, his chafing expression branded itself in her brain.

"I enjoy your body, Brehan. That *is* all that matters."

Her eyes flashed him a warning, but they couldn't camouflage the inner turmoil she was suffering. Erth nearly abandoned his resolve. He was on the verge of pulling her into his arms when she abruptly fled from the room. The E wall sealed behind her.

Erth's shoulders sagged as if they carried the weight of the universe.

"How can I deny that which makes me whole?" he murmured disparagingly, and sank onto the edge of his bed.

ROMANCE FROM FERN MICHAELS

DEAR EMILY   (0-8217-4952-8, $5.99)

WISH LIST   (0-8217-5228-6, $6.99)

AND IN HARDCOVER:

VEGAS RICH   (1-57566-057-1, $25.00)

Available wherever paperbacks are sold, or order direct from the Publisher. Send cover price plus 50¢ per copy for mailing and handling Penguin USA, P.O. Box 999, c/o Dept. 17109, Bergenfield, NJ 07621. Residents of New York and Tennessee must include sales tax. DO NOT SEND CASH.

ROMANCE FROM JO BEVERLY

DANGEROUS JOY   (0-8217-5129-8, $5.99)

FORBIDDEN   (0-8217-4488-7, $4.99)

THE SHATTERED ROSE   (0-8217-5310-X, $5.99)

TEMPTING FORTUNE   (0-8217-4858-0, $4.99)

Available wherever paperbacks are sold, or order direct from the Publisher. Send cover price plus 50¢ per copy for mailing and handling to Penguin USA, P.O. Box 999, c/o Dept. 17109, Bergenfield, NJ 07621. Residents of New York and Tennessee must include sales tax. DO NOT SEND CASH.